WISHING FROM THE HEART

Annie Dillon doesn't know what else could possibly go wrong. First her dream of turning a Texas ghost town into a tourist attraction left her broke and stranded in Deadend. And now a freak whirlwind has granted her wish for better, simpler times—by sweeping her off to an earlier century . . . and depositing her into the arms of an arrogant, infuriating bounty hunter named Sam Noble.

WANTED ACROSS TIME

At last he's caught the feisty lady outlaw known throughout the West as "Rotten Rosie"! But the crafty criminal whom Sam has apprehended is more than brazen and beautiful, she's plumb loco to boot—claiming to be the *great-great-granddaughter* of the hellcat he's been searching for! But while her wiles and willfulness have his head spinning, her fiery sensuality is turning his rage into desire. And though the law wants Rosie dead or alive, Sam knows he wants her only one way: for always!

EUGENIA RILEY

Wanted Across Time

An Avon Romantic Treasure

AVON BOOKS ◆ NEW YORK

WANTED ACROSS TIME is an original publication of Avon Books. This work has never before appeared in book form. This work is a novel. Any similarity to actual persons or events is purely coincidental. All Indian folk medicines and remedies described herein are used strictly within a historical context. No endorsement is made, or intended, regarding the safety or effectiveness of any such medicines or remedies, and readers are cautioned not to use them.

AVON BOOKS
A division of
The Hearst Corporation
1350 Avenue of the Americas
New York, New York 10019

Copyright © 1997 by Eugenia Riley Essenmacher
Inside cover author photo by Lienna Essenmacher
published by arrangement with the author
Library of Congress Catalog Card Number: 96-96878
ISBN: 0-380-78909-4

First Avon Books Printing: February 1997

AVON TRADEMARK REG. U.S. PAT. OFF. AND IN OTHER COUNTRIES, MARCA REGISTRADA, HECHO EN U.S.A.

Printed in the U.S.A.

RA 10 9 8 7 6 5 4 3 2 1

This book is dedicated to my editor,
Ellen Edwards, with warm thanks
for her friendship, enthusiasm,
and support over the years.

The author acknowledges, with gratitude, the following sources consulted in the writing of this book: *A Dictionary of the Old West*, by Peter Watts; *The Cheyenne Indians* and *The Fighting Cheyennes*, both by George Bird Grinnell.

Chapter 1

Annie Dillon drove into Deadend pushed by a killer wind.

Although fall had not yet officially arrived, winter had already dispatched a first, bitter chill to nip the stark, desolate mesas high in the Texas Panhandle on this, the coldest recorded September day in more than a decade. A fierce blue norther howled down the dusty main street of the old, abandoned town, rattling clapboard facades, sending roof shingles flying, and gobbling up every smidgen of dust in its wake.

The gusts were so powerful, they buffeted Annie's small blue sports car. Gingerly she maneuvered her vehicle along the rutted lane, wincing as a craggy tumbleweed bounced off her hood. She eyed the rattletrap structures flanking her, remnants of a western cattle town that dated to the late 1870s—the old apothecary, general store, dressmaker's, hotel, stable, saloon, and small sad church at street's end—spectral images of a time gone by standing forlornly here on the Staked Plain.

All of the buildings had been abandoned amid restoration, as suggested by sawhorses cluttering the boardwalks, stacks of lumber and cans of paint strewn about, and the ragtag appearance of the storefronts themselves, many left half-painted, with shutters hanging askew and windowpanes missing. With the wind baying like an evil hound, red dust swirling in nasty torrents, and not

1

another soul in sight, the atmosphere seemed downright spooky.

So *this* was her dream come true!

Annie circled back behind the saloon and parked on the dusty, pebbled ground. Climbing out and locking her car, she shuddered at the force of the chill biting her face, and lifted the hood of her heavy wool car coat against the icy onslaught. Digging her hands into her pockets, she donned her wool gloves.

Her teeth rattled. She glanced at the landscape beyond the town, viewing stark red mesas, blowing prairie grass, more swirling red sand, and tumbleweeds. A dirty blue haze hung over the vista, blurring the distant horizon into a muddy gray.

She'd arrived in hell, and a damn cold hell at that! Shivering at a new blast, Annie quickly crossed to the saloon's back steps, grateful she'd also worn a thick sweater, corduroy jeans, long johns, and fleece-lined boots. She sprinted up the stoop and creaked open the scarred back door. Inside the storage room, she paused against the closed panel, pushed back her hood, removed her gloves, and stuffed them back inside her pocket. With the door quaking against her back, she glanced with distaste at the clutter strewn everywhere: cans of paint, boxes of nails, a toilet and sink someone had neglected to install, abandoned trash, and beer bottles. Spying a mouse scurrying across a smudged tarp, she grimaced. She could hear and feel the entire structure shaking with the power of the wind, even as frigid tentacles penetrated the thin walls and pierced through her thick clothing to her very skin.

"Oh, Larry," she muttered.

Now as never before, Annie realized she never should have entrusted her older brother with the renovation of her ghost town. A successful commercial real estate broker from Dallas, Annie had hoped Deadend would become her biggest triumph, a restored Old West town attracting many tourists. She had gambled two years' earnings, plus her own considerable inheritance, on buying and renovating the old town. A new state highway pushing through from Amarillo should have brought many tourists.

But the project had been plagued by difficulties from the outset. Annie, busy in Dallas trying to earn more money for the venture, had relied on Larry, an unemployed carpenter, to carry out many of the day-to-day operations, but Larry lacked Annie's organizational skills and genius for business, and had bailed out when problems arose.

Now Annie could not even find her brother. Her lead contractor had also abandoned the project, after performing substandard work and neglecting to pay his subcontractors, who had in turn filed liens on Annie's property. And all of these woes had come before the Indians had declared war in the courts, suing her and the federal and state governments, claiming Deadend as part of their tribal lands and blocking the planned highway. Her first court date loomed only two weeks away.

What a mess! Annie desperately needed a huge infusion of cash. If only she could sell one of her bigger commercial projects—such as the ranch she had been pushing to developers as a housing tract—she might still avoid bankruptcy. Her partner in Dallas had promised to oversee all her ventures while she was away, but she couldn't count on a fat commission to pull her butt out of this deep crack.

Stepping over discarded beer bottles and trash, Annie proceeded through the storeroom to the main room of the saloon. Emerging at one end of the long oak bar, she glanced ahead at tables and chairs strewn haphazardly about. A startled gasp escaped her as she spied the shadowy figure of a man seated in one of the old chairs, his feet propped on a rickety table. She cautiously stepped closer, eyeing the stranger's lined, leathery face and hawk nose, his high cheekbones and pronounced chin, his braided gray hair. Clearly of Native American heritage, the man wore a high-crowned black hat with a snakeskin band, ragged jeans, and an Indian blanket poncho; he was whittling some kind of animal figure—

quite possibly a bird—and humming under his breath, a singsongy, Indian sort of chant.

Annie wondered if this was Thomas Windfoot, a representative of the Cheyenne band whom she was supposed to meet this morning. If so, how had he arrived? She'd not spotted another vehicle parked outside.

Moving closer, she tentatively called, "Mr. Windfoot?"

The old man craned his neck to stare at her, then slid his booted feet off the table. Setting down his knife and piece of wood, he stood. "Miss Dillon?"

"Yes." Annie moved closer and offered her hand.

Removing his hat, Windfoot shook her hand, his grip rough and strong. "Welcome to Deadend."

"Thank you," Annie replied with a perplexed smile. "May I ask how you got here? There's no other car outside."

The old man chuckled. "I parked my pickup in the stable next door, out of the wind. My truck, well, she is very old and temperamental, a '53 Chevy, and I must pamper her."

"I see." Annie was amused that Windfoot would give his vehicle human qualities. "Well, I've been to Deadend before, and I'm sorry to say I don't find it much improved."

Windfoot glanced about and sighed. "Your contractors have not served you well, miss. You are fortunate to have the Silver Wind band of the Cheyenne to take this white elephant off your hands."

Bristling, Annie drew herself up with pride. "Mr. Windfoot, I've invested every dime I have into what you call a 'white elephant.' This property is mine, and I don't intend to give it up without a fight—despite your tribe's frivolous lawsuit."

"Frivolous?" Windfoot shook his head. "This land belongs to the Silver Wind, Miss Dillon. Back in the late 1860s, President Grant signed an executive order ceding more than four million acres in Indian Territory to the Cheyenne and the Arapaho. A small portion of the Texas

Panhandle was included in the grant, and allocated this property to our band."

"I've never heard of such a provision," declared Annie.

"You are a scholar of revisionist history, then, as are so many of your kind," he replied bitterly. "You will see the truth for yourself in court."

"My lawyer thinks otherwise. He says your band's claim for land in Texas is pure exaggeration and distortion, and he expects to see your suit dismissed on the first day of trial."

Windfoot sighed, shifting from foot to foot. "Ah, the white man is eager to forget and forsake his promises. Again and again, he has broken his treaties and cheated the red man. But this time I am determined to see my people prevail."

Annie groaned. She had not intended for the meeting to turn into a confrontation. Indeed, she sympathized with the plight of Native Americans, but was also sure she was in the right here. Her lawyer had told her he could discover no treaty term or other precedent that would cede her land to this particular band of the Cheyenne.

She flashed Windfoot a placating smile. "Look, Mr. Windfoot, isn't there some way we can compromise, some way we can all profit from this property? As things now stand, your lawsuit could tie up my ghost town for years in federal and state courts. And, given the litigation, the state has postponed the planned new highway. Which means that unless you and I can reach some sort of consensus, no one will benefit from Deadend."

But Windfoot merely shook a finger at Annie. "Ah, you White Eyes. You think of nothing but exploiting the land and profiting from it. It is left to the red man to consider matters of the spirit, preserving the land and the birthright of the Tsistsistas."

"Tsistsistas?" repeated Annie.

"It is what we Cheyenne call ourselves—'the people' or 'the slashed ones,' wounded by the White Eyes, no less."

Annie fought to hold on to her patience. "Why are you so determined that Deadend should be in Cheyenne hands?"

He grew wistful, staring off at some point in space. "I will tell you a story, Miss Dillon. Many moons ago, my beloved grandson, a young warrior of the Silver Wind, journeyed high into Black Mesa on his traditional vision quest, to speak with the gods in the earth and sky and seek his spiritual totem. The lad strayed well into the wilderness, where he vanished like smoke rising from the mesa on a clear summer day." Windfoot moved his hands in a dramatic smoke sign. "That was fifteen years ago, and the boy has not been seen or heard from since."

"I'm sorry," said Annie sincerely.

"I believe my grandson disappeared because the White Eyes have stolen the soul of the red man, just as you have stolen our sacred lands. But this time you will not win. This time I will reclaim Deadend as my grandson's birthright, for the day he returns."

Annie ground her jaw. Although she could understand the old man's frustration, his fanatical claims regarding a grandson who was surely dead made her wonder if he wasn't unhinged. In any event, his band's legal maneuvers were ruining her life.

She eyed him in supplication. "Are you sure there can be no compromise in this?"

"There have already been too many compromises," pronounced the old man. "Every time the red man yields, the white man further exploits him and decimates his heritage. In the past the Cheyenne were defeated through massacre, as at Sand Creek. Today the red man is destroyed more subtly, through economic repression." Windfoot held up a fist. "But this time my people will make a true stand, as of old. This is our land, and there will be no surrender."

Annie flung a hand outward in exasperation. "Then why did you agree to meet with me if you had no intention of listening to reason?"

He smiled. "Because I had hoped to make *you* see the light, Miss Dillon. Perhaps it is you who needs to go on a quest for spiritual enlightenment."

Annie was tempted to roll her eyes.

He clapped on his hat. "At any rate, I must go." He paused as timbers rattled about them. "The Hevovitas-tamiutsts will arrive soon, I think."

"The *what*?" gasped Annie.

"The whirlwind," pronounced the old man.

"Ah," she murmured cynically. "You know, I think it's already here."

Smiling ruefully, Windfoot tipped his hat to her. "Farewell, Miss Dillon. May the Wise One Above guide your journeys."

Annie nodded; Windfoot meant well, she supposed. She shivered as his departure sent a new blast of chill air in through the front doors. She stood hugging herself. A moment later, she could hear his old truck snorting and backfiring as it lurched out of town.

Alone in the drafty saloon, Annie felt more depressed than ever. She had already lost her shirt on this venture, and now even her ownership of the land had come under fire. She was ruined at the tender age of twenty-six.

She strolled about, eyeing the shoddy workmanship of the contractors: substandard doors and windows, water stains on the "new" ceiling, nails protruding from the plank flooring. Heading toward the bar, she glanced at an aged oil painting hanging above it, of a blond, voluptuous naked beauty who appeared to be having a lot more fun than she was. Glancing at the gray plank wall surrounding the chipped, gilded picture frame, she realized the contractors had not even tried to refurbish the paneling. Still peppered with bullet holes, the wood appeared to be at least a century old.

Feeling gloomy, Annie rested her elbows on the bar and propped her chin in her hands. She wondered where everything had gone wrong. She had bought Deadend out of her love for the Old West, her longing to bring a bit of frontier times to this modern age. She had been born to parents rich in oil and land, and raised on their ranch outside Dallas. Her father had been pure Texas cattleman at heart, and Annie had learned to ride, rope, and shoot with the best of his ranch hands. Her mother had been the more refined one, insisting Annie be provided the best education and a background in the arts. Thus Annie's nature had become divided between the wild and the civilized, a dichotomy she had banked on well when she had turned to commercial real estate as a career. Annie had found herself at home in some of the most sophisticated board rooms in Dallas, able to speak the crusty jargon of the good-old-boy oilmen or the more sophisticated language of bankers, accountants, and developers.

Even as she had achieved career successes at an early age, she had lost both her parents—her father three years ago to a heart attack, her mother only last Christmas, to emphysema. Her brother had seemed even more devastated by the deaths than she was, leaving Annie to be the strong one, to settle her parents' estate, sell their ranch, and even take on her folks' traditional role of trying to coddle and reform Larry.

Six months ago, when a banker friend had mentioned that the property in the Texas Panhandle was on the market, Annie had felt compelled to drive out and see the ghost town. From the moment she'd first laid eyes on Deadend, she'd felt a connection to this land deep in her soul, and had dreamed of bringing the desolate town back to life. Her friends in Dallas had declared she was crazy to make an offer on this forlorn, bleak property smack in the middle of Tornado Alley. But Annie had always relied on her instincts, and she'd had a feeling Deadend could become a cash cow, especially with the new state highway connecting the town to Amarillo.

Fundamentally, she'd bought Deadend out of a desire to return to the natural setting of her youth. She had thought reviving the ghost town would have pleased her parents, particularly her father, and she'd purposely involved Larry in the project to give his life new direction.

But everything had turned sour.

She smiled bitterly, longing for simpler times, when disputes were settled at high noon on Main Street, when Indians went on the warpath rather than to court. She wished she could have lived in those gritty and more honest times, and laughed at an image of herself as an

Annie Oakley–type character in the Old West, shooting it out with her thieving contractor.

Even better, she could have become a grand lady like her great-great-grandmother, Rosanna Dillon, who was once a pillar of Victorian Denver society. Annie had long admired Rosanna; indeed, she was Rosanna's namesake and greatly resembled her. She remembered her mother showing her Rosanna's picture and bragging about what a true lady she had been.

Oh, how wonderful it would be to go back to those romantic times and escape her current troubles! And of course, if she could have lived in such a dashing era, she would have needed the right man to share her old-fashioned world—a true, rugged individualist with character and grit, a man at home in a genteel parlor or shooting it out on the trail—not one of the homogenized, shallow types Annie had been dating for the past ten years. God knows, she could use an Old West hero to rescue her from her current plight!

Annie sighed. Enough daydreaming. There were no heroes to come dashing in to rescue her. There were just problems to solve, only her own wits to depend on. She may as well leave Deadend, go back to Dallas, and consult further with her attorney. . . .

Annie was about to leave the saloon when the wind began to roar more savagely than ever; she cried out in fear as the front saloon doors blasted open and a chair sailed across the room toward her! She dashed out of the missile's path and covered her face with her forearms as all around her timbers began to rattle and shriek and glass shattered; she feared a tornado could be brewing.

Was this what old Windfoot had meant by "the whirlwind"? Indeed, the wind now roared so violently that chairs and even tables were sailing about like so many matchsticks!

Annie staggered across the room, gripped the front door handles, and tried to push them closed. Standing there trembling, boot heels dug into the floor and body lashed by the wind, she felt as if she were wrestling with a demon. After several moments of frustrating struggle, she gave up and retreated, dodging additional flying debris as she dived behind the bar, where she cowered as the terrible howling and crashing continued.

Then a large object thudded down onto her back, prompting her to cry out in fear and pain. Shoving the item away, she saw that the portrait had landed on top of her. The naked beauty was still smirking, mocking her.

Damn it, not even her hiding spot was safe!

Annie struggled to her feet. Whirling toward the wall to dodge a rusty beer can hurtling toward her, she suddenly found herself face-to-face with an ancient-looking wanted poster that had been concealed behind the painting.

What in hell . . . ! With a gasp, Annie recognized the picture on the poster as that of her own great-great-grandmother, the ancestor she'd been thinking off mere seconds earlier, a woman whose face was so much like her own. What on earth was going on?

Annie's ancestor was glowering back, her pretty features fearsomely set, her long hair in pigtails. Wide-eyed, Annie read the caption: "Wanted, Dead or Alive, for Murder and Other Crimes Most Foul: Rotten Rosie Dillon."

"Rotten Rosie!" Annie cried.

She was appalled, not sure what to make of the wanted poster, which was yellowed and curled, and did appear quite old and authentic. But the notice made no sense: Her great-great-grandmother had been a grand lady, never an outlaw or a murderess! Had Larry played some kind of weird practical joke on her? And why was she looking at the amazing wanted poster mere seconds after thinking about Rosanna?

Before Annie could further contemplate the mystery, she was distracted by a banging behind her. She spun about just as the saloon doors crashed against the wall and a huge, ruggedly handsome man strode in. The very sight of him put a shiver down her spine.

The stranger was dressed in old-fashioned buckskins and wore a large round brown hat with a snakeskin band and an eagle feather at the back. He sported dark, collar-length hair and a short, scruffy beard. He held a Winchester rifle in one hand and a crumpled piece of paper in the other. The wind whipped his buckskins about a massive, hard-muscled frame that oozed menace. A huge Colt was strapped to one sinewy thigh, a long knife to the other.

And his eyes! Even from across the room, Annie could tell they were dark and ruthless. That merciless gaze was fixed on her with riveting intensity; the man radiated an aura of danger and raw sensuality that staggered her on a deep, elemental level.

There was something almost savage about his visage, and she wondered if he might be part Indian. Indeed, he appeared as if he had materialized from another time or had been lost in the wilderness for ages. Could he be a rancher from the area? If so, that would explain the rifle. But his manner of dress was so bizarre!

As the wind quieted a bit, he spoke in a deep, charged voice. "Step out from 'round that bar, sister. Slow like." He pointed his rifle toward her.

Annie gulped. Although it wasn't that unusual to see a man with a rifle in these parts, having it pointed at her was another matter altogether! Nonetheless, she lifted her chin, stepped forward, and faced the newcomer with bravado. "Well, hello, mister. Who are you? And hasn't anyone told you it's a federal offense to possess eagle feathers?"

Appearing less than amused, the man uncrumpled and held up the piece of paper, which Annie was astounded to see was a newer-looking copy of the very wanted poster she'd just spotted hanging above the bar!

"This you, lady?"

"No, of course not—it's my great-great-grandmother," Annie retorted.

The stranger laughed and shoved the poster into his coat pocket. "Well, that's an original story if I ever heard one. Come on, sister, let's go. My grandpappy always said you gotta reap what you sow. You broke the law and I'm haulin' you in. I've come a long way to find you, and it's time for us to head out."

Annie's mouth fell open as feelings of unreality swamped her. "Head out? Where?"

"To Central, Colorado, to bring you to justice."

"To Colorado? To justice? Are you out of your mind? Why, that's the craziest—"

Annie stopped cold as the man lifted his rifle, threw the lever, and chambered a round. "All right, lady, enough palavering. Get your butt moving out them saloon doors. You're wanted dead or alive, and it makes no nevermind to me."

Annie's heart galloped with fear. Oh, God, this nut was serious! Clearly he was prepared to kill her if she didn't cooperate. What kind of lunatic was he? She observed the deadly determination in his stance, his eyes, the rifle in his huge, tanned hands. Although she'd been trained in self-defense, she knew a no-win situation when she saw one, and realized her only recourse was to humor this maniac.

Cautiously she moved toward him.

He held up a hand, nodding toward the purse hanging from her shoulder. "What's that, sister?"

"My handbag."

"Give it over."

"Not on your life!"

"Do it, or it's fixin' to have several big holes blowed in it." He smiled nastily. "If I don't miss and shoot you instead."

Glaring murder at him, Annie removed the bag from her shoulder and hurled it at him.

He caught it without taking his eyes off her. Backing up slightly, juggling his gun and her bag, the stranger opened the purse and rifled through it. He tossed her nail file on the floor, then flipped the bag shut and threw it back at her.

"You satisfied now?" she hissed.

"No. Lift your coat."

"*What*?" she shrieked.

"You heard me. Hitch it up, sister, or I'll do it for you. I gotta see if you're packin'."

Seething with defiance, Annie hiked her car coat halfway up to her bosom, then lowered it. She glanced at the stranger to see amusement and some darker emotion gleaming in his eyes. "If I did have a gun, I'd kill you."

He made no direct comment, only pointed with his rifle. "Out the door."

"You have got to be—"

"I said, out the gall-durned door!"

Sick with fear and certain the man was delusional, Annie proceeded outside onto the saloon's porch just as the violent wind gusted again. Choking on dust, she gazed in horror at two brown horses tied to the antique hitching post. Both animals sported canteens and bulging saddlebags that suggested preparedness for a long journey.

But horses! Appalled, Annie turned to her demented captor. "You *must* be kidding."

"You don't listen too well, do you?"

The rest happened in a flash. With a curse, the man set down his rifle, seized a handful of Annie's coat, and hauled her down the steps. Planting one strong hand squarely beneath her rear, he hoisted her, none too gently, into the saddle of the first horse. Before she could even react, he pulled a length of strong twine from the saddlebags and securely bound her wrists to the pommel. He then retrieved his rifle, grabbed her reins, and mounted his own horse.

Annie's features were frozen in terror as the two galloped off into the wickedly howling wind.

Chapter 2

"Are you crazy?" Annie yelled, her words all but drowned out in the roar of the wind.

"Keep ridin', lady," came her captor's obdurate reply.

Annie ground her jaw and gripped the horse's flanks with her thighs, hanging on to her precarious perch in the saddle as best she could. The rough twine binding her wrists cut cruelly into her tender flesh with each lunge of the horse. She was a skilled rider, but not when someone else held the reins. And it seemed this madman held the reins not only to her horse but to her life as well!

They were riding north hell-bent-for-leather, galloping across a long red mesa dotted with yucca and prickly pear, clumps of prairie grass, and a few patches of yellow and violet wildflowers bravely challenging the fury of the elements. Along craggy arroyos, the stunted forms of mesa oaks stood misshapen by the wind. As they passed through a brake of buffalo grass, a flock of pheasants flapped and screeched their way into the cold, somber skies.

Annie could have screamed herself. She could not believe what was happening to her, that this bizarre stranger had kidnapped her. Was he truly insane, accusing her of being both an outlaw and a dead woman? Would he take her off into the hills somewhere and murder her now?

Icy tentacles of fear gripped Annie's heart, threatening to throw her into full-fledged panic. *Get a grip*, she silently scolded herself. *You'll never get out of this situation alive if you freak out completely.*

She studied her captor covertly, noting the hard line of his jaw, his broad shoulders and muscular arms, his easy seat in the saddle, and the way his hard thighs molded to his horse. Whether he was sane or not, she was clearly up against one hell of a powerful adversary. Even if she managed to get the drop on him, his raw physical strength might easily subdue her.

Where had he come from? How had he acquired the wanted poster, the same one that had been on the barroom wall? Why was he convinced she was her own great-great-grandmother? Even as Annie's mind spun with the overwhelming questions, her kidnapper caught her eyeing him.

Annie lifted her chin. "Who are you, mister?"

To Annie's surprise, the man laughed. "Well, I 'spect since you and I are fixin' to be trail buddies for a spell, you have a right to know. I'm Sam Noble, a bounty hunter based in Denver. I'm here pursuing a warrant for your arrest issued by Judge J. D. Righteous of Gilpin County."

Annie's jaw dropped in amazement. "You have got to be kidding! There is no warrant for my arrest. Besides, there are no bounty hunters living in this century—certainly not fools dressed like you and riding horses!"

He chuckled. "Sure, sister. There ain't no bounty hunters, just like there ain't no outlaws and murderesses like you."

Annie stared daggers at him. "I'm not an outlaw and a murderess, and you have absolutely no right to shanghai me at gunpoint. Furthermore, why did you accuse me of being my own great-great-grandmother back at the saloon?"

He scowled. "Now don't go trying to confound me with your wabash. As any fool can see, you're Rotten Rosie in the flesh. It's your face on the wanted poster, so I'm taking you up to Central to be tried for your crimes."

"B-but that's the most absurd story I've ever heard!" Annie declared. "First of all, there's no way I can be my

own great-great-grandmother, Rosanna Dillon. I'm Annie Dillon, an entirely *different* person. Besides, my
great-great-grandmother has been dead for more than
half a century—not to mention the fact that she was a
grand Denver lady, never an outlaw or a murderess.
Furthermore, if you take me off to Central City claiming
I'm some woman who lived over a century ago, you'll
only make a laughingstock of yourself."

"And you're only trying to hornswoggle me with your
loco talk," the man retorted. "I say you're Rosie and
you're headin' for Central—and a meeting with the
hangman, I 'spect."

Annie gulped. "The h-hangman! But no one is hanged
in this day and age!"

"Tell that to the judge, honey." He grinned. "J. D.
Righteous has been punishing lawbreakers in Gilpin
County for over a quarter of a century, ever since gold
was discovered at Gregory Gulch back in '59. Couple
weeks ago, J.D. handed me your wanted poster and said,
'Sam, why don't you hunt down this here female desperado? She's a bad 'un, I'll allow.'"

Annie was flabbergasted. "My God—you talk as if
we're living in the late nineteenth century!"

The man appeared perplexed. "We are."

Annie was rendered speechless. She was clearly in the
clutches of a lunatic. Again she struggled to ward off
panic, realizing hysteria would not serve her well in her
current desperate situation. She glanced about, trying to
gain her bearings. They were still galloping along at a
mean pace, and she judged they must be in the Oklahoma Panhandle by now, for Deadend was only two miles
from the border. In the distance she spotted the dramatic outline of Black Mesa, the rugged, high plateau that
stretched for miles along the western horizon. She knew
the Oklahoma Panhandle was less than forty miles wide,
and the way they were plowing the trail, they would
likely make it into Colorado before nightfall. From there
Central City must be another three hundred miles or so,
albeit through more rugged and mountainous terrain—
a good ten days' trip if they remained on horseback.

Horseback! This was nutty as hell!

Annie glanced at her abductor, sizing up his determined gaze fixed on the horizon ahead. Surely there was
some way to get through to this man, to convince him
she was not Rotten Rosie.

Before she could contemplate the challenge further,
her captor called out, "Whoa!" and brought their horses
to a halt at the edge of a narrow stream lined with
cottonwoods.

Dismounting, he said gruffly, "Reckon we'll stop here,
fill the canteens, and water the horses. These animals
ain't been rested for a spell."

"Will you release me from my bonds?" Annie asked
shrilly.

"I reckon you can stretch your legs—if you'll promise
to behave yourself."

She glowered, but he relented nonetheless, striding
over to her horse and untying her hands. Annie rubbed
her chafed wrists and hopped to the ground. A sudden
smile lit her face as she spotted her handbag dangling
from the pommel. She grabbed it and pulled out her
billfold.

"Here—look at this!" she declared, extending the
wallet toward Sam Noble.

A frown furrowed his brow. "What's that?"

"My billfold. Open it and you'll find proof that I'm
not the woman you're looking for."

His scowl deepened. "How so?"

Annie flipped open the wallet and held it up. "This
contains my driver's license and other items of identification proving I'm not the woman you're seeking but her
great-great-granddaughter, and that we're living in the
1990s, not the 1880s."

Her captor only sneered. "The 1990s?"

"Yes."

Muttering an expletive, Sam grabbed Annie's wallet,
snapped it shut, and stuffed it back inside her bag.
"Sister, I have no intention of listening to your hokum or
going through your satchel. Everyone knows all about
Rotten Rosie and her bag of tricks. You're some storyteller, spinning yarns to save yourself from the gallows—
either that, or you're plumb haywire."

"And you're not?"

He pulled the wanted poster from his pocket, uncrumpled it, and waved it at her in disgust. "How many times do I gotta say it? It's *your* picture on this here poster. So don't go trying to sway me with your wild talk. If you're like every other criminal I've ever hauled in, I suspect you're a liar rather than crazy. But if I know J. D. Righteous, he'll make you pay for your crimes, loco or not." He paused, his dark, merciless gaze sliding over her with contempt. "'Sides, if I ever seen a female outlaw, it's you, sister—from them britches on your butt to the sass spillin' from your mouth."

"Why, you . . ." Fuming, Annie waved her bag at him. "Why won't you listen to me, or even look at my identification?"

He was breathing hard. "Unless you want me to toss your treasure trove into the next arroyo, you'd best hush up."

Annie did so, clenching her jaw as he turned and strode away, leading the horses to the stream. She gazed around the rock-lined gulch, sizing up her chances for escape.

"And don't go gettin' no smart ideas about hightailing it," he called over his shoulder. "I'll shoot you in your tracks. Like I told you, makes no nevermind to me."

Annie stuck out her tongue at his back and contemptuously mouthed his words, "Makes no nevermind to me." Grateful he hadn't seen her display of contempt, she cleared her throat and called, "Hey, I—er, need to see to my business."

He turned and grinned. "Toss me your coat and boots, and have at it."

"I'll freeze to death!" she yelled back, outraged.

"Not if you rattle your hocks. And you sure as hell won't try an escape in your stocking feet, with no coat."

He was right and Annie knew it, to her fury. Muttering under her breath, she pulled off her boots and coat and hurled them at him. Then she ducked into a stand of skinny, shivering cottonwoods.

When she emerged, he threw the items back at her.

"Well, the horses is watered and the canteens is full. Ready to mount up?"

Shuddering from the cold, Annie yanked on her coat, then plopped down on the ground, pulling on her boots. "I'll see you in hell for this, Samuel Noble," she hissed through chattering teeth.

He strode over and pulled her to her feet. "Hell, sugar, I reckon you'll beat me there."

Had she not been assured of brutal retaliation, Annie would have slapped his arrogant face. As he led her off to her horse, she feared he might have spoken the truth about her beating him to the next life. She mounted her filly, her spirits sinking when he again tied her wrists to the saddle pommel; her skin was already smarting from the abrasion of the rough twine.

Still, as they rode off, Annie realized she couldn't afford to give up. Glancing ahead at Black Mesa, she tried a placating tone. "Look, mister, I think we got off on the wrong foot, and we can easily clear up this little misunderstanding. Why don't you just admit you've made a mistake, one for which you're bound to pay dearly? You know what you've done amounts to kidnapping, pure and simple. You could spend the rest of your life in prison for abducting me—"

"Abducting you, my butt," he sneered. "I've apprehended an outlaw, lady."

Annie's patience snapped. "Well, you have the wrong damn woman! Now, why don't you just leave me at the state park up ahead, and we'll call it even?"

"State park?" he scoffed. "What in hell state is that? We're in Indian Territory, sister. Smack dab in the middle of the *mal país*."

"The *mal* what? Indian Territory! Mister, you're about fifty-two cards short of a deck!"

"And you'd best hush up for a spell," he snapped back. "I'm sick of your babble."

Annie cursed under her breath and stared stonily ahead.

Across from Annie, Samuel Noble, bounty hunter from Denver and true man of the West, felt baffled by this female outlaw he had just captured. Of course it was this woman's face on the wanted poster—a countenance he had memorized and sought for weeks now. Indeed, his grandmother, a very wise Cheyenne medicine woman, had urged him to heed the words of the band's sacred idiot, that his quarry would be found beyond the Numhaisto, the wind of the south. Well, he had ridden south, way south, and now he had found his quarry just as the sacred man had foretold. He was determined to take this wildcat to justice and secure his reward. But she sure was an odd one, talking out of her head about being someone else, a woman from the next century. Surely it was just reckless jabber from a desperate woman trying to escape her fate.

She was also far prettier than he'd expected, and tall, close to his own height of six feet. She had a nicely endowed bosom and long legs that gripped her horse well; she was clearly an expert rider, just as any outlaw must be. Her face was especially lovely, with a broad brow, large blue eyes, a straight feminine nose, a wide full mouth, and a pointed chin. Her thick swath of brown hair was shot with highlights of gold and bound in a single braid, tempting him to loosen those thick strands and run his fingers through the rich tresses.

He grunted, warning himself that he was venturing into dangerous territory. Although he'd never before taken a female to face such grim charges, he'd been entrusted with bearing this lawbreaker to justice, and he could not afford to develop softer feelings toward his quarry. Though she was a woman—and a fiery, beautiful one at that—she would likely end her life as all murderers did, dancing at the end of a rope, and he was a fool to think of her as anything but the dangerous desperado she clearly was.

He was jerked from his thoughts as he heard her gasp beside him. "Burr in your saddle, sister?"

Features white, Annie nodded toward three distant riders stirring up clouds of dust. "Look! Who are they?"

Shading his eyes with a hand, Sam stared ahead and spotted three Indian braves cresting the horizon on their paint ponies. "'Pears like a bunch of young Indian bucks out on a hunting pass. Comanche by the look of them."

"Comanches!" Annie exclaimed.

"Didn't I tell you we're in Indian Territory?" He grinned. "It's a well-known fact that only the brave or the crazy venture forth here in No-Man's-Land—"

"Well, I certainly agree you're crazy!" she blustered.

"—even with Judge Parker trying his best to hang every scoundrel hiding out in a rustler's roost," he finished with forbearance.

Annie regarded him in disbelief. This was preposterous! She was well aware that the hanging judge, Isaac Parker, had lived over a century ago.

Warily she eyed the approaching warriors. "Judge Parker, my foot. Just look at those braves. Why, they appear as if they just materialized out of a John Ford western."

Scowling at her comments, Sam remarked, "The Comanche are supposed to be peaceable now that the redskins have been gathered up on the reservations. Hell, these days, even old Chief Quanah spends more time in Washington than he does here in the Llano Estacado."

"So the braves are no threat?" Annie asked, confused and apprehensive.

Sam watched the warriors gallop toward them. "Well, I wouldn't go that far. The Comanche'll still try to steal a horse or rustle cattle if the fancy strikes 'um. Best let me handle 'um."

"Oh, be my guest."

With the warriors drawing ever closer on their prancing ponies, Annie stared at them in fear and wonderment. She realized the braves were little more than teenage boys, dressed in Indian buckskins and quilled moccasins, wearing copper or silver beads around their necks and eagle feathers in their braided hair; yet the orange and black paint on their hawkish faces was daunting. Were they simply adventuresome adolescents out playing cowboys and Indians? A feeble possibility, especially since the braves appeared as if they'd just stepped out of Custer's last stand!

As the ponies snorted and stamped, one of the warriors addressed Sam in an Indian dialect, his tone loud

and arrogant. To Annie's amazement, Sam replied with
rapid signs and Indian words of his own. Watching the
brisk, decisive movements of his hands, the way he
motioned toward his eyes, nose, ears, or mouth, the way
he waved his fingers or pounded his fists together, Annie
found the exchange downright eerie. Several times during the spirited conversation, one of the braves pointed
impudently at Annie while the others laughed. She got a
sick feeling from the many frank looks and sneers the
Comanche braves directed toward her.

Finally Sam tossed one of the braves a small sack, and
the three whooped their Comanche yells, wheeled their
ponies, and galloped away.

Choking on the dust they stirred, Annie turned, wide-
eyed, to her captor. "What was *that* all about?"

"It's like I thought. They're just a bunch of young
whippersnappers, still wet behind the ears and bored at
the reservation. They're out on a hunting pass, looking
for quarry, and trouble. They wanted to know if we'd
seen cavalry, and I told 'um no."

Cavalry, hunting passes . . . Annie's head was spinning! "Thank God you were able to get rid of them so
easily," she muttered. "How did you know how to talk
to them?"

He shrugged. "I'm one-quarter Cheyenne. Over the
years, my grandmother's band has adopted a Comanche
or two. Being around the people, you learn the lingo—
and the signs."

Annie was still struggling to digest everything, with
little luck. "So you're part Indian. . . . What did you
give those boys?"

"Beef jerky." He grinned. "Actually, we got off easy.
They wanted you."

As he galloped off, tugging along Annie's mount, it
took her a moment to absorb the impact of his statement. At last, she retorted saucily, "Well, maybe I should
have gone with them."

He laughed with contempt. "Yeah, I'd imagine you're
the type who would bed down with redskins to escape
the gallows."

Fury all but blinded Annie. "Oh, you beast! If my wrists weren't tied, I'd slap your insolent face. And to think you're a quarter Indian yourself—and ridiculing your own people."

He turned in the saddle to look her over slowly, and crudely. "I wasn't insulting my people," he drawled.

His inference was obvious, and her blistering reply was drowned out by a sudden gust of wind.

They rode at a breakneck pace for the remainder of the day, crossing the wagon-wheel-rutted expanse of the old Santa Fe Trail, and stopping only to water the horses along the sandy banks of the Cimarron River and to eat a brief, unappetizing meal of hard biscuits and cold, greasy bacon. They continued across windswept mesas, through fields of waving buffalo grass and along jagged arroyos that resembled small canyons. Toward sundown, Annie felt exhausted, her face burning from the wind, her wrists raw, her bottom sore from the brutal pounding. She was about to protest to Sam when her gaze was arrested by a small band of humpbacked cattle moving across an escarpment to the west. About a half dozen in number, the mystical beasts glided across the stark mesa, their hulking forms backlit by the eerie red glow of sundown.

"My God, are those what I think they are?" Annie's words came out the merest whisper.

"Yep. Bison are growing scarce as hens' teeth in these parts, but I allow there are still a few small bands left here on the Staked Plain. I reckon them braves we spoke with are on their trail."

Annie reeled. Indians hunting buffalo? This was downright spooky. Plus, she was so physically and emotionally drained from her ordeal that she couldn't begin to understand it all. She desperately needed a break, a respite so she could gather her wits and try to make sense of the incomprehensible.

"Hey, Noble, are we ever going to stop?" she called irritably. "I'm exhausted and starving, and that 'lunch' you fed me was about as appetizing as cow chips. Besides, we can't make Central City tonight."

"True, but only a fool lingers in Indian Territory. We're just inside the Colorado border now, so I reckon we can stop for the night soon."

Annie was about to comment when she heard a voice shouting in the distance. "Hey, Noble! Samuel Noble!"

Glancing ahead, Annie spotted two riders moving toward them from the next rise. She glanced at Sam and spotted recognition, along with a certain wariness, in his eyes. As Sam reined in their mounts, she studied the approaching men, two more characters straight out of the annals of *How the West Was Won*.

One rider was young, slim, and handsome; he wore a white Stetson, a checked shirt, and jeans; in awe, she spotted an old-fashioned lawman's star glittering on his chest. The other man was older and scruffier, dressed in a ratty blanket poncho and buckskins. Studying his whiskery face, she fought a wince as she observed that the tip of his nose was missing, the bridge ending in a deformed stump with two misshapen nostrils.

The four met in the valley, their horses puffing and neighing.

"Well, Sam Noble," greeted the young one. "If you ain't a sight for sore eyes." He glanced at Annie, appreciation glinting in his gaze. "And tugging along such a pretty filly."

"Hello, Billy," replied Sam. "What are you and Stub Nose doing in these parts?"

"Just headin' back to Indian Territory after a little fandango over at Trinidad." Again, the man's gaze settled on Annie. "You folks been through there today? We're trackin' a gang of whiskey peddlers for Judge Parker."

Judge Parker again! Annie thought sinkingly.

Sam answered, "Yeah, we just rode through the *mal país* and only spotted a few Comanche bucks out huntin'."

"Comanches!" scoffed the one named Stub Nose. "I'll scalp 'um and string 'um up by their innards!"

Annie grimaced at the man's grisly descriptions and the venom in his tone.

"Now Stub Nose," scolded Billy, "you can't lynch

every redskin we come across, even if one of Sitting Bear's braves did burn off the tip of your nose and slice off two fingers."

An *Indian* had chopped off some of this man's extremities? Annie was getting a *very* bad feeling from this conversation!

Billy slanted Sam a reproachful glance. "Hey, Noble, ain't ya gonna introduce us to the lady? And how come you got her hog-tied?"

To her astonishment, Annie watched Sam's fingers move to the butt of his Colt, an obvious warning to the other men. "This here is the outlaw Rotten Rosie, wanted dead or alive for murder," he informed them in charged tones. "I'm takin' her up to Central for the reward money . . . and you can't have her."

Billy chuckled. "Rotten Rosie, eh?" He winked at Annie. "Well, she looks pretty damn fresh to me."

Sam shot Billy a menacing glance, and Stub Nose squinted at Annie. "Know what, Billy? I'm thinkin' she be Rotten Rosie. Thought she looked familiar. Reckon I seen her wanted poster last time I was up at Central."

"Well, what a plumb shame," lamented Billy. "But we're still being unmannerly toward a lady." He pulled off his hat and spoke with silvery charm. "Ma'am, I'm Billy Singletree, deputy U.S. marshal out of Fort Smith, and this here's my partner, Stub Nose Pete. We're mighty pleased to make your acquaintance."

Annie acknowledged the man's words with a stiff nod. Although everything sounded demented, she was smart enough to recognize a friendly face, and an opportunity to enlist aid.

In a hoarse, near-desperate tone, she addressed Billy. "Look, mister, I don't care who you are. But if you are a lawman, you're duty bound to help me." She hurled a glare at Sam. "This lunatic abducted me!"

To Annie's frustration, all three men laughed. *Laughed*—now that was an understatement. They all but split their sides.

Billy shook his head at Sam. "You got a feisty one on your hands, don't ya, Noble?"

"Sure do," he grimly agreed.

Billy focused his amused gaze on Annie. "Ma'am, I'd purely love to take you off Sam's hands, and not just for the reward money. But the fact is, Sam nabbed you first, so you're his prize. That's the code among us lawmen here in the West, and Sam'd kill us if we tried to interfere."

"Damn right," seconded Sam.

Annie's spirits sank.

Stub Nose addressed Annie. "Case you don't know it, ma'am, Samuel Noble's a legend in these here parts, 'specially in No-Man's-Land and up around Denver. He ain't one to tangle with, nossir. Honey, you couldn't a'picked you a better man to take you to the hangin'."

"Thank you," muttered Annie with a frozen smile. "You just made my day."

As the men continued to shoot the bull about the gang of whiskey peddlers Billy and Stub Nose were tracking, Annie's mind began to whirl again. *What* was happening to her? Nothing was making sense. She could barely think.

But she knew one thing: This was *serious*. This could be actually happening. She was caught in the throes of a nightmare . . . yet no dream could be *this* real!

Chapter 3

⟶⟩◯◯⟨⟵

In a sheltered arroyo near a tiny steam, Annie sat wan-faced, her wrists lashed to a scrawny mesa oak. They'd left Billy Singletree and Stub Nose—whoever in hell *they* were—moments earlier, and now they had stopped for the night.

Although the killer wind had mercifully died down, Annie was exhausted, her body covered with dust and her wrists stinging from the twine. Glancing down at her bonds, she realized numbly that at some point during this bizarre day—probably when she'd struggled with the bounty hunter back at Deadend—she'd lost her wristwatch, and she had no idea what time it was.

No idea what time it was. Now *that* was funny!

A few paces away from her, Annie's captor was moving about, calmly setting up camp, acting perfectly normal, as if the Looney Tunes festival wasn't still going on. Under other circumstances, Annie might have admired this man across from her: his robust strength, his lithe grace as he moved, the way his buckskins pulled against the muscles of his hard thighs as he hunkered down to place a pot of beans on the fire. She'd always felt drawn to cowboys, to men of the West. She even found whiskers appealing. She was conscious of her captor's brash masculinity even now, but she simply had much more pressing priorities.

Survival was pretty near the top of the list. Correction—survival was the *entire* list. Night was ap-

27

proaching, and she had no idea what kind of man Samuel Noble really was. Correction, she *had* learned from the inimitable Stub Nose that her captor was a legend. How fortunate she was to be escorted to the gallows by a legend. It was daunting to realize that so much male power stood between her and escape. Self-defense training or not, this huge man would be very hard to throw off.

And it didn't help one bit that her head was splitting, her mind again careening with outlandish information she could make no sense of: Indians and buffalo; the *mal país*, aka No-Man's-Land; Stub Nose, with his penchant for lynching Comanches; Billy Singletree, with his antique marshal's badge.

Of course, nothing in this crazy montage could even exist unless she had somehow landed in the nineteenth century. She'd still been in the 1990s the last time she had looked, so where in hell *was* she? And who else would they run across on this mad trek through *The Wild, Wild West*? Perhaps Butch Cassidy and the Sundance Kid? Or Charlie Siringo chasing them? Sitting Bull and Georgie Custer having a tea party? Anything seemed possible here in *The Outer Limits*.

And to think that mere hours ago, she had assumed her captor was crazy. Well, everyone couldn't be crazy. Perhaps *she* was crazy.

Annie groaned, mentally ordering her mind off the Tilt-A-Whirl. She had to think rationally. She must use her wits.

So what was happening? A really sick practical joke came to mind, but who could engineer this kind of cinematic spectacle? That must mean . . . Had she *really* crossed over into the nineteenth century? It seemed incomprehensible, but how else could she explain not seeing a pickup truck or a telephone pole, an asphalt road or an airplane all day long? Annie had driven through this country before and it wasn't *this* desolate. There were farms and ranches, eighteen-wheelers barreling along. And if she hadn't crossed through some time barrier, how else could she explain encountering all these crusty characters straight out of *Lonesome Dove*?

But *how* could this be possible? Only this morning, she'd been in Deadend wishing she could have lived in frontier times and could meet a man with "true grit."

A sick feeling washed over her. Could her wishes have caused this misadventure to happen? Or had she lost her mind? Annie suspected her "journey" through time was real—as real as the noose that might soon hang around her neck! She had wished for an Old West adventure and instead had been granted an Old West nightmare!

Yet . . . if a flight of fancy had prompted this bad dream, couldn't she escape the same way? Annie concentrated fiercely, trying to "wish" herself back to the present. She shut her eyes and beseeched the fates to allow her to awaken from this larger-than-life ordeal.

"Care for some beans and coffee?"

The bounty hunter's voice jerked Annie back to reality. So much for the wish theory, she thought glumly. This particular voyage through Hades showed no signs of ending soon.

She eyed the very real man standing above her, holding a plate of beans and a cup of coffee. The smell of the food reached her nostrils, and she realized she was hungry. Life went on, she supposed—at least on some level, and assuming she *was* still alive.

Had she been feeling courteous, she might have even acknowledged that it was kind of her captor to prepare dinner. Only Annie wasn't feeling cordial at all. She was tired, scared, shaky, miserable, on her way to the gallows—and all because of *him*.

She jerked her head toward her bound wrists. "Do you expect me to lick the plate and lap up the coffee?"

A half smile tugged at his lips. "God, I never heard a female with a mouth like yours. I'll let you loose long enough to eat. But you'd best behave."

"Believe me, I'm not up to tackling you at the moment."

Staring down at his captive, Sam Noble had to agree. This woman didn't look like a hardened outlaw. She looked sad and bewildered—and too damn pretty, of course. Oh, there was still a flicker of spirit left in her, but the pale creature seated before him bore quite a contrast to the feisty woman who had confounded him with her crazy talk.

Indeed, reality seemed to have hit her hard. He'd been watching her as he'd set up camp. That look on her face . . . What would he call it? Like she was lost, in a trance or something. Her chin might have been lifted in pride, but her eyes had seethed with fear and confusion. Then, while he was shoveling up her beans, he'd watched her shut her eyes and squinch up her face real tight, like she was praying.

The sight of it had made Sam feel right sorry for her, though he knew he could ill afford such perilous feelings. Still, her vulnerability had tugged at his conscience.

Why the change in her? Guess it must have been some shock, being captured, realizing she must finally pay for her crimes. It was hard not to feel some compassion for a woman caught in her plight.

But she was an outlaw, and Sam knew he mustn't forget this. Lawbreakers were skilled at fooling others and enticing their sympathies. Once they gained a man's confidence, they'd knife him in the back in an instant, without a flicker of remorse.

Keeping a wary eye trained on his captive, Sam leaned over and set down her plate, then unbound her wrists. Straightening, he caught a tantalizing whiff of her hair. He didn't like what *that* did to him, either. He hastily backed away.

Annie rubbed her wrists and watched Sam abruptly step back. Why was he so edgy? Surely he wasn't afraid of her. She watched him serve himself and sit down across from her. Picking up her own plate and cup, she supposed the polite thing to do would be to thank him for the food and for freeing her wrists.

Only she *still* wasn't feeling very gracious.

She took a long sip of the strong, hot coffee. The taste reassured her a bit. She glanced over to see Sam staring at her, his expression unreadable.

She cleared her throat. "So, who were those two delightful characters we encountered—Billy and Stub Nose?"

A grin softened his features. "Oh, Billy Singletree is a passably decent sort, I reckon. I knew him when we was both deputy marshals for Isaac Parker, and Billy's still trackin' for the judge."

Annie stifled a groan at yet another mention of the illustrious Judge Parker. God, her head was throbbing so!

"But why Billy hooked up with that piece-of-trash partner of his is beyond me," Sam finished with distaste.

Remembering the incident, she shot him a hard look. "You know, you seemed to tense up when we came across those two. You didn't want them to take me away and deny you your bounty, right?"

He laughed harshly.

Her voice rose a notch. "You find that amusing, do you?"

His gaze bored into hers. "Lady, if Billy Singletree had gotten his hooks on you, he might have turned you in for the bounty, but he damn well would have had his way with you first. As for Stub Nose Pete—that rodent would have raped you within the first two minutes and slit your throat the next."

Annie shuddered. Was he saying things could actually be *worse*? "So you were protecting me," she muttered ironically.

"I'm doing my job, and I don't take advantage of women along the way," he replied heatedly.

Although his words did provide some measure of reassurance, Annie was still far from in a mood to be appeased. She realized there were a million questions she should ask this man, but at the moment she was just overwhelmed.

Staring into the fire, she muttered in the barest whisper, "This is really happening, isn't it?"

He fell silent, regarding her in bemusement for a long moment. "Yeah, it's really happening. You're really caught and you're really gonna face justice."

Annie glanced up at him sharply. She should have laughed in his face, only her sense of humor was wearing thin.

Chapter 4

❦

"So, Mr. Noble, tell me a little more about the mess this 'Rotten Rosie' is in."

It was morning—a bleak, overcast day, but mild enough that Annie had shed her coat. They were on the move again, heading west across a vast grassland.

After going around the bend last night, Annie was rested and back in her strong-woman mode, ready to tackle the dauntless bounty hunter riding beside her and divest him of his ridiculous notions about her. The fact that she might have crossed over some time barrier still all but unhinged her each time she thought about it— but however she may have arrived here, she was clearly in grave danger. She could no longer dismiss Sam Noble as some sort of crackpot; indeed, Stub Nose and Billy had confirmed for her that her captor meant business, that he really intended to take her to the gallows. She had to learn more about the immediate threat she faced, try to get a handle on how to save her life.

After frowning over her question for a moment, the bounty hunter raised a dark brow. "You mean the mess *you're* in."

Annie chewed her lower lip in betrayal of her irritation. "Mister, I already told you yesterday, only you don't listen too well. I'm not Rotten Rosie. I'm Rosie's great-great-granddaughter, Annie Dillon."

"Who lives in another century, right?" he finished dryly.

"Right."

Sam's gaze beseeched the heavens. "Rosie or Annie, it makes no nevermind to me. I'm still taking you to Central and turning you over to justice."

Annie spoke through gritted teeth. "Why? What exactly is Rosie wanted for?"

"You mean what are *you* wanted for?"

"Damn it, Sam Noble!"

He waved a hand. "All right, don't pop your cork. I'll tell you." He paused for a moment as the skies rumbled overhead. "According to Judge Righteous, two years ago, you and your bridegroom come through Rowdyville on your honeymoon."

Feeling a cold, fat raindrop splash on her nose, Annie scowled. "Rowdyville? Where's that?"

"It's a small former mining town northeast of Central, kinda cattywampus between there and Denver. Anyhow, scuttlebutt is, your husband deserted you on your wedding night. Afterward, you went plumb loco, shooting up the town and killing a man named Bart Cutter just because he stepped into your path. Ever since, you been terrorizing Rowdyville, robbing stages and rustlin' cattle, and you're wanted for murder and bank robbery, among other crimes."

Annie's mind whirled with these revelations, which she could not reconcile with what she remembered of her family history. For one thing, if her great-great-grandfather really had deserted her great-great-grandmother on their wedding night, then she never would have been born. She'd also seen pictures of Rosanna Dillon as a grand lady in Denver. How could this be if she was a murderess and an outlaw?

Unless she'd been sent back to a period in time *before* her great-great-grandmother became a revered lady, she realized with a sudden, sinking feeling. Had she possibly been sent back to help Rosanna in some way? As bizarre as the prospect seemed, Annie realized she'd be well-advised to try to find this Rosie person, or her family history might well go the route of the dodo bird. Indeed, her only recourse at the moment seemed to be uncovering the truth about this outlaw Samuel Noble assumed was her.

Which meant she must either win her captor over to
her point of view or find a way to escape him. Taking in
his implacable expression, and the Colt strapped to his
side, she decided to try reason first.

"You know, Sam, your story makes no sense."

"How come?"

"Why would this Rosie go on a rampage against a
town that had done her no harm?"

"Everyone knows Rotten Rosie is crazy."

"But there's just no reason my great-great-
grandmother would have murdered a complete stranger!
Can you tell me anything about this Bart Cutter?"

"I hear tell he was Royce Rowdy's main henchman."

"And who is Royce Rowdy?"

"He's the man who established Rowdyville fifteen
years ago, back when he hit a major vein of gold there.
He owns a big cattle ranch and most every building in
town."

"What kind of man is Rowdy?"

Sam sighed. "Truth to tell, he's known as Ruthless
Royce. Rumor is, he's a bully who has exploited the
town, especially since his gold mines became tapped out.
Got a bad case of gold fever, that one."

"He sounds like a prince of a fellow."

"Well, I'll allow not even old J.D. thinks much of
Royce," Sam continued. "J.D. has suspected for some
time that Royce jumped his daddy's claim out beyond
Black Hawk, but he never did have no proof, since his
daddy was found dead in the wilderness. Still, after you
went on your rampage, Rowdy brought forth a herd of
witnesses that seen you killin' Cutter, and Rowdy even
put up the reward money hisself, I hear. Since J.D. is as
honest and right as rain, he had no choice but to uphold
the law and issue the warrant for your arrest."

"But can't you see there's clearly more to this story
than meets the eye?" she cried.

Sam appeared unmoved. "It's my job to enforce the
law. The courts can sort out the rest."

"Not if we're dealing with a man of questionable
character!" Taking a steadying breath, Annie continued

in calmer tones. "And another thing. If I'm Rotten Rosie, what was I doing in Texas?"

"Heck, that's easy," he replied with a grin. "Hiding out from me, of course. J.D. warned me you've been known to lay low on occasion."

Annie made a sound of exasperation. "You have an answer for everything, don't you, Sam Noble? Well, maybe I'll just have a little chat with old J. D. Righteous myself. He can't possibly be as mule-headed and stubborn as *you*!"

Sam gave a shrug. "Suit yourself. Tell it to the judge if you want, sister. I'm still haulin' you in."

Annie fell silent, struggling to respond in a calm manner. "You know, there's only one thing to do, only one way I can prove to you that I'm not a murderess. We must go to Rowdyville, investigate Royce Rowdy, find the real Rosie, and discover the truth."

Sam only laughed humorlessly as the skies again reverberated and more scattered raindrops began to fall. "Lady, I've already found the real Rosie, and she's riding right across from me. You can lie and make up tall tales, try to weasel out of this all you want, but like my granddaddy always said, a bad girl'll reach a bad end every time."

Annie's patience snapped. "And I say I'm sick of hearing about you and your granddaddy!"

And she clamped her mouth shut.

Across from Annie, Sam Noble noted the expression of frustration on his captive's face. He felt more perplexed and unsettled by this woman than he cared to admit, for this feisty female challenged his beliefs and even stirred his blood.

He knew this woman who called herself "Annie" greatly favored the fugitive on the wanted poster. He knew any criminal would lie to escape justice. Given the fact that she dressed and rode a horse just like a man, and smarted off to him like no decent female he'd ever known, she must be the outlaw he had sought.

But this girl was also beautiful and proud, and seemed sincere. He'd even felt moved by her helplessness and confusion last night. Could she be telling the truth? The daunting possibility left him shifting uneasily in the saddle.

Naw, he quickly decided, she must be a liar. Otherwise, her resemblance to the "real" Rosie would be too much of a coincidence. His doubts must stem from the fact that he was unaccustomed to turning females over to justice, and he couldn't allow her feminine tricks to cloud his better judgment.

Nonetheless, his gaze strayed back to her, drinking in the proud tilt of her face, the loveliness of her wide mouth, and how wisps of her gold-shot brown hair had pulled loose from her braid and were whipping about her pretty face. Again, those forbidden urges coursed through him, man-woman sort of longings he could ill afford to have.

Imagining that supple neck snapping as she dangled at the end of a hangman's rope, he groaned as if his gut had been punched. At her frankly curious stare, he hastily jerked his gaze away. He would do his job, all right, but it was going to be a damn shame to hang her.

He was frowning over this gloomy prospect when a tremendous booming of thunder wrenched him from his thoughts. Wincing as a gust of wind sprayed rain in his face, he glanced overhead. How had he managed to become so distracted that he'd taken no note of the elements?

Her, that's how! Turning, he hollered, "Hold on, sister, we're gonna have to ride hard. I don't like the look of them skies. There's a town called Prairie Stump up the road a piece, and we're gonna hafta pray we can make it."

"Make it before what?" Annie asked.

"Before all hell busts loose."

Glancing at the skies as rain began falling harder, Annie felt a shiver of fear. "Do you mean hell or— Ouch!" she finished as a small hailstone bounced off her forehead.

"Shit!" yelled Sam.

Next Annie heard an ungodly, terrifying roar, and with her hands bound to the saddle horn, she could only cringe and wince in pain as a barrage of hailstones pounded her. She heard her horse's high whinny, felt it lurch forward.

"Damn it, woman, let's ride!" shouted the bounty hunter.

Pummeled by hail, they galloped as far as the nearest arroyo, the spooked horses shrieking and bucking much of the way. At last Sam managed to bring both mounts to a halt. In an instant he was down, cutting Annie's hands free. By now she was trembling, soaked, recoiling as nature continued to batter her.

He pulled her off her horse. She barely heard his voice over the clamor of the elements. "Hunker down, woman. I'll tie up the horses."

Hunker down *where*?

Glancing about wildly, Annie spotted an indentation in the craggy hillside beyond and made a dive for it, wedging her body into the opening and wrapping her arms about her head. At least the front of her was safe now, though hail still peppered her backside.

She heard the horses scream and stamp. Then something extraordinary happened. She felt Sam Noble's body sliding into place behind hers, covering her. Inexplicably, she felt warmed, even touched, that this hardened lawman would care enough to shield her from nature's fury. Indeed, even as she shivered, she felt his strong arms coming around her.

Oh, God. She shouldn't feel this searing tenderness, not now, not toward *him*! But, all at once, the life-and-death struggle between them receded, and they were just a man and a woman, fighting the elements, taking refuge in the earth and in each other.

Sam, too, felt the instinctive pull as he held Annie. Yes, this girl was an outlaw, but she was also a human being, a woman—wet, cold, frightened, and vulnerable. As they'd galloped to the arroyo, her cries of pain and fear had shaken him, arousing his manly instincts to protect her. When he'd joined her and found her shivering so fiercely, he'd been unable to resist putting his arms around her to warm her.

Now her lush curves felt so tempting against him that

he was hardly even conscious of the hail hammering his back.

As the storm continued to roar, Annie illogically felt safe for the first time in twenty-four tension-fraught hours. She ceased her shivering and became even more aware of the hard, warm, masculine body cocooning hers. After a while she relaxed enough to shift her hand from its cramped, uncomfortable position. In doing so, she unwittingly brushed Sam's thigh and heard him grunt.

Then her fingers encountered something very hard. His knife. That contact brought Annie spinning back to reality, to the threat against her life. Yes, Sam Noble was being a nice guy at the moment, but he still intended to bear her to her death. This daunting reality redoubled her determination.

When thunder roared with such violence that he flinched, Annie smoothly eased his knife from its sheath.

Chapter 5

❝**Y**ou ready to get up now?❞

An eternity later, Annie felt Sam's body leaving hers, then heard his deep voice. She twisted about, shaking off mud and hailstones, squinting as incredibly bright sunshine all but blinded her. The air was sweet, and a mourning dove was cooing, as if nature's fury had not just shaken the entire world to its core.

Not to mention what had happened to *her* world.

Sam Noble towered above her, filling her vision. He might be her captor, he might be mud-spattered, but, God, he was a man, his soaked buckskins clinging to the rugged beauty of his body, his damp hair curling about his face. One large, tanned hand was extended to her. Again, he was being a gentleman, trying to help her. Something deep inside her had to admire this, even respond to it.

But he also was her enemy, and Annie didn't like these feelings.

Still, she almost reached out to accept his assistance, then remembered his knife concealed beneath her body, in the muck where she was entrenched. Panic swamped her. There was no way she could stand without his noticing the weapon. Taking charge of herself, she shoved the blade deep into the mushy ground beneath her.

"Thanks," she muttered, reaching out, letting him pull her to her feet.

He held on to her hand for a split second too long, and Annie felt something sensual jolting them both. He moved back and for a moment they simply stared at each other, physical awareness heating the atmosphere between them. Something powerful and irresistible held them riveted. Something scary as hell.

At last, he reached out to wipe a dab of dirt from her nose. He grinned. "Lord, you look a sight."

Feeling extremely self-conscious, Annie took note of her mud-encrusted jeans. "Yeah, I do."

"You all right?" he added awkwardly.

Remembering his true motives, Annie was beset by confusion, tempted to ask him if he cared. But then he *had* just protected her with his body. God, this was unnerving! She didn't want to like this man or feel drawn to him—couldn't afford *any* softer emotions under the circumstances.

Maybe she was simply unused to this type of man, and that's what was rattling her so badly. She supposed Sam's protecting her was a nineteenth-century-guy thing to do. He didn't allow a woman to be pounded by hailstones—even if he was taking her to the gallows.

"I'm okay," she muttered at last. "How about you? You took the brunt of it."

"Oh, I'm pretty toughened and hard."

She had noticed. Again they stared at each other almost helplessly. Something was sizzling on the air— no, melting.

He cleared his throat, then glanced about the hail-strewn landscape. "Ah, shit."

"What's wrong?"

"One of the horses got loose."

Annie looked at a nearby scrub oak and saw that, indeed, only one animal remained tethered. "You're right. My horse is gone."

Shading his eyes with a hand, Sam perused the countryside, then smiled. "Hey, I think I see her in the distance. Maybe I can coax her close."

Gazing in the same direction, Annie spotted her filly chewing on prairie grass. "Good thinking." This man could likely coax *anything* female close.

"Hope I can get a rope on her," he continued. "Otherwise, we'll be riding double to Prairie Stump."

Annie reeled. She didn't think she could bear *that* particular torture, not after what they had just shared.

Although Annie assumed Sam would tie her up before proceeding, he surprised her when he merely retrieved his hat from a pile of hailstones, then strode directly to his horse. She watched him trot off toward her brown filly, working his lasso, whistling and coaxing all the while; her horse whinnied and shied, but soon began moving toward him. Annie smiled as she watched Sam throw out his rope with poetic grace, lassoing the animal on his first try.

She shook her head with grudging admiration. Damn, but this man had a way with horses, and a rope; she never could have lassoed that filly on her first try.

As he started back, tugging along her horse, she remembered the hidden knife and sucked in a shaky breath. She hated the thought of tusseling with him after he'd protected her. But this was her one chance to escape, and she knew she'd be a fool to blow it.

Thankfully, he was far enough away that she could still retrieve the knife. She quietly backed up to the hillside, knelt, and pulled the weapon from the muck. Securing the knife behind her, she straightened and warily watched him grow near.

She tried to plot her next move, fighting the instinctive fear rushing through her. How best could she use the weapon? She didn't want to knife Sam. If she was lucky, she might be able to approach him from behind, press the tip of the knife to his spine, and demand his gun. Then she could tie *him* up and escape.

Sure. In her dreams. He'd likely kill her within the first three seconds. But her life was at stake, so she had to give it a try.

About five yards away, he reined in both animals and grinned at her.

She flashed him a stiff smile. "So you got her. That's great."

Nodding back, Sam dismounted and removed his lasso from the filly's neck. As he stood next to the horse gathering up his rope, Annie's heart raced. Sam was distracted, and this might be her one chance, a moment when he was turned away from her and she was almost completely out of his line of vision.

Her mouth went dry. Well, it was now or never. Cautiously she started toward him, the knife raised and ready.

Then he froze. Then she froze, swamped by sickening dread.

In the next instant he whirled and threw out his lasso—this time at *her*. A split second later, the knife was snapped out of Annie's fingers and went spinning through the air even as she watched in stunned disbelief.

Annie was staggered by the spectacle. Who on earth *was* this character? It wasn't as if he were using a bullwhip to snap a cigarette out of someone's hand! He was using a lasso, and no man could be *that* skilled! Again, she remembered Stub Nose calling Sam Noble a legend, and her stomach took a nosedive.

In the next instant he loomed before her, grabbing her by the shoulders and shaking her until her teeth rattled.

His eyes blazed with anger. "Trying to get the drop on me, were you, sister?"

"I—" Annie recoiled at his blinding fury.

"Try a low-down stunt like that again, and . . . By damn, it'll be one long, brutal ride to Central with you cinched up facedown over your horse, but that's exactly what you'll get!"

Annie was speechless.

"You're lucky I don't drag your lousy butt to Prairie Stump!"

In short order, Sam hauled Annie over to her horse, plopped her into the saddle, and lashed her wrists to the pommel. Watching him retrieve his knife, gather his lasso, and mount his own horse, she seethed. Yet on another level, she supposed she should thank him.

Sam Noble had made things so simple for her. She was back to hating him again.

* * *

Sam cursed himself as they rode off. He *should* drag this woman's no-good hide to Prairie Stump; it was the least she deserved under the circumstances. Thank God he had sensed her approaching him and realized his knife was missing—and not one damn second too soon. Otherwise, she would have gotten the drop on him, and he would have been one dead, stupid bounty hunter with his own knife stuck in his back!

Danged fool! How could he have let down his guard that way, allowing a few moments of temptation to rob him of all good judgment? And to think he had sheltered her from the hailstorm, felt sorry for her, even lassoed her damn horse for her. To think he had wanted . . .

Big mistake, Noble. He had thought of her as a woman and vulnerable, yet clearly she was just like the rest of the outlaws: a liar, a clever and resourceful killer who wouldn't hesitate to knife a man in the back. To a man of the West, nothing was lower than back-stabbing or back-shooting. And unless he had shit for brains, he couldn't afford to forget that again.

Chapter 6

〜〜◯◯〜〜

The sun was waning by the time they crested a rise and Annie spotted a quaint Old West–style town in the distance. She supposed this must be Prairie Stump, the place the bounty hunter had mentioned—the newest and brightest attraction in their trip through the looking glass. At the moment, she was almost too exhausted and overwrought to care.

Again they'd ridden all day, stopping only for a brief lunch. As had happened yesterday, Annie had seen no indication that they might still be in the twentieth century. To the contrary, they'd passed several riders on horseback, a farmer in his hay wagon, and a couple in their old-fashioned buggy—all trappings of the nineteenth century.

The hours had passed in sheer misery for Annie. She had dried off totally, but this was no blessing. Dirt was now caked on her clothing, grit clinging to her skin and hair. After two days in the same garments, this particular set of clothing was beginning to feel like a way of life. Her bound wrists were on fire, her face burning from the wind and sun. Never had she so yearned to take a bath, to draw out the small bottle of lotion that she'd mercifully included in her bag and slather it all over her face, wrists, and hands.

Even her mouth tasted like grit. Being raised on a ranch, Annie had spent many a day out riding her horse. She was accustomed to what others might call inconve-

44

niences, to taking a nap on the grassy ground or relieving herself behind a tree. But this was *ridiculous*.

To make matters worse, the bounty hunter had been terse and uncommunicative all day, ever since he'd caught her sneaking up on him with his knife. Even now his features were fixed in a granite stare. Annie wanted desperately to beg him to stop, to find her a bath, find *something*. But she knew she was hardly in his good graces at the moment.

They drew closer to the small burg, and Annie spotted a sign that read PRAIRIE STUMP, COLORADO. POPULATION 272. She gazed ahead at a potholed street lined with ancient clapboard storefronts, a hamlet that much resembled Deadend—except that here, horses and buggies were traveling the rutted red avenue, and men and women in pioneer clothing were trooping along the boardwalks. A few doors down, a cowboy staggered out of the saloon, whooping loudly and firing his pistol into the air before he mounted his horse and galloped away.

Annie shook her head. God, this was weird! So she really *had* crossed over into another century. She supposed she had already accepted this intellectually . . . but it was still one big emotional leap! She glanced at her captor and saw no reaction on his face. Obviously, this sort of scene was commonplace to him.

They continued into the town. Along the boardwalks Annie spotted three frontiersmen ambling along in buckskins and mountain hats, two blanket-draped Indians sitting on a bench, and a man in an elegant black frock coat entering the saloon. At the door to the dry goods store, a housewife in calico, heavy shawl, and slat bonnet emerged with two small children clad in brown homespun; next door on the porch of the general store, three old-timers in overalls, flannel shirts, and battered hats huddled over a small table, playing dominoes. Out in the street Annie spotted a mule, two horses, a buggy, one barking dog, a bearded prospector with his burro, even a prairie schooner filled with a pioneer family. The smells of horse manure and dust cloyed the air.

Amazing! Still, they were riding right past what served

for the comforts of civilization here. Annie realized she *must* say something to her grumpy captor or there wouldn't be a prayer of her getting any relief from her physical torment.

"So this is Prairie Stump," she ventured. "Tell me, where's the stump?"

He cast her an irritable look.

"It does look like an inviting place," she added hopefully.

He grunted. "Reckon Prairie Stump's not much to look at, but considering the sorry state we're both in, reckon we'll call it a day. There's a right respectable hotel that'll do."

A hotel! Annie could not contain the surge of relief rushing through her. At last they would stop and she would have a chance to feel clean and reasonably human again.

But would they share the same room at the hotel? Uneasiness tugged at her, but again, Annie felt almost too wretched to care. "So what kind of town is this?" she continued conversationally.

Sam tipped back his hat. "Reckon Prairie Stump's just a trail town, where folks stop off to rest or buy supplies before heading out to the Rockies to search for gold."

"Then I suppose I can't hope it's some sort of living history exhibit?" she quipped.

In response, he gave her another one of those cranky looks. God, he *was* in a mood!

He pointed ahead at a stylish storefront. "We'll bed down yonder."

Sam brought their horses to a halt before a handsome building with an elegant shingle proclaiming THE JEFFERSON HOTEL. He dismounted, tied their animals to the hitching post, removed his saddlebags and tossed them over a shoulder, then approached Annie's horse and began untying her wrists.

"I'm warning you to be on your best behavior now— or else," he said sternly.

Annie bit her tongue. Damn, but she was getting sick of his testiness! He had kidnapped her, for God's sake. Although his insolence tempted her defiance, as she eyed the huge Colt Peacemaker holstered at his side, she decided her chances of escape at the moment were little to none. Besides, after he'd blown a gasket back at the arroyo, she wasn't feeling particularly suicidal.

He hauled her down off the horse and tugged her to the boardwalk. Though annoyed, Annie had to admire the Victorian facade of the brownstone hostelry. Two large, square windows embellished the ground floor; a large yellow cat was curled up in one, and a lush window garden filled the other. Rows of tall, narrow windows, accented by white bricks, distinguished the second and third stories, culminating in a classical roofline with ornate cornice and carved Grecian pediment.

Stepping inside, Annie gaped at the opulent lobby filled with tufted red velvet Victorian settees, thick blue-and-gold Oriental rugs, vibrant ferns on wicker stands, and oil paintings picturing Rocky Mountain scenes. A handsome black marble fireplace graced a far wall, with a large brass-framed mirror hanging above it; a wrought iron chandelier with large frosted glass bulbs glimmered overhead. Hearing a sputtering sound, Annie realized with awe that the fixture must be lit by gas. She glanced at a cowboy who sat snoring on a settee, his western hat tipped over his face and his booted feet propped on a marble-topped table, then took in the lobby's carved oaken staircase and massive front desk, and the quaint mustachioed clerk standing behind it. The odd little man wore an antiquated black suit with velvet lapels, and his slicked-back hair was parted down the middle.

It was all out of this world. Clearly, so was she!

Sam's grating voice broke into her thoughts. "Come on, sister, quit standing there gathering flies. You look like you ain't never seen a hotel before."

"Not one like this."

"Let's register," came his impatient response as he hauled her over to the desk.

The clerk grimaced at the sight of the bedraggled newcomers. "Good afternoon, sir. May I help you?"

Sam eyed the man narrowly. "You new here?"

"Yes, sir. Mr. Fulcrum died."

Sam nodded. "Too bad. One room for the night. Two beds."

Although Annie's anxieties were partly assuaged by Sam's request for separate beds, she was still not anticipating spending the night in the same room with this temperamental man.

She glanced at the clerk, who was regarding Sam with pinched, disapproving features. "Sir, are you wed to this here female?"

Sam laughed harshly. "If I was, would I be askin' for two bunks?"

The little man glanced at Annie, then blushed. "But, sir, it just ain't seemly—"

"I ain't married to her," cut in Sam. "Fact is, I'm a bounty hunter doing a job for Judge J. D. Righteous out of Gilpin County. This here woman's my prisoner, a dangerous female outlaw, and I'm fetchin' her up to Central for a reckoning with the law. In the meantime, I sure as hell ain't letting her out of my sight."

The words "dangerous female outlaw" set Annie's blood boiling. Meanwhile, the clerk shook his head. "I'm sorry, sir, but it just don't seem proper, the two of you sleeping in the same room, lessen' you're hitched."

Annie was quick to pick up on this cue. "Yeah, maybe I don't want to share the same room with *you,*" she haughtily informed Sam.

He smiled nastily. "If you'd rather spend the night down at the hoosegow, sister, it makes no nevermind to me. But I'm warning you it's a fleabag, full of drunkards and road agents, plus the sheriff . . . well, that rascal has a fondness for the ladies, if you know what I mean." His gaze raked over her, making his message clear.

Annie felt frustrated enough to scream. "You snake."

She realized her mistake as she heard the clerk's scandalized gasp. Sam hauled her up by the collar of her shirt, and she winced as she found herself staring into his formidable dark brown eyes.

His cold, hard voice shot a chill through her. "Lady, one more insult and I'm draggin' your britches down to the calaboose for the night, and to hell with you. Got it?"

Gulping, Annie nodded.

Sam released her so abruptly that she tottered. He turned and slapped a gold piece down on the counter. "And I ain't takin' no more hokum off you neither, mister," he curtly informed the clerk. "That's one room for the night. Two bunks. Got it?"

"Yes, sir." The chagrinned little man hastily flipped open his register book, spun it about, and shoved it toward Sam.

"We'll be needing our horses stabled, too," Sam added, taking a pen from the inkwell and signing his name with bold strokes.

The clerk nodded. "I'll have our stable boy take your mounts to the carriage house and see they're tended."

"Much obliged."

Taking his key from the clerk, Sam ushered Annie up to the second floor. He unlocked the third door on the right and shoved her inside ahead of him.

Regaining her balance and shooting him a rebellious glance, Annie turned to examine her surroundings. The room was actually lovely, large and airy, with two old-fashioned, twin iron beds sporting yellow chintz coverlets. The windows were curtained in matching lace-trimmed fabric, the handsome oak dresser topped with white marble and accented by a ceramic basin and pitcher painted with roses. Under other circumstances, Annie might have found the setting charming.

Not now. Not only did she feel unsettled to be in the same hotel room with this dangerous, cantankerous man, but she was uncomfortable as hell. Her gaze settled hungrily on the pitcher of water.

At last she glanced at Sam and felt unnerved to note him intently watching her. "I—I need a bath," she said miserably.

"Not now," he replied, setting his saddlebags on a chair. "You can wash up for supper, but then we need to grab some grub and get over to the dry goods store before it closes."

"The dry goods store?" she asked hopefully.

He pocketed his key. "Yep, I reckon we'd best buy you a couple changes of clothing." At her pleasantly surprised look, he eyed her filthy clothing and added gruffly,

"It's a long ride up to Central, and I reckon you'll never make it to the trial in them muddy duds."

Annie's gratitude over his generosity faded at his new reference to her fate. "So you propose providing me with a new wardrobe? Guess you want to turn me over to be hanged in prime fashion, huh?"

He didn't respond.

"I suppose that's only fair, since you took me away in quite a hurry and I didn't get to pack a thing, did I?"

A belligerent frown brought his brows rushing together. "Quit spoutin' off that smart mouth of yours and scrub your face and hands if you're gonna."

Hating him more and more, Annie went to the basin, at first recoiling when she caught her own reflection in the mirror—her grimy, sunburned face and soiled clothing. With a groan, she wet a towel and cleansed her face and hands. The cool water felt wonderful against her chapped skin, but she still seethed with resentment.

Remembering Sam's scolding her, she sighed. She probably was spouting off to him more than was wise under the circumstances, but then she'd been raised to speak her mind. To Sam's credit, he had saved her from a night with the nefarious characters down at the jail—but he'd just been so arrogant about it! What woman wouldn't bristle if caught in her current plight?

When she moved away from the basin, he took her place there, wiping the dirt from his own hands and face without ever taking his eyes off her. Annie took out her hairbrush, unbound her hair, and tried to rake some of the dust from her heavy tresses. Glancing up, she saw that the bounty hunter had finished washing up and was again watching her. God, he was unnerving! As she rubbed lotion on her chapped face, neck, hands, and wrists, his eyes never once left her.

Great! She had an entire night of *this* to look forward to, combined with those confusing, devastating memories of his tenderness in the ravine. He made her want to scream, and not just from anger.

She snapped her purse shut and faced him bravely.

"Let's go," he said.

"Sure."

Downstairs, he ushered Annie inside the hotel's small dining room. They passed a linen-draped table where a stylishly dressed couple sat eating roast beef and mashed potatoes. The woman, in a silk dress and flowered hat, glanced askance at them in their grungy clothing. Annie noted that the man was scowling over a copy of the *Rocky Mountain News.* Squinting, she spotted the date and shuddered—it was September 15, 1885!

She winced. So she was right; she really had gone over the rainbow. *Welcome to the year 1885, Annie girl. . . .*

"You all right?" she heard Sam ask gruffly.

Raising an eyebrow, she regarded his tense face. "You're saying you care?"

Coloring slightly, he grabbed her arm and steered her toward a corner table. "Well, you went kinda pale there, and for a moment I thought you was one of them lily-livered females that has fits of vapors."

"Oh, don't worry, Mr. Noble. I'm still in prime shape to be executed," Annie retorted. "I'm just hungry as hell."

Amid this charged atmosphere, they took their seats. A waitress stepped up, wearing a dark broadcloth dress, a long white apron liberally stained with coffee and gravy, and a dingy white cap. She possessed a long, narrow face with a receding chin, but her expression was pleasant.

"Evenin'. What can I get you folks?" she asked in a frontier twang.

Sam frowned and stroked his jaw. "How 'bout coffee, fried beefsteak, and potatoes?"

"Sure." The waitress turned to Annie. "That all right for you, too, ma'am?"

"I'd prefer something less loaded with cholesterol," Annie replied with distaste. "Fish perhaps?"

The woman cackled and slapped her sides. "Honey, don't you know you're still plumb in the middle of the Staked Plain? Ain't no speckled trout swimming in the arroyos hereabouts. If it's fish you're a'pinin' for, you'd best head out to one of them fine restaurants in Denver."

Annie noted Sam's equally bemused expression. "Then chicken?" she suggested hopefully.

The woman nodded. "Chicken and dumplings it is, then. Coffee all right, ma'am?"

With a sigh, Annie nodded, and the woman walked away. She glanced back at Sam. He looked ruggedly handsome though trail-worn, his face heavily whiskered, the collar of his buckskin shirt coated with dust. She found herself wondering if he would want a bath, too.

Oh, she didn't want to think about that now! Besides, she was daunted enough by the menacing frown that still sculpted his face in rigid lines. Even so, she had to admit there was something sexy about the smoldering state he was in. She decided she may as well bite the bullet and find out why he was being so cross.

"All right, what's eating you?" she asked.

He glanced up in surprise, and Annie felt a surge of pride that she'd managed to catch him off guard.

"Nothin'," he replied tersely.

"Oh, don't give me that," she chided. "You've been acting pricklier than a porcupine ever since—well, the hailstorm. So what's stuck in your craw?"

His expression grew even more formidable. "If there was somethin' stuck, why would I discuss it with you, woman?"

Exasperated, she waved a hand. "Fine, don't discuss it. Why should I care, anyway?"

He fell into brooding silence as the waitress returned with their dinners. For several tense moments they ate without speaking.

Suddenly Sam's fist slammed down on the table, rattling the dishes. "There's nothin' more low-down than back-stabbing!"

At his totally unexpected explosion, Annie almost jumped out of her chair. Dropping her fork, she cried, *"Excuse me?"*

"You heard me. There's nothin' worse than a back-stabber."

"What are you talking about?"

"You was gonna knife me in the back."

"Where? When?"

His dark eyes blazed into hers. "This morning, after the storm."

Annie was flabbergasted. "I didn't stab you in the back!"

"No, but you was gonna. My daddy always said if you're gonna kill a man, show some decency and do it to his face."

Annie was stunned speechless. What was going on here? What had she done to deserve this diatribe?

Then she remembered: the nineteenth-century man, the code of the West. Back-stabbing probably *was* a pretty serious offense here.

Well, what about taking the wrong woman to the gallows? Wasn't that pretty despicable, as well?

Still, it was satisfying on some level to see Sam Noble in a slow boil over something she'd done. Studying his proud, indignant face, Annie couldn't resist a knowing smile.

"Aren't you riled because a mere woman almost got the drop on you?"

From the ire darkening his face, she'd definitely hit a nerve. "That's beside the point."

"Can you blame me for trying to escape you, when you refuse to believe a single word I say?"

He gave a cynical laugh. "Well, you showed me your true colors today."

Annie struggled to retain her patience. She was smart enough to realize she had no hope of winning Sam over to her point of view if he remained convinced she was a back-stabber and lowlier than the low. Plus it bothered her that he thought of her this way . . . even though it shouldn't.

With utter sincerity, she said, "Look, I wasn't going to knife you in the back."

"You expect me to believe that?"

She stared him straight in the eye. "I was going to try to get the drop on you, tie you up, then escape."

He held her gaze for a charged moment but gave no sign of relenting.

Instinctively, Annie reached out and touched his hand. "Sam, I *wasn't* going to knife you in the back, okay?"

He pulled his fingers free. "Eat up. We gotta get down to the dry goods store."

Annie released a seething sigh and returned her attention to her food.

Sam churned in confusion. Annie's touch had burned him, and those big blue eyes of hers had set his gut twisting. Damn, but she could play a man like a Missouri fiddle. One minute he was ready to string her up himself, the next he was tempted to believe her.

Believe her and what else? The thought staggered him.

Besides, how crazy could he get? How could he trust a word she said after she'd almost knifed him? He stole a wary glance at her, taking in the proud tilt of her face and the graceful motions of her hands as she ate. She had that beguiling way about her, all right, and damn, but she was lovely.

Was she right that he was riled because a woman had almost bested him? But why should his feelings, his pride, be involved at all?

Because he'd held her in that arroyo and something about her helplessness had touched him. Only this little schemer wasn't *really* helpless at all. She was one smooth desperado, sliding his knife out of its sheath without his even noticing it. Made him wonder what *other* talents she might have with a man. Fool that he was, he'd forgotten all about the dangers and had become totally focused on the tantalizing woman he held, the soft bottom nestled against his loins, making him throb.

And he had to admit that something carnal had contributed to his anger and frustration all day— reckless yearnings that might well cause him to drop his guard and lose his life. The bounty hunter in him recognized this, but the man in him . . . well, the man in him generally wanted something else.

Even now he was consumed by memories of being upstairs with her, watching her wash that pretty face, brush out that fiery hair, and rub lotion all over that smooth skin.

Shit. He'd be sharing the same room with her all night long.

Damn it! She was an outlaw. She was a *woman*. Women were dangerous as hell, unpredictable as rattlers. Sam had hauled in the most despicable desperadoes, but perhaps he never should have tried to tackle a *female*.

Chapter 7

As they stepped inside the dry goods store, the smells of sizing and pomander balls filled Annie's nostrils. She glanced from the quaint ready-made clothing on racks to the bolts of calico, wool, and broadcloth neatly stacked on tables.

A buxom woman in green gingham, her brown hair in a bun, stepped up to join them. "May I help you folks?"

Appearing ill at ease, Sam jerked a thumb toward Annie. "Yeah. The lady here needs two changes of clothing for the trail—flannel shirts, denim britches, long johns, and a hat."

The woman glanced at Annie and smiled. "But your wife is so pretty, sir." She pointed toward the window, where a mannequin sported a stylish fitted dress of blue-sprigged calico with a small bustle. "Wouldn't she like a lovely new frock as well?"

Annie noted to her pleasure that, on seeing the gown, Sam actually grimaced and appeared very put on the spot. Again she took perverse delight in watching him squirm.

"Your wife is tall, but I haven't hemmed the garment as yet," the lady continued with excitement. "It shouldn't take me long to tack it up if your missus wants the dress—and I'll give you a real good price, sir."

Sam's face had darkened by several shades. "Heck, I reckon we'll take it. She'll be needing somethin' respectable to wear for the—er—"

"The hanging?" Annie provided sweetly.

Tossing a menacing look at Annie, Sam addressed the proprietress, who stood with her mouth hanging open. "She's some kidder, ain't she?"

The woman nodded, appearing too baffled to reply.

Sam cleared his throat. "Yeah, throw in that there frock in the winder, and I 'spect she'll be needin' a nightgown or two."

The woman smiled in obvious relief. "Yes, sir. Excuse me a moment, I think I may have just what your wife needs. . . ."

As the proprietress walked toward some shelves, Annie smiled poisonously at Sam. "Why didn't you correct her when she assumed I'm your wife?"

He grunted. "You seem to be doin' a fine enough job flappin' off your mouth. 'Sides, after what happened back at the hotel, it seemed simpler to leave it be."

Annie laughed. "What's this? A dauntless bounty hunter taking the easy way out?" She crossed her arms over her bosom and raised her chin. "I really think I should tell the woman the truth: that I'm an innocent victim and you're a cruel bully who has abducted me and is taking me off to be hanged."

He shook a finger at her. "You do it, woman, and you'll be wearing them very muddy britches all the way to Central."

The two were glowering at each other as the woman returned with a stack of pretty Victorian lingerie boxes. Setting them down on a table, she opened the first and pulled out a whisper-thin white nightgown edged with exquisite lace. "Look at this, sir—the finest Irish linen, complete with convent lace, imported all the way from Belfast. And I've some lovely undergarments here that will be so pretty on your wife. Just wait till you feel these fabrics."

As she held up a pair of lacy drawers, hot color shot up Sam's face, much to Annie's pleasure. Appearing miserable, he shifted from boot to boot and avoided the very sight of the enticing lingerie. "Reckon they'll do. You two females decide what's best."

He strode away, stationing himself near the front

door, shoved his hands in his pockets, and stared sto-
ically at the back wall of the store. Observing him in
puzzlement, Annie realized he was standing sentry, like
one of the famous guards at Buckingham Palace. Obviously he couldn't bear to look at her selecting lingerie,
but he wasn't about to turn his back on her, either. Once
again, she took pride in the fact that she might be getting
to him. Indeed, when the shopkeeper strolled up to the
window to retrieve the dress, Sam didn't even glance in
the woman's direction.

When the shopkeeper returned, Annie held the pretty
calico dress up to her shoulders while the woman
crouched at her feet with needle and thread and tacked
up the hem. Annie had to laugh as she caught her own
reflection in a nearby floor-length mirror. At this angle it
looked almost as if she were wearing the dress, with its
high neckline and dozens of tiny, bead-shaped buttons.
She appeared as if she had just stepped out of an episode
of *Dr. Quinn, Medicine Woman.* How her girlfriends
back in Dallas would laugh if they could see her now!

Dallas. It seemed another world and a lifetime away.

When the hem was done, she and the proprietress
filled several boxes with the dress, shirts, jeans, a trail
hat, and new lingerie. The two chatted all the while.

At the last moment the shopkeeper tossed several
brightly colored silk scarves into one of the containers.
"This is my gift, dear," she informed Annie. "If you're
going to be out riding in that wind all day, you'll need
these to protect your neck." Glancing at Annie's throat,
she sighed. "I can already tell your lovely skin is getting
windburned."

Annie touched her chafed neck, which still stung a
little, despite the lotion. "You're right—and thanks."

The woman smiled. "Well, I reckon we'd best call your
mister to pay the bill."

When Sam and Annie emerged on the boardwalk,
Sam carrying the stack of boxes, she had to smile. "I
suppose I must thank you. You were generous."

"I just aim to get you where you belong."

"Ah, yes," she quipped. "Now I'll have a pretty calico
dress to wear when I swing at Central City. Tell me, do

they have a really skilled hangman, or is slow strangulation still the norm these days?"

He shot her a look that would curdle milk.

"At any rate," she continued sweetly, "I've always said it's great to have something to look forward to."

Next to Annie, Sam groaned. If she wasn't a fine one to stoke his guilt, especially after he'd just spent all that money on her.

What had happened to him back at the store? One glimpse of a pair of lacy drawers had reduced him from dauntless bounty hunter to gutless sissy. All at once it had seemed simpler to let the proprietress assume Annie was his wife than to admit the truth, even though he was only doing his job and there was no shame in that.

Who was he kidding? Truth to tell, he had lost his composure in the face of all that enticing feminine finery—and especially at the prospect of *her* wearing any of it. Or all of it. Or none of it.

Shit. Why should a wispy nightgown set him reeling? Why should he care if she hanged in a gunnysack?

But Sam realized he did care, at least on some level. Yes, he was upholding the law, but he'd also been raised with a conscience. The thought of a woman—correction, *this* woman—hanging bothered him more than he would have thought. Especially when this girl was so adept at tormenting him about it. She might be a pain in the neck, but she was spirited, proud, beautiful . . . and she was getting under his skin.

Chapter 8

"**D**on't you dare," Annie said.

Up in their room, she shot Sam a warning look as he prepared to light a cigar. He was standing near the dresser, she sitting on her bed near the window. She felt very conscious of the intimacy of their situation, especially since, before they'd come upstairs, he'd asked the desk clerk to send up hot bathwater.

At least the bounty hunter hadn't been in quite as nasty a mood since she'd informed him that she hadn't intended to back-stab him. She wasn't sure he believed her, but he must have been somewhat appeased, or he'd never have bought her all those clothes. She half smiled at the memory. He'd been so miserably put on the spot—probably why he'd allowed the shopkeeper to do such a job on him.

Now they had the night together to look forward to. . . . Oh, joy.

But he wasn't going to smoke, not if Annie had anything to say about it. Her feelings there were bitter and strong. And if it made him mad, so be it.

To her astonishment, he appeared amused, lifting a handsome male brow. "You saying you mind if I smoke?"

"Hell, yes, I mind." Annie fought a painful tightening in her throat. "My mother smoked for decades, then died of emphysema."

He appeared very taken aback. "What in tarnation is that?"

"Let's just say it's not a pretty way to die. If you want to kill yourself, that's your business—but I'll not have you inflicting your secondhand poison on me."

Sam burst out laughing. "You say the queerest things, woman. 'Sides which, you're likely to . . ." He paused, the expression of pleasure fading from his face. "That is, if I was in your shoes, I wouldn't be frettin' over no cigar smoke."

Resentment roiled in Annie. "Thank you for reminding me. I'd forgotten about my imminent execution for all of thirty seconds. Now take that cigar and—"

He silenced her by holding up a hand, then stuck the unlit cigar back inside his pocket. "All right, don't pop your cork. You happy now?"

"Release me and I'll be ecstatic."

The two were tensely regarding each other when a knock sounded at the door. Sam strode over and opened it. "Yep?"

A large woman in a long apron and droopy house cap ambled inside carrying a bucket of steaming water. Puffing from the strain, she asked, "You folks wanted a bath?"

"Yes, indeed," he answered.

The woman lumbered across the room to a porcelain tub that was wedged in a corner, with a folded dressing screen leaning against the nearby wall. She dumped her water then headed back toward the door.

"I'll be needing to make several more trips, sir," she informed Sam wearily.

"Fine," he replied.

After she left, Annie stared perplexedly at the tub, and at the chamber pot sitting not far from it. "It's the 1880s, right?"

Sam guffawed. "You know damn well it is."

She pointed at the tub. "One would think you'd have indoor plumbing by now"—she glanced at the oil lamp glowing on the night table between their beds—"as well as electricity."

"They do in Denver," Sam replied. "But this here's the frontier, woman."

"Ah. How could I have forgotten?"

The maid made several more trips with buckets of hot water until the tub was filled. Before leaving, she set up the old-fashioned, calico-printed screen in front of the tub.

Closing the door behind the woman, Sam turned to Annie. "You want to scrub first?"

"With you in the room?"

He gave a rueful laugh. "Do you really think I'm gonna leave and let you hightail it?"

In reply, Annie hauled off a boot and hurled it to the floor, gritting her teeth as she heard Sam's chuckle.

She grabbed a nightgown and her bag, ducked behind the screen, stripped off her clothing, and unbound her hair. Although Sam couldn't see her, she felt unnerved to be naked in the same room with him. She also felt awkward because she needed to use the chamber pot. Never had she so longed to be back in the twentieth century—with bathrooms, electricity, and no ruthless bounty hunter taking charge of her life; no grim reckoning awaiting her in Central City, where the judge might, or might not, be sympathetic toward her plight.

At least Sam had insisted on separate beds, which meant he likely didn't have rape on his mind. That's right, all this had already been explained to her: He didn't take advantage of women; he only escorted them to the gallows.

So, she was likely safe from assault. But undressing, bathing, and sleeping in the same room with this intense man was another matter altogether. Again she remembered Sam's holding her in the hail-battered gully, his passionate outburst at dinner. He was clearly as sexy as he was dangerous.

Despite her anxieties, as Annie stuck her toe into the steamy tub, she found the warm water felt marvelous. The tub was small and cramped by modern standards, but she enjoyed a good soak nonetheless, and the old-fashioned vanilla soap smelled good and felt marvelous against her skin. She scrubbed all the grime from her body and washed her hair. For a few lazy moments she forgot the insane crisis she was caught up in.

Afterward, she dried off her body and hair and slipped on the handkerchief-linen nightgown. Noting how sheer the garment was, she grimaced. As tall as she was, the nightie only covered her to midcalf. A shiver of uneasiness and sexual awareness shook her at the thought of Sam seeing her this way.

Brushing out her damp hair, she wondered if she would have any chance to escape him during the night. If only she had a weapon.

She could always bludgeon him with her hairbrush. Replacing it in her bag, she rifled through the interior for any other item that might help her. Her wallet and car keys would be of little use, and Sam had already disposed of her nail file.

But in typical male fashion, he had not searched her bag as thoroughly as he should have, she realized triumphantly. Deep inside, Annie's fingers closed over the small metal and cloisonné sewing kit her mother had given her years ago. Annie had always treasured the accessory, with its artwork of a cherub, and she usually tossed the kit into her bag whenever she traveled. Heck, this particular seraph might become her guardian angel tonight. She chuckled at the possibility.

Opening the small, hinged container, she stared at an array of possible, though admittedly minuscule, weapons: needles, straight pins, safety pins, and, most promising of all, a pair of very small, very thin, very sharp scissors. Scowling, she removed the scissors from the kit and replaced the container in her purse.

At about two inches in length, the scissors weren't much of a weapon, and might never cut through the tough twine Sam had used to bind her wrists today, but they were surely the most potent choice of the lot. If Sam tried to thwart an escape attempt, they could prove a minor distraction—especially if she stuck him good and hard. She struggled against a smile. At least she needn't worry that a sharp jab with the world's tiniest pair of scissors would qualify as the despicable "back-stabbing."

But how would she conceal the weapon on her body? Glancing down at the large lacy collar of her nightgown,

she at once had her answer. Folding the collar back, she
pointed the sharp tips of the scissors away from her neck
and shoved the blades deep inside the lining, much as
she would do with a large straight pin. Smoothing down
the collar, she felt at least a trifle better prepared for
potential combat.

She was about to leave the safety of the screen when
she remembered the birth control pills she carried in
a zipper pocket of her bag. Although Annie was not a
promiscuous young woman—she hadn't even had a
steady boyfriend for a while—she was realistic enough
to faithfully take her pills, and she saw no reason to stop
now. Who knew what might happen to her over the
coming days?

Unfortunately, she had only a few weeks' supply of
pills left. She laughed at her own absurdity. Here she
was, stranded in another time and worried about next
month's refill. Heck, the way things were going, she
might be swinging at the end of a rope by then!

She downed a small pill, grimacing as it slid down her
dry throat. But she was not about to draw attention to
herself by asking Sam for water.

With her folded clothing and purse in hand, she finally
emerged from behind the screen—to the sound of Sam's
whistle. She stopped in her tracks, blushing, and spotted
him standing across from her, devouring her with his
dark eyes.

She hurled her clothing and bag down on a chair.
"This another part of your job, bounty hunter?"

He chuckled. "I can look, can't I? Ain't no law against
that."

"Look at me that way again and I'll be writing new
law."

He only grinned and began shucking his buckskin
shirt. She gulped at the sight of his beautifully muscled
arms and chest, the tufts of dark hair swirling downward
toward his trim belly.

"You gonna undress in front of me?" she asked in
trembling tones.

"Not entirely. And no one's askin' *you* to look,
woman."

While she stood frowning with arms crossed over her bosom, he strode over to his saddlebags and pulled out a pair of handcuffs.

Suspiciously, Annie watched him move toward her. "Getting kinky, are we?"

He scowled. "Don't know what you mean by that, but you sure as hell ain't gettin' the drop on me while I wash. Reckon I gotta shackle you to your bed."

He was about to grab one of her wrists when Annie remembered how ropeburned her skin was and held up both hands. "No, please! Just look at my wrists—they're already raw from that sadistic twine you've been using for two days now. I can't wear those torture devices all night long."

He actually hesitated, a muscle working in his jaw as he studied the ugly welts on her flesh. "Well, what do you expect me to do, woman?"

Annie stared at him for a moment, then squelched a telltale snicker as inspiration dawned. She remembered her tiny, concealed pair of scissors and, even more blessedly, the shopkeeper's generous gift.

"Use the scarves," she suggested.

"What scarves?"

"The silk scarves the shop lady gave me. She said they're so much better on chafed skin."

Eyes suddenly wide and mouth falling open, Sam appeared downright comical. "Shit, woman! You was discussin' me tyin' you up with the shop lady?"

"No, silly," she replied, rolling her eyes. "She just gave me some scarves to protect my chafed neck." Annie pointed at the dresser. "They're in that box."

He sneered. "Yeah, and if I tie you to the bed with 'um, it'll be a mite easier for you to try to escape again. Right?"

Her laughter mocked him. "Easier to escape? Well, you're a cowboy, aren't you? Don't tell me you don't know how to tie really good knots? Hell, my wrists are living proof of it!"

For a moment he remained indecisive. Then a blistering sigh escaped him. "All right, sister. Remember, you asked for this."

He strode to the dresser and pulled two long silk scarves from a box.

His low chuckle as he approached gave her pause. "So you think I know how to tie *really* good knots. . . ."

He did know how, Annie soon discovered to her dismay. Sam first ordered her to lie down on her bed, then to place each hand near a specific rod on the iron headboard. He tied one end of a scarf to each wrist, then secured the other ends onto the rods—which turned out to be far enough apart that Annie couldn't possibly untie one hand with the other.

He pulled back and winked at her. "Well, I reckon you're about the most fetchin' sight I ever seen."

"Oh, go drown in your bath!"

The rascal grinned and strode away.

Annie glanced disparagingly at her bonds. Damn, but he had done an excellent job of restraining her. Even though the loops binding her wrists were loose enough to prevent further pain, Sam's knots were incredibly hard and tight—somewhat like the man himself, she reflected ruefully—and would be impossible to loosen with the fingers of one hand.

She heard Sam get into the tub. This was a strange situation indeed, she thought ironically. Forty-eight hours ago, she never could have envisioned herself spending a night this way—lying here powerless, tied to a bed, while a powerful, sexy man bathed only a few feet away. She felt rattled, and not just on an intellectual level.

She ground her jaw as he splashed about while loudly singing "Wait for the Wagon." He had a fine, deep baritone voice. Then, only minutes later, she gasped as she watched him step from behind the screen, a scant white towel wrapped about his trim middle. Her mouth went dry—for Sam truly was a glorious male specimen, his legs long and hard-muscled, covered by coarse dark hair, his satiny back and shoulders gleaming from the bath, his damp brown hair curling about his ears and nape. Captivated, she watched him stride to his saddle-bags, remove a tin cup with shaving paraphernalia, then go to the basin, whip up some shaving soap, and lather his face.

Oh, God, he was all but naked, so handsome and virile.

At last she found her voice. "Where are your pajamas?"

Sam carefully slid the old-fashioned straight razor up his neck. "I ain't got none."

"Then what do you sleep in?"

"In what God gave me."

"Ah, so you're a religious man?" she asked in quivering tones.

He tossed her a forbearing glance over his shoulder.

"You sleep naked?" she demanded.

He smiled.

"Not in this room, you won't!"

"Woman, don't you ever shut up?" he asked in exasperation.

She did so now, tensely watching him finish shaving, his strokes long, rhythmic, and strangely sensual. She shook her head, wondering what her friends back in Dallas would think if they could see her now.

She smiled. Actually, most of Annie's girlfriends, on sight of a "hunk" like Sam, would have gone into a feeding frenzy. They were all such shameless wenches. She could almost hear Ginger, the most outrageous of the lot, shrieking, "Who cares if he's taking you to a hanging? Rip off that towel and attack him! He's gorgeous. I'll surrender to him *any* day!"

Of course Annie was above such wanton lapses. Of course.

But as Sam wiped off the residue of the lather and headed toward his bed, her pulse fluttered. Well-scrubbed and clean-shaven, he was incredibly handsome—from the sexy notch in his chin to his sensual mouth, strong nose, high cheekbones, deep-set eyes, and broad brow.

Under other circumstances, she *would* have been hard-pressed not to yank off his skimpy towel and attack him.

He paused between the beds. "You'd best look the other way."

"And why is that?"

" 'Cause I'm gonna drop this here towel, snuff out the lamp, and get in bed."

"Indeed?" she mocked. "A gentleman would snuff the lamp first, I would think."

"Who said I'm a gentleman?" He paused, a sly look crossing his face. "And you're not turning the other way, neither. Curious, are you, sister?"

Annie's heart raced at his shrewd barb. "Not in the least. It seems you're not only stubborn and pig-headed, but an exhibitionist, as well."

"What in hell is that?" he growled.

"A man who likes to flaunt himself to offend women."

His handsome features darkened. "You sure as hell got some mouth on you! I should use some of that there soap to scrub your smart tongue and teach you some manners."

Annie seethed at his threat. "You have all kinds of distasteful tendencies, don't you, Mr. Noble? Too bad you have so little sense that you mistake me for your real quarry."

With angry movements, Sam strode to the night table. "If you know what's good for you, woman, you'll quit baiting me with that viperous tongue. Hell, I'm bushed. It's time for some shut-eye. So hush up."

"You gonna make me?" she asked sweetly.

Annie realized her mistake too late, for Sam's ruthless smile, the flash of his even white teeth, proved downright devastating. God, when would she learn to control herself? While her heart thrummed wildly, he closed the distance between them. His strong hand gripped her chin—and his mouth seized hers.

The rough, hot contact jolted Annie. Sam's kiss bruised and punished, but also strangely delighted. Like one unexpectedly seared by an electrical current, she went weak. She couldn't seem to think or breathe, much less fight him. He smelled of vanilla and shaving soap, and he tasted so delicious, so warm. So ready and determined.

Then strangely the punishment stopped and the glory began as Sam's kiss mellowed and grew tender, his tongue gently pushing inside her mouth, probing against her own with tantalizing insistency, sending a riot of delicious heat shooting through her body. She made a low sound, both whimper and plea, deep in her throat, and he responded with bolder strokes of his tongue.

And she had thought he'd been wonderful when he'd held her in the gully this morning! This man was too sexy for words. Annie actually hurt her bound-wrists as she instinctively struggled to pull free to embrace him.

Abruptly Sam backed away, both of them breathing hard as he stared, awestruck, into her flushed face. His gaze lowered to her taut nipples, prominent through the thin gown, and a knowing grin settled in.

"Who woulda thought?" he quipped. "Passionate little critter, ain't ya? Well, sugar, you can put anything you want on the table tonight, and it ain't changin' a thing."

"Oh, you beast!" she cried.

Irate though she was, Annie still winced as Sam turned his back and dropped his towel. Oh, God. Maybe she *was* as shameless as her friends. For her gaze became riveted on his hard, beautifully shaped male buttocks as he walked confidently to the night table and snuffed out the wick. She heard the squeak of bedsprings as he lay down.

In the darkness, the tension between them remained thick enough to cut. Annie was still reeling. Her pride railed out at the power Sam held over her life, her emotions, yet her traitorous woman's body hungered for more of his hot, sexy kisses. She felt bewildered with herself, her own feelings. Macho bullies were not usually her thing.

Until now. Until Sam Noble.

In the other bed, Sam lay clenching his fists, silently scolding himself for losing control. Twice now this woman had managed to penetrate his defenses in a very physical way. This morning, tenderness had overcome his good judgment. Tonight, pure lust. How was he going to turn her over to justice if he first gave in to his passions? He would be the one captured and defeated—not her.

Lord, the woman was pure temptress. Even when

she'd been bathing behind the screen earlier, her sweet scent had drifted out to tantalize him. Bathing in the water she had used had been an almost sexual experience. Seeing her curves through that thin gown, watching her damp hair curl about her face and shoulders, kissing her just now had all but decimated what remained of his defenses. Such a damn soft mouth she had, and skin like a baby's. And when he'd watched her nipples pucker hard against that thin gown, his mouth had ached to claim those tight little pebbles. It would have been so easy to pull off that wisp of a garment, tangle a hand in that mane of thick, wet hair, and bury his aching maleness deep inside her.

Damnation! He should have left her at the jail for the night. He could still smell her in the darkness. If he didn't gain better control of himself, this feisty filly would soon be leading him around by . . . well, by a very swollen portion of himself!

Chapter 9

$\sim\!\!\!\sim\!\!\!\diamond\!\!\!\sim\!\!\!\sim$

In the darkness, Annie's mind continued to churn, especially when she heard the sounds of Sam's soft, occasional snores. She knew she must try to escape, but logic argued she must wait a while until she was certain he was deeply asleep.

How dare the big beast snooze anyway while she lay here in bondage? How could he be so content with himself, knowing he intended to take her to be hanged?

And he'd had some gall to ogle her in her nightgown, then kiss her to "shut her up," plus all but accuse her of trying to seduce him in order to gain her freedom! Oh, he made her mad enough to chew nails. But what still daunted her most was how much she'd enjoyed his kiss, how she'd gloried in the sight of him parading his magnificent backside in front of her.

Annie had never been one to indulge in casual sex, but neither was she a starry-eyed virgin. She considered herself a sexually liberated woman. For some time, however, she simply hadn't met a man with whom she wanted to have a love affair.

Though on another level, perhaps she hadn't allowed herself to become vulnerable. It had been such hell, losing both her parents. Self-preservation had become the key—much as it was here. Focusing on business had helped Annie to alleviate the pain. Plus, there had always been Larry to worry about.

Larry! Anxiety needled Annie at the thought of her

itinerant older brother, his problems with drinking and everything else. Was he all right back in the present?

For that matter, did that faraway world she'd left even exist?

Sorry, pal, she thought to herself as bittersweet emotion welled. *Sis is caught up in purgatory. Hope I'll make it back to you one day. . . .*

Well, there was no hope of *that* unless she first saved herself from her predicament and got the hell out of Dodge. Of course she had no reason to believe a return trip through time was even possible—yet nothing would be possible if she was dead. Which meant she still had Sam Noble to contend with.

She did feel rattled by him, shaken from her normal self-control and composure. Usually when Annie desired a man, her feelings centered on trust, rapport, and emotional intimacy; danger, lust, and heated conflict did not enter into the mix at all. But Sam Noble had changed all that. Never before had she met a man quite like him— brazen and brash, yet principled in his way and, above all, supremely confident and sexy. A legend of the Old West.

She smiled. Under different circumstances, it might have been nice to hook up with a legend, with the type of man she might never meet in the twentieth century.

But not when she was his hostage and he believed such awful lies about her. Sam Noble's cocksure manner infuriated her, confused her, agitated her senses, but also compelled her. Lord, when he looked at her in that intense way, with such animal magnetism, she could feel herself melting, her senses opening to him. And when he had kissed her . . . Annie hated herself for her weakness, but there it was. It was exquisite torture to be lying in the same room with him—another reason she *must* get out of here.

When Sam's breathing at last grew deep and regular, she decided she must make her move now or never. At least when he had tied her up, Sam had allowed enough slack in the scarves that she had a little maneuvering room. She twisted about, awkwardly trying to reach beneath the collar of her gown, then froze as the bedsprings loudly protested and, across the room, Sam's snores stopped.

For a moment, Annie lay motionless, half nauseated by fear. But thankfully she heard no sounds of Sam actually stirring. She remained immobile until he resumed his even breathing; then she reached the tiny pair of scissors and gingerly withdrew the implement from the lining.

She began cutting not at the impenetrable knots but at the length of material hanging between them. Snip, snip, snip. Her scissors were so small that it seemed to take forever to make the tiniest progress through the bunched silk, especially with her hand cocked in such an unnatural position as she worked. Plus her heart was beating so fiercely, she feared Sam might hear *her*.

At last the silk gave way and one hand was free. Annie breathed a sigh of relief. Rending the other scarf proved much easier. After a few snips, she was able to rip through the silk, making only the merest sound.

Thank God, she was loose! Elation roared through her blood. With infinitesimal movements, she slipped from the bed, this time prompting only the weakest complaint from the bedsprings.

Creeping across the darkened room, she located her clothing and purse on the chair. She decided not to bother with the knots on her wrists—these would take time to undo, a task best saved for later. Quickly she dressed. Thank God she knew how to move around all but soundlessly. When her mother had become so ill with emphysema, Annie had often cared for her on weekends. Toward the end, Marian Dillon had been a very light sleeper, her breathing tortured, her body restless and pain-racked. During her mom's brief but merciful hours of slumber, Annie had gotten in the habit of creeping around the bedroom as quietly as a church mouse, tidying up and gathering her mother's laundry.

That training paid off now. Fully dressed in boots, jeans, shirt, and coat, Annie hooked her bag over her shoulder, then felt around on the dresser, searching for Sam's pistol. She grimaced as her fingers contacted the

cool metal of the still-open handcuffs. She touched a pile
of Sam's clothing, then located his gun belt and pistol.
Easing the heavy Colt Peacemaker from its holster,
feeling its weight and coldness in her hand, it occurred to
Annie that the easiest solution to her dilemma—indeed,
the safest route to take—would be to grab a pillow, place
it over Sam's face, and shoot him.

Overwhelming horror made her dismiss this possibility
at once. Granted, Sam Noble had unlawfully kidnapped
her and placed her life in peril, but she couldn't resort to
cold-blooded murder any more than she could have sunk
herself to back-stabbing this morning. She would simply
have to pray she could outfox him—and outrun him.

She replaced the pistol in its holster and fastened
Sam's gun belt low on her hips. Turning to his trousers,
she hesitated only a moment before retrieving his wallet
from the back pocket and flipping it open. Even though
she couldn't see the money, she could feel the crisp bills,
and she took out several. Much as her conscience nagged
her for stealing from Sam, she knew she must have the
nineteenth-century greenbacks to survive. The
twentieth-century cash and credit cards in her purse
would do her no good.

Of course Sam would be livid to discover she had
robbed him—if he even noticed in his fury over her
escape, which was bound to be tenfold. Besides, she was
already wanted for murder and bank robbery. Adding
theft to her list of sins could hardly make matters worse.

Setting down Sam's wallet on the dresser, Annie
decided she would take not just his pistol but also his
trousers and coat. A wry smile curved her lips. That
should slow him down.

As she stealthily opened the door to the hallway, soft
light spilled in. She turned and caught an image of Sam
asleep, his features innocent and peaceful. The sight of his
wrist positioned close to a rod on his iron headboard
proved irresistible to her. Much as she knew she was a
fool even to approach him now, her desire to torment him
as he had tortured her won out. Annie carefully retrieved
the handcuffs from the dresser, then tiptoed to his bed,

attached one cuff to an iron rod on the headboard, and ever so gently snapped the other around Sam's wrist.

The big dolt never even stirred!

Resisting an urge to laugh in triumph, Annie slipped from the room.

Chapter 10

❦❦

"**W**hat in hell . . . !"

Shortly before dawn, Sam jerked awake to find his right wrist shackled to an iron rod on his headboard. Cursing vividly and yanking futilely against his bonds, he glanced wildly at the other bed, spotted the tatters of silk scarves waving in the breeze, and realized his quarry had escaped.

Damnation, how could he have been so stupid, letting her talk him into showing mercy and using the silk scarves to tie her up! The gal had hornswoggled him even as he slept. He'd always been far too sound a sleeper for his own good. Now, too late, he was fully awake, only to face the disgrace of having been outwitted by a female outlaw!

How would he get out of this mess? Again he perused the room but could not spot his trousers or gun. That left but one alternative.

"Help!" Sam shouted at the top of his lungs. "I said I need some help in here!"

To Sam's consternation, it took a good five minutes of hollering before a timid female voice called out from the hallway. "Sir, it's the maid. Are you all right in there?"

"Shit, no, I ain't all right! Go find the desk clerk and tell him to rattle his hocks and get up here—now."

"Yes, sir," replied the scandalized voice.

Two minutes later, the clerk burst in, reddening as he spotted Sam handcuffed to one bed, the remnants of the silk scarves fluttering on the other.

The little man's nostrils flared in distaste. "May I help you, sir?"

Sam ground his teeth to find himself facing the same sanctimonious pipsqueak who had registered them yesterday.

There was bound to be the devil to pay over this shameful spectacle.

Nonetheless, Sam roared back like a raging bull. "Hell, yes, you can help me! Find the key to these here handcuffs. It's in my trousers pocket."

The man did not even budge, his features a picture of pious contempt. "May I ask how you got into this disgraceful predicament, sir?"

"You sure as hell may not!"

Wide-eyed, the man shook a finger at Sam, his voice ringing out shrilly and self-righteously. "I knew I never should have allowed you and that—that *female*—to stay in this hotel. You both had the look of heathens and sinners about you. It's obvious what the two of you have been doing in this room."

"Oh, yeah? And what's that?"

The man's thin lips twisted into a sneer. "Do you actually think I would speak of such evil doings? I'll have you know this is a Christian establishment, sir."

"Are you sayin' I ain't had no Bible larnin'?" Sam bellowed back. "You think I was hatched up under some rock? God a'mighty, mister!"

The man appeared to be too outraged to respond.

"Now get your no-account butt moving and find me the gall-durned handcuffs key!"

"Yes, sir." Though he shot Sam a look of seething scorn, the clerk dutifully searched the room. "Sir, I see no trousers."

"Damnation! The witch must have taken them."

With a superior air, the clerk turned back to Sam. "You know, that is odd. When the stable boy came on duty a few minutes go, he mentioned seeing a man's trousers and coat floating in the horse trough outside."

"The goddamned horse trough?" yelled Sam.

The man drew himself up with dignity. "No, sir. Just the horse trough."

"Cute," Sam sneered. "That's real cute. The hellcat! You go fetch them trousers right this minute and get that key—or a hacksaw."

"Yes sir."

"I'll kill her," Sam gritted, pounding his free fist on the mattress. "Hell, I'll string her up and save Judge Righteous the trouble!"

She was going to make it. She must!

This was Annie's desperate thought as she galloped down the sagebrush-strewn arroyo, toward the stand of cottonwoods surrounding a narrow stream at the bottom of the gulch. Although the morning had dawned briskly, she was thankful the atmosphere was clear except for clouds of red dust billowing from the trail she cut. The rising sun had painted the eastern horizon spectacular red and gold hues; the pastoral quiet was broken only by the thunder of her horse's hooves and the distant scream of an eagle.

Escaping Prairie Stump had been easy enough for Annie. No one had been on duty when she'd crept inside the stable and saddled her horse. But her progress riding in the darkness through sometimes rugged territory had been tortuous at best; she'd proceeded with great care, fearing her filly might stumble into a gopher hole. Finally, exhaustion had overtaken her, and she'd stopped to catch a few hours' sleep.

She'd made better progress since first light. Granted, she didn't know this terrain as well as Sam Noble did, but surely she had a good chance of making it back to Texas before he could catch her.

What then? She could only hope that the time warp that had transported her into the Old West in the first place was still there, and would carry her safely back to the present—and out of this nightmare. The prospect seemed outlandish—but then, so was her traveling through time in the first place!

She was galloping through the cottonwoods when a flash of motion sent her heart crashing in her chest. Before she really saw the man, Annie felt a steely arm clamp around her waist and haul her off her horse. With a high whinny, her mount galloped on, splashing into the shallow river while Annie thudded to the ground with a force that knocked the breath from her.

Sam Noble leaned over and snatched his Colt from her waist, then straightened and shoved the weapon into his belt. He towered above her, all muscle and menace, calmly puffing on a cigar.

"Ain't so easy to escape me, is it, sugar?"

Annie's breath, along with blinding fury, returned simultaneously. Sucking in an agonized gulp of air, she struggled painfully to her feet and knocked the cigar out of his mouth. "You bastard! You could have killed me!"

His expression turned ugly. "Who says I don't want to throttle you after what you gone and done? When I woke up and seen your dirty work, you had me swearing so bad I'm sure my poor mama's rolling over in her grave. Plus, when that pious runt of a desk clerk come up and seen the shameful state I was in . . ." He paused, breathing hard. "You plumb humiliated me, woman!"

"Good." She lifted her chin in pride. "Outsmarted you, didn't I?"

"Now who's outsmarted?" he sneered back, lunging for her.

He would have grabbed her, but Annie's self-defense training spurred her to act on instinct. Neatly side-stepping the bulk of his weight, she engineered a perfect over-the-hip throw, sending him crashing down onto his back.

From the ground, he stared up at her, stunned. "Damnation, woman!"

But Annie was already running, intent on stealing his horse and making good her escape. She glanced over her shoulder to watch him leap up and pursue her.

A second later he grabbed her right arm, pivoting her body toward him as he tumbled her to the ground beneath him. She winced as the weight of his massive frame crashed down on her own.

She struggled to get free. "Damn it, get off me, you big bully!"

"When I'm good and ready!"

"Does brutalizing women make you feel like a man?" she sneered, still struggling to squirm away.

She watched his face purple with rage. "You got some nerve, lady. Shackling me to my bed, stealing my clothes and my gun—"

"And you're one dumb bastard to let me get away with it."

With a blistering curse, Sam shoved his revolver beneath her nose. Annie froze and her eyes went wide; her heart skidded to a stop, then resumed galloping fanatically.

"Oh, yeah?" he sneered, blinking at her in his fury. "Who's got the upper hand now, lady? Seems to me you ain't so smart after all."

Annie breathed hard, hating him to the marrow. "How did you find me, anyway?"

Smiling nastily, he moved the pistol away from her face. "Figured you'd head back the same way. And I know a few shortcuts."

"Like I'm your shortcut to the reward money, right? You're low-down enough to haul in anyone, aren't you? Even a woman!"

"Well, sugar, you're a woman all right," he replied.

Annie didn't like the sound of Sam's voice; indeed, the abrupt lowering of its timbre shot a shiver through her. She gulped as a change crossed his features. His expression grew intent, his eyes gleaming with a different emotion—something darker, more passionate. A predatory gleam that was scary as hell.

"Hold still," he ordered.

The soft warning made her heart skip a beat. Annie wasn't about to resist—not with the lethal Colt .45 still in Sam's hand—though she seethed with helpless frustration.

Sam moved his free hand to her thigh, then began exploring the curve of her hip, his fingers teasing and tantalizing her through her denim jeans. She sucked in a scandalized breath. Then his hand slid between their bodies, his fingers settling on her crotch.

Raw outrage overwhelmed Annie's fear. "What in hell are you doing?"

His fingers began working the buckle on the gun belt that lay low on her hips. "Unfastening my gun belt from you."

"You mean you're feeling me over!"

He didn't deny it as he slowly unfastened and pulled the heavy belt off her hips. Annie clenched her teeth so hard, her jaw muscles hurt. As if his bold touch wasn't bad enough, she was painfully conscious that he was becoming *aroused,* his manhood growing hard and thick against her pelvis. Even more humiliating was the deep, treacherous aching he stirred inside her.

She was flushed and breathless by the time he moved off her, stood up, replaced his pistol in its holster, and fastened the gun belt around his own hips. The scoundrel appeared entirely too pleased with himself.

She could have killed him.

"Get up," he said.

With a grimace, she sat up and eyed him mutinously. "I see you're wearing a different coat—and trousers."

He didn't comment. "I said get up. We're leaving."

"On one horse?"

He grabbed her hand, hauling her to her feet. "I oughta make you walk all the way to Central. But I reckon I can round up your filly. She won't stray far from this here water hole."

That's right, the legend of the West at work again with his trusty lasso, Annie thought cynically. Tottering on her feet, she winced and rubbed her aching backside, then shot Sam a fuming look.

To her surprise, he sighed, a muscle working in his jaw. "You know you shouldna gone and pulled this stunt. I didn't mean to hurt you."

Although his humility was unexpected, Annie was in no mood to be appeased, her emotions raw from their very physical and provocative encounter. "No, you don't want to hurt me," she mocked, fighting the sting of tears. "You just want to turn me over to be executed for the reward money. You're a real prince of a fellow, right?"

"It's my job," he blazed.

"Is it your job to rape me along the way?"

Outrage darkened his features. "Woman, I oughta gag that sassy mouth of yours. Besides, who was panting and blushing on the ground just now?"

"That's beside the point."

"Oh, is it?"

Stepping closer, she yelled, "Is it your job to profit on the death of an innocent woman?"

His laugh was more of a jeer. "You sure as hell didn't act innocent when you escaped—or beneath me just now."

Despite her flaming face, Annie shook a fist at him. "I'm acting like a woman whose life has been threatened! And make no mistake about it, Sam Noble—this is a life-or-death struggle as far as I'm concerned. And if I have to kill you to save myself, then so be it."

Annie spun about and stalked off to retrieve her purse.

"Guess I've been warned," Sam muttered, starting after her.

He felt stunned by how quickly he had lost control again, how his raging temper had escalated into ruthless desire. He didn't usually respond to women in such an unbridled way. But this woman stoked his desire on every level. She might be wanted dead or alive, but now she was wanted by Sam Noble even more.

Chapter 11

❦❦❦

"You gonna pout all day?" Sam asked. "At least I agreed to stop back off at Prairie Stump and let you gather the rest of your gear."

Hours later, Sam posed his questions as they trotted their horses through grasslands north of Prairie Stump. The landscape was subtly changing—the high mesas and yawning arroyos of yesterday giving way to flatter terrain broken by an occasional rocky gulch and distinguished by more yellow soil. Fewer scrub oak, more clumps of cedar, and immense expanses of buffalo grass mingled with the ever present cacti and sagebrush. The scents of tangy evergreens, fresh dew, and prairie wildflowers sweetened the air. Vibrant mountain bluebirds and scores of horned larks flitted about through endless yellow fields.

Annie had been giving Sam the silent treatment ever since they'd left the hotel for the second time; she was pleased to see how uncomfortable he'd become. "Am I going to pout all day?" she repeated sarcastically. "My, and I don't have any reason to act the least bit sulky, do I?"

He glowered.

She took a long, deliberate moment to adjust her hat. "First, you kidnap me, a woman who has committed no crime, and drag me through three states. Despite my numerous denials, you decline to believe I'm not an outlaw or a murderess. You refuse even to look at the identification in my handbag that would prove I'm not the person you're seeking. To wit, simply because I resemble a face you've seen on a wanted poster, you're determined to turn me in for the reward money. Not to mention the fact that you tried to jump my bones at the hotel last night, then subjected me to—er, new indignities—on the trail this morning. After all the outrages you've heaped on me, you expect me to be *pleasant* as well?"

He ground his jaw. "I'm just saying it's a long trek up to Central. Why snip at each other every step of the way?"

"You're suggesting a truce?" she asked in disbelief.

"Things would go a mite easier on you if you'd quit defying me at every turn. Hell, even if you could escape, there's a lot of rugged country between here and Gilpin County. You're a woman, and out here alone, you'd likely die of exposure."

Indignation charged Annie's voice. "Now wait just a minute, Mr. Samuel Noble. Seems to me you're contradicting yourself. I thought I'm supposed to be some hardened criminal, a female desperado who would hardly be daunted by an odyssey through the wilderness. Don't tell me you're starting to believe I'm telling the truth?"

To her satisfaction, she watched his face darken a shade. She smiled in grim triumph. "Well? Which is it, Mr. Noble? Am I a ruthless murderess or some fragile hothouse flower?"

"I'm just saying you don't know the terrain," he grumbled.

"If I don't know the terrain, how in hell did I get from Rowdyville, Colorado, to Deadend, Texas, in the first place?"

He had the grace to appear embarrassed, glancing away and scratching his jaw. "Reckon you got a point. Still, you're a female—"

"We've more than established *that*," Annie cut in. "And although you obviously think of yourself as the superior species, I assure you I'm hardly the helpless wilting violet you assume most women must be."

"You're determined to be a thorn in my side, ain't you?" he burst out in exasperation.

"Can you blame me?" she shot back. "Oh, I'm perfectly willing to be agreeable—the instant you start believing me and let me go!"

He scowled, clearly at a loss, and returned his attention to the trail.

Annie inwardly seethed. Sam Noble was so maddening—refusing to believe her, ridiculing her as a defenseless woman, and then suggesting they be *pleasant* to one another while he took her to be hanged! Oh, she'd be amiable, all right. She might even have a few kind words to say after she shoveled him six feet under.

They exchanged barely a word that morning, or at noon, when they stopped for lunch. Annie had just gotten back on her horse, and Sam was standing beside the filly, about to rebind Annie's wrists, when all at once a curse escaped him.

He glanced up at her in alarm. "Damnation, woman! Your wrists are bleeding. Why didn't you say something?"

His abrupt expression of concern seemed to catch Annie off guard, and hoarse emotion roughened her voice. "Have you given me any reason to believe you would have cared?"

Gazing up at Annie's expressive face, Sam was struck by her turmoil and even wondered if she might be on the verge of tears. Self-loathing roiled up in him, especially as he again studied the ugly, oozing welts on her wrists. Why hadn't he given more thought to what the twine was doing to her? He'd been too damn angry, of course.

But he should have considered that her woman's skin was much more delicate than a man's. Lord, hadn't he touched that baby-soft flesh of hers? Hadn't he tasted that incredible, warm mouth? Part of him hungered to kiss those angry welts even now.

He stifled a groan. He was getting into trouble with this woman. Big trouble.

And she was right. He hadn't given her any reason to

assume he would care if her wrists were bleeding. But he did care. He wasn't an animal.

Still, he was caught in quite a pickle. After she'd attempted two escapes, he had no reason to assume he could trust her. Yet he couldn't continue to bind her wrists. Out here on the trail, dirt would seep into those wounds; with the twine further irritating her raw flesh, those welts would quickly fester. Folks had died of less.

Given the fact that this woman's fate might already be sealed, some men might not have cared, either. But Sam Noble did. Annie was a human being, after all, and she deserved basic human consideration.

He looked up to see her regarding him with turbulence and confusion. He extended his hand. "Get down."

Though she appeared wary, she accepted his assistance.

Once she was beside him, Sam placed his hands on her shoulders and spoke soberly. "Look, I gotta have your word you won't try to escape again."

An incredulous laugh escaped her. "You do?"

"I gotta have it so I can quit binding your wrists. I don't like the look of them welts. Not at all."

Observing the tense expression on Sam's face, Annie was surprised, even touched, by his show of compassion. She was also quick to recognize an opportunity.

"All right," she replied evenly. "I promise."

Skeptically, he raised a brow. "You're sure now?"

Annie muttered a supplication to the heavens. "What do you mean, am I sure? You're the one who just made the suggestion, aren't you?"

"I don't want you taking sick before we reach Central," he continued gruffly. "But if you try to hightail it again, I may have to shoot you."

Bitter disappointment lanced Annie. Sam Noble wasn't really concerned about her; he was only being practical. If her wounds festered and she took sick, she might slow him down!

"Don't worry, Mr. Noble, I've been warned," she replied harshly. "I know you're determined to turn me in—dead or alive—to get your blood money. Makes no nevermind to you, right?"

Annie half expected him to lash back at her, but although his features tightened, he merely grunted and took her by the arm.

"Reckon we'd best wash them wounds and wrap 'um before we hit the trail again."

As they rode off, reason began to prevail over Annie's hot head. Whatever Sam's motives, it *had* been kind of him to unbind her wrists. He'd also helped her cleanse the wounds and had even torn some strips from one of his clean shirts to cover the welts and shield them from trail dust. At his surprisingly gentle doctoring, Annie had felt herself softening toward him, coming perilously close to tears again. It was such a relief to be riding without the constant, stinging torment of the twine abrading her oozing flesh.

Granted, she was still fuming over her fate, at being Sam's captive when she'd done nothing wrong. But she was smart enough to realize that his earlier suggestion that they be more congenial toward one another might be her one real chance of getting out of this mess alive— *if* she could win his confidence and trust, and convince him she wasn't Rotten Rosie. Certainly, that was one helluva big "if," but she had to admit defying him had gotten her nowhere fast.

It was time to cultivate some patience, perhaps even try to humor or charm him—which would likely get her in *deeper* trouble, she mused cynically, recalling her shameful response to Sam's fiery kiss and bold caresses. Still, what did she have to lose? It wasn't as if the man were a monster. He'd demonstrated basic decency, protecting her more than once now. And although his motives were at least partly self-serving, he *had* freed her wrists when he'd had no reason to trust her. Not to mention the fact that he hadn't raped her, when other men in his shoes surely would have.

Perhaps she might still appeal to him. And learning more about her enemy could only enhance her chances.

Clearing her throat, she said casually, "So tell me about yourself, bounty hunter."

He eyed her dubiously. "You're speaking to me again?"

"Aren't you the one who suggested we be more pleasant?"

He gave a shrug. "So what do you want to know?"

"About your family, where you grew up, that sort of thing." She eyed him curiously. "You mentioned being part Indian. . . ."

"One-quarter Cheyenne."

"So tell me how that came about."

A thoughtful smile curved Sam's lips. "Well, reckon it all started with my grandpa, who fifty years ago was a missionary to the tribes in Indian Territory."

"Your grandfather was a minister?" Annie asked, amazed.

"Yep, a Baptist preacher. He met my grandma, a Cheyenne squaw, in No-Man's-Land. They was married, and my pa was born along the trail as they headed west. My grandpa became a circuit rider in California. My pa growed up out west and married young. When I was just seven, Pa moved the family to Colorado, back when gold was discovered at Pike's Peak."

"Your father was a miner?"

"Nope, a gambler hoping to win his fortune the easy way, fleecing gold nuggets off'n the Fifty-niners. My ma was a schoolmarm. She taught at New Eden, the mining town where we settled."

Annie shook her head in wonderment. "A gambler and a schoolteacher. What a combination!"

Sam's jaw tightened. "My pa was gone a lot, always heading off for the nearest boomtown, hoping for easy pickins among the miners." His mouth twisted with contempt. "Unfortunately, he squandered much of his winnings on red-eye and loose women."

"I'm sorry," said Annie.

His expression wistful, Sam clucked to his horse. "My ma was left to raise me and my sister."

Annie stifled a laugh. "Pardon me for saying it, but you don't sound like a schoolteacher's child."

He grinned. "My younger sister Betsy does, though I was pretty much a wild hare from the start. My ma tried

to give me book larnin', but I preferred spending my
time huntin' and fishin', or hanging around town lis-
tenin' to the old-timers."

"Ah, so maybe there's a little of your pa in you?" she
suggested wryly.

"Maybe a smidgen," he conceded, pressing together
his thumb and forefinger.

"Well, at least you weren't raised entirely without a
male influence."

"Yep. Plus a few years after my folks settled in
Colorado, my grandpa moved back, I 'spect to bring
redemption to the sinful hill rats and sage-nutties . . .
and of course to my pa. When Grandpa died, Grandma
went back to live with the Cheyenne. She's still among
her people to this day, though they're a renegade band
ever since the Indians was officially removed from
Colorado."

"Was she happy going back to her Native American
roots?" Annie asked.

Though he appeared perplexed by the term she'd used,
Sam nodded. "She loved my grandpa more'n life, but
never really fit into his white world—one reason they
kept moving 'round, I reckon."

"And your parents? Did your father ever settle down,
or quit gambling and philandering?"

Sam shook his head. "When I was thirteen, we got
word that he'd been shot in an argument over a game of
five-card stud."

"What a shame," murmured Annie.

"My ma passed on from the ague two years later.
That's when my sister and I went to live with Grandma
and her band."

"You lived with the Cheyenne? How did that work
out?"

His face lit with pleasure. "We made out just fine.
Betsy was thirteen and still needed a woman's influence.
She stayed there even longer than I did, then up and
married a white trapper. She moved off with him to
Wyoming Territory, and I get a letter from her ever now
and again."

"Do you miss her?"

"Sure I do. She's the only kin I got left, 'ceptin' for my grandma." He sighed. "I enjoyed my years with the Cheyenne and also learned a lot from their braves—how to hunt and fish the Indian way, how to track. Thanks to my Cheyenne brothers, I found purpose for my life when I went on a vision quest."

"Vision quest?" Annie repeated, remembering someone else who had mentioned that term to her only days before. "What does that mean?"

"It's traditional among young Cheyenne males to go into the wilderness for a *awuwun,* a starving. After days of fasting and meditating, the brave's spiritual sign or totem is supposed to appear. I went on my quest when I was sixteen. It was then I seen the hawk that pointed me toward my life as a bounty hunter."

"Did you leave the tribe then?"

"I did later, though I've never severed my ties. I still visit my grandma and her people several times a year. I'm grateful for the direction the Cheyenne gave me."

"I see," murmured Annie, mulling over his words. "So you really believe in what you do?"

He regarded her solemnly. "I believe in right and wrong, in upholding the law."

A smile pulled at her lips. "You must also have a big conflict in your nature, having a circuit rider preacher for a grandfather, a Cheyenne Indian for a grandmother, a schoolteacher for a mother, and a gambler and womanizer for a father. Where does all of that leave you, Sam Noble?"

He chuckled. "Well, when I meet up with a feisty filly like you, I'm not sure whether I want to preach to you, teach you, scalp you, shoot you, or take you to bed."

Annie struggled not to laugh. Then a more thoughtful expression drifted in. "I'm not used to being around men who have a code."

"Code? You mean like Billy Singletree was talking about?"

"Yes. A sense of justice and fair play, a feeling of purpose in your life. You *do* want to do what's right, don't you, Sam?"

"I try to."

"Well, I can tell you you're dead wrong in apprehending me," she declared passionately.

He sighed. "Annie, must we start up again?"

"We must. Tell me, what makes you so certain I'm the one you're seeking?"

He appeared mystified. "Why, your face is on the wanted poster, woman."

"Yes, but why did you come all the way to Deadend to find me?"

"You know, that was odd," he admitted. "You see, there's a white man, Moon Calf, the sacred idiot, living among my grandmother's people. Some time back, three Cheyenne warriors out hunting come across him in the woods. The man was in bad shape, wandering around without a memory. Truth to tell, he's not right in the head, but the Cheyenne think he possesses powerful spiritual medicine, 'specially since he can charm animals."

"How fascinating."

"Before I headed out to track you, I stopped off to visit my grandma's people, and Moon Calf had one of his visions. He told me and my grandma I must ride south till I found you. He even told me I should bring along an extry horse. At first I thought it was just more of his crazy ramblings, but my grandma insisted I should heed the sacred idiot's words." He glanced pensively at Annie. "My grandma knows of these matters, so I figured you was hidin' out again."

Annie could only shake her head. "Then there was something mystical about your finding me."

He scowled. "Yep, I reckon you could say that."

Annie made a gesture of pleading. "If you believe in Indian mysticism, then why won't you believe I'm from another time?"

He fell grimly silent.

She spoke with utmost sincerity. "Sam, when are you going to believe me? I'm from the late twentieth century, and you somehow rode across time to find me."

"And that's the most loco story I ever heard!"

She maintained her patience with an effort. "I don't claim to understand everything, but perhaps I've been sent here to the past for a reason. Maybe I'm supposed to find my great-great-grandmother and help her—especially since my family history may hinge on whatever happens to her."

Sam shook his head. "Woman, you're talking haywire again. Travel through time just ain't possible, which means you have got to be the most accomplished liar I've ever heard."

Annie was outraged. "Oh! And you're the most stubborn man, determined to cling to your wrongful beliefs no matter what! It would be so easy to prove I'm telling the truth—all we have to do is to go to Rowdyville and find the real Rosie."

"Lady," he reiterated, "I already found her."

That comment proved the final straw for Annie. She knew she had to get away from the infuriating bounty hunter before she said something really unforgivable. Muttering a curse, she spurred her horse and galloped ahead.

For a moment, Sam watched her departure in disbelief. Tarnation, this woman was plumb crazy! So much for trusting her. How could she promise not to escape, then pull a stunt like this? Fuming, he spurred his own mount and galloped after her, coughing as he inhaled her dust.

At last he reached her side, grabbed the reins, and brought both horses to a halt. Quickly he dismounted. Even as he hauled her down beside him, her expression seethed with defiance.

"Do you want me to shoot you, woman?" he yelled, fingers digging into her shoulders.

She faced him down unflinchingly. "Why not? Why don't you just admit that's exactly what you want?"

Oh, she was a siren, tempting him with her heaving bosom, blazing eyes, and that big, lush mouth as the wind whipped sexy little tendrils free from her braided hair. He wanted to shake her till her teeth rattled, but even more, he burned to establish his dominance over her.

He couldn't hit a woman, of course, but he *had* to do something. He had to . . .

"I'll show you what I want," he said roughly, and hauled her into his arms.

He heard the strangled sound rising in her as his lips seized hers. The taste of her, the incredible softness of her wet mouth, sent desire raging through him, making him even more determined to master her. Damn, but he'd been starved for this ever since he'd tumbled her beneath him this morning. He molded her womanly curves close and slipped his hands beneath her coat to caress her shapely bottom.

She writhed against him, unwittingly rubbing her pelvis against his manhood—arousing him to agonized hardness. Out of control, he kissed her with ruthless desire until he could taste the melting in her, until her sounds of panic faded into frantic little moans. Her surrender sent wild passion roaring through his veins. He took all she offered, plundering deep with his tongue, crushing her so close that they seemed to be one aching, throbbing being.

He was on the verge of tumbling her to the ground when some remnant of decency and self-control stayed his trembling hands. What was he doing? After years spent hunting desperadoes, hadn't he learned never to become personally involved with a prisoner? Would he stoop so low as to exploit a woman he was taking to the gallows?

At last reality penetrated his crashing heart and reeling senses, and he wrenched his mouth from hers, staring into her bewildered, flushed face.

"What was the meaning of *that*?" she asked breathlessly.

He reached out to brush a tendril from her soft cheek and spoke huskily. "I don't know, but you make me so blame crazy, woman, I don't know my head from my butt. Crazy to control you, to punish you, and . . ." He raked his hot gaze over her.

Though her cheeks turned a deep, enticing pink, she shoved him away, hard. "Not on your life!"

He shook a finger at her. "You ain't much for keeping your word, are you, woman?"

"I didn't escape!"

"You damn sure tried to!"

"I needed to blow off some steam."

"You mean you needed to make *me* choke on your dust."

The siren smiled then. "That, too."

Sam felt a vein throbbing in his temple at her relentless baiting and narrowly resisted an urge to horsewhip her. "You're damn lucky I didn't shoot you. You gonna mind now, or do I gotta hog-tie you regardless of the sorry state your wrists is in?"

"I'll be happy to cooperate," she retorted, "if only to forestall more of your odious advances." She mounted her horse. "By all means, bring on the execution."

Glaring at one another, the two continued their ride in silence. Annie felt frustrated with herself for allowing Sam to provoke her again, and more deeply jarred by the intimacies they had just shared. Never before had she felt such an intense pull, such an overpowering need to mate with a man. Sam Noble was a wicked kisser and clearly the strongest and sexiest guy she'd ever met. She blushed at the very thought of how wantonly she might have responded had he hauled her down to the ground with him.

Admittedly, there was a strong sexual attraction between them. Yet Annie was realistic enough to know that mutual lust, while satisfying in its way, would never win her freedom, for she didn't doubt for a moment that this remorseless bounty hunter would bed her, then cheerfully claim his blood money. Seducing her would be little more than a perk to him. If she was to save her life, she had to depend on her wits and not this overwhelming chemistry.

Still, Annie was beginning to despair of ever getting through to her mule-headed captor. Sam refused to waver one iota from his obstinate stand that she was Rosie. What was she to do? At the rate they were going, they'd likely be in Central City within a week, where she might be subjected to swift and barbarous frontier justice. How could she persuade him to give her a chance to prove her claims?

Although Annie wasn't aware, Sam, too, felt beset by

turmoil as he rode beside her. He still ached for her, was still shaken and confused by the passion they'd shared.

He stole a glance at her proud, angry face and stifled a groan. She was a handful, but she was also damned near irresistible. And she'd gone and done it again, tormenting him until she popped his cork, centering all his emotions in a part of his anatomy that had no place in bounty hunting. Either she was a very hot and passionate little critter, or she was the best damn tease since Jezebel.

Despite his bravado, Sam remained conflicted, not certain what to believe. Logic argued that she was his quarry, a rough-and-tumble female fugitive who wouldn't hesitate to stoop to lies or deceit, or to provoking him sexually to get him into bed and off the path of justice. Yet his gut still urged him to believe her—his gut or some instinct far more primitive.

Chapter 12

At sundown, they made camp in a clearing next to a cool, rushing stream shaded in the slope of a craggy gulch. Sam rubbed down, watered, and fed the horses, laid out bedrolls for them both, then began preparing himself and Annie a trail supper of beans, bacon, corn dodgers, and coffee. Annie washed up at the stream, brushing out and rebraiding her hair, and changing into a fresh shirt and jeans. She rinsed out her dusty clothing, spreading the wet items out to dry over several small cedar trees.

Night had fallen by the time she returned to camp, the light of the fire guiding her path. She entered the clearing to spot Sam hunkered down by the blaze, stirring a steaming pot of beans. He was hatless and appeared very sexy with the firelight shooting glimmers into his dark hair and the fabric of his shirt and jeans pulled tight against his muscled body. The smells of bacon and strong coffee laced the crisp night air.

When he glanced frankly up at her, her heartbeat quickened and a pulse surged to life between her thighs. Heavens! The tension between them was still thick enough to cut.

"Well, you look a mite better all scrubbed up," he greeted her. "Hungry?"

Placing a small bundle on her bedroll, Annie plopped down Indian style not far from him. "Sure."

He handed her a cup of cool water. "Grub'll be ready in a moment."

"Thanks."

Remembering her nightly ritual, Annie grabbed her purse, opened it, and took out her birth control pills. She removed a pill from the container and downed it with water, then glanced up to see Sam regarding her suspiciously.

"What's that you just swallered?"

Annie replaced the packet in her purse and set it aside. "A pill."

He regarded her with a deep scowl. "You ailing?"

"Nope." Feeling a stab of resentment, she added, "Don't worry, it wasn't cyanide, and my wrists are already healing as well. Looks like I'll make it to the gallows in perfect health—so I won't be slowing you down, bounty hunter."

He regarded her darkly. "I wasn't worried about you slowing me down."

Knocked off kilter by his response, Annie glanced away. She felt a stab of guilt for assuming Sam had quit binding her wrists more out of expediency than true concern.

He shoveled food on a plate and extended it toward her with a fork. "Here, take this."

"Thank you." She took a bite of beans. "This is good."

"Well, it ain't the Windsor Hotel in Denver, but it'll do."

Intrigued, she asked, "Is that where you stay when you're in the city?"

"I keep a suite there."

Annie laughed in pleasant surprise. "Ah—then you're not completely rootless, or unfamiliar with the trappings of civilization?"

He appeared bemused. "I reckon not."

"How long before we get to Central City?" she went on casually.

He glanced up at the gray night skies. "A week, I reckon, weather permitting," came his strained reply.

Annie was pleased to hear that note of tension in Sam's voice. Perhaps he wasn't entirely comfortable with the prospect of watching her swing at the gallows.

Perhaps she was managing to weaken his defenses that first, tiny bit. If so, she had best keep up her friendly assault.

"So tell me, bounty hunter—how long have you been hunting desperadoes?" she ventured.

"Oh, nigh onto twelve years."

"What kind of criminals have you nabbed?"

He scratched his jaw. "Lemme see. . . . Dozens of train and bank robbers. A good score of murderers. Assorted claim jumpers and road agents. During my years working for Judge Parker, I hauled in killers and rapists, whiskey peddlers and horse thieves."

"Did you ever meet him?"

"Oh, yeah. I'll allow the judge is a good-natured sort, if a staunch Methodist. I once went to services with him and his Mary, and they even invited me to Sunday dinner afterward."

"Why aren't you still working for him?"

Sam glanced away uneasily. "Parker's a fair man, but unbending in enforcing the law. I reckon after a spell, watching all them multiple hangings didn't go down too well."

Annie laughed humorlessly. "Yes, hangings do that to a person."

They regarded each other warily for a moment.

Sam cleared his throat. "After a few years trackin' for Parker, I concentrated more of my efforts in Colorado, doin' work for Judge Righteous, and for the sheriff of Arapahoe County."

"So, tell me about your activities in Colorado."

"Well, I once nabbed a flimflam man who drove 'round the Colorado hillside in his bandwagon, selling hundreds of bottles of sugar water to a gullible public, claiming all the while that he had discovered a miracle blood restorative that would cure all their ills. He was a character, that one. Entertained me all the way to Central with stories of his exploits. Even old J.D. couldn't bear to sentence him to more than a few weeks in the county jail."

Annie couldn't restrain a smile, especially at this hint

of leniency in Judge Righteous. "But most of the desperadoes you nabbed weren't nearly so nice?"

"Nope." His gaze narrowed. "One of the worst cases I
ever worked was in the hills above Colorado City. At the
time, I was staying with an old friend, Ben Kenton, a
U.S. marshal, and I helped him with the investigation.
We was called up to a miner's cabin in the Rockies,
where we found a woman and her six daughters horribly
slaughtered."

"How awful!" Annie cried.

He nodded grimly. "Jim and I tracked the father clean
to Wyoming Territory. When we caught the bearded old
fanatic, he claimed Jesus told him in a vision that his
wife and daughters was defiled, and only their blood
could cleanse them. He said we should rejoice 'cause
they was in heaven now."

"My God—how sick!" Annie gasped. "Why do you
suppose he did something so terrible?"

Sam stared into the fire as in the distance a coyote
began to howl. "Maybe he was just mean crazy. Sometimes the mountains, and the isolation, makes folks
touched. Anyhow, it was clear to me he'd been consor-
tin' with Satan incarnate, not any deity. It sure was hard
to take him back alive—but it was a pure pleasure
watching him swing in Colorado City."

Annie sipped her water, keeping her fingers steady
with an effort. "Have you killed many men, Sam?"

His features grew taut. "A few that wouldn't come
along peaceably. I prefer takin' them in alive—and they
smell a heap better."

She blanched.

He glanced up at her quickly, his expression contrite.
"Hey, I'm sorry, I shouldna said that. You know what
I'm doin' . . . well, it ain't nothing personal, Annie."

Annie's restraint evaporated. "Sure, it is. I take losing
my life for something I didn't do *very* personally. Let me
tell you something, bounty hunter. If you're looking for
absolution from me, you're not going to get it."

He glowered, then turned away, pouring them both
cups of coffee.

"You killed many women, Sam?" she continued with deceptive mildness.

He drew a heavy breath and handed her a cup. "Truth to tell, over the years, I've apprehended very few females—only a few whores stealing from their customers, that sort of thing. I've never before tracked a female wanted for murder."

"Ah—then you do squirm a bit at the prospect of watching me hang?"

"I ain't saying I relish it, Annie."

She fell silent, toying with the remnants of her meal with her fork. "What do you intend to do with your life, aside from tracking desperadoes?"

"You sure do ask a lot of questions," he grumbled.

"You mean you don't have an answer?"

"Just what are you asking?"

She waved a hand. "Well, you must like to do *something* besides bounty hunting—something for intellectual enlightenment or fun."

His eyes glinted with amusement. "You mean women?"

She might have known that would be the first response from a rascal like him. "Well, yes."

He glanced at her wryly. "I'll allow there've been a few."

She raised a brow. "Any of them you liked enough to settle down with?"

He chuckled. "Reckon I've done most of my lovin' on the run."

"Have you ever wanted something more than just a few minutes upstairs at the local saloon?"

He glowered. "Hey, I ain't that desperate."

"Neither do you have a woman who means more to you than the fleeting pleasure she can bring you. Am I correct?"

She could tell by his perturbed expression that she was making him think. For a long moment, he gazed soberly out at the star-dotted heavens. "Maybe I can't afford to have a woman who means too much," he admitted at last.

"Oh?"

He drew a deep breath. "The life of a bounty hunter is wild, rough, and usually brief. I reckon someday before I get too old, I'd like to have a wife, and a son to carry on my name. But my missus will have to be a docile type and accepting of my wandering ways." He glanced at her meaningfully.

"Ah, so you wouldn't want a headstrong creature like me?"

A sensual grin lit his features. "Well, sugar, guess that depends on what you mean by 'want.' But it's true: When I marry, I'm wearing the pants and making the decisions for my family, and my wife will have to be a real lady who knows her place."

Annie made a sound of outrage. "Oh, you're such a throwback! And to think I bought into the myth of the Old West hero, that I even wanted to meet a retrograde jerk like you! I always assumed a strong man would want a strong woman. But that's too much of a threat to your vanity, eh, cowboy? Instead of wanting a wife who is your equal, you set your sights on a spiritless 'little woman' who will keep the home fires burning while you trot off on your adventures and have all the fun."

Sam was scowling formidably. "I ain't saying my wife should be spiritless, only feminine and uncomplaining like my ma." His expression softened. "She was the one my sister and I could count on when our pa was off gambling, drinking, and womanizing." He shot her a fervent look. "And if you think she wasn't a strong woman, then you best think again, sister."

"Of course I agree that what your mother did was admirable," Annie quickly assured him. "Especially since she had every right to chase down your father with a shotgun. But was what your father did—deserting and betraying your mother—fair to her? She raised the children and shouldered all the responsibilities while he did as he pleased, shutting her out of his life completely. That's what I find so unjust. Why can't a woman share a man's world?"

"I ain't claiming my pa was fair to my ma," Sam replied heatedly. "But it is a decent woman's lot to support her man and raise his family."

Annie threw a twig at him. "Oh, give me a break!"

Grinning, he batted away the missile. "It's the gospel truth. Any female with other notions in her head has got to be a temptress and a Jezebel."

"Like me?" Annie snapped, eyes bright.

"Well, you're a temptress, all right."

"And you're a sanctimonious bigot," she retorted. "Don't you realize you're really just like your father? Do you also have a woman in every town?"

Sam raised a fist and spoke vehemently. "I ain't like my pa at all. I earn my living respectable, upholding the law. My woman will have to accept that I won't be home often. But I'll always provide for her and our children."

"Oh, yeah, you're really Mr. Perfect, aren't you?"

"Didn't you say I live by a code?" he demanded through gritted teeth.

Their hot gazes locked for a long, meaningful moment. "You have a point," she conceded, setting aside her dishes with a rattle. "I'll concede you're not like your father in every way. Still, if you're away from your wife a lot . . ."

"Yeah?" he prompted.

Annie could feel her face heating as she irresistibly looked him over. "Well, a man of strong urges like yourself . . ."

Something very sensual and dangerous flared in his eyes then. "What do you know about my urges, woman?"

A shudder shook Annie as she realized she'd pushed Sam a bit too far. This man was getting to her, and the attraction she felt for him was clouding her judgment. His hot look rattled her, making her realize how close he was—how close they both were—to losing control.

Her gaze shied away from his. "I—I think it's time to call it a night."

His arm reached out and seized hers. "I said, what do you know about my urges?"

His touch burned her. She gulped. "Nothing."

He laughed. "Right. Are you trying to tempt me, woman?"

Annie fought the confusion welling up in her. "I'm trying to get through to you any way I can!"

He smiled.

"But I don't want to talk about your urges!"

"You brought it up."

She eyed him steadily, though she was trembling badly. "Sam, please let go of my arm. I'm tired, and I want to get ready for bed."

He released her at once, but when she stood, he was there beside her. His long arm caught her about the waist and he pulled her close. Even as she tried to wiggle free, he seized her face in his large, rough hands and tipped it up toward his.

Annie spotted the intensity blazing there and was riveted. Oh, God, she was in deep trouble now! Her heart roared.

Desperately, she whispered, "Sam, please, no—"

He didn't respond, only lowered his passionate face toward hers and brushed his lips over her mouth. Annie winced as if he'd seared her with a flame.

"You tempt me, Annie," he whispered, "whether you intend it or not."

Annie wasn't even conscious of who made the next move; she only knew this fevered longing was bursting inside her. Suddenly their lips met with sweet, blinding passion. Sam pushed his tongue inside Annie's mouth with brazen eroticism, giving no quarter as he gently probed and tormented. Dizzying torrents of heat shot down her body, tingling in her breasts and settling deep in her belly. Annie felt unnerved, exhilarated, and very vulnerable. She ached everywhere Sam's heat touched her. She clung to him, reeling with desire.

Sam's fingers found the tie on her braid and pulled it free. At his boldness, a hot shiver racked her to the core. Instinctively she shook her head as he parted the loose plaits, then buried his lips in her unbound hair. His incredibly sexy gesture filled her with aching tenderness.

She felt his long, warm fingers sliding through the tresses and heard his hoarse voice. "You make me so plumb crazy, woman, I don't know myself no more. You look at me with them big blue eyes, like you're tempting me to melt you. Well, sugar, ask for it and you're gonna get it."

Annie's mind struggled to conjure up a denial . . . but what was the point when her hungry woman's body was already losing the battle? She could feel the demanding passion coursing through Sam as well when he kissed her again. She wasn't sure just how they ended up on the ground together, side by side, and tightly embraced. She only knew the pressure and heat of Sam's solid body felt wonderful against her own, that his male scent heightened her yearnings to a fever pitch. Heaven help her, she'd been ravenous for more of him ever since he'd kissed her earlier today. She was surely wanton, but she felt hypnotized, out of control.

Abruptly his mouth left hers and he grazed his lips over her cheek. Chills consumed her and she panted for breath. His huge palm settled over her breast, arousing her nipple even through the fabric of her shirt. And the need inside her built to unbearable fervor.

This time, Annie kissed Sam, possessing his mouth with her hungry lips, her eager tongue. He rolled and pulled her on top of him, roving his hands down her spine, exploring the curves of her bottom. His fingers moved to the buttons on her shirt, pulling impatiently.

A whimper escaped her as Sam drew the tip of her breast inside his hot, wet mouth and wickedly caressed her with his tongue. She cried out, writhing at the unbearably pleasurable sensation, and his steely arms clamped down hard to restrain her wiggles. He drew her breast deeper inside his mouth and relentlessly resumed his erotic stroking. Harsh little cries escaped her. His fingers slipped inside her jeans, caressing her bare bottom, tilting her pelvis into his rigid erection.

Releasing her nipple, he buried his face in the valley between her breasts, the roughness of his whiskered skin sensually abrading her. "God, you're so soft, so sweet," he rasped.

And he was so male, so hard!

He rolled her beneath him, his fingers unbuttoning her jeans. Annie was on fire and couldn't wait to be filled by him. Distantly, some voice of sanity warned she could be making a terrible mistake, but she refused to listen. She was reaching between their bodies to unbutton him when all at once his hand caught hers. She could feel his entire body tensing, could hear his tortured breathing as his mouth abruptly released hers.

"Shit," he said.

"Sam, what's wrong?"

He rolled off her, sat up, and ran his fingers through his hair. He appeared to be a man in agony, his breathing tortured, veins standing out on his neck and in his temples.

"I don't know what come over me," he muttered. "I can't do this."

Intensely frustrated, Annie sat up beside him. "What do you mean you can't do this? Isn't it the woman's prerogative to be coy?"

He reached out to pull a small twig from her hair. He drew a ragged breath. "I'm caught between what my pa would no doubt find irresistible and what my granddaddy would call a moral dilemma. I can't go to bed with you then take you to Central to be hanged. What's worse, I think you know it and that's exactly what you're banking on."

Outraged, Annie shoved his shoulder. "Oh! Of all the arrogance! I think in your convoluted way, Sam Noble, you just called me a whore."

"I did not!"

"You did so! You're saying I'd trade my body for my freedom, aren't you? Well, if I'm that ruthless, you tell me this: Why didn't I just shoot you in the head last night at the hotel when I had the chance?"

She watched an exquisite struggle cross his face, his jaw trembling, his eyes seething with turmoil.

"Well, Sam? Has it occurred to you that I might be turned on by you, too, that a woman can have passions equally strong as a man's?"

He shot to his feet. "It's time for us to turn in. We've a lot of ground to cover tomorrow."

Annie bolted up beside him, balling her hands on her hips. "That's right, be a typical male. If you can't win an argument, bury all your emotions and just walk away from it."

He waved a hand in exasperation. "What do you want

me to say, Annie? That I was out of line? All right, I behaved like a scoundrel. There, are you satisfied?"

"Satisfied that you're a ruthless soldier of fortune who considers his reward money above all else? Yes, I'm satisfied."

"What in hell do you expect me to say? You know I'm doing my job—"

"Oh, don't give me that lame excuse!"

"What excuse?"

"Throughout history, too many men have hidden their evil deeds behind a shield of following orders—by being blindly loyal to wrongful causes, doing just what they were told, refusing to question, or to even consider the possibility that they could be making a mistake."

He was silent, clearly at a loss.

Annie caught a steadying breath. "You know, Sam Noble, all day long, I've been trying to get to know you better. Has it occurred to you that you haven't asked a single question about *me*?"

All at once his gaze avoided hers. "Getting to know you wouldn't make what I have to do no easier."

Tears clouded her eyes. "And how about having my breast in your mouth? Does that leave you slightly conflicted as well?"

Contrite, he reached out to touch her arm. "Of course it does."

She flung off his fingers. "Especially since, if you listened, it might open your mind a bit."

He appeared bewildered. "Open my mind to what? Annie, it's your face on the wanted poster."

"Damn it, you're like a broken record." With a fierce sigh, she went to get her bag, then returned to his side. Taking out her wallet and opening it, she thrust her driver's license into his hand. "Take a look at this."

He pushed the card back toward her. "I said I ain't interested in your bag of tricks."

"And I say look at it, damn you! After what just happened between us, you owe me at least that much."

Coloring, he glanced at the plastic card, then emitted a low grunt, as if his stomach had been punched. "My God! What's this? This has a picture of you—in color."

"Keep looking," she ordered.

He was shaking his head in bewilderment. "But a color picture ain't possible."

"Then why are you holding it? I said, keep looking!"

He stared at the card, his expression growing thunderstruck. "'Texas Department of Public Safety'? 'Expires 1998'?" He paused, running his fingers over the smooth surface. "And what in hell is this made of?"

"Something you've never seen. It's called 'plastic.' And I've more proof where that came from—credit cards, my Social Security and medical IDs—"

"Bah!" His expression unnerved, he tossed the driver's license back at her, as if it had burned him. "It's gotta be a trick."

Annie was tempted to stamp her foot. "It's no trick. You've simply got all the stubbornness—and sense—of a mule."

Sam was blinking rapidly in betrayal of his agitation. "Put that haywire doohickey away," he ordered gruffly. "I swear if I see it again, I'm throwing your entire bag of tricks into the fire."

Gritting her teeth, Annie shoved the card and her wallet back inside her bag. She stalked away, climbed inside her bedroll, and turned her back to him.

Sam sat gazing into the fire for a long time. What on earth was going on here? Why couldn't he figure out Annie? Why couldn't he keep his hands off her, or control his own raging needs and emotions? Even now he was still burning for her, still tasting that hot, velvety mouth, still smelling that intoxicating hair that had spilled through his hands like heavy silk.

She'd spoken to him about finding a woman who meant more to him than just a quick roll in the hay. This woman was beginning to, he realized. And it scared the living hell out of him.

Could she be telling the truth? Sam had never before seen anything like this "plastic" card she had just showed him, complete with a color picture of herself.

But if she was telling the truth, that would mean she had traveled across time. How could that be possible? Worse yet, if she was being honest, that meant he was wrong—dead wrong. Instead of apprehending a murderer, he would have kidnapped an innocent woman . . . and would have violated everything he believed in! His pride recoiled from that horrifying possibility.

He drew his fingers through his hair and groaned. He realized his head was splitting. Surely what Annie claimed was impossible. He stared at her back, gazed at her bag lying beside her. Part of him wanted to grab that witch's poke and learn every secret she kept inside there.

Part of him was scared to death of the unholy object and wanted to hurl the cursed satchel into the fire.

What was he going to do? He couldn't seem to figure out the truth or understand the strange power this woman held over him. Was she a clever liar and brazen seductress, or simply a victim of his own misguided obsession for justice?

Chapter 13

Morning found them continuing west over a rutted wagon road. Annie viewed signs of encroaching civilization: They crossed a cattle ranch where several drovers were gathered about the chuck wagon having breakfast while others were already riding the range and rounding up longhorns and Herefords; they passed a large double freight wagon loaded with bags of grain, with a bullwhacker driving a team of eight oxen toward Durango; they followed the dust of a northbound Wells Fargo stage until they overtook it.

Although the weather remained cool and crisp, Annie's thoughts were hotter by many degrees. Each time she stared at Sam riding so quietly beside her, memories of last night's torrid encounter rose to torment her. How could she have almost given herself to a man who was determined to bear her to her death?

The fact was, as much as Sam Noble maddened her, he was incredibly sexy and virile, and she wanted him more with each passing day. There seemed to be a mystical link between them, first indicated by the Cheyenne holy man, the sacred idiot, who had told Sam where to find her. And, assuming there was some divine order at work here, why had *Sam* been sent after her? Was he part of her destiny, or was she here strictly to help her great-great-grandmother?

She felt so drawn to Sam. Indeed, it galled her that he'd broken things off last night. He'd said he couldn't have sex with her, then take her to be hanged. Well, wasn't he noble to a fault? He didn't hesitate to collect a blood bounty on her neck, but he drew the line at seducing her first.

Still, part of Annie had to grudgingly admire Sam Noble for having integrity, for refusing to exploit a woman he was taking to justice. Indeed, in an ironic sense, Sam might have become his own worst enemy through admitting his vulnerability: It was dangerous and tempting knowledge for a woman who was, despite all, already a little in love with him.

How far *would* she be willing to go to win him over? The question left her squirming in the saddle. Then she slowly shook her head. She was determined to break through Sam's resistance, but she wouldn't stoop to whoring herself to gain her freedom.

Around noon, they were about to cross a rushing stream when they spotted a small family who had parked their mule-drawn prairie schooner beneath the branches of a large cottonwood tree shading the bank. The woman, dressed in a long nutmeg-colored calico dress and a slat bonnet, was rolling out sourdough on a flour-covered wagon gate; the man was building a fire beneath an iron tripod. Four children—twin girls of about four, and two somewhat older boys—were gathered at the base of the cottonwood, all yelling frantically, "Erasmus! Erasmus!"

Sam slanted Annie a quizzical glance and both halted their mounts. Spotting them, the man brushed off his hands and stood. Annie noted that he was tall and gangly, with deep-set, fiery dark eyes peering out of a gaunt face, and a chest-long black beard.

"Can I help you folks?" he asked in a deep, frontier-accented voice.

Sam dismounted and offered Annie a hand. "Looks like your young 'uns are the ones needing the help."

"Blame cat is up the tree again," grumbled the man. "I told them kids the creature is unholy, that they never shoulda rescued it from the hills." He stepped closer. "Name's Nehemiah Cooper. The Reverend Cooper of the Southern Baptists. Yonder's the wife, Myrtle Ruth.

By the tree's our young 'uns—sons Ezra and Micah, and the twins, Mary and Margaret."

"Pleased to meet you folks," said Sam, shaking his hand. "I'm Sam Noble and the lady is Ro—that is, Annie Dillon."

The reverend tipped his hat to Annie. "Pleased to meet you, ma'am."

"And you, Reverend," she answered.

The preacher leveled a stern glance on Sam. "You two traveling alone without benefit of holy wedlock?"

Sam and Annie exchanged a secretly amused glance. Then he answered, "I'm escorting the lady up to Central. She—er—has a compelling reason to git there pronto, and she couldn't make the journey by herself."

He scowled. "Well, it don't seem fitting. The Good Book says, 'Abstain from fleshly lusts, which war against the soul.'"

Sam winked at Annie. "Yep, and it also says, 'Blessed is the man that endureth temptation.'"

The man's gaze narrowed. "You a scholar of the Good Book, sonny?"

"My granddaddy was a sin-buster," Sam answered proudly.

The woman stepped forward, a friendly smile gracing her round, pretty face. "Nehemiah, don't you always quote Deuteronomy to your flock? 'Every man shall give as he is able.'" Nudging her husband with her elbow, she asked, "Should we not extend our hospitality toward our fellow travelers?"

Clearly not appeased, the reverend frowned formidably. "I prefer the passage from Hebrews: 'Whoremongers and adulterers God will judge.'" He slanted another pious glance at Annie and Sam.

"Nehemiah, really!" scolded Myrtle Ruth.

Glancing at the children, who continued to beseech the cat a few feet away, Sam pulled a wry face. "Well, now that we've aired the scriptures, Reverend, don't you think your young 'uns could use some help with their pet?"

The reverend glanced at the youngsters and shook his

head. "That Erasmus is definitely a sinner and not a saint. The creature's been a worse plague than the destruction the heavens unleashed on our flock back in Silver Plume."

"Wasn't Silver Plume hit by a terrible fire last November?" Sam asked. "You folks are lucky to have escaped with your lives."

"Praise the Lord, when the tragedy struck, the entire family was away at a revival meeting over in Georgetown," put in Myrtle Ruth.

"Afterward, we come home to find our house and church gone," Nehemiah finished sadly.

"How terrible," put in Annie. "At least your family was spared."

"Indeed, the Lord be praised," put in Myrtle Ruth feelingly. "Since then, we've been visiting with my people in New Mexico Territory." She eyed her husband with features aglow. "Now Nehemiah has received the call to preach the Word to the good folk of Greeley."

"Lucky for them," agreed Sam with a stiff smile.

"Well," Myrtle Ruth continued brightly, "won't you folks join us for dinner?"

"Oh, no, we couldn't impose," protested Sam.

"We reckon it's our Christian duty not to let you go on your way hungry," put in the reverend sanctimoniously.

Sam glanced at Annie, and she wrinkled her nose at him. "I reckon we're much obliged then," he told the reverend. Turning to Myrtle Ruth, he added, "Only, ma'am, maybe you could help me with something."

"Why, of course, if I can."

"I've an extry pound of coffee in my saddlebags that I know will go to waste before we reach Central. Could you take it off our hands?"

The woman's eyes lit with pleasure. "Why, we'd be much beholden! The fact is, we haven't been able to afford—" Blushing miserably as Nehemiah cast her a stern glance, she finished, "That is, we're running low on coffee."

"Consider it our contribution to the meal," said Sam gallantly.

Cupping a hand around her mouth, Myrtle Ruth

called, "Children, come away from that tree! We've company, and I need your help to cook the stick bread."

The four youngsters bounded over, and Annie observed how adorable they were—the boys with freckled faces and dark, bright eyes, wearing overalls and homespun shirts, the twin girls with darling pink cheeks and curly black hair, decked out in calico dresses that matched their mother's.

"But, Ma," protested the oldest boy, "Erasmus won't come down out of the tree."

"Oh, he'll come down when he smells my stew," said Myrtle Ruth wisely.

"Either that, or he can stay there and repent his wayward ways," pronounced their father.

A chorus of protests rose from the children. They jumped up and down, clutched at their parents' clothing, and moaned their distress, their little faces pictures of dismay.

When the youngsters failed to budge Nehemiah and Myrtle Ruth, one of the girls rushed over and tugged at Sam's sleeve, beseeching him in her plaintive voice. "Mister, you look big and strong. Would you rescue Erasmus?"

As Annie looked on in delight, Sam grinned. "Why, of course, honey. I was just waitin' for a pretty lady to ask me." Amid the gleeful laughter of all four children, he turned to their father. "All right with you, sir?"

"Do as you please," intoned the reverend. "I shall say only, 'A fool returneth to his folly.'"

Sam waved an arm at the children. "All right, young 'uns, let's go!"

The children cheered and tugged Sam off toward the tree.

"Excuse me. I've got to see this," Annie informed the Coopers, hurrying off after the group.

She arrived at Sam's side to see him staring up at the tree, his expression mystified. She soon discerned the reason for his amazement. On a limb about five feet above his head was perched a scrawny gray-and-brown animal, a decidedly unfriendly "cat" that was hissing viciously at Sam and baring its sharp claws.

"My God—is that what I think it is?" she whispered to Sam.

"Hell and hog-wallows," he muttered back. "It's a blame bobcat all right."

Annie gulped as she continued to study the cub with its lithe, spotted body. It wasn't much larger than a full-grown house cat, yet its feral features and large, savage eyes made it look particularly ferocious.

"He looks none too happy," she murmured.

"No kidding," Sam replied. "He's the fiercest, ugliest critter I ever seen. Reckon I'd rather rescue a wood pussy."

"A what?" asked Annie.

"A *skunk*."

"Shhh!" she warned, glancing at the youngsters' anxious faces. "The children will hear."

Sam turned to grin at the children. "Don't worry, young 'uns. We'll get him down."

"He's only scared, mister," called one of the girls, her precious face pinched with concern. "He's really very nice."

"Sure, honey, I can tell that," Sam reassured her solemnly as the bobcat emitted a bloodcurdling snarl. "Don't worry, I'm right good at taming wildcats."

Annie playfully kicked him in the shin.

Flashing her a chiding glance, Sam turned his attention back to the task at hand. "How did you young 'uns say you got him?"

"We found him when he was a starving baby, abandoned in the snow above Grandma's place in New Mexico Territory," replied the oldest boy. "Pa said the sinful critter should be—er, destroyed—but Ma wouldn't hear of it."

"Good for Ma," Sam muttered. He flashed Annie a brave look. "Reckon I'd best start climbing."

Annie glanced up and grimaced. "And what do you think that cub's going to do—give you a hand? He's a wild animal, for heaven's sake."

Annie paused as she felt a tug at her shirt. "Miss, he's really tame," insisted the other twin. "He purrs for Sister and me, and eats out of our fingers."

"Thanks, we'll keep that in mind," Annie replied. Turning back to Sam, she rolled her eyes toward the cub. "Soon as you start climbing, he's going to take off."

"You an expert at bobcats, are you, woman?" he teased.

She waved a hand in exasperation. "I've been around enough animals, and I haven't lost my common sense. This tree's gotta be fifty feet tall, and I have a good idea where that cub's going to end up. You aren't exactly Tarzan, you know."

He appeared taken aback. "Who's he?"

"King of the jungle."

He chuckled. "I ain't saying it'll be easy, but I promised them kids. And a promise is a promise. I grew up with a daddy who sometimes didn't keep his word, and I swore that as a man, I'd stand by mine."

Annie smiled. Despite herself, she was liking Sam more by the moment, even though it was implied that "keeping his word" also meant bearing her to justice. "Very well, Tarzan, have at it."

Sam began clambering up the tree. At first the cub eyed him warily with its bright, alert eyes. As soon as Sam got within reaching distance, the cat let out a venomous scream and bolted away, much as Annie had predicted.

"Oh, no!" wailed the children in unison.

"It's all right," Annie reassured them. "Really it is."

Sam continued to climb upward and made two more attempts to nab the cat; each time, the cagey animal let him get within a foot or two, then hissed and scampered away.

By now, Annie judged, Sam was at least twenty feet up the tree. He shimmied down closer to her and spoke intently. "Annie, I need you to get my rope and a saddle blanket."

She was appalled. "Don't tell me you're going to try to lasso that cub? This is no time to be showing off! You could hang the poor thing!"

"Annie, all I'm seeing is that blame cat's rear end. Maybe I can lasso it round its hind flanks the next time the critter tries to hightail it. I ain't gonna lynch it. All right?"

In a sarcastic whisper, she said, "That's right, you just like to hang women, eh?"

"Only if they're tried and convicted. Now go get my gear before them young 'uns bust out cryin' and you have to tend 'um."

Annie glanced at the children, all of whom did appear close to tears. From the boys' desperate expressions, they were ready to panic; the twin girls had knelt and clasped their tiny hands together in prayer.

That heartrending sight was all it took to spur Annie into action. She hurried off to Sam's horse and unhooked his lasso. She was reaching for the bedroll to get a blanket when she spotted his Winchester in its scabbard.

Her heart raced and her mouth went dry. What was she doing? Here was her perfect chance to escape! Sam was up a tree. All she had to do was mount his horse, tug along her own, and ride off. He'd never be able to track her, even if the preacher lent him a mule. Assuming he did manage to pursue her, she had the rifle to defend herself.

Except she'd promised him—twice now—that she wouldn't try to escape again. Just as he'd promised the children he would rescue their cub.

Glancing over at the distraught youngsters, she bit her lip. She just couldn't do it. Grabbing the blanket, she returned to the tree.

She handed Sam the rope, and she and the children watched tensely as he climbed up after the cat and prepared the lasso. He inched slowly up to the limb where the cat was perched. As it again turned and tried to speed away, he gently hooked the rope over the animal's back legs.

The captured animal snarled, screamed, and fought against its bonds, turning and trying to strike out at Sam. Watching him struggle to hang on to the rope while dodging the cub's lethal claws and sharp teeth, Annie knew he needed help. She threw the blanket over her shoulder.

"Sam! Wait right there! I'm coming up."

Relying on skills she hadn't used since childhood, Annie quickly clambered up the tree. Finally she settled just beneath Sam's feet. At his look of mingled astonishment and pride, she quipped, "Just call me Jane."

"Jane? That your latest alias?" he teased.

She shot him a forbearing look. "Pass me the rope and I'll give you the blanket. I'll hold on to the little monster while you wrap him up."

"Yes, ma'am," said a very relieved Sam.

He passed her the rope and she held on tight, stunned at the strength of the small cat. Quickly Sam threw the blanket over the struggling animal. Within seconds, the cub was rendered harmless, wrapped tightly in the thick, coarse blanket as the two began their careful descent to the ground. The children cheered as Sam placed the precious bundle in one of the girls' arms. She folded the blanket away from the cub's face, and it gazed about warily, appearing no worse for its ordeal.

The reverend and Myrtle Ruth rushed up. "Well, I'll be a Presbyterian," declared the reverend. "You are a determined man, Mr. Noble."

"You've both certainly earned your dinner," added a beaming Myrtle Ruth.

Annie helped one of the twins brown stick bread over the fire while Sam and the reverend drank coffee and visited. Annie enjoyed the dinner with the Coopers, despite the reverend's subtle and not-so-subtle references to temptation and sins of the flesh.

She had more fun watching the children with their "cat." Just as the youngsters had predicted, the cub was as docile as a domestic house cat, going from one child to another and plaintively wailing for scraps. Observing the astounding scene, Annie mused that one would never know that moments before, this same animal had been a hissing, spitting miniature dragon. She wondered what would happen when the animal grew too big to be a pet, and was glad this was the Coopers' dilemma and not her own.

When the time came for everyone to depart, the reverend magnanimously said, "If you folks ever decide to wed, just get your license and come on up to Greeley. I'd be right honored to hitch you up, free of charge."

"Thanks, Reverend," answered Sam solemnly. "We'll keep your kindly offer in mind."

Annie and Sam thanked Myrtle Ruth for the meal, and both felt touched when all four children rushed up for hugs. As the two of them rode off, Annie glanced back at the Coopers' mule wagon plodding along behind them. "They're nice people, even if the reverend is something of a prig."

"Oh, he's passable kind, I suppose," Sam said. "Reminds me of my grandpa."

"You know, I'm wondering. . . ."

"Spit it out."

"Why didn't you tell them I'm a criminal you're taking to justice?"

His jaw hardened. "Reckon it ain't none of their affair."

The two rode along in silence for a moment.

"I'm wondering something, too, Annie," Sam added with unaccustomed tentativeness.

"What's that?"

Gravely he met her eye. "How come you didn't escape when you had a chance? You could have taken both our mounts, plus my rifle."

"So you noticed that," she murmured with an ironic smile.

"Shit, yes, I noticed."

She met his gaze boldly. "Did you want me to escape, Sam?"

The question left him scowling. "You know, I reckon I ain't rightly sure why I let my guard down. Neither do I know why you passed up the chance—'ceptin' you ain't stupid."

"You're right."

"Then why, Annie?"

To her amazement, Annie felt tears burning her eyes, but she didn't shy away from his troubled gaze. "Because I made a promise to you, Sam, just like you did to those children. Because I have a code, too, just like you do."

His eyes blazed with some unnamed emotion. "Criminals don't have codes, Annie."

"That's right," came her bitter reply. "Think about that, Sam Noble. You just think about that."

Sam could think of little else.

Chapter 14

A new tension sizzled in the air as they rode along. Annie knew she had risked death in order to keep her word and stay with Sam. Part of her was convinced she was a fool. Part of her felt she'd had no choice. Seeing him with those children, risking the wrath of a frightened bobcat in order to forestall their tears, had affected her deeply. She hadn't expected a ruthless bounty hunter to be so sensitive. To some, the experience might have seemed silly, frivolous. To Annie, it meant more proof that she was falling in love with the wrong man.

That afternoon the landscape began to evolve again, with scattered buttes popping up to the south and west of them. The terrain became gently rolling, with more deep gulches and high crests, denser clumps of cedar, and reemerging stands of mesa oak—all evidence that they had reached the foothills of the Rockies.

When they descended toward another stream in a large clearing with plenty of shade, Sam turned to her. "Reckon we'll stop here for the night."

Annie glanced at the sky. "Really? I'm shocked at you, Sam Noble. There's still plenty of daylight left."

"I reckon this is a good place to camp," he reiterated.

She reined in her horse. "Yeah, but we could still cover more ground, get me that much closer to Central City."

Abruptly, he dismounted, strode over to her horse, and hauled her down. She moaned shamelessly as her body slid down the hard length of his. His hands settled on her shoulders.

He just looked at her in that intense way that made her stomach curl. "I said we'll stop here."

Annie could barely force out a response over her thrumming heart. "Sure. Fine."

He fell back a step and spoke gruffly. "I'll gather some wood."

Watching him stride away, Annie shook her head and struggled to control her rapid breathing. Sam was acting so strange. She'd felt bonded to him by their experience with the children and the bobcat, and she knew those moments had touched him, too. But he'd hardly spoken to her all afternoon, though something was clearly smoldering inside him, and what she suspected—that he wanted her as much as she wanted him—made her uneasy.

After building a fire, he sat down on a boulder and watched her every movement—rattling her once again.

She cleared her throat. "If it's all right with you, I'm going to go wash up."

"Come here first."

Oh, God. The husky note in Sam's voice—its territorial timbre—unnerved Annie. Warily she approached him. His long arm snaked out and he pulled her onto his lap.

"Sam!"

"Hold your horses. I gotta ask you something."

"What?"

He cupped her chin in his large hand. "In a minute."

Annie could barely hear his words over the mad pumping of her heart, for Sam sounded like a man intent on getting precisely what he wanted. She struggled to force out a protest, but the sound faded into a moan of ecstasy as Sam captured her lips in a passionate kiss. His hard desire swelled against her bottom as his tongue made slow, wicked suggestions inside her mouth. The erotic torment left her weak and trembling.

God, he was out of control, and she wasn't far behind him!

Breathless, she broke away. "Sam, I thought you said you couldn't do this and—"

"Why'd you do it, Annie?"

"Do *what*?"

"It's been eating me up all afternoon," he continued fervently. "I was so caught up in helping them kids, I really let down my guard this time. Why didn't you run? Hell, you had both our horses and my rifle. You could have done most anything under the circumstances."

All at once Annie bolted out of his lap as his words touched a nerve. "*Anything?* Are we back to the nefarious back-stabbing again?"

He grinned. "What are you babbling about, woman?"

"Do you think I would have shot you in front of a Baptist minister, his wife, and four children?"

Shocking her, riling her even further, he laughed. "Lord, you're pretty when you're mad."

Annie regarded him in disbelief. "I'm—*what*? How can you say such a thing in the middle of an argument? What do my looks have to do with it?"

A lot, Sam thought to himself. *A damn lot.* Annie was so feisty and desirable, so tempting, with her bosom heaving, her blue eyes blazing at him.

But, Lord, she was ready to fry his bacon. "Naw, I don't think you woulda shot me," he assured her. "I'm just saying you clearly had the upper hand. And you still haven't answered my question. Why didn't you run?"

Annie crossed her arms over her bosom. "Guess I'm just crazy."

"You're making *me* crazy," he admitted.

She smiled.

"Does that please you, woman?"

She released a shuddering breath. "Maybe I'll drive you so crazy that you'll let me go."

Sam was on his feet. "Not a chance."

Annie reeled. Sam was close to her now—too close. An even hotter tension charged the air.

She glanced away, her lower lip trembling. "Yeah, I guess you're right. You still have to get me to that hanging, don't you?"

Sam lifted her chin with his fingers. "Maybe I ain't so eager to see you hanged."

That statement hung between them like a live electrical

current. Annie regarded him with helpless bewilderment. "What do you mean by that, Sam? You're confusing me."

"Hell, I'm confused, too," he confessed with surprising humility. "You're supposed to be an outlaw, but you sure don't run like one. Yet you expect me to believe the most cock-eyed bull I ever heard."

Although Annie's features tightened, she bit down an angry retort. "I can understand your frustration, Sam. I'm pretty damn frustrated myself."

He smiled, reaching down to draw a teasing finger along her proud jaw. "Oh, are you?"

She sucked in a sharp breath and backed away. "I— think I'm going to go wash now. That stream looks inviting."

You look inviting, Sam thought, watching Annie stalk off, her hips swaying seductively, the setting sun outlining the glorious curves of her body. God, he was frustrated as hell! One minute he wanted to do his job. The next, he wanted to let her off with a kiss or two . . . and maybe six or eight babies. He had to do *something* to calm himself down before he did something really rash.

Annie was heading toward her horse when a loud crackling sound almost had her jumping out of her skin. She whirled to see Sam about ten yards away from her, working his lasso in huge circles up and down his body. She shook her head in amazement. "What are you doing now?"

"Oh, just practicing with my lasso," he called back. "Helps me blow off energy when I'm tied up in knots."

Incredulous, she asked, "All that riding today and you still need to blow off energy?"

He grinned.

Annie also had to smile. "Guess it's all that frustration, huh?"

"Yeah. Could be."

Annie thought it best not to comment further. Gathering her towel and soap and heading for the stream, she found the things Sam had said to her still spinning through her mind. Was he really starting to come around to her point of view? He'd said he wasn't so eager to see her hang. Was he contemplating letting her off the hook? Just the fact that he was wavering made her soften toward him. And too damn much.

As she finished washing, Annie continued to hear Sam's lasso snap and whiz. In the fading light, she was heading back for camp when she heard an ominous rattle not far away from her feet.

Shit, a rattler! Annie froze, her heart galloping in fear.

Before she could even call out to Sam, she watched him spin, saw his lasso slice through the air. A split second later the rattlesnake went flying off a nearby rock, its head cinched up tight at the end of Sam's rope.

In amazement, Annie watched the snake land, saw Sam rush over and slaughter it with his knife. Shuddering, she eyed his rapid approach.

"You all right?" he asked anxiously.

Annie gulped. "Are you trying to scare the life out of me?"

"That rattler woulda done a heap more'n that had he gotten his hooks in you."

"Right," she readily admitted, drawing a hand to her racing heart. "But wouldn't it have been simpler just to shoot it? Must you be—so dramatic?"

He chuckled. "Well, that rattler was coiled and ready to strike. I had the lasso in hand, and my first instinct was to get that viper away from you."

"Good thinking," Annie muttered. She glanced over at the gruesome sight of the headless snake and felt herself staggering.

Sam caught her arm. "You scared? The critter didn't bite you, did it?"

Shaking her head, she regarded him helplessly. With a groan, he pulled her trembling body close.

"There, there," he murmured, stroking her back. "The snake can't hurt you now. All right?"

Annie sighed. It felt good having Sam hold her after the fright she'd just had. Indeed, it was only now hitting her how close she'd come to being killed! For a long moment she let him comfort her.

"Coiled and ready to strike, eh?" she quipped at last.

Sam pulled back and touched the tip of her nose with his finger. "Rattlers like to come 'round at twilight to steal some heat from the rocks. The next time one tries to get its hooks in you, woman, I'll shoot it, if it'll make you happier."

Annie was enjoying his teasing and feeling rather playful herself. "You won't shoot; you're too busy showing off with your lasso. You're probably a bum shot, anyway."

His mouth fell open. "You think I can't shoot?"

Annie smiled, challenging him to prove it.

Sam dug in his pocket and pulled out a silver dollar. "Here, toss this up in the air."

Annie did as he bid, tossing the silver coin high. Sam whipped out his Colt and made the coin dance six times before it fell to the ground.

Annie whistled.

"Well, woman?" he demanded.

She stared at him through the haze of smoke. "You're a good shot."

"A *good* shot?"

"Okay. The best damn shot I've ever seen."

He appeared ready to bust his buttons with pride. "Now you're talking."

"Better even than any of my father's ranch hands."

He raised an eyebrow. "You was raised on a ranch?"

She nodded. "You aren't the only one who spent your youth around the old-timers. I was raised among some pretty crusty, outspoken characters."

He grinned. "No wonder you got such a mouth on you."

She raised her chin. "I'm used to holding my own with some real legends."

"Oh, yeah? And what did them legends teach you?"

Annie smiled. "All about the Old West."

"Which old West?"

"*This* Old West."

He appeared perturbed. "Like what?"

"Well, all the famous tales of frontier days. You know, Butch Cassidy and the Sundance Kid, the Dalton gang."

She paused, taking note of his bewildered expression. "But maybe I'm getting ahead of us. Let me see. . . . You ever heard of a road agent's spin?"

Secret amusement danced in his eyes. "Maybe I have. Maybe I ain't."

His words were a challenge, and Annie knew it. "One of my father's hands taught me the gun trick when I was ten. Want me to show you?"

"Think I'm gonna give you my Colt?"

She shrugged. "Why not? All the bullets are gone. I should know. I just counted them."

Hooting with laughter, Sam shook his head, then handed her his Colt, butt first. "All right. Show me."

Annie first checked the cylinder to ensure she'd been correct in assuming no bullets remained, then she shut it and set the hammer in safety position. She balanced the heavy weapon in her hand. "Well, a road agent's spin comes into play when an outlaw is *supposed* to be surrendering to a sheriff. In handing over his weapon butt first, he keeps one finger on the trigger guard . . ." She paused, extending the Colt toward Sam in such a fashion. "And that's where the fun part comes in."

In triumph, Annie neatly spun the Colt backward on its trigger guard. In a flash, the weapon came to rest with its barrel pointed squarely at Sam.

He whistled, raising his hands in mock horror. "Hot damn, woman! I surrender."

She giggled.

"What other tricks did them old-timers teach you?"

Annie's lips twitched. "Well, I might know a few, but maybe I'm saving them."

"Yeah, that's a woman for you." Sam carefully eased the Colt from her hand. "You ever heard of a border shift?"

Enjoying their little game, she said, "Maybe I have, maybe I haven't. You gonna show me?"

"Damn right." He holstered his gun. "A border shift is a distant cousin of the famous border draw. You see, if a man is wounded in a gunfight, he's gotta shift his weapon—and damn fast."

Pivoting slightly away from Annie, Sam drew and

made several harsh, guttural sounds as if he were firing at some point off in space. While she laughed, he staggered and groaned, grabbing his right shoulder and pretending to be hit. Then he spun his weapon into his left hand, cocked the Colt, and pointed it ahead.

"Border shift," he announced proudly.

Annie drew a shuddering breath. "Yeah, you're cocked and ready, all right."

He turned, and for a long moment they stared at each other. Annie was sure Sam must hear her roaring heart.

Then he holstered his Colt, and a devilish smile lit his face. "You know there's a price to be paid for rescuing a woman from a snake."

"Oh, yeah?"

"Yeah. A kiss."

"You mean you haven't stolen enough kisses yet, bounty hunter?" she asked in mock indignation.

"Not by a long shot."

All at once the atmosphere was sizzling again. Annie felt riveted by the sight of Sam's dark, impassioned face as he leaned over and touched her lips with his own. It was a kiss that started out gently, teasingly, then began to burn. His strong arms coiled around her. She clung to his rugged strength. They kissed deeply, ravenously . . . and finally moved apart just to breathe.

Sam swallowed hard. "Reckon it's time for us to fix some grub before that fire fizzles out. All this blowing off steam has worked me into quite an appetite."

Yeah, me, too, thought Annie dazedly.

Chapter 15

∽◦∾

"**R**eckon you can cook tonight."

"Me?" asked Annie.

Sam chuckled. "And I thought you was so capable of taking care of yourself."

They were standing by the fire. Annie set her arms akimbo. "Well, I'm used to riding and shooting, but not to cooking—particularly not under these primitive conditions."

"You mean none of them legends at your daddy's ranch taught you how to fire up the chuck wagon?"

She eyed him askance.

"Guess you was too busy learning how to flap off your mouth."

"Guess so."

Sam gestured toward the fire. "I already done all the hard stuff. All you got to do is prepare the pots and hook 'um onto the tripod."

"You make it sound so easy," she mocked. "So now you expect me to become an obedient female like Myrtle Ruth Cooper?"

"I'm just saying it's your turn to shovel the grub."

He had a point, Annie had to concede. "Remember, you asked for this," she warned, heading off toward the horses.

Going back and forth, Annie unloaded utensils and food. Soon she was squatting on the ground, staring mystified at the collection in front of her—a can of beans, a sack of cornmeal, a tin of baking soda, salt and pepper, a parcel of bacon.

"Need some help?"

She glanced up to see Sam regarding her in amusement. "I told you I can't cook."

He hunkered down beside her. "And this is the lady who can take care of herself just fine, thank you, sir."

"I sure can!"

He pulled out his knife. "Tell you what, I'll open this here can of beans while you make up the corn dodgers."

"How in heck am I supposed to do that?"

"Well, you make up some corn batter, then drop spoon-size dabs onto a greased frying pan. Then you just fry 'um up."

"And how do I make up the corn batter?" she pursued miserably.

Setting down the can he'd opened, Sam reached out to tug at her braid. "You put some cornmeal in a dish, add some water and some soda . . ."

With Sam doing more of the work than Annie, they managed to prepare a supper of beans, bacon, and corn dodgers. "Well, it's palatable," Annie pronounced as they sat together eating. "If a repeat of last night."

"Just what was you expectin'—some fancy steak?"

"Broiled redfish might be good—or fillet of sole."

Sam shook his head. "What is it with you and the fish?"

"It's much healthier for you," came her prim reply.

They consumed their supper in silence for a few moments. Thinking back to his dashing rescue, Annie had to smile. Sam had been wonderful—saving her life, comforting her, even cajoling away her fright. Lord, she was moving closer to this man, but she still wasn't sure she should be making that perilous journey.

"What are you thinking, woman?"

At his soft question, she smiled shyly. "Oh, I think I may have forgotten something earlier."

"What's that?"

Sincerely, she said, "Guess I didn't—well, in all the excitement over the rattlesnake, I forgot to thank you for saving my life."

He winked at her. "Your kiss repaid me."

Blushing, she glanced away. "Yes, I suppose it did, you rascal. But I still should have said it." She eyed him soberly. "Thank you, Sam."

"You're welcome."

Annie felt her throat tightening. "When I think about it, it's really an ironic thing to say to you. My fate is in your hands, isn't it?"

He didn't immediately reply, though his face reflected as much turmoil as Annie was feeling.

At last, he said, "Annie, I'm trying to sort through all this."

"But you aren't telling me where I stand, Sam," she continued in an emotional voice. "Is that fair to me?"

He didn't reply.

"Plus you keep kissing me, and—"

"And?" he cut in tensely.

"I don't know what it means, or what you're really thinking!" she burst out. "Are you discovering things about me that are threatening your beliefs? Are you wrestling with your conscience, with having to abandon your previous assumptions about me and admit you made a mistake?"

A muscle worked in his jaw. "This ain't no time to be pushing me, Annie."

Annie realized this but pressed on nonetheless. "Is it because you desire me, and you can't figure out how your noble conscience would allow you to lust after such a bad girl? Because your feelings are at war with your intellect?"

Blinking rapidly, he glanced away. "I'm warning you, Annie."

"Oh, I know, you're so hardened and mean." Features reflecting her hurt and bewilderment, she leaned toward him. "Sam, you know I'm no killer. You know I've had at least three opportunities to knife you or escape you, and I let all of them go. All of them, Sam. Why won't you just admit it?"

Again, no response.

"Why is it I get the feeling that now that you have me, you don't know what to do with me?"

He laughed and set down his dishes. "Is that what you really think?"

"Didn't I say you can't handle a really strong woman?"

In a flash he was beside her, his passionate gaze boring into hers. "Well, maybe you can't handle a really strong man."

"Yes, I can."

The reckless words left Annie's mouth almost of their own volition, and she regretted them the instant she spotted the fervent, volatile passion gripping Sam's features.

"Oh, yeah?" he replied. "Then show me."

Annie's heart skipped a beat. Sam's intent face was close, too close. Belatedly, she realized she had pushed him too far, that she'd laid herself wide open for his heated response. They were no longer blowing off steam with pistols and lassos. This man was no longer her captor but a smoldering stranger who wanted her.

Drawing a shaky breath, she replied, "Sam, don't you push me, either. We're not playing cowboys and Indians anymore."

He gripped her face in his hands. "I'm aware of that, Annie. And I said, why don't you show me?"

Annie could only stare back at him in trembling uncertainty.

Drawing a ragged breath, Sam caressed her cheek with his fingertips, making her shiver. "God, what a little witch you are. Do you have any idea how much you've tempted me, knowing you didn't run when you could have, that you laid your life on the line to stay with me? Why didn't you run, Annie? You gonna show me or not?"

Annie squeezed shut her eyes and clenched her fists. "Sam, please don't confuse me this way."

Sam heard the helpless anguish in her voice and it tore at his gut. What had come over him now?

At once he dropped his hands. "I—wasn't trying to scare you, Annie. Guess we'd better—"

Her shaky words cut him off. "Good night, Sam."

* * *

Long after Annie was in bed, Sam lingered by the fire,
trying to make sense of his jumbled thoughts and
feelings about her. Along the distant horizon, he spotted
a streak of lightning—probably not an ominous sign,
since the skies had not appeared threatening all day.

The turmoil raging inside him was another matter
altogether. He had to admit Annie had raised some valid
points as they ate, driving home something that already
bothered him a lot. Although she possessed all the
feistiness and skill of a female desperado, she lacked the
ruthlessness, the meanness, that he'd found to be innate
in most lawbreakers. This ate at his conscience. Hell,
even if she *was* an outlaw, wasn't she also a woman
worth saving?

A woman he couldn't understand!

He glanced at her mysterious bag, which sat nearby.
He focused on the fearsome object for a long moment
until he finally realized he *had* to know more about
her—he had to learn the truth.

He picked up the reticule and dumped out its contents. Scowling, he examined her keys then her wallet,
glancing again at the bizarre card she called her driver's
license. He perused her other cards one by one, finding
strange names, strange shapes, weird writing. One card
was named "Visa," another "Social Security," another
"Blue Cross/Blue Shield." And all of 'um bore dates
from the 1990s!

Replacing the cards in their pockets, he pulled out
money engraved in a manner he'd never seen before—
crisp green bills, bearing dates from the next century,
along with a few more current notes. He chuckled to
himself, realizing she'd likely stolen those particular
greenbacks from him. He'd thought he'd had some
money missing ever since Prairie Stump.

So she'd taken the currency from him in order to
survive while on the run, he mused ruefully. Obviously
those other bills would do her no good here. Where had
they come from?

Scowling, he stuffed all the money back in the wallet
and replaced it in her bag. He inspected other items: a
bizarre black tube containing some sort of lip rouge; a

round, thin green object that opened to reveal a miniature mirror, a cake of powder, and a powder puff; a tiny
sewing caboodle; and a really odd pink container, the
one he'd seen her taking a pill from more than once. On
its back were written more curious terms he couldn't
understand. Flipping open the case, he spied rows of
pills arranged beneath some slick, transparent substance
and resting on an even stranger silver material. Several
of the pills had been removed, and the term "Exp.
10/1998" had been raised in the silver.

Another date from the future!

Snapping the container shut and replacing all the
items in her bag, Sam thrust his fingers through his hair.
Hell, he was so blamed confused he didn't know what to
think. Was Annie telling the truth about coming from
the next century? Or was she some kind of witch?

His mind still argued that travel through time was
impossible. But one thing was becoming crystal clear—
something here was not as it seemed.

He really did need help with this. *They* needed help
with this, and he had a notion where they might turn—
to his grandmother. After all, wasn't Medicine Woman
the one who had insisted he should heed Moon Calf's
prophecy that he would find Rotten Rosie beyond the
southern wind? Although Sam wasn't particularly mystical himself, he did respect his grandmother's power and
vision, and she hadn't steered him wrong yet.

Then why would she have sent him after the wrong
woman? It made no sense at all. Hell, maybe Medicine
Woman could help them sort this out—before it drove
them both loco. He could still hear Annie's tormented
voice: *Sam, please don't confuse me. . . .*

She was right, he realized. He should tell her where
she stood. And he couldn't straddle the fence between
enforcing the law and becoming her lover. He had to
choose one or the other, to decide what he wanted.

He smiled. At last, an easy question to answer.

He wanted *her*.

Chapter 16

The sound of an ominous rattle echoed through Annie's dream. Her heart pumping with terror, she spotted the snake, its angry fangs ready to sink into her. She cried out in fear.

Annie jerked awake to the sound of thunder. She glanced at the western skies to see lightning flashing. A chill had permeated the night and she was trembling badly.

At once Sam was beside her on her bedroll. "What's wrong? I heard you crying out!"

She twisted about to regard his anxious face in the moonlight. "Did I?"

He nodded.

"I . . ." She shuddered. "Had a nightmare. Guess I've been on edge ever since . . . well, the rattlesnake."

Sam wrapped an arm about Annie's shoulders and nuzzled her cheeks with his lips. "God, sugar, you're shivering so. Here, let me warm you. It'll be all right."

All at once, Annie become intensely conscious of the sexy man beside her, his scent, his heat. "Er—Sam?"

"Yep?"

"You've gotten in bed with me."

He chuckled.

Her fingers touched his bare arm. "And you don't have a shirt on, either. Guess you larger-than-life legends stay hot even on a chilly night, eh?"

"Now, Annie, I'm wearing my britches. And I came

over here to see what was wrong—not to start up no hanky-panky."

Despite her anxieties, Annie had to smile. "That's right, you're a man with a code. You do your job; you don't rape and pillage along the way."

He was about to comment when thunder rumbled and she again tensed. "Boy, that rattler really did fluster you, didn't it?"

Annie felt a lump rising in her throat. "I remember once when I was twelve, out riding my favorite horse. A rattler spooked him, and he threw me off."

"Were you hurt bad?"

She released a shaky breath. "I got out of it with a broken ankle, and neither of us got bitten. But my horse took a nasty stumble, broke his foreleg, and we had to . . .

He knew enough about horses that she didn't have to finish. "I'm sorry, sugar," he said.

"God, I loved that horse," she went on, feeling her eyes sting. "He could run like the wind, and when the sun hit him, he had flanks like copper and a mane like cream."

Sam's arms tightened about her and his lips brushed her hair. "Yeah, I seen a few beautiful manes in my time."

His tender charm touched her, and for long moments, Annie just let Sam hold her. It was so comforting being in his arms again. Feeling safe. Her nightmare, the rattler, the thunder, had all demonstrated to her how on edge she truly was.

Of course, most of the time during this ordeal she'd managed to remain strong. But at quiet moments like this, her fears crept up on her and she felt lost, far away from home. Staring out at the vast heavens, she wondered what had happened to the world she'd known, to her brother, her friends, her *life*. Did anyone know she was gone? Was anyone worried? Would she ever make it back to her own time, or would she be stuck in another century forever?

She felt vulnerable. She needed a friend. Sam was

there, warm and real. She was coming to care for him, even though technically, he was still her enemy.

His lips brushed her forehead and she winced. Perhaps in the night, even an enemy could be a friend. . . .

Annie's reverie was shattered as lightning danced across the distant horizon. "Do you think it's gonna rain?" she asked fretfully. "God, I don't think I could take another hailstorm."

Sam scowled up at the skies. "Naw, sugar, I think all we're lookin' at is ghost lightning."

"Ghost lightning?"

He regarded her tenderly. "The skies can be just like a woman, sometimes contented and serene, sometimes all pouty like, moody and threatening."

That description prompted Annie to wrinkle her nose at him. "You would blame it all on a woman."

Chuckling, he gazed overhead. "One of the greatest joys of my life is sleeping out under the stars like this, looking up at the dazzling heavens."

Annie sighed. "They're awesome, all right."

"There's no finer pleasure a man can know"—his voice grew husky—"unless it's having a beautiful woman in his arms."

Oh, he was driving her crazy with his sweet talk! As thunder again boomed out, Annie cuddled closer to him. In a small voice, she asked, "And what would this man do if the woman in his arms was scared?"

He twisted about to stare at her. "Scared of the thunder?"

Annie's throat burned. She realized she'd been scared of so much more, but she couldn't tap into that wellspring of emotion right now or she'd fall apart. "Yeah, scared of the thunder."

Sam raised himself on an elbow to look down at her. He moved a finger teasingly along her chin. "Why, he'd comfort her, of course. Try to distract her."

"How?" Again, Annie found herself speaking without conscious volition.

"Maybe with a little kiss." He leaned over and brushed his mouth over hers.

Just the merest touch of his lips set Annie on fire. "How else?" she asked breathlessly.

Sam's gaze darkened perceptibly. "Maybe a tender caress." He rubbed his rough cheek against her own.

God, he felt so wonderful, so male. "How else?" she whispered desperately.

She heard Sam's groan of frustration. "Annie, darn it, if you keep this up, I'm gonna—"

"*How else,* Sam?"

"Like this."

It was as if something broke in them both. Sam's mouth descended on Annie's with devastating passion. Their tongues collided, hungrily seeking penetration. Their arms coiled tightly, fiercely around each other. They clung together, kissing feverishly.

At last Sam nuzzled his lips against Annie's throat. "God, Annie, you shouldn't say such things to a man," he whispered roughly. "You make me crazy—crazy with wanting you."

"Just hold me, Sam," she whispered back. "I'm tired of fighting, and I just want you to hold me."

"God, you're so sweet."

Again, he kissed her, clutching her tight. He felt so good, especially with his warm, naked chest crushing her breasts. Sweet desire spiraled through her body. His hands slipped beneath her, the fingers molding to her bottom, gently kneading. Her breasts ached pleasurably and a throbbing need invaded between her thighs. She arched her hips into his teeming erection and heard the deep groan in his throat.

But as thunder again boomed out, he stiffened and stared down at her, his expression solemn.

"What is it, Sam?" she asked.

"Annie—uh, darlin', we need to talk."

"Talk?" Suspicion and hurt knifed through Annie.

"Yeah. There's something I gotta tell you, that is before we—"

"What, Sam?" She regarded him accusingly.

"Well, like I told you, I been mighty confused," he continued. "I keep thinkin' 'bout everything you said and all that's happened, and well, I need to tell you—"

"Yes?"

"I can't do it."

Anger and bitter disappointment roiled up in Annie. Close to tears, she shoved him off her and sat up. "You go to hell, Samuel Noble!"

"What? What's gotten into you now?" he cried, sitting up beside her.

Her words came out choked. "You just have to rub salt in my wounds, don't you? You just have to say it one more time!"

"Say what?"

"What you said last night. You can't go to bed with me and take me to the gallows!"

There was a moment of stunned silence. Then Sam burst out laughing. Annie started hitting him.

"Ouch!" Sam grabbed Annie's wrists and struggled with her. "You stop that, now! You ain't listening to me!"

"Oh, I hear you loud and clear, bounty hunter!"

He wrestled her down on the bedroll, holding her immobile with his powerful body, pinning her with his menacing gaze. "You're gonna listen to me, woman!"

"Well?" she demanded.

Sam stared her in the eye and drew a convulsive breath. Then something truly wondrous happened: His features softened into a breathtaking smile.

"Annie, I can't take you to be hanged."

Chapter 17

I *can't take you to be hanged.*

There they were at last, the words Annie had prayed to hear for what had seemed an eternity, over days of agonizing over what Sam might do. She'd finally gotten what she wanted from this man. She'd won.

She should have laughed in triumph. She should have shouted her elation.

Instead she burst into tears. Not just tears, but wrenching, humiliating sobs—and this for a woman who couldn't bear the thought of crying in front of any man. But somehow, Sam's smile and the sweet way he'd spoken had touched something in her, bursting a dam of emotion, sending tenderness piercing through to her core when she'd thought her defenses were impenetrable.

He reacted in panic. "Oh, God! What's wrong? What'd I do?"

"Nothing," she wailed. "It's just I'm so—"

"So what?"

"Relieved."

"Relieved?" he cried incredulously. "And that's why you're bawlin' your eyes out?"

Staring down at Annie, Sam felt heartsick at the sounds of her sorrow. He'd seen this woman angry and feisty, but never falling apart. The sight was devastating. He could only clutch her close and groan as emotion shook her.

Her anguished voice reached him. "I've had to be so strong."

"Of course you have, sugar."

"I've been running on adrenaline."

"God, what is *that*?" Had he driven her over the edge?

"Guess I didn't realize I've been—"

"What, sugar? What?"

"So scared," she finally admitted in a choked voice.

Something inside Sam died at that moment. He could have shot himself. There it was at last—the cause of her pain. Of course she'd been strong—she'd had no choice with her life on the line. Now at last all the fear and vulnerability were pouring out of her. Fear *he* had caused.

And he loathed himself for it through and through.

"Christ, I'm a bastard," he whispered. "I'm so sorry."

Inexplicably she clutched him tighter. "Just keep holding me, okay?"

Tenderness tore at the deepest reaches of Sam's heart. She was so sweet, so trusting when he so little deserved it. He could have wept with her. All he could do was to try to soothe her as she'd asked. He roved his lips over her face, tasting her tears.

"Sugar, please don't cry. Don't be afraid. It's over now. We'll get through this somehow—together."

A little sob escaped her, and Sam couldn't bear it. His lips caught hers in an aching kiss. He pushed his tongue inside her warm mouth, and something in him claimed her.

Hands trembling with need, Sam unbound Annie's hair and kissed the soft tresses. He roved his lips down her smooth throat and pulled at the buttons to her shirt. She did not resist and, if anything, only encouraged him with sweet kisses and soft shudders. Emotion tightened his throat as she stroked the flesh of his chest with her soft, tantalizing hands and kneaded the tight muscles of his shoulders with her fingers. Impatiently, he tugged off her shirt, his eyes growing near black with desire as he stared at her bare breasts, at the nipples already tight with arousal. He leaned over and hungrily took one of the tautened peaks in his mouth. She sobbed in ecstasy.

"Easy, darlin', easy."

By now, Annie wanted Sam so badly she hurt with the sheer intensity of it. The overwhelming intimacy of their joining—his wet mouth on her breast, his hard belly crushing hers, his manhood imprinting her pelvis—was almost more than she could bear. The roughness of his whiskery skin against her delicate breast sent shivers streaking all over her. She whimpered with the force of her desire, thrusting her fingers into his thick, soft hair. Even as she tried to catch her breath his mouth passionately seized hers, his kiss so intimate and drugging.

When he pulled back, she leaned forward to kiss a tuft of dark hair on his chest, then planted her lips in the sexy notch in his chin, thrilling to his harsh moans. She reached upward to catch him about his nape, and she drew his mouth down to hers, inviting his plunder with her tongue.

She could feel the passion shaking him then. When his fingers moved to the buttons at her waist, she shivered with anticipation. She reached between their bodies to touch his manhood through his trousers, feeling its proportions, its rigidity. Her mouth went dry.

"Oh, God, you're going to feel so good."

Sam sucked in a sharp breath, his fingers reaching down to clasp Annie's. God, he was drowning in her. He kissed her ravenously as he pulled off her jeans and drawers, and quickly freed his stiff manhood. He reached down to caress the warm, downy place between her thighs, glorying when she opened to him and writhed shamelessly against his finger.

"You're damp. You want me," he whispered raggedly. "Now I want to feel all of you wrapped tight around me."

"You will," she promised hoarsely.

Kissing her again, Sam pushed his aching member inside her. Such heaven. There was no virginal membrane, but she was tight, warm. He penetrated her slowly, struggling to rein in his raging desires, listening to her little sighs and whimpers, alert to any sound that he might be hurting her. At last, with a frantic groan, he buried himself in her, felt her hot velvety womanflesh grip him, heard her ragged gasp . . . and looked down to see her face all lit up!

Incredible joy pulsed through Sam. "What are you smiling at, woman?"

"You, bounty hunter," she whispered back. "You're larger than life in *every* way."

Sam's reply was a shout of jubilation, and then he became lost in her again.

Annie reeled in pleasure as Sam withdrew and plunged. Incoherent moans escaped her as she felt the throbbing tension of her own tissues, the glorious pressure of being possessed by him so thoroughly. She tossed her head and shuddered, sensual shockwaves rippling downward through her body and ending in a sensual wiggle at the base of her spine. That unconscious provocation brought his mouth down hard on hers as he pulled back, then thrust repeatedly, devouring her.

She tossed her head and cried out, a sound caught between desperation and a wild need for fulfillment. His mouth eased over hers, both comforting and tenderly demanding her surrender.

After a moment she looked up to see him smiling at her, and overwhelming love welled in her. Wild, fierce, sexy, and strong, her bounty hunter possessed her with riveting power and vitality. How wondrous it felt to be one with him. Their bodies grew slick with sweat as he moved to and fro, rubbing her breasts, her belly, and deliciously abrading the velvety sheath that tightened about him even as he swelled relentlessly inside her.

Neither could bear the building excitement, their frantic cries finding release in an aching kiss. Annie felt the exquisite melting deep inside herself even as the first convulsions of her climax carried her away; she locked her thighs about Sam's, mated her mouth with his, and eagerly met his thrusts.

Perched above her, Sam could barely breathe. Annie was incredible, so hot and snug and passionate, her supple body coiled about his with an eagerness that touched his heart and stoked the hot fever inside him. He had known women before, but he'd never made love with a woman who had given herself to him so completely. His restraint broken, he held Annie to him desperately and pressed home, losing himself in a paroxysm of rapture that shook him to his core. . . .

Later, while Annie slept, Sam donned his jeans and shirt and sat down on the blanket next to her, smoking a cheroot. He smiled at the sight of her lovely, content face outlined in moonlight, and reached out to smooth her mussed hair away from her face. Such pleasure she'd brought him tonight, even as her turmoil and vulnerability had torn him apart. He felt such tenderness toward her, and—dare he even think it?—such love.

He drew the cheroot to his lips with trembling fingers. This woman had certainly turned his life, and all his emotions, topsy-turvy. She had given herself to him in genuine passion, and he wanted to believe everything she'd told him; yet she hadn't been a virgin, a fact that argued against her being a righteous innocent. Of course, Sam would have expected an outlaw to be a soiled dove, but in his experience, decent women were always virtuous and maidenly.

But then, Annie Dillon had certainly defied all Sam's previous notions about decent womanhood. Although she had broken through his defenses, he still wasn't sure he could believe her. Was she a liar, or could there be a grain of truth in the bizarre story she was telling him? Was she right that he couldn't deal with a woman who was as strong as he was? Assuming he could get her out of the mess she was in, could they make a go of a life together, or would they be like two shooting stars, colliding and burning each other out?

Sam had no easy answers. He only knew he recoiled at the thought of losing her now.

Chapter 18

The scent of strong coffee awakened Annie. She opened her eyes and stretched dreamily. Although a chill gripped the landscape, the sun was up and mourning doves were cooing.

Sam was gone. Glancing about, she spotted him sitting nearby on a fallen branch, fully dressed, sipping the brew from a tin cup. The sight of him made her heart thrum with joy, her senses pulse with provocative memories.

"Good morning," she called.

He smiled. "Good morning to you. How you doin', sugar?"

"Fine." She sat up, drawing the covers about her.

Setting down his coffee, Sam came to her side and knelt, cupping her chin in his hand. "You're not scared no more?" he asked anxiously.

She reached out to ruffle his hair. "How could I be, with a legend of the West here to protect me?"

Eyes lighting with pleasure, Sam leaned over and kissed her. Then he sat down beside her, draping an arm about her shoulders.

"You're up early," she ventured.

"I had a lot on my mind."

"Oh? So tell me what's on your mind, Sam Noble."

"You, of course," he replied earnestly. "Thinkin' about everything you've said, about us."

"Go on."

He eyed her in uncertainty. "Well, last night before we made love, I—er, looked in your bag."

"You did?"

"You said I could," he hastily reminded her. "Remember?"

She nodded. "So was going through my bag what changed your mind?"

He pulled his fingers through his hair. "Well, you might say that. Though in some ways, I'm more confused than ever." Abruptly, he got up and began to pace. "That's one haywire treasure trove you got, Annie— money that claims to be from the future, weird doodads with even weirder dates on 'um. I couldn't make no sense of any of it."

Annie was getting a bad feeling from this conversation. "What do you mean, you couldn't make any sense of it?"

"Just what I said."

"Now, wait a minute," she cut in tensely. "Am I missing something here? Didn't you tell me last night that you can't take me to be hanged?"

"Yep, and I meant every word."

"But—when you said that, I thought it meant you believe me now!"

He turned to her, appearing miserably torn. "I want to believe you, Annie, but you got me so befuddled I ain't sure what the truth is. You say you're from the future when I know that ain't possible. You say you're innocent when . . ." He drew a shuddering breath. "Well, you ain't so innocent in bed."

Ice chilled Annie's voice. "Is that a complaint?"

"Hell, no," he quickly reassured her.

"Then what are you saying, Sam?"

He eyed her steadily. "If you ain't Rosie, how come you weren't a virgin?"

"Oh!" she cried, indignant. "You haven't listened to a word I've said, have you, Sam Noble? If you had, you'd never ask such an insulting, chauvinistic question!"

"Come on, Annie," he cajoled. "I ain't blaming you for nothin'. I'm just trying to understand."

"Well, understand it all by yourself."

"Besides, a man likes to feel like a woman is his alone."

"Aha! So that's what's really stuck in your craw, isn't it?" she asked with anger and hurt. "You just can't stand the fact that you weren't my first. You'd rather think of me as a bad girl and murderess than accept the fact that I come from another time when women are more sexually liberated."

Sam flung a hand outward. "If you don't say the gall-durnedest things!"

Annie was blinking at tears. "Why did you make love with me, Sam, if you still think I'm an outlaw and a liar? I know why I made love with you—because you touched something in me, as much as I tried to fight it. Why did you make love with me?"

Eyes filled with turbulent emotion, Sam went to her side and knelt beside her. "Because I wanted you, too, sugar."

"Did you?" Her words were hoarse.

With a groan, Sam pulled Annie onto his lap, arranging the blanket around her shoulders and cuddling her close. "It's like I told you last night. We're in this together now."

Though his nearness was sweet and drugging, Annie still needed reassurance—and answers. "Tell me why you wanted me."

He smoothed down her mussed hair. "I want you because you're beautiful, proud, and strong. Because you touched me, too. Because you had your chance to escape me and you didn't take it."

Despite herself, Annie smiled.

He pressed his mouth to her cheek. "You chose me, didn't you, Annie?"

She nodded, tender emotion welling inside her.

"You risked your life to do it, too," he continued with quiet pride. "And you made love with me because you wanted to." He lifted her chin with his fingers and stared down into her eyes. "*That's* why, Annie."

He kissed her then, and for a moment, the fight in Annie died away in a welling of poignant emotion. She rested her head against Sam's shoulder; his arms tightened about her.

He caught a shaky breath. "Can't you see how different things are now, that what we done last night changes things?"

Annie still felt torn, twisting about to look up at him. "Sam, how different can things truly be when you still haven't changed the way you think about me?"

His gaze settled on her meaningfully, and his finger stroked her lower lip. "Oh, I haven't? You think I don't see you different at all after you cried in my arms? After you gave yourself to me like you did?"

Annie released a shuddering sigh and clutched his hand. "It meant a lot to me, too."

He cuddled her closer. "And you think it ain't occurred to me that you could be carrying my baby now?"

The very thought of bearing his child brought a wondrous smile to Annie's lips. Still, she slowly shook her head. "Those pills I keep taking prevent conception—at least as long as I don't run out of them."

"A pill can do that?" he asked, amazed.

"Yes." She regarded him in compassion. "Sam, I can understand how everything I'm saying must sound bizarre to you, how the story I'm telling is difficult for you to grasp. I come from the future, from a world that doesn't even exist as yet, a place you probably can't even imagine. I know I'm asking you to believe the impossible. But it's also who I *am*, Sam—and when you don't accept who I am, that hurts."

He was silent, bemused. "I'm trying, Annie."

"Are you starting to believe me even a little?"

His expression was troubled. "I believe something here ain't as it seems. But them stories you tell . . ." He gestured helplessly. "I'm sorry, Annie, but they still sound haywire to me."

"Then we're stuck at an impasse, aren't we?" she asked sadly. "You say you don't want to take me to be hanged—"

"Damned right, I don't," he cut in vehemently.

"Then what *do* you have in mind for me, Sam?"

"For us, Annie."

"All right, for us."

He frowned thoughtfully. "I think we need to go see my grandma."

"Your grandmother?" she asked, surprised. "You mean the one who is Cheyenne?"

He nodded earnestly. "Yes, she's a medicine woman, and very wise. She can help us get to the bottom of this mess, maybe even help get you straightened out."

All at once Annie was bristling. "What do you mean, get *me* straightened out?"

He slanted her a chiding glance. "Darlin', I care for you, but you've still got to be the most gall-durned liar I've ever met."

"Oh!" Outraged, she clambered off his lap.

"I want you, anyway, sugar," he continued, "and part of me can't blame you for lyin' to save your own hide. You know you don't gotta do that no more."

"Damn it, Sam, I've been tellin' you the truth all along!" she burst out in frustration.

Although his features appeared conflicted, he calmly forged on. "The fact is, we made love and now I'm responsible for you."

"Responsible?" she cried. "Of all the gall! Damn your self-righteous hide, Sam Noble! I don't need you to be responsible for me—or to save me from my wayward ways!"

"Well, I gotta see things different, whether you like it or not," he retorted stubbornly. "I gotta get you back on the path of righteousness."

Annie made a sound of raging exasperation. "If you think I'm so cunning and deceitful, why don't you just let me go? Why don't we shake hands and call it a day?"

"Not a chance, woman!"

"But you still think I'm deliberately deceiving you!"

He drew a steadying breath. "Annie, my grandmother and her band's sacred idiot told me where to find you. Why would *they* lie to me? My grandmother's prophecies have never been wrong that I can recollect."

Perplexed, Annie could only stare at him. He had a point, and she could again understand his frustration. She couldn't really grasp this mystical link to her time-travel experience, either.

"Then I find you and you look exactly like the outlaw I'm trackin'," he continued sternly. "What *do* you expect me to think?"

She released a heavy sigh. "We really are at cross-purposes, aren't we, Sam?"

He placed his hands on her shoulders. "Sugar, let's go see my grandma, see what she says, see if she can help us."

"Very well," she conceded.

"Glad that's settled." Smiling, he lifted her chin. "Do I get a kiss now?"

Though tempted, she replied, "You really like to push your luck, don't you, bounty hunter?"

Sam pulled her up onto her knees beside him. With a tenderness that made her wince, he leaned over and gently brushed his lips over her own.

"Annie," he whispered, her name half a groan.

Feeling his manhood throbbing against her, Annie felt hot desire stirring within her and realized the situation could easily get out of hand. "Sam, not now," she said quietly, pushing her palms against his shoulders.

His hand slid confidently over her bare leg, her hip. "Annie, you know how much you want this. There's something between us that's too powerful for either of us to fight."

Oh, yes, she felt that intense pull, even as tears of hurt and pride flooded her eyes. "Maybe you're right, but this is not the time."

With a groan, he pulled back. "Why not?"

She blinked at tears. "Because nothing has really changed."

He flung a hand outward. "Ain't you heard a word I said? Everythin' has changed."

"Making love is supposed to bring two people closer together."

"You're sayin' it didn't?"

"I'm talking about something that goes far beyond the physical. I'm talking about true intimacy, understanding, and trust. Accepting the other person as he or she really is. Our bodies may have come together last night, but in too many ways that count, our hearts and minds are still apart. I can't sleep with a man who thinks I'm lying to him. So . . ." She paused helplessly. "I think we're going to have to settle some important issues first."

His hands dropped and a ragged breath escaped him. "If that's what you really want, Annie."

Annie really wanted *him,* of course. But too much still stood in their way.

Chapter 19

~❧~

They rode off again, lost in their own doubts and hurts.

That day the countryside grew increasingly craggy, with blue mesas spawning buttes and ledges to the north and south of them. As they crested a rise bedecked with hackberry, sage, and cedar, Annie caught her first glimpse of the full face of the Rockies in the distance. Jagged blue mountains erupted out of the earth, their peaks arcing skyward, capped in glistening white, with shafts of mists spiraling off the pinnacles to melt into incredibly blue skies above. The sight was awe-inspiring, though her mood remained bittersweet, her mind still focused on the troubling impasse between her and Sam.

Finally he broke the silence. "You still mad at me, sugar?"

She slanted him an admonishing glance. "You're saying I don't have cause? When you're planning to take me to your grandmother, so she can reform me of my deceitful ways?"

"I'm just sayin' my grandma's a mighty wise woman," he reiterated. "She'll be able to make sense of this."

"And you can't?"

Sam pulled off his hat and ran his fingers through his hair. "Annie, I'm a simple man. I ain't as smart as you. I can't grasp all this far-fetched stuff you keep telling me."

"Nonsense," she replied. "You're much smarter than you think, Sam. You could understand a lot if you really

151

tried. You're just too proud and stubborn to admit you're wrong."

She watched his jaw harden. "We'll see what Medicine Woman says."

Annie bit back her next retort. There was no sense making Sam miserable. He seemed sincere and was obviously as troubled as she was; perhaps for now it *was* beyond him to accept what she was saying. And she had to love him for being willing to help her anyway.

Still, she felt frustrated and hurt at the wall of mistrust and anguish looming between them. That barrier kept her from him when she wanted nothing more than to fly into his arms and love him to death. Especially when memories of last night kept rising to torment her—of how wonderful and sexy Sam had been, how close they'd drawn. But now she'd awakened to the sobering reality that things weren't nearly as perfect as she had assumed and they had a long way to go before they could be close again. This thought made her features tighten with turmoil.

Sam noted that expression of pain and it tore at his gut. He could feel the emotional distance stretching between him and Annie. God, he burned for her, memories of her sweet surrender driving him mad. He hungered to take her in his arms again and melt that look of hurt from her lovely face. He longed to lie naked with her in a dusky hollow, to kiss and caress every inch of her, to thrust into her all day long until she begged for mercy.

But he couldn't seem to bridge this vast chasm between them. And he wouldn't lie to her to get her back into his bed. He couldn't say he believed when he didn't. And as much as he knew that hurt her, *he* hurt, too.

Her voice, forced and cheerful, cut into his thoughts. "So, how far is it to Grandma's place?"

He smiled. "A few more days. She and her band are hiding out in a valley beyond Central."

Annie frowned. "You mean there are still Indians roaming free in Colorado in 1885? I would have thought most of the Indians in this area would have been gathered up on the reservations by now—or have fled further west."

"You're right there," Sam admitted. "The few free Indian bands left are mostly in Nebraska, Wyoming, and Dakota territories." He sighed. "With the buffalo all but extinct, they won't be roaming for long. Those that don't starve will be forced to go to the reservations."

"And your grandmother's band? How did they manage to remain free here in Colorado?"

"They have quite an interesting history," he related. "I reckon I'll let her tell the story."

"Can you at least tell me how they've eluded the cavalry?"

"By never staying in one place too long. They've been roving for nigh onto six years now—with my help, and that of another white man."

"You don't mean Moon Calf?"

Sam laughed. "No, a former mule skinner named Whip Whistler. Whip's been living with my grandma's band for these last six years. When we get to my grandmother's camp, you'll learn all about it."

"This is promising to be an interesting tale," she replied.

The atmosphere between them remained strained as they continued toward the Cheyenne village. Soon after they passed the small town of Trinidad, they found themselves among the Rockies in earnest. Amid the falling of a light, cold mist, they followed a well-marked trail that took them steadily higher, past massive, gray stone dikes that sliced across mountain ranges, dramatic rock walls springing inexplicably from the face of the Rockies. Annie was amazed to glimpse a mountain lion soberly watching them from one of those high, jagged ledges. She also caught her first close-up glimpses of thick ponderosa pines and thin, ramrod straight aspens that were downright poetic in their symmetry. Brilliant mountain bluebirds and colorful sapsuckers flitted among the trees; Annie heard woodpeckers drilling, as well as the harsh cries of ravens. Mule deer and bighorn sheep frequently crossed their path.

Although they did not make love again during this phase of their journey, the enforced intimacy of the trail—watching Sam wash and dress, knowing he slept just across from her at night—was almost more than Annie could bear. From the confused yet burning looks he cast her way, his agitation was equal to her own.

Their second night on the trail was particularly difficult for her. She had just returned to camp after washing her hair at a stream. She stood struggling to brush snarls out of her wet curls while Sam sat on a nearby granite boulder, intently watching her. After a moment, she muttered a curse.

Without a word, Sam pulled her onto his lap, took the hairbrush from her hand, and began smoothing out the tangles with infinite care and patience. Annie found she couldn't meet Sam's eyes. It was all so sweet and sexy that she almost succumbed to him then and there. She almost burst into tears again.

When he finished, he tipped her face up to his and gently kissed her. Annie bolted away like a spooked deer, certain she would have fallen apart had she stayed.

Oh, yes, Sam had the ability to get to her that way, to make those feelings rise up in her: how much she missed her parents and worried about her brother; how much she needed something in her life. Home, a family. A man.

A man like Sam. Was he the one perfect mate for her, the one she'd come across time to find? She was so drawn to him. Yet they were so different, they wanted vastly different things from the opposite sex, and she had no idea how long this would last, or if it would last. And he still wouldn't accept who she was.

The weather remained cold, with frequent mists or even light rain dampening their passage. But Annie found that the spectacular setting more than compensated for any discomfort caused by the elements. They continued along crude trails and over well-traveled wagon roads, sometimes snaking through breathtaking passes and along sheer cliffs. They observed remarkable granite formations, huge, glistening pink boulders tossed into deep valleys like so many pebbles haphazardly thrown into baskets. They rode through small, bustling communities and past spooky ghost towns. They wended their way through an endless morass of abandoned mines, as evidenced by crumbling mine heads and broken-down sluices, deteriorating rail beds, and massive piles of tailings mounded along the hillsides. They crossed shallow rivers, icy mountain streams, quiet farms, and busy cattle ranches. They viewed beavers working on dams, mule deer foraging for food, chipmunks scurrying up trees, bighorn sheep grazing in meadows.

The sheer beauty and magnitude of the Rockies was almost too much for Annie to absorb. Everywhere she looked were spectacular splashes of color: the misty purple of the mountains, the bright green of grassy meadows, the flaming yellow of aspens, the sapphire blue of a lake, the fiery rust of a rufous hummingbird flitting at the delicate lilac of a late-blooming columbine.

Finally one morning the mist broke, and a brilliant sun heralded the advent of a crisp, clear day. As they crossed a high Alpine meadow dotted with yellow sunflowers and purple gentians, Sam made an abrupt announcement.

"Reckon we'll be at Grandma's village soon. It's in a hidden valley beyond the next pass."

Taken aback, Annie glanced at him. "We're really that close?"

"Yep."

"How many Indians live at the village?"

"About twenty. Before we get there, I wanted to tell you a little about their traditions."

"You mean me being a White Eyes and all?" Annie quipped. "Believe me, I wouldn't want to insult anyone."

"That's good—because the purpose of my grandmother's band is to preserve the Cheyenne way of life, which is dying off at the reservations."

Annie nodded. "I'm aware that the reservation system is a dismal failure, that it has decimated the Indian culture."

"I just wouldn't want you to violate any taboos while we're at the tribe."

"Such as?"

He eyed her soberly. "Well, when you enter a lodge, you as a woman must always step to the left."

"The left?" she repeated, puzzled.

"Yep. Men always step to the right."

Annie's gaze implored the blue heavens. "I should have known."

"After you're inside the lodge, you must remain standing until the host invites you to sit down. Also, you must never walk between an Indian and the fire—it's considered bad medicine. Walk behind them instead."

"Aye, aye," she responded cheerily.

He affected a stern look. "My grandmother's band often has open councils, where all are invited, though my grandmother is the only woman who is allowed to speak, being the honored medicine woman. Otherwise, only the men talk."

"Well, since I don't speak Cheyenne, I'm sure you needn't worry about my interrupting the council."

"Most of the band members speak English as well as Cheyenne," he replied. "Just remember, if you can't contain yourself and must speak out, it's considered an insult to interrupt another speaker—or a storyteller."

Annie was frowning, trying to absorb all the admonitions. "Anything else?"

"Yes. It is forbidden to point at any heavenly body, or to watch members of the Quilling Society at work, or to burn the feathers of an owl."

"Oh, gee, and I was planning an owl-feather barbecue tonight."

He scowled.

"Sam, I was being silly," she replied, laughing. "I can't even bear the prospect of any animal or bird being harmed."

"That's good," he commented. "The Cheyenne respect the powers of nature and only use its bounties as needed. In fact, Cheyenne women believe that golden eagles possess such powerful medicine that if they touch such a bird, some affliction will befall them."

She wrinkled her nose. "How peculiar—but also fascinating."

He snapped his fingers. "Oh, and women, except those in a special society, aren't allowed to handle wolves."

She smirked. "Too late for that now."

He shot her a mock-scolding look. "When it comes to meals and stuff, there are other rituals and blessings. Just follow my lead."

She made a strangled sound. "Good grief, Sam, you're making me feel like some naughty child being lectured by her auntie before being taken to tea."

"Truth to tell, you're gettin' off easy," he teased back. "At least there ain't no Contraries in this camp."

"What on earth are Contraries?"

"They're members of a warrior society that do everythin' backwards. So, if you want a Contrary to go north, you gotta tell him to go south, and so forth."

"You're kidding."

He slowly shook his head.

Annie waved a hand. "So how am I supposed to remember all this stuff? And if I violate some taboo, will I be burned at the stake?"

He chuckled. "Cheyenne are peaceable by nature. It's the encroachment and broken treaties of the whites that has forced them to fight. Still, if you violate a taboo, it won't go down well."

"I'll do my best to be circumspect."

All at once, Annie strained in her saddle as they crested a rise. In the valley below she spotted half a dozen white lodges gathered in a circle; beyond the tepees, a makeshift corral teemed with pinto ponies and brown cattle. Flanking the camp to the west was a gleaming blue lake; to the east rose a forested mountain.

"Good gracious, we really are here."

He smiled. "With the exception of my grandmother, you'll find the Cheyenne are suspicious of most whites, at least at first. You'd best let me do the talking for now."

Watching Indians emerge from their lodges to view their approach, Annie replied, "Oh, by all means."

Chapter 20

A s they guided their horses down a rocky incline, Annie continued to gaze in wonder at the small Cheyenne village stretching below them. Half a dozen tepees—decorated with stars, eagles, hunting scenes, and Indian symbols—were arranged in a circle, with a large fire pit at the center and an opening facing the east. An old man in a buffalo robe was tripping along from tepee to tepee, yelling out as he went, several yapping dogs at his heels. Annie figured the man must be the camp crier, for as he made his rounds, additional Indians emerged and moved forward to observe their approach. In the distance, a couple of older girls who were harvesting corn in a small field ceased their labors and walked back toward camp, followed by three large mule deer.

Sizing up the band, Annie judged they numbered around two dozen—old men and women, younger couples, a few adolescents, and perhaps half a dozen children of various ages. One young woman, who stood beside her husband, appeared to be great with child. Among the group were two white men: an older man wearing buckskins and a mountain hat similar to Sam's, and a younger fellow with a very long beard, who wore a buffalo robe and seemed to be holding some sort of bird in his hands.

Even when Sam and Annie maneuvered their mounts to within a few feet of the Indians, they did not speak but fixed their dark gazes solemnly on her. Though the scrutiny made her uneasy, she maintained a confident facade. She figured the Indians were accustomed to Sam; she was the newcomer, a White Eyes, and thus the threat.

Seen at closer range, Annie found the people exotic and comely, the men tall and slender, attired in practical buckskin shirts and leggings, the women shorter and squatter, dressed in exquisitely beaded and quilled deer-skin dresses. Although the smallest children were barefoot and wore little more than breechclouts, the rest of the band sported an assortment of magnificently quilled, colorful moccasins. Indeed, Annie was amazed at the array of jewelry the Indians wore: Elaborate charms adorned the hair of the men; beads, bracelets, nose rings, and earrings beautified the women. She observed that even the smallest children had the entire length of their ears pierced and heavily beaded.

A tall woman with long white hair moved through the throng and paused before them. She wore a plain deer-skin dress, and a large leather pouch was tied to her waist. Looking into her heavily lined face, Annie could see both traditional Cheyenne features, and wisdom and kindness in her dark eyes.

Sam dismounted and approached the woman, and she grinned almost toothlessly at him. "Welcome, Grandson," she said in English.

Sam beamed and hugged her. "Hello, Grandmother. You're a mighty pleasing sight, as always." He gestured toward Annie, who had remained on her horse. "I brought a friend."

"Let us meet her," the woman urged.

Sam strode over to Annie's horse and helped her dismount. As they moved toward the woman, he winked at her and whispered, "Easy, sugar. She don't bite."

Annie tossed Sam a long-suffering look, then smiled at the woman.

Sam announced, "Grandmother, this is Annie Dillon."

"Welcome to our camp," she said.

"Thank you," replied Annie.

"Annie," Sam added, "this is my grandma, Medicine Woman."

Glancing again at the pouch hanging from the woman's waist, Annie judged it must contain medicinal herbs that were surely the source of a certain pungent odor in the air. "I'm very pleased to meet you."

Medicine Woman smiled.

The older man in fringed buckskins strode up to Sam and slapped him across the shoulders. "Well, ain't you a sight for sore eyes." He tipped his hat at Annie. "And showing up with a pretty filly, too."

Throwing the man a chiding glance, Sam said, "Annie, this is my old friend Whip Whistler."

Annie smiled at the man, who appeared to be in his sixties and was potbelied, with a large square face covered by a graying beard. "How do you do?"

"Right fine, ma'am, thank you."

The other white man, with his buffalo robe and long beard, moved warily toward Annie. As she turned to regard him in bemusement, he grimaced and recoiled, a muscle jerking spasmodically in his right cheek.

Feeling very taken aback, Annie glanced at Sam questioningly, but he only shrugged. After a moment the peculiar man began creeping toward her again, this time furtively eyeing her. She observed his approach in equal caution, not wanting to spook him again.

At last, without saying a word, he paused before her and stared at her searchingly, his gaze both unnerving and haunted. Though his curiosity was obvious, so was the tension in his features and body. He reminded Annie of a cat sniffing out a newcomer and fully prepared to bolt at the first sign of aggression. She glanced downward to see that he held in his hands a beautiful brown-and-yellow meadowlark. Amazed that any wild creature would be so docile in human hands, she watched the songbird peer about as the man stroked its downy head.

Annie wondered if the person standing before her was Moon Calf, the white sacred idiot and animal charmer Sam had told her about. If so, why was he so fascinated with her? Indeed, she struggled not to cringe at the intense light emanating from his dark, deep-set eyes.

Although he was gaunt and bearded, Annie could see a shadow of handsomeness in his features—the long, well-etched nose, broad brow, and finely drawn jaw. He appeared to be a relatively young man, perhaps thirty or so.

And, judging from those feral eyes, he was mad as a hatter!

Even as Annie conjured the troubling thought, the man clutched the bird to his breast with one hand and jerked his free hand upward, raising a forefinger toward the sky. As the meadowlark trembled against him, his voice boomed out, sending shivers down Annie's spine.

"The deliverer has come. It is written in the stars that she will come and now she is here."

Annie could only watch and listen in horror.

The man swung about toward the others. "The Wise One above foretold that she would appear from the rock, appear from the autumn and the morning, and now she is here."

Finishing his speech, the man dropped his hand, turning and walking away from Annie as abruptly as he had come. He released the bird, which flapped off so suddenly that she flinched.

"My God," she muttered, looking around to see many of the Indians whispering among themselves and staring at her.

Sam took Annie's hand, flashing her a reassuring look. "Sugar, don't mind Moon Calf. He don't mean no harm. He don't speak much, but when he does, he talks out of his head—even if the People do think he has powerful medicine."

"That was Moon Calf?" she asked. "The white man who told you where to find me? But he doesn't talk like a white man—he talks like an Indian."

Medicine Woman flashed Annie a sympathetic smile. "That is because Moon Calf only knows the Cheyenne way now. When he came to us, that one, he was like the Great Plains after they were raped of our good friend, the buffalo. All traces of his white life had been wiped from his soul."

"You mean he had amnesia?" asked Annie.

As Whip and Sam exchanged mystified glances, Medicine Woman continued. "For the past years, the sacred idiot has spent time with our ancient warriors, smoking or meditating in the lodges, learning our ways."

"He really has gone primitive," Annie muttered. "And he does seem to have a talent with animals."

Medicine Woman nodded. "He roams the prairie, that one, even at night. He sings to the birds and speaks to the animals, to our sacred wolves and coyotes. One time he charmed a skunk into our camp." She grimaced. "That creature was worse than a Contrary on the war-path. After the foul cat mercifully left our village, we had to burn several lodges."

Annie stifled a giggle.

"As you must see, the ways of the white man are lost to Moon Calf," Medicine Woman concluded, turning to smile sadly at Sam, "just as those ways became lost to me when my white life journeyed to the place of the dead."

Sam wrapped an arm about Medicine Woman's shoulders. "Just so you don't forget your mostly white grandson."

Appearing outraged, she stepped away and shook a finger at him. "Forget blood of my own blood? Forget the one who protects us? Never."

"That's my girl," said Sam proudly, hugging her again.

Medicine Woman grinned. "You and the woman are tired and hungry?"

"Well, I reckon some of your stew would sit well with us right now."

She beamed. "We shall make a big fire and have a feast to honor your arrival."

"Don't go to no trouble now," Sam scolded.

Medicine Woman cast him a haughty look. "We can do no less to welcome you, Grandson." She turned to the others, who had been so quiet, and spoke in rapid Cheyenne, clapping her hands and gesturing.

Annie presumed Medicine Woman had announced the celebration, for at once the other Indians cheered and ran off to make preparations.

Sam sauntered up to Annie and hooked an arm

around her nape. "Well, here we are, sugar—alone at last," he teased.

"Alone, with two dozen of your grandmother's people?" she replied in mock astonishment. "Plus, you're forgetting the taboo about my fraternizing with wolves," she added, removing his arm from her shoulders.

"Annie, gall-durn it," he replied in exasperation.

Seeing his agitation, Annie sighed. "Sam, how can I forget why you really brought me here—so the liar can be reformed? How do you think that makes me feel?"

He groaned. "I know, sugar. But ain't you through roasting my chops about it yet?"

Looking him over, she struggled against a smile. "Actually, Sam Noble, there's a lot of you to roast." Her features tightened. "Guess I'd best go join the others . . . and see to my redemption."

Sam shook his head as he watched Annie stride away. Boy, she still had a burr in her britches. Over the past days, the distance between them had made him crazy. And unfortunately, the more aloof she acted, the hotter he became. Even now, seeing the saucy tilt to her head and tempting sway of her bottom made him wild to gobble her up.

And it wasn't just physical passion that was tormenting him. He wanted this hurt and distance to end for them both. He wanted things right between them; he wanted to make some sense of their lives together. Wasn't that why they were here?

He sure hoped the two of them could find some answers, for he was having a devil of a time keeping his hands off her. He grinned ruefully. It was so ironic. He may have tracked her, but now *he* was the one caught.

Chapter 21

Annie was fascinated by the celebration. All of the Indians gathered in a large circle, many of them still watching her solemnly. Holding a tin plate, cup, and fork one of the Indian girls had given her, Annie sat next to Sam, with Whip Whistler and Medicine Woman completing their end of the circle. Moon Calf, the white man who had so startled and amazed Annie, sat across the fire from her. Once again petting his meadowlark, the sacred idiot rocked to and fro, his eyes tightly closed as he chanted to himself in Cheyenne.

Two older women and two young girls brought forth the food. First the oldest woman, bearing a tin plate heaped with morsels of meat, solemnly approached Medicine Woman. Medicine Woman held up both hands and the server placed several small pieces of meat on her right palm. Medicine Woman pressed her hands together and began motioning as she sang softly in Cheyenne.

"She is making a sacrifice to the four directions called *nivstanivoo*," Sam whispered at Annie's side.

"Ah," Annie murmured, fascinated by the ritual.

Once Medicine Woman finished her prayer and placed her pieces of meat on the ground, the server offered the remaining tidbits to the others. Watching each Indian, including the sacred idiot, take a small piece, raise it toward the sky, then place it on the ground, Annie followed suit and caught Sam winking at her.

The other servers began to circulate, and the feast started in earnest. Annie found it interesting that every-

164

one ate with white men's implements and that the Indians conversed in Cheyenne interspersed with smatterings of English. She relished the main dish of calf stew flavored with chopped roots and corn; pemmican and dried berries completed the repast.

After a while, Whip turned to Sam with a grin. "So what brings you folks up our way?"

"To see how all of you are doin', of course," answered Sam.

"And the lady?" Whip added, glancing eagerly at Annie.

Sam clutched Annie's hand. "It's up to her to tell her own story, I reckon."

Feeling a number of dark eyes again focused on her, Annie was uneasy.

Medicine Woman spoke up. "The woman is our guest, and her story is her own to share. To force the giving up of one's story is to make the spirit confront its own shadow."

From the gasps sounding out around her, Annie figured that seeing one's shadow must be a serious matter indeed.

"You're right, Grandma," agreed Sam. "But you know, I sort of promised the lady you'd tell her your story."

Medicine Woman smiled at Annie. "What do you wish to know?"

Feeling rather put on the spot, Annie nonetheless spoke up. "I suppose what Sam means is, I had remarked to him that it seems odd that your band is still on the move, with so many Cheyenne on the reservations by now."

"Our nation has become like a large wolf herded into a cage," the old woman replied gravely. "Only its tail remains free."

At the apt description, Annie struggled against a smile. "How did your situation come about? That is, if you don't mind my asking."

Medicine Woman's eyes grew solemn. "No, I have told the story many times. After my white life died, I

returned to the People. I joined a large band of northern
Cheyenne, whose Dog Soldiers had battled the blue
coats after the devil Chivington massacred our southern
brothers at Sand Creek. Many moons later, Sam and his
sister came to live with us. Sam studied our ways for a
time, then returned to his white brothers. My grand-
daughter followed this same path, marrying a white
trapper. Afterward I roamed far with our people as our
warriors searched fruitlessly for the buffalo the white
hunters had pillaged from our plains. Even as we tried to
live in peace, the blue coats still hunted us. After our
braves helped defeat the Indian-hater, Custer, the blue
bellies tracked us into Wyoming, and MacKenzie forced
us into the winter hills, where we took refuge with our
brothers, the Sioux. There we all but perished, and our
great chief, Dull Knife, was forced to surrender his
people at Fort Robinson."

As Medicine Woman paused, staring grimly into the
fire, Annie almost exclaimed, *My God, you were part of
Custer's last stand!* then remembered the taboo of never
interrupting a speaker or storyteller.

"At Fort Robinson, we were locked up in the cold like
dogs, with no water or food," Medicine Woman continued soberly. "Finally, our own leaders bid us escape, and
we stampeded like wild horses. Those of us the soldiers
did not wound or capture, the winter plains killed. There
was no food, no water, no buffalo to be had."

Again Medicine Woman hesitated. Although her lined
features remained stoic, Annie sensed her inner pain.
She was dying to ask what happened to the group next,
but again kept her silence.

Medicine Woman nodded at Whip. "Buffalo Driver
will take up the story now."

Annie felt secretly amused to hear Whip Whistler's
Indian name as the older man cleared his throat. "I
reckon Medicine Woman wants me to tell how I found
her and the others. You see, I used to be a bullwhacker,
haulin' buffalo hides for the white hunters. Only the
pickin's was gettin' mighty poor by '79. The hunters kept
pushin' further north along the plains, and findin'
nothin' much left 'cept bones. The group I was with

slaughtered one of the last herds up north of the Platte. I was haulin' a load of hides south to Kansas City when I come across a group of starvin' Cheyenne." He shuddered, his dark eyes filled with private anguish. "I seen 'um—men, women, and children dressed in rags, shiverin' in the cold—and I thought, this is what me and the others done to 'um. We've taken their land, their food, their clothing. Even though I weren't a hunter, I was a hauler, and I reckoned I was as guilty as the rest. So I vowed then and there that everything in my wagon belonged to the Cheyenne, and I turned it over to them, just like I turned my life over to them." He gestured about the camp. "Some of them hides was used to sew these lodges and to make the clothing we're wearin'. The rest we traded for food, and the band has been on the move ever since. Sometimes we stay put long enough to plant corn, like we done this last time. Sometimes we end up moving before all the rocks is laid to hold down the tepees." He grinned at Sam. "Sam helps us, too—he has ever since '79."

Annie looked at Sam with admiration as Whip fell silent and everyone continued to eat. She studied the group, watching a laughing little boy feed scraps to several frisky mongrel dogs and a couple of tame mule deer, seeing a young man draw out dice and start a game with several other braves.

She observed an old man pulling out a hand drum, beating it softly, and beginning a singsongy chant. Several Indians got up to dance. One young man shook a rattle in time to the drum while two young women sang and waved stunted ears of just-harvested corn. Clutching his bird to his breast, Moon Calf got up to join the others, whirling, dancing, and chanting, twirling his robe about him wildly. Annie's eyes widened as the edge of his robe trailed over the fire, sending sparks shooting into the atmosphere. Fortunately the pelt did not ignite.

Sam's hand clutched hers again, and the two exchanged a smile. Turning back to observe the ritual and the magic, Annie was filled with a tremendous sense of awe at the courage and simplicity of these remarkable people who had triumphed in preserving their way of life over tremendous odds, who had lost so many of their brothers along the way but could still be peaceful and productive.

She had clearly stepped into another world, and yet in her life, it seemed finding new worlds had become an everyday occurrence.

Once the feasting ended, Sam and Annie strolled off toward the lake together, passing the corral filled with ponies and cattle, and the small field where young girls were again plucking ears of rather anemic-looking corn. A fresh breeze blew toward them off the crystal blue waters ahead; Annie smiled at the sight of several mallards and teal ducks flapping about in panic as a peregrine falcon swooped through their midst.

Near the shoreline they paused. Annie glanced at Sam, admiring him in a blue-plaid flannel shirt and jeans. At the moment he was hatless, the breeze whipping dark brown hair around his face. She noted that his beard had really grown since the last time he had shaved in Prairie Stump; she remembered that rough face abrading intimate parts of her when they'd made love days before, felt herself aching for him . . . and hastily tugged her thoughts toward safer territory.

She cleared her throat. "I like your grandmother."

Sam smiled. "She's an amazing woman. She likes you, too, sugar."

"You'll be talking to her soon?" Annie added meaningfully.

"Yes," he replied soberly. "About everything."

"I guess if you think she can help us, we may as well get started," Annie murmured.

"I reckon so."

"I must say everyone here has been so nice to me," she continued. "Though I'm rather surprised the Indians didn't ask more about my background. They all kept staring at me so curiously during the feast."

He chuckled. "Oh, they're mighty interested, but it's not the Cheyenne way to pry."

"But your grandmother told her story so willingly."

"That's cause everyone else in the circle knows it by

heart. And she only told you what she wanted you to know."

"That's not the Cheyenne way," Annie replied. "That's a woman's way."

"Amen," he agreed with a chuckle.

She took a deep breath of the crisp air scented of earth and evergreens. "Why is your grandmother called Medicine Woman?"

Sam gazed out at the lake. "Because she's a healer and has always possessed great spiritual powers. Now she has pretty much become the chief of this small band."

"Is it unusual for Cheyenne to have a woman chief?"

"It's rare, but hardly unheard of," he replied. "In Cheyenne tradition, certain women with powerful medicine have always been allowed to speak at council, to doctor, to act as chiefs, even to kill in battle."

"They are quite an enlightened people, then," Annie remarked. "Although I find it fascinating that she says her white life died."

His gaze darkened with remembered sadness. "She never speaks of her time with my grandpa, though I reckon she'll love him till the day she dies."

"Theirs must have been an extraordinary marriage. You say they met in Indian Territory?"

Sam kicked at a twig with his boot. "Yep. She grew up there with her family, way back in the twenties while the bands still roamed free. She was eighteen when my granddaddy rode into her band's camp. She once told me she'd never seen a braver man—him in his fine black suit, facing many hostile, suspicious braves. He won the respect of the People, even converted a few of them—and stole my grandmother's heart."

"Did she become a Christian?"

He shook his head. "She went through the motions but stayed in the background throughout their marriage. It wasn't easy for her—hell, many a frontier congregation that had seen Indian massacres rode Granddaddy out of town on a rail when they learnt he had a 'squaw' for a bride. I think the hardest thing for her was being unable to practice her medicine due to the fear and ignorance of the whites. There were times when she sorely wanted to help sick folk but wasn't allowed to. And of course my pa bore the stigma of bein' a half-breed—maybe why he turned to liquor and cards, and why not even a good woman could save him."

"I'm really sorry," Annie said sincerely.

"Thanks. To return to Grandma's story, she lived with my grandpa for thirty years and went back to her people after she buried him. It's just as well, since she never did fit in the white world."

Annie nodded; she could hear the bitterness in Sam's voice.

"A few years afterward, Betsy and me come to live with her. After we drifted away, I didn't see her for a time. Then one day almost six years ago, Whip Whistler come looking me up in Denver and told me the story of how Medicine Woman and the others had escaped from Fort Robinson, how they was on the run from the cavalry and low on resources. I been helping the band ever since—seeing they have food and cattle, finding them new places to roam and hide."

"You're an amazing man, Sam Noble." Impulsively, Annie stepped into his arms.

He clutched her close, regarding her with surprise and delight. "Hey, that's a big improvement, sugar. A mite friendlier, I must say."

She raised an eyebrow. "Don't go getting any ideas, now. Things aren't resolved between us, Sam. I just think a man who champions the cause of a band of lost Indians deserves a hug."

He chuckled and cuddled her close. "It's not that much to do," he said modestly. He gestured toward the circle of tepees. "This small group of Indians is keeping alive the old traditions and culture, a way of life that is dying off at the reservations. As long as there's breath left in my body, I'll see that they roam free."

"And what about Whip Whistler? Why has he stayed with the Cheyenne so long?"

Sam broke into a grin. "He's in love with my grandma, of course. I know she's old, but Whip sees through to her soul. He's learned the lesson that spirit matters most in life."

"But you said she still loves your grandfather."

"That's right. She and Whip share a deep kinship, but she's the kind who will only love once."

The words sent a chill down Annie's spine as she thought of a possible parallel to her own life. Was she, too, a woman who would love only once? Was Sam truly the man of her destiny? If so, would they find a place together, or would the forces that had brought them here ultimately rip them apart? Being in his arms now, feeling his warmth, his strength, smelling his manly scent, made the question all the more heart-wrenching for Annie. Sam was a wonderful man, a strong and kind man who in every way lived up to his "noble" name, even if his blind spots regarding her proved frustrating and painful.

Sam's hand rubbed her back, and his voice broke into her thoughts. "You're shivering, sugar. Are you all right?"

"Yes," she replied tremulously. "I was just thinking of what great devotion Whip possesses—to support Medicine Woman and her people for all this time, even though his love will always be unrequited."

Sam pulled back and playfully tweaked her nose. "That's how it is when a man finds the right woman. He's plumb lost without her."

Annie couldn't bear the look of stark longing on Sam's face. Heavens, she was shameless. Because if he didn't kiss her, she'd—

But he *did* kiss her, easing his mouth over hers with possessive ardor. Annie curled her arms around his neck and pressed herself into his heat. Sam roved his hands over her back, her hips, while his tongue caressed the inside of her mouth with shattering tenderness.

They clung together for a long moment. His lips trailed over her warm cheek. "Um, Annie, there's something I've been meaning to—er—"

"Yes?" she murmured.

Awkwardly, he said, "We need to talk about our—er—sleeping arrangements tonight."

That remark pulled her back to reality. "Do we?"

He scratched his jaw and regarded her sheepishly. "You see, among Cheyenne women, chastity is greatly prized. So, you and me—well, we would not be expected to share the same tepee—that is, unless . . ."

Annie frowned. "Are you assuming I'd want to share the same tepee with you?"

"No, I ain't assuming nothin'," he hastily replied.

"Then are you suggesting we lie to the others and pretend we're husband and wife?"

He groaned. "No, I ain't proposin' that, neither. It's just that—I'm missing you somethin' fierce, sugar." He pulled her close again. "Can't we figure some way to be alone?"

Hearing the fervent desire in his voice, Annie swallowed hard. Sam might never know how close she was to dragging him off into those glorious yellow aspens. But they'd still be at the same impasse: he, convinced she was a liar; she, left with the same hurts. They'd been lovers now, and Annie found she couldn't bear the thought of being intimate with him again until they moved to a new level of trust.

With the long seconds ticking past, his expression grew bewildered. "Don't you want me, Annie?"

"Of course I do," she answered honestly. Still, gathering all her fortitude, she pulled away. "But the next time we make love, you're going to have to know who I really am."

Sam could only watch in misery as Annie turned and walked back toward the center of camp.

Chapter 22

Returning to camp, Annie felt at a loss, uncertain what to do next. She smiled at a couple of elderly squaws who were chopping roots outside a tepee, and skirted a group of loud, rambunctious boys, who were tossing a ball while a younger lad tried to catch the missile with a mesh-lined hoop.

Annie was grateful when a young Indian woman, the one whose belly was so large, came up towing along a boy who appeared to be no more than four. The squaw wore a white deerskin dress, heavily quilled and beaded, and knee-high moccasins that were also lavishly decorated. Her long hair was parted down the middle and bound in many braids embellished by deerskin charms and plant sprigs that smelled like sage. The woman was pretty in her way, her skin honey brown and smooth, her features even, despite the jarring presence of a silver ring in her nose and heavily beaded earlobes. Her child was dressed only in a breechclout, his straight black hair spilling down upon his shoulders, his round face solemn. Although the afternoon had grown mild, Annie had to wonder if the boy was cold.

"Visitor, I bid you greeting," the woman said in English. "I am Sits on a Cloud, and this is my son, Little Fox."

"How do you do?" replied Annie. She smiled down at the lad, who gave a shy grin before disappearing behind his mother's skirt. "Your boy is beautiful, and it looks as if he'll soon have a new brother or sister."

For a moment, Sits on a Cloud did not reply, and Annie fervently hoped she had not violated some taboo in speaking so frankly of the woman's pregnancy. Then the squaw giggled. "Oh, yes, soon my family will be blessed again. My husband, Red Shield, is most proud."

"I'm sure he is, and I bet he loves your cooking, too," Annie replied. "I enjoyed the pemmican you brought me at lunch."

The squaw modestly averted her gaze. "I will teach you how to grind it if you wish."

"I would love that. Everything about your life here fascinates me."

The woman smiled, reaching out to take Annie's hand. "We will learn to grind pemmican on another sunrise. For now, I know you must be tired. I will take you to your lodge."

Pleasantly surprised by the offer, Annie followed Sits on a Cloud to a large white tepee decorated with hunting scenes. A gorgeous, multicolored, quilled star hung over the entry flap.

"What a lovely decoration," she murmured, pointing at the intricate adornment.

Sits on a Cloud beamed. "I am Meenoistst, one of the Quilling Society. I quilled the star in tribute to the Wise One Above, to bless our lodge and bring our family good fortune."

"You mean this is your lodge?" asked Annie, taken aback.

"It is yours while you are here," the woman replied.

Annie was horrified, vehemently shaking her head. "Oh, no, I cannot put you and your family out of your home—especially not with you about to give birth to another child!"

The woman appeared confused. "But it is a great honor to offer one's lodge to a visitor, especially a revered friend of He Who Protects Us."

Bemused, Annie repeated, "He Who—"

"Sam," the girl explained.

"Ah, yes. But I still cannot take your home! Where will you and your family sleep?"

"In the lodge of my husband's parents." The girl hung

her head. "If you refuse our hospitality, it will bring my family great shame."

"Oh, heavens." Remembering Sam's warnings about taboos, Annie touched the girl's arm. "Believe me, Sits on a Cloud, the last thing I would want to do is to insult you. I was just so touched by your generosity, I wasn't sure how to respond at first. But of course I'd be deeply honored to sleep in your lodge."

The woman beamed. "Good. Then come."

Sits on a Cloud moved aside the entry flap and motioned for Annie to precede her inside. Ducking through the opening and moving to the left as Sam had advised, Annie straightened to view a shadowy interior with a central fire pit; around it were arranged several beds of pelts. The furnishings were completed by two benches composed of grass woven over sod bases and a cupboard made of buffalo hides stretched over a wooden frame. A water skin was attached to one of the anchoring poles, and several parfleches were stacked neatly beneath it.

"Your home is so cozy," Annie remarked.

"Thank you. As long as you are among us, it will be yours alone."

"And Sam?" Annie couldn't resist asking.

Sits on a Cloud smiled. "He will sleep in Medicine Woman's lodge." She gestured about the tepee. "Please make our home your own. Perhaps Little Fox and I should leave you to rest."

"After that wonderful feast, I am a bit sleepy—and still getting accustomed to this thin mountain air, I suppose," Annie confessed. "But before you go—I'm curious. Where did you get your name?"

The young woman's face lit with pride. "When I was a very young child, I disappeared high into the mountains. My mother was panicked, and everyone in our tribe tried to find me. Only there was a terrible fog that morning. Finally one of our elders, Spotted Wolf, spied just my head peaking out of the mists. He brought me back to my mother and pronounced, 'I name this child Sits on a Cloud.'"

"What a fascinating story," replied Annie. "And your son?"

Sits on a Cloud ruffled the boy's hair. "A red fox came across our camp, jumping over the fire on the night he was born."

"Amazing," said Annie.

Sits on a Cloud rubbed her stomach. "Perhaps if this child is a female, we shall name her for you, the one who slept on the mat before her."

"You are too kind," said Annie.

"You must rest now," the squaw replied, taking her son's hand and leaving the tepee.

Annie lay down on one of the surprisingly comfortable pelt beds. She could not believe the kindness and trust of these humble people. And Sam protected them—this endeared him to her, as had his earlier kisses and pleas.

She felt so torn and wanted him so much, wanted them to be close again. Still, she couldn't forget that he didn't trust her.

Whatever he had in mind, the next move was clearly his.

"How have things been, Grandmother?"

Sam sat with Medicine Woman in her lodge. Well-remembered, pungent aromas cloyed the atmosphere inside the tepee. The old healer was perched on her haunches, a mallet in hand as she ground up dried whiteweed in a bowl. Sam knew she used the plant in a poultice for her rheumatism, although she never complained about the affliction. Around her were small deerskin pouches containing various herbs, weeds, dried roots, and flowers that were used in her medicines.

She looked up from her labors, regarding him with a grandmother's pride. "Buffalo Driver says we must move on soon. We have been here for too many moons—now the corn has been harvested, such as it is here in the high country."

Sam nodded soberly. "I reckon Whip is right. If you squat here much longer, the government's bound to get wind of your whereabouts and send the blue coats after you."

"The old ways are dying, anyway," Medicine woman lamented. "Our men no longer meet in the medicine lodge or sacrifice themselves to the pole in the sun dance ritual. Our women no longer wear the painted signs of their husbands's coups in their hair, for the days of our battles are over. Now we herd the cow, where before we hunted the buffalo."

"Still, you're keeping many of the old customs alive here, Grandmother," Sam remarked, "like living simply off the land and practicing the miracle of your healing. I remember when I was with you as a kid and had that terrible nosebleed. You stanched the bleeding with some kinda berry powder. You made a believer out of me that day."

Medicine Woman smiled faintly. "Those were good days, Grandson, when our band still roamed free. Now we are hunted like a pack of dogs."

Sam sighed. "I just wish I had enough money stashed away to buy you a huge ranch and let you and your people live on it however you please."

"Your heart is generous, Grandson," Medicine Woman replied. "You have given much to us already, food and beast and seed. You cannot give your life."

"I would gladly," said Sam sincerely.

"That is not your path," she replied wisely. "You have chosen the trail of the white man. Even in your dream of giving us land, you dream as a white man. The Cheyenne cannot be owned by the land, nor bound to it. It is our destiny, our spirit, to roam free."

Sam reached out and touched her hand. "Think on it, Grandma, please. If I can find a way . . . You need a place of your own. Otherwise, the cavalry will hunt you down until there's nowhere left to hide."

Medicine Woman nodded. "I will think on it, Grandson." She brightened. "Now tell me of this woman—this Annie—that you have brought with you."

Sam gathered his thoughts so that he might approach the subject tactfully. "She's the one I tracked—you know, the one Moon Calf said would be found to the south."

"Ah," murmured Medicine Woman. "You mean she is Rotted Rosie?"

Sam smiled at her mispronunciation. "Yeah. Well, that's who I thought she was, anyhow."

Medicine Woman frowned. "Your mind has changed?"

He groaned. "She's like no one I've ever met, Grandmother. She's brave, she's beautiful, she's feisty. But she also has to be the most gall-durned liar I've ever known."

"The woman speaks with forked tongue?" Medicine Woman frowned. "I think you must tell me this entire story, Grandson."

Sam spilled out everything to Medicine Woman, telling her how he had tracked Annie to the Texas Panhandle, just as she and Moon Calf had advised; how he had borne her away, kicking and protesting; how she had claimed that she was not his quarry, Rotten Rosie, but a woman from another time.

"She claims she's from the future," Sam finished, "and she's got some mighty strange stuff in her bag— like doodads and money with dates from over a hundred years ahead of us in time. Still, if she is from another century, that'ud mean she'd gone and traveled through time . . . and that ain't possible, right?"

Medicine Woman scowled. "Many things are possible in the realm of the spirit."

"Perhaps, but it ain't possible to move through time more than a hundred years . . . is it?"

She was quiet for a long moment. "There are many paths in this world, Grandson. Who can say where all of them lead?"

"But you and Moon Calf told me where to find this woman!" Sam burst out.

Medicine Woman spoke calmly. "Grandson, I urged you to heed the wisdom of our sacred idiot, that your quarry was to be found beyond the Numhaisto, the wind of the south. Sometimes, however, there is a message in a vision that goes far beyond what we hear with our ears, just as deep currents can move beneath the surface of a placid pond."

"What are you saying?" he asked, frustrated.

Carefully, she replied, "Our sacred man may have had another purpose in sending you south—perhaps to fulfill a destiny of your own."

Sam stared at her, dumbfounded. "Well, now's a fine time to be telling me!"

"Grandson, I have always spoken my heart to you. Why would I stop now?"

He shook his head.

Observing his agitation, she sighed. "What do you wish me to do?"

Sam drew his fingers through his hair. "Hell, I don't know—maybe you can perform some type of purification rite, make Annie sit in your sage smoke like you used to do with me when I violated the taboos and stuck a stick in the fire or somethin'. Maybe you can cleanse the lyin' from her soul."

"Perhaps," conceded Medicine Woman, "but first I must get to know this woman and judge her story for myself."

"Yeah, I reckon that's only fair." Sam's expression grew even more torn. "Are you sayin' you think she might be tellin' the truth?"

"I do not know." Medicine Woman regarded Sam thoughtfully for a long moment. "You have given your heart to this woman, have you not, Grandson?"

Sam grinned. "I reckon I have."

"That is why you did not take her to the white man's justice?"

"I just couldn't," he replied tightly.

"Then perhaps you already believe her a little yourself?" Medicine Woman pressed.

Sam mulled over the question. "I believe that at heart, she's a good woman, but mighty confused and misguided."

"What of you, Grandson?" the old woman asked wisely. "Are you perhaps a little confused and misguided?"

Sam's features grew sheepish. "I allow I've had a doubt or two. Like, am I being too stubborn with Annie? Could she be telling the truth?" He sighed. "But you know all that, don't you? No one knows my heart and mind better than you, Grandmother."

"Ah, but perhaps this woman will?"

"Perhaps."

"I think your Annie has great heart and spirit," Medicine Woman pronounced.

"Indeed she does."

The old woman frowned. "But the two of you need help along your path."

"We'd be mighty obliged."

The healer poured the pulverized whiteweed into a small sack. "This is a complicated matter, and I have many more remedies to grind today. I will ponder your difficulty as I prepare the milk medicine for after Sits on a Cloud's birthing. After the sunrise, I will speak with your woman."

"Thank you, Grandmother."

Sensing Medicine Woman wanted to be alone, Sam kissed her wrinkled brow, then got up and quietly left the tepee. His mind still churned. What had Medicine Woman meant when she'd said Moon Calf could have had another purpose in sending him south? Had he been sent to find the woman of his destiny rather than his true quarry, Rotten Rosie? If so, why did Annie look just like Rosie—unless she really was the outlaw's relation from another time?

God, what if he really was wrong? He would have made a shameful mistake. Would Annie ever forgive him?

At sunset, the group again gathered at the central fire. Berries, jerky, and cornbread were passed, along with cups of cool spring water. Annie was touched when Moon Calf came up to her, solemnly presenting her with a small bouquet of yellow and violet mountain wildflowers. Accepting the blooms, she smiled and thanked him. After staring at her intently for a moment, he withdrew to sit across the fire from her. He continued to regard her for a moment before he went back to his ritual of rocking and chanting.

Sam nodded toward the bouquet in Annie's hands.

"That fella's gonna make me jealous if he don't watch it."

She chuckled. "Well, wasn't he the one who told you to head south after me? Now that I'm here, you can't expect him to ignore me."

Sam grunted and took a bite of jerky. "Oh, yeah? Well, maybe I'm starting to wonder about his *real* interest in you."

Annie shot him a baffled look but didn't comment.

The atmosphere of the evening meal turned out to be much quieter than at the noon feast. One old warrior played a flute and another droned out a soft tattoo on a drum while Whip Whistler told the children a story of a buffalo calf lost on the great prairie and searching for his family. Annie found it ironic that in fiction, the ending of the tale was happy, with the calf reunited with his parents' great herd, whereas in reality, the plight of these people was far more tragic, their fates sealed in the demise of the great and noble beast that had once provided them with virtually all food and shelter.

Soon darkness fell, a deep chill settled over the valley, and a thousand stars glittered to life in the black heavens above them. Catching Annie yawning, Sam gave her a nudge, and the two slipped away from the others, heading toward her lodge.

"I don't know why I'm so sleepy," she admitted. "I already had a nap this afternoon. Like I told Sits on a Cloud, it must be this thin mountain air."

Sam nodded. "Red Shield told me quite proudly that you had been given their lodge."

"I know," she replied with a groan. "I didn't want to inconvenience their family, but when I tried to refuse, Sits on a Cloud seemed downright insulted."

Sam chuckled. "It *is* an insult to refuse the offer of hospitality."

"Well, I think I managed to smooth things over." She paused by her tepee to regard him sincerely. "These are good people Sam—your grandmother, Whip Whistler, Sits on a Cloud—everyone here has been wonderful to me."

He reached out and stroked her cheek. "You sure look pretty in the moonlight, sugar."

"Thanks," she replied almost shyly.

"And you're comfortable in the lodge?"

"Oh, yes."

"Then you don't mind staying here for a spell?"

Annie hesitated. "So your grandmother can reform me?"

He gripped her by the shoulders. "Annie, I already spoke to her today, and she's thinking on our situation now. I reckon she'll want to talk to you soon. Won't you trust her to figure out what's right?"

"Fair enough," Annie conceded. "But what if what she decides goes against what you already believe?"

"I'll abide by her judgment," came Sam's sincere and immediate response.

Annie nodded and extended her hand. "Then we've got a deal, cowboy?"

He cocked a brow at her. "A handshake, Annie? By damn, if you think I'll *ever* settle for that—"

The rest of his words were drowned out as he gathered her close and kissed her, his mouth trembling over hers with sweetness and hunger. Annie could only moan in helpless longing as feelings flared powerfully between them.

Finally, Sam pulled back, tucking her head beneath his chin. "Annie, let me come to you tonight, after the others are sleeping," he whispered, his voice rough with need.

Again, Annie felt powerfully tempted. Even though the larger issues between them remained unresolved, the events and emotions of the day had bonded them. Nonetheless, she quietly replied, "Sam, while we're here, I think we should honor the traditions of your grandmother's people."

He pulled back and wagged a finger in admonition. "That's not why you're saying no, and you damn well know it."

She regarded him in anguish. "Then let me put it this way: I don't think our worlds can meet again physically until they meet spiritually."

He stood with fists clenched. "Annie, can't you meet me halfway?"

"I've already given as much as I can," she replied, her voice thick with emotion. "The rest is up to you, cowboy."

Annie slipped inside the tepee, and Sam was left to grind his jaw and stare beseechingly up into the cold heavens.

Chapter 23

The old crier's voice awakened Annie just before dawn. She could hear him running about the circle of lodges, yelling some important pronouncement in Cheyenne, the barking of dogs a shrill accompaniment.

Wrapping herself in a pelt, Annie stepped out of her tepee into the cold, damp grayness that would soon give way to morning. Feeling the need to relieve herself, she headed away from the lodges toward the wooded hillside, only to pause in her tracks, enchanted by the amazing spectacle taking place just a few yards beyond her.

In a small open space beneath the slope of the hillside, Moon Calf was crouched on the ground, at the center of a throng of wild creatures. With his pet meadowlark perched on his shoulder, the sacred idiot was tossing out seed to a host of birds hopping about him: striking red-breasted nuthatches, bright gold and rosy finches, brilliant bluebirds, yellow-and-black evening grosbeaks. The birds were chirping happily and scooping up the seed, a bold Steller's jay even pecking it out of the holy man's fingers. Only a few feet away, two cottontail rabbits, four striped chipmunks, and several mule deer happily munched on piles of clover that the sacred idiot had obviously laid out.

Annie was entranced by the sweet, pastoral scene, especially as she watched one of the vibrant grosbeaks flit upward to perch atop Moon Calf's head and launch into lilting song. Moon Calf closed his eyes and trilled

out a response. For the first time, Annie saw the poor
man smile, an expression exquisite in its innocence and
joy. The sight touched her heart. Moon Calf appeared
totally in harmony among the wild creatures, as if he
were a part of their untamed world. Awed by a sense of
magic and mysticism, Annie dared not move closer,
fearing she would spook the precious creatures and spoil
the delightful scene.

As she stood transfixed, Moon Calf seemed to sense
her presence; he opened his eyes and stared at her. Annie
smiled back shyly; he continued to gaze at her but did
not otherwise react. After a moment she turned away,
giving the endearing vignette a wide berth as she moved
off toward a different section of the woods.

Moments later, as she emerged from the trees, dawn
was painting the landscape with glorious shades of red
and gold. A man's exuberant yell and a loud splash
turned her attention toward the lake. First she spotted
several women squatted along the shoreline, filling water
skins. The females seemed oblivious of the fact that,
nearby, the men were bathing. Moving closer, Annie was
astounded to watch Red Shield, Sits on a Cloud's
husband, dive naked into the crystal blue water. Several
other men and young boys, gathered along the shore,
were shucking their clothing. As Annie looked on in
mystification, Sam and the old crier strode up to join the
group.

Shamelessly, she watched Sam strip nude, saw the rays
of dawn play over the splendid muscles of his back, his
beautifully shaped buttocks, and his long, hard thighs.
Desire raced through her body with unexpected intensity, warming her, making her tremble. Watching him dive
in and imagining how cold the water was, she couldn't
contain a shiver or restrain thoughts of warming his
chilled flesh with her too hot body. She stood riveted as
he swam about for a few moments, then began to emerge
from the water, revealing first his handsome, whiskered
face, then his tanned neck and broad shoulders, followed
by his muscular, hair-covered chest, and then . . .

A feminine voice behind Annie roused her from her

near hypnotic state. "It is tradition of the men to bathe at dawn."

Red-faced with embarrassment, Annie whirled to view Sits on a Cloud standing behind her, holding a filled water skin. "Oh—I didn't mean to eavesdrop."

Sits on a Cloud laughed. "It is a shocking sight for she who has not seen it before. The men are brave to venture into the lake, especially with water monsters about."

"Water monsters?" Annie repeated.

"There is *mihn* and *ahke*, who devour brave men alive. We must frequently sacrifice a lamb or a calf to keep them appeased. And there are the people that live under the water. They have strong medicine, and are revered. They do not harm us like the monster lizard and the bull."

"I see," murmured Annie. She nodded toward the water skin the squaw held. "The women are out and about early, too."

She nodded. "We must gather living water each morning. Water that sits all night is considered dead."

"How fascinating."

The squaw grimaced and rubbed her lower back.

Annie stepped forward. "Are you okay?"

Sits on a Cloud nodded. "I have this aching. . . . I think my time may soon be upon me."

"Oh, bless your heart," said Annie, mentally wincing at the thought of the young woman having to deliver her baby in such crude conditions, with no doctor, other than Medicine Woman, to attend her. "I wish there was something I could do to help."

"Medicine Woman will know what is to be done," the squaw replied. "And you must be famished. Come over to our camp and I will serve you gruel and warm berry tea."

"But shouldn't you be resting?"

Sits on a Cloud stared at Annie as if she had lost her mind. "I am fine. Come."

Annie accompanied the young woman to the lodge of her in-laws, where she was offered hot gruel, tasty Indian nut bread, and warm berry tea. When Sits on a Cloud slipped inside to help her mother-in-law straighten the lodge, Annie decided to explore the camp. Just beyond the lodges, she watched Sam, Whip, and several braves gallop off into the hills, waving their fists and yelling exuberantly. She wondered if they were going hunting.

To the north of the corral, several children were involved in a lively game of "bear," an older boy dressed in a bearskin stalking about trying to terrorize the younger ones, much to their delight. Annie chuckled, watching the youngsters dash about everywhere, screaming gleefully and trying to hide under junipers or behind lodges. Heading back toward the common area, she observed women busy at work, some airing bedding, others tending fires or chopping roots. She studiously avoided passing directly before a lodge where two elderly squaws were quilling moccasins, remembering Sam's admonition that the quilling process was considered sacred. She paused by a mother and daughter who were sewing rawhide shirts and felt warmed when the pair invited her to join them. In broken English, the duo struggled to instruct her in sewing. Annie tried her best to mimic the women and sew a simple seam by making holes in both pieces of rawhide with a sharp awl, then trying to draw the tough sinew thread through the two layers of hide to bind the seam. All three laughed over her clumsiness.

After leaving the two, she paused before Medicine Woman's lodge; the old woman squatted near an outside fire, putting the finishing touches on a small cradle, sewing a beaded deerskin to a wooden frame.

"What a lovely cradle," Annie said. "Is that for Sits on a Cloud?"

"Yes," replied the old woman. "Her time will be soon. I have already prepared the herbs to ease her labor, and the milk medicine for afterward." She pointed toward the hillside, where Red Shield was raising an isolated tepee. "The birthing lodge will be ready soon."

Annie found it odd that the tepee was set apart from the others but didn't comment.

Medicine Woman gestured to the ground beside her. "Sit for a time."

"Thank you."

Annie squatted beside the old woman, watching her skilled fingers work the hide. "Have Sam and the others gone hunting?"

The woman nodded. "I think he wished for us to talk."

Hearing a meaningful inflection in Medicine Woman's voice, Annie wondered how much she already knew. "Has he told you my entire story?"

"He has told me some," Medicine Woman replied. "You do not have to say more if your heart directs otherwise."

"No, I want you to know," replied Annie frankly. "Especially since I feel so frustrated with Sam."

The old woman chuckled. "My grandson is a proud and determined man—yet his heart is good."

"I realize this," Annie assured her. "But has Sam told you he refuses to believe me?"

"Yes."

"Will you hear what I have to say with an open mind?"

She nodded. "That is only just. But I must hear the entire tale from your lips."

"Fair enough," agreed Annie.

Annie launched into her account, telling Medicine Woman in broad terms about the world from which she had come, a world of the future over a hundred years ahead of them in time. She explained how she had grown up in Texas and had lost both her parents. She told of her work on the ghost town in the Texas Panhandle and of how Sam had tracked her there, unwittingly crossing some barrier in time, then taking her back to this century with him. At this point in the story, the healer looked up from her labors to gaze at Annie oddly, though she did not interrupt.

"I know it sounds strange," Annie continued, "but Sam is convinced I'm someone else, a criminal named Rotten Rosie, just because my face resembles one on a wanted poster. Even stranger is the fact that the real person he is after is my great-great-grandmother, and I know she must be in terrible trouble. In fact, in some bizarre mystical way, I think I may have been sent here to help my ancestor. Sam and I—well, we've become very close, and he's no longer set on taking me to justice. But he won't believe who I really am, and how can I straighten out this mess, or rescue my ancestor, until he does?"

Annie fell silent, staring at Medicine Woman, whose expression was once again impassive. At last she looked up and said quietly, "I would hear more of your world."

Annie hesitated. How could she make this woman, who had lived in primitive conditions much of her life, understand automobiles and spaceships and weapons of mass destruction? Nevertheless, she made a valiant try, describing the world of the late twentieth century, spinning images of marvelous modern wagons without horses that carried people for many miles, rockets more powerful than shooting stars that bore man up into the heavens, and bombs destructive enough to destroy entire civilizations. She portrayed how pictures could move across screens, how voices could travel vast distances over circuits. Turning to territory more familiar to Medicine Woman, she spoke of how modern potions could stop pain and cure illness. She continued on and on, trying to depict everything from computers to skyscrapers to stereo headsets in terms the old woman could understand.

Finally, Annie could think of no more to say and gazed at the woman in uncertainty. "Do you believe me? Will you help me?"

Having finished the cradle, Medicine Woman was putting away her sewing implements. "I know that a message from our spirits brought you here. This is surely why our sacred man had his vision and told Sam where to find you. We both recognize this, but my grandson cannot see the full truth as yet. He is a good man, but his totems are the gods of the White Eyes. He has abandoned the Cheyenne in his soul, and he needs to rediscover the way of the spirit. I will meditate on these matters. The Wise One Above will guide me. When the truth is shown to me, I will speak with Sam."

Annie touched the old woman's hand. "Thank you. That's very fair, and all I can ask."

Chapter 24

A nnie lingered for a while with Medicine Woman, enjoying her company and the mild day. The two women shared a lunch of berries and pemmican.

Early that afternoon, hearing laughing children, Annie glanced off toward the hillside and observed six of the camp youngsters—three boys and three girls—proceeding in a caravan toward a wide ledge, tugging along heavily laden dogs and even a mule hauling a travois. The boys, including Little Fox, were armed with small bows and miniature quivers filled with tiny arrows; the girls bore deerskin dolls on cradle boards. In a whimsical touch, Moon Calf followed at the rear of the echelon, his posture regal as he held high a smoldering stick. Several mule deer trailed behind the sacred idiot.

Annie was perplexed. "What are the children doing? Running away?"

Medicine Woman laughed. "They are going camping."

"Camping?" Annie repeated with an astonished laugh. "And why is Moon Calf with them?"

"He carries the ceremonial fire stick. He will start the fire and bless the lodges."

"Lodges?"

"Yes, the children have their own small tepees that their mothers made for them."

"How charming."

"After the lodges are raised, the girls will begin preparing the meal while the boys go hunting."

"Amazing."

"Go and watch," the wise old woman directed. "Only do not linger too close. For the children, this is serious business."

Flashing the woman a smile, Annie rose and went to observe the youngsters from behind a clump of cedar. While the girls unloaded the packs and travois, the boys erected three miniature lodges no more than four feet tall at their centers. The play tepees were decorated with smaller animals such as beavers, raccoons, and foxes. One of the girls arranged a pile of buffalo chips in the central area, and Moon Calf went into great ceremony, chanting and dancing with his smoking stick, before he lit the fire. Then, as the children reverently watched, he blessed the lodges, rubbing them down with sage.

The girls brought out bowls and knives and began chopping roots while the boys tested out their bows and arrows, shooting shafts into a tree stump. All at once they paused as Sam, Whip, and several braves galloped into view, turkeys tied to their saddles. Waving the others on, Sam dismounted and brought the boys one of the slaughtered fowl. The lads accepted the gift with hoots and laughter, one of them taking it to the girls, who began plucking off its feathers. The boys continued to congregate around Sam, chattering rapidly in their native Cheyenne, obviously beseeching him as they tugged at his sleeves and motioned toward his horse. Annie wondered if they were begging him to take them hunting.

A moment later her curiosity was assuaged when he strode back to his horse and got his rope. As he moved toward the children, they backed away, surrounding him in a circle. Annie watched, enthralled, as Sam began performing rope tricks, twirling his lasso in circles high in the air, then whipping the loop up and down his body. The children cheered wildly and jumped up and down. After a moment, he flung the lasso outward, creating a huge sideways hoop. The boys began dancing through it. Pandemonium erupted when one of the dogs leaped through the loop! Sam continued to enchant the youngsters, gently lassoing several of them about the waist and pulling them forward as the others laughed. He even used his lasso to snap a bow out of Little Fox's hands, much to the joy of all.

Then he turned and his eyes met Annie's. She froze, embarrassed, realizing she had unconsciously strayed closer to the fascinating scene. Sam grinned, threw out his rope, caught Annie about the hips, and hauled her carefully but firmly toward him. The children howled with laughter, and even Annie giggled as Sam pulled her close.

"Know what this means, sugar?" he whispered, eyes dancing with mischief.

"What?"

"I've reeled you in and now you're mine," he murmured back huskily, leaning over and kissing her.

Annie kissed him back, unable to resist his sexy words and rugged charm. He smelled of the outdoors, and even his whiskers felt manly against her skin.

Pulling back, he winked. "That's what you get for spying on us."

Annie was about to scold him, but several children burst forward to tug at his hands and clothes. Grinning, he removed the lasso from her hips and strode away with the youngsters.

Still smiling, Annie walked back to rejoin Medicine Woman, who was pounding dried berries into powder. "Your grandson has many talents." She laughed. "In fact, he recently used his rope to rescue a bobcat cub and even to save me from a snake. How did he become so skilled with a lasso?"

Medicine Woman banged her mallet rhythmically against a wooden bowl. "Sam always loved his rope. When he was still a lad and lived among our people, he entertained us all with demonstrations of his magic. He also shoots and rides with greater skill than any man I have ever seen, red or white. Now he uses his mastery to seek the white man's justice."

Beset with bittersweet emotion, Annie strained to catch another glimpse of him with the exuberant youngsters. She had such doubts that her world and Sam's would ever truly meet. Yet everything she learned about this amazing man only made her love him all the more.

The waning day brought a deep chill, and Annie donned her wool car coat. When time came for the evening meal, all members of the encampment, including the children, returned to the central area. For Annie, it was her first chance that day to spend any real time with Sam, and she was secretly thrilled when he plopped down next to her. She realized she truly had missed him that day—too much.

"So, did you enjoy your day as a natural man?" she teased.

He raised a dark brow. "What do you mean by that?"

"I mean you spent your day communing with nature. Let's see—you began by diving naked into the lake—"

"So you watched that, did you?" he asked with a grin.

"The splashing caught my attention," she replied primly.

He leaned over and whispered, "The splashing or my naked butt?"

"Oh!" She felt chagrined by the telltale blush heating her cheeks. "Sir, your naked butt holds no appeal for me."

He hooted with laughter. "You can't fool me, sugar. I know better."

Annie glanced away to conceal a guilty expression. "Well, your backside is kind of cute, even if you are a shameless exhibitionist."

He wrapped an arm about her shoulders. "I'm just proud of what the good Lord gave me, sugar." Leaning closer, he added, "You should be, too. *Mighty* proud."

She shot him a chiding look but spoke with a quiver. "Enough of that. To get back to your day in the wilds, you went hunting, then entertained the kids with rope tricks—"

"So you're really keeping track of me, are you, woman?" he taunted, appearing pleased. "Maybe you miss me. Heck, maybe you like me a bit more than you're letting on."

Annie was saved from replying as Moon Calf came up

to present her with a new bunch of flowers. She smiled. "Are those for me?"

Appearing miserably put on the spot, the holy man shoved the bouquet toward Annie's nose and stammered, "W-welcome."

Thrilled that he had actually spoken to her, Annie accepted the blooms with a look of pride. "Thank you. You're very kind."

Moon Calf almost smiled back, then caught Sam's scowl and hastily backed away.

Annie shot him a chiding look. "Sam! Why did you stare at him so coldly? He's harmless."

"Harmless?" Sam blustered, scowling. "He's got his eye on you all the time, when he ain't fawning at your feet like a lovesick puppy dog."

"That's not true! He spent a lot of time camping with the kids today—you know, blessing their lodges and such. And he actually spoke to me just now, instead of ranting or chanting."

Sam's menacing look deepened. "I just ain't sure about him."

"Well, I am," Annie argued. "He's sweet and friendly, and I think he's a dear to bring me flowers. Besides, there's enough segregation of the sexes around here."

"Complaining, are you?" he asked with a sudden, avid gleam in his eyes.

"Not really," she replied demurely. "But I have noticed how the men spend the day doing their thing, leaving the women to perform much of the labor. Although I did have a very good talk with your grandmother."

"Did you?"

Annie was about to elaborate when she again spotted Moon Calf standing over her, extending a bowl of stew. She reached out, took it, and smiled. "Thank you."

Annie was stunned to watch Sam shoot to his feet. "You leave her alone," he gruffly ordered the other man.

Blinking in fear, the bearded man dashed away.

"Sam! How could you?"

Sam fell back down beside her, his expression bemused. "Annie, he's got some kinda strange fascination with you, and I just don't like him coming around."

"Well, maybe I don't like *you* around me!" she retorted.

Sam groaned and met her eye soberly. "Annie, he's never taken an interest in a female before. First he told me where to find you . . . now this. The man is right touched and we both know it. Lord only knows what's really on his mind or what he might do."

"Well, I'm not afraid of him. He's a dear, nonviolent man and you should apologize to him right now—or sit somewhere else!"

He appeared incredulous. "Annie, you can't mean that."

"Damn right, I do. Sam, you were mean to him, and it's totally unlike you to be cruel. What's going on?"

Glancing off toward the lake, he groaned. "Annie, it's just that . . . I miss you somethin' awful, sugar, and then I see you smilin' at him all nice like, and I guess it just twists somethin' up inside me." In a low, husky tone, he admitted, "Reckon I need you to clip my horns."

Although she fought a smile, Annie replied crisply, "Then go tell him that."

Sam's mouth fell open. "Woman, have you gone plumb loco? I can't tell *him* that. Hell, he'll think I'm one of them funny fellers that likes lace hankies and gold-tipped walking sticks."

Annie raised a hand to cover her giggles. "I mean, go make him understand why you acted so ugly."

Sam rolled his eyes. "Annie, I could talk all night and he ain't understandin' nothin'."

"Well, go try."

Waving his arms, Sam got to his feet and trudged across the central area toward Moon Calf. Spotting the other man's approach, Moon Calf almost bolted away, until Sam laid a hand on his shoulder and spoke quietly with him. Before long Sam returned to Annie's side, grinning smugly. She glanced across to see Moon Calf examining a coin from many different angles.

"Well?" she asked Sam.

"I gave him a five-dollar gold piece to amuse him—
though he'll never know the difference—and thanked
him for helping me find you. So there. Do I get a kiss
now?"

Annie harrumphed. "You're going to have to mind
your manners a lot better than that to get a kiss from
me."

Sam scowled, then ducked down and stole a kiss
anyway while nearby several children chortled and
cheered.

Chapter 25

Not long after the evening meal ended, excited whispers spread through the camp as a young woman raced up to Medicine Woman and began gesturing and speaking in rapid Cheyenne. A moment later the old healer joined Annie and Sam, who stood talking near one of the lodges.

"White Owl has informed me that Sits on a Cloud's time has come," the woman told Annie. "She has requested that both of us attend her in the birthing lodge."

"Me?" asked Annie in pleasant surprise. Having been raised on a ranch, Annie was not unfamiliar with the cycle of life, though she wasn't sure how much practical advice she might offer on the delivery of a child. Still, she felt honored to be asked. "Well, if she wants me there, I'll be happy to come."

With Annie following her, Medicine Woman stopped by her lodge to gather various medicines and pick up the cradle she had made. Then the two women hastened toward the isolated birthing lodge higher on the hillside. Following the healer through the tepee opening, Annie first saw the birthing chair, a low, bottomless rawhide-and-wood contraption, placed a few feet away from the fire. She spotted Sits on a Cloud lying beneath the far eaves on a bed of pelts. The girl was curled up on her side, her face covered with sweat and convulsed with pain.

"Oh, you poor dear!" cried Annie, rushing over to kneel by her side and take her hand.

Sits on a Cloud did not reply, but Annie took heart when she smiled faintly and squeezed Annie's fingers.

Medicine Woman was untying the bag from her waist. "I will make up the bark medicine to ease her pain."

While Medicine Woman stirred the drink, Annie helped the laboring woman sit up. After Sits on a Cloud sipped the concoction, her discomfort seemed to lessen for a time. Medicine Woman took out her rattle, danced, sang, and made various gestures to the spirits. When she threw crushed sage on the coals, creating both thick smoke and an acrid, unpleasant odor, Annie almost protested, certain the fumes were not good for a laboring mother. But she bit her tongue, realizing that for these people, the ritual of burning sage was sacred as a ceremonial blessing.

Annie was deeply moved to note that as Sits on a Cloud's labored deepened, she did not cry out, though she never let go of Annie's hand and her features contorted with intense pain. Medicine Woman brewed additional pain potions, rubbed the laboring mother's belly with pungent salves, and finally placed a stout piece of rawhide between her teeth, so she could clamp down when the worst of the contractions gripped her. Soon Sits on a Cloud's fingernails dug into Annie's flesh, but she did not pull away, convinced that no matter what discomfort she might feel, her friend's agony was a hundredfold greater.

When Sits on a Cloud's contractions became constant, Medicine Woman knelt by her and said, "Come now. It is time to go to the birthing chair."

Annie watched in wonder as the woman sat on the chair and, with skirts raised, strained to push out the child, her features dark and twisted from the effort. At last, as Sits on a Cloud emitted a single, harsh cry, Annie watched the tiny blood-smeared infant fall into Medicine Woman's hands. The healer cut the cord with a knife, then placed the child in a bowl of warm water. It was a girl! The baby gave a lusty cry as Medicine Woman wrapped her in a blanket. Annie glanced at Sits on a Cloud to see her eyes wide open in wonder.

"You have a girl," Annie said, her voice thick with tears.

The squaw smiled. Medicine Woman turned and handed the baby to Annie. "Place the baby in the cradle while I attend to the afterbirth."

But Annie was not about to let go of the precious bundle in her arms. She couldn't believe how tiny and adorable the child was. The little brown infant was squirming and flailing its small fists. Tenderness clutched at Annie's heart as for a moment, the child opened its eyes and stared up at her in a baby's sober, unfathomable way.

"Welcome to life, little one," she whispered, touching the baby's soft cheek with her finger, feeling a new rush of sweet emotion when the baby grabbed her finger in its tight fist.

After a moment Annie looked over to see that Medicine Woman had again settled Sits on a Cloud in her bed, and was feeding the girl another drink.

"Your daughter is beautiful," Annie said.

Sits on a Cloud managed a weak though radiant smile.

Medicine Woman turned to Annie. "You will take the child to see its father?"

Almost as if it had heard the question and protested being parted from its mother, the baby's little body tensed and it let out a wail. "But aren't you going to allow the baby to nurse and bond with its mother first?"

Medicine Woman appeared shocked. "The child may not nurse from its mother for four days. I will find another mother to nurture it until then. Such is Cheyenne tradition."

As the baby's cry threatened to become a high-pitched scream, Annie saw the exquisite yearning reflected on Sits on a Cloud's face. "But this is not right. These first few hours are when the child bonds with its mother. This should not be done with a stranger. Besides, I read once that the first secretions from the breast include many antibodies that the mother can transfer to the child."

"Antibodies?" repeated Medicine Woman, appearing bemused.

Annie struggled to explain this so that the healer could understand. "Powerful protection against evil spirits."

"Ah." Medicine Woman continued to mull this over as the child's wail reached a terrible, heart-wrenching keening and Annie failed to quiet her. Sits on a Cloud's features grew fraught with anguish. Finally, the healer turned to Sits on a Cloud and pronounced, "We shall try Future Woman's way. Perhaps she brings us wisdom from her world beyond the wind."

The new mother beamed and Annie's heart lit with gladness at this evidence that Medicine Woman believed her and was accepting her guidance. She carefully maneuvered on her knees across the tepee and placed the baby girl in her mother's arms. The child at once rooted to its mother's breast and grew content and quiet.

All three women's eyes shone with happy tears.

A while later, Annie emerged from the tepee carrying the infant, now peacefully asleep in her arms. The night had grown chill, and a snowflake tickled her nose.

Sits on a Cloud was resting in the tepee, while Medicine Woman gathered her potions. Annie was finally taking the child to meet its father.

Finding Red Shield was not difficult; Annie at once spotted him standing with Sam near the large fire at the center of the lodges. She also spotted Moon Calf hunkered down in the shadows near one of the tepees.

All three men silently watched her approach. She went directly to the husband. "Red Shield, you have a beautiful daughter, and Sits on a Cloud is well."

The warrior beamed and took the bundle from Annie's arms, staring down at the infant with a father's pride. "Little Fox will be pleased to have a sister."

Sam was watching the father with his child. "That's a right pretty young'un, Red Shield."

Red Shield nodded respectfully to Sam. "When she is grown, she will turn the heads of all our eligible warriors and demand a bride price of many fine horses."

"I reckon that 'un will fetch you in a herd," agreed Sam.

Red Shield extended the baby toward Annie. "You will take her now so I may see my bride?"

"Of course." Annie carefully accepted the child.

"I will return," the brave said.

Annie and Sam smiled at each other. "How was it tending the birth?" he asked.

She laughed. "I didn't do much tending, though I was deeply honored that Sits on a Cloud wanted me there for moral support." She sighed. "These are such simple people, Sam. They have such pride, dignity, and purpose. When Sits on a Cloud delivered her daughter, she cried out only once."

"The Cheyenne are stoic about pain."

"I find their various rites so interesting," she went on. "Ignorant people call them savages, yet they have a well-defined culture with all sorts of rituals and taboos."

"Kind of like white man and his ways, eh?"

Annie nodded. Staring down at the sleeping infant, she blinked at a tear, remembering her own family—the parents she'd lost, the brother she'd left behind in another century. She drew a quivering breath. "You know, when I watched this tiny, miraculous life emerge, it reminded me that I've missed out on some pretty basic things in my life. I've had . . . well, other priorities."

"It's not too late," he murmured.

She smiled sadly. "Perhaps. Though I've my doubts, considering the mess my life is in at the moment."

The two were staring at each other in uncertainty when Moon Calf tentatively approached Annie. She turned to see the sacred idiot's eyes filled with heart-rending yearning, his arms extended in entreaty.

"What does he want now?" Sam asked, tension in his voice.

"I think he wants the child—perhaps to bless it."

Sam scowled. "I ain't so sure about that."

But Annie relied on instinct and placed the child in Moon Calf's arms. The man gently accepted the baby and cuddled it protectively against his chest. Annie's heart caught in her throat as, for the second time, Moon Calf smiled.

Hoarsely, she addressed Sam. "Don't worry. He won't harm her. He knows how precious she is."

Sam fell silent as Moon Calf, cradling the infant in his arms, began to dance around the fire, his movements as delicate as those of a floating cloud. Large snowflakes began to fall, sizzling on the flames, creating a spooky aura in the night. Moon Calf glided about, singing an Indian chant, a song of joy and exultation. As the light of the fire caught his face, Annie spotted tears streaming down his bearded cheeks. In that moment, she could see his humanity, his frailty, his inner pain. If she lived to be a hundred, she would never forget that dear sight.

"Oh, Sam."

"I see, sugar." He caught her close, his arms trembling about her. "I reckon you're right about him. And I'm sorry for every unkind word I ever said to him."

They stood embraced, watching Moon Calf dance, hearing his soul-sweet song, all of them locked in a mystical moment beyond time and space. Sparks rose to the heavens as downy snowflakes blanketed the earth.

At last the sound of a neighing horse drew their attention from the celestial scene. Annie watched Red Shield approach, leading a magnificent pinto pony covered with a gorgeous beaded blanket and saddle.

Grinning broadly, the warrior extended the reins toward Annie. "In honor of my daughter's birth, I give you this horse."

She was flabbergasted. "Me? But I didn't do anything."

"My wife and Medicine Woman have agreed that our child must be named for you, Future Woman," he went on. "For this you must be honored."

Annie was already warmed to her soul to be called Future Woman by the People. To have the baby named after her was another great honor. Yet she still wasn't certain whether to accept the horse. Wavering, she glanced at Sam.

He leaned over and whispered at her ear. "Annie, it is Cheyenne tradition for a father to give away a horse when he is blessed with a baby. You don't have to do nothin' to deserve it, but it's an insult to refuse."

Grateful for the explanation, Annie turned to Red Shield. "I accept with pride. Thank you for the magnificent gift."

The brave grinned and handed her the reins. Moon Calf came forward, extending the baby toward Annie. Giving Sam the reins, she took the infant. "I'd best take her back to her mother now," Annie told the men. "Take care of my horse, Sam?"

"Sure, sugar," he replied.

Annie reached the birthing lodge just as Medicine Woman was emerging from it. "How is Sits on a Cloud?"

"She is fine. I must find Sam now."

Annie inclined her head toward the men. "He's over by the fire with the others. I'll sit with mother and baby while you're gone."

Medicine Woman nodded and walked off toward the men.

Sam spotted his grandmother's approach and came out to meet her, leading Annie's pony. "Hey, you sure done a fine job of bringing that baby into the world tonight," he said. "Red Shield gave Annie this fine horse in tribute."

A faint smile curved the old woman's lips. "I must speak with you about your woman, Grandson."

"Sure," he said. "Just let me tie up this pony and I'll join you at your lodge."

By the time Sam arrived at the tepee, Medicine Woman was seated outside by the fire, and the snow had tapered off. He plopped down beside her. "So, did you talk to Annie?"

"She spoke to me."

"And what do you think?"

Medicine Woman's sober gaze met Sam's. "I have pondered much the story your woman has told."

"And?" he asked tensely.

Medicine Woman frowned at Sam. "Grandson, why do you refuse to believe that which you do not understand?"

"I ain't sure I follow you," he replied with a scowl.

Medicine Woman stared into the flames. "I am wondering why you do not believe your woman. I have meditated long on this, and it is clear to me now that your Annie is telling the truth."

Sam grunted as if his gut had been punched. "You believe her?" he asked, stunned. "But what she says is plumb haywire."

Medicine Woman's expression grew deeply troubled. "Grandson, do you believe in our ways?"

Sam shrugged. "Well, I reckon so."

"You came here many moons ago as a young man. You rode with our warriors and starved yourself to see visions of our gods." Her features fraught with sadness, Medicine Woman shook her head. "Once, you were Tsistsistas, but I fear you have lost the connection with the Cheyenne in your soul. You have abandoned the world of the spirit."

Sam appeared deeply distressed, reaching out to touch his grandmother's gnarled hand. "If I've lost touch with the old ways, I didn't mean to."

"You refused to believe our sacred idiot when he told you where to find your woman," she pointed out.

"But didn't I listen when you urged me to heed Moon Calf's advice?"

"That is true," she conceded. "But now that you have brought your woman here, you refuse to see the truth beyond your own eyes."

Sam frowned over her words.

Passionately she continued. "Grandson, how can you claim to believe in the Wise One Above, the Place of the Dead, and the people who live under the water, yet not believe your woman has seen yet another place beyond our vision?" She gestured at the black heavens. "Look above you at the stars—how can you know what beings dwell there, in other worlds? Look around you at your brothers—see our life here. This band is lost in time. Why do you not believe your woman can be lost in time, too?"

Sam gazed up at the heavens, electrified by his grandmother's uncanny wisdom. "Well, I never quite thought of it like that."

"You must believe in your woman, or the two of you are doomed," advised the grandmother. "You love her, do you not?"

Sam smiled. "Oh, yes. I do."

"I can see it in your eyes when you look at each other. I know it is difficult for you to admit your mistakes, but you must listen to her story and believe. Pride and arrogance are a good path for the warrior, but a disastrous path for a husband and provider."

Sam mulled over Medicine Woman's dire pronouncement. "What can I do?" he asked at last.

"You must stand by her. You must go find the real Rotted Rosie and uncover the truth."

Sam fell silent. Could Medicine Woman be right? Had Annie been telling the truth all along? It seemed outrageous, yet he could not deny Medicine Woman's shrewd words, or his deepening feelings for Annie, which kept arguing that she was anything but a murderess.

Oh, Lord, if he *was* wrong, then no wonder Annie had held herself apart from him. He considered his own proud, stubborn behavior and groaned. Well, he was a man of honor, and if he truly had erred, then he'd just have to swallow his pride and set things right between them.

Chapter 26

*After a restless night spent at war with himself, Sam rose early and went for a ride around the lake. He galloped his horse through the cold morning mists, past towering pines and spruces along the water's edge. Hearing a chorus of ducks, he spied a flock of mallards sailing past on their way south.

His grandmother's words—"Your woman is telling the truth"—reverberated through his brain. It *was* hard for Sam to admit he might have been wrong about Annie up until now, that her outlandish tales of being from another time could be true.

Yet, hadn't he known for some time that she was different, honest and genuine, unlike the other desperadoes he'd apprehended? Still, he hadn't believed her—it had taken his grandmother's intervention to bring him to his senses. And to think he might have actually taken her to be hanged. The very possibility filled him with self-recrimination.

What were they to do now? He supposed, as his grandmother had advised, they needed to go to Rowdyville to investigate, to get to the bottom of the mystery surrounding the real Rotten Rosie. But, crazy though the notion seemed, that might mean he'd end up taking Annie's great-great-grandmother to justice, and if he did that, Annie might still hate him forever. He seemed damned every way he turned.

And Rosie was only the beginning of their troubles. If Annie truly had come from another time, wouldn't she

206

at some point want to return to her own world? The prospect seemed absurd—but so was her ability to move across time in the first place.

He groaned. All he wanted was to love her, as different as the two of them were, and even though, with the life he had chosen, he could offer no real permanency. But when he looked at the paths confronting them, it seemed that no matter what choices they made, he was destined to lose her.

Annie rose, dressed, and went to wash up at the lake. Before returning to camp, she stopped in at the birthing lodge to find mother and daughter blissfully asleep together. The sight of the baby dozing in Sits on a Cloud's arms tugged at Annie's heartstrings, arousing the same maternal instincts she had felt last night. She picked up the water skin and took it back to the lake, filling it with "living" water for Sits on a Cloud to have when she awakened.

After leaving the filled skin inside the new mother's lodge, Annie returned to camp, intending to fetch breakfast for her friend. Walking into the large central area, she gasped as she spotted most every other member of the band, including all of the children, Medicine Woman, and Moon Calf, seated in a large circle, eating breakfast together. All of them paused to stare at Annie.

Self-conscious, she approached Medicine Woman. "Why is everyone together so early?"

The old woman gestured toward a vacant spot beside her. "Please join us, Annie."

She did as bid. A smiling White Owl came forward with a bowl of porridge and a spoon, handing both to Annie; she accepted the food with a nod, yet hesitated to eat.

"You must break your fast," directed Medicine Woman.

"Could I take this to Sits on a Cloud instead? She has had no breakfast yet."

The old woman patted Annie's hand. "You are kind, but I think Sits on a Cloud needs much rest. There will be plenty left, and I will see to her needs later."

Annie began eating, feeling even more put on the spot as the others continued watching her. At last she protested to Medicine Woman. "Why is everyone staring at me?"

The old woman laughed. "By now they all know you are Future Woman. They would hear your stories of the world from which you come."

"My, news travels fast, doesn't it?"

"They are quietly waiting because it is considered rude to ask for a guest's story," continued Medicine Woman. "The decision is yours, of course."

Annie glanced about the circle at the many sets of dark eyes watching her with such avid expectation. She set down her empty bowl. "Well, if you put it that way . . . how can I refuse?"

Medicine Woman beamed her happiness, and then snapped her fingers. An adolescent boy came forward with a lit wooden pipe whose bowl had been carved in the shape of a bird. With a smile, the lad handed the pipe to Annie.

Annie glanced askance at Medicine Woman. "What am I supposed to do with this?"

"There is a ceremony to storytelling," Medicine Woman explained. "First you must take the pipe and perform *nivstanivoo*." She took the pipe from Annie and demonstrated, saluting each of the four directions in turn by first tapping the pipe on the ground, then raising it toward north, south, east, and west. "Can you do this?"

"I think so," muttered Annie.

"Good," declared Medicine woman, handing the pipe back to Annie. "Afterward you must smoke."

"Smoke?" Annie gasped.

The old woman grinned. "You must at least try, or your storytelling will not be blessed. Then you must pass your own hands over your arms, head, and legs. This is your prayer for guidance from our spirits, and your vow to speak truthfully."

With a nervous frown betraying her anxiety, Annie took the pipe and performed *nivstanivoo* as best she could, feeling very awkward as she tapped and pointed four times. Afterward, with a grimace, she raised the pipe to her lips and gagged on a couple of breaths of acrid smoke, much to the amusement of everyone else. After the mirth died down, she waved her hands over various parts of her body as instructed.

"Very good," said Medicine Woman, taking the pipe. "Now the stories may begin."

When Sam rode back into camp, it was to spot Annie standing at the center of a circle of enthralled Indians. Dismounting and approaching the group, he noted she held aloft two sticks tied together like a cross and was moving the apparatus through the air as she described to the others something she called an "airplane." He hovered just beyond the group, watching her. For an instant their eyes met, his questioning, hers uncertain. Then she lifted her chin and continued her lecture.

She spoke about vast highways as smooth as the surface of the lake, and lodges that stretched into the sky as far as the eye could see, and magical baskets that bore people upward to the top of the tall lodges. Every eye in the camp was riveted on her—even Sam became caught up in her astounding tales.

The group finally dispersed just before noon. Sam strode quickly to Annie's side. "We need to talk, sugar."

"Do we?" she asked.

Sam grinned sheepishly. "Come on, let's get out of here before someone else grabs you to hear more."

They walked up into the hills, not touching, each eyeing the other with unassuaged longing. At last, Annie cleared her throat. "Sits on a Cloud and her baby are doing well. I looked in on them this morning."

"I'm right pleased to hear it."

"Did you have a good ride?"

"Yep." He shoved his hands into his pockets. "I been doin' some thinkin', Annie."

"Yes?"

He smiled at her almost shyly. "You sure had the whole village captivated with your stories."

A defensive edge crept into her voice. "They're not stories. They're the truth. And your people believe me. I find I really connect with them."

"I know what you mean," Sam admitted. "I always felt the same way. Reckon it's my Indian blood."

Her reproachful gaze met his. "But you don't connect with me, Sam. Why can't you accept what I say as your brothers do?"

He groaned. "Annie, my brothers also believe in gods under the earth, water monsters, and folks that live in the lake."

"So what is your point?"

"I'm just saying that with their heritage, the way they believe, it's easier for them to accept your outlandish notions."

Her voice echoed with hurt. "Well, maybe they can just observe my face, or look into my eyes, and see I'm telling the truth—while you've always doubted me."

A look of pain crossing his features, Sam glanced away. "That's fair enough. I'll warrant I deserve the criticism."

She let out an incredulous breath. "What's this? The mighty Sam Noble displaying humility?"

He waved a hand. "Damn it, Annie, this ain't easy for me."

"Then why don't you tell me what's on your mind?"

He removed his hat and thrust his fingers through his hair. "I spoke with my grandma last night."

"Yes?"

He met her eye. "And she made me see you been tellin' the truth all along. You really are who you say you are—and Rosie's someone else."

A stunned gasp escaped Annie. She walked away a few paces, struggling within herself. On one level, she was grateful that Sam at last believed her—yet her pride argued that he should have all along, and this realization made her throat burn.

"So you've finally seen the light," she muttered.

"I'll admit I've been proud and stubborn," he went on, approaching her and laying a hand on her shoulder. "But I promise I'll believe you from now on if you'll just give me a chance."

Her expression wounded, she turned to him. "It

shouldn't have taken your grandmother to bring you to your senses."

"I know, sugar," he admitted. "I'm sorry. But you know the tale you told me was mighty strange."

Annie's mouth tightened.

Contrite, he reached out to caress her cheek. "Forgive me?"

She was quiet for a long moment. "You hurt me, Sam."

"I know." His thumb tenderly stroked her underlip. "I'm fixin' to take care of that, darlin'."

His words were charged with sexual meaning, and even his gentle touch unnerved Annie. Trying to swallow a knot of wounded pride, she pulled away. "Are you?"

Even as she backed away, he followed her, his intent gaze holding her riveted. "What do you want me to do, Annie? Should I swing myself from the torture pole?"

Fighting a smile, she reached out and ran her fingertips over his hard pecs. "And scar up that pretty chest? I don't think so."

He broke into a grin. "So you don't hate me completely."

"I never hated you, Sam."

He lifted her chin with his fingers and met her gaze solemnly. "What will it take to win your forgiveness?"

"Will you help me find my great-great-grandmother?"

He drew a heavy breath. "Sure, I reckon I'm willing, if you're set on it. But what if she really is guilty of murder and all them other crimes? What are we going to do then?"

She bit her lower lip. "You mean could I let you turn her in?"

He nodded.

"I don't know, Sam," she admitted honestly. "I guess it would depend on the circumstances."

Both fell silent, anguish stretching between them. At last he asked, "Is that what you really want, Annie?"

"Sam, I have to try to help her."

His voice shook with emotion. "Do you know what I want?"

"No."

He hauled her against him, tucking her head beneath his chin. "I want to keep you here forever. I don't know why I found you, sugar, though I'm blessed to have you. I do know that wherever we go from here, it's for damn sure gonna tear us apart."

His tormented words and tender nearness reached Annie, and her arms coiled around him. Oh, he smelled wonderful and felt so warm and strong holding her. And she feared he had spoken the truth, that they would be torn asunder if they proceeded as she wanted. She felt so tempted to take refuge in him, to hide from the world—indeed, from *both* their worlds—but that would never solve their problems.

"We can't just turn our backs on this, Sam."

"Why not? You like it here, don't you?"

"Well, yes, but—"

"You want me."

Annie's heart thundered in the explosive silence as Sam's gaze held hers. She didn't just want him—she was dying for him. She wanted to lose herself in their love and never let him go again.

Still, she sadly shook her head. "Sam, wanting you is not going to help my great-great-grandmother. And we've already wasted so much time. . . ."

His tone turned bitter. "You still gotta punish me, don't you?"

"No! That has nothing to do with it!"

He dug his fingers into her shoulders and spoke vehemently. "Don't it? You told me I couldn't have you 'cause I wouldn't believe you. Well, I believe you now, Annie, and I'm through waiting."

At his fierce, possessive words, something melted inside her. Even as she opened her mouth to speak, Sam's lips captured hers. Like sweet madness, desire jolted through her, her famished body coming alive with awareness of him, of how much she had missed him, of how desperately she needed him now. Sam felt it too, she knew—felt her mouth melding into his, her breasts seeking the heat of his chest, her pelvis arching to feel his hard erection.

With a tortured groan, he tumbled her down onto the soft pine needles with him, his mouth locked on hers in a deep, drugging kiss. His fingers made quick work of the buttons on her shirt. His lips moved feverishly down her throat, to her breast. He gently tongued her tautened nipple. She winced in pleasure.

"Say you forgive me, Annie," he said hoarsely. "I want to hear it from your lips—*now*."

"I do, Sam. I forgive you," she answered in choked tones.

"It's settled. It's behind us. You understand?"

"Yes."

He pulled back, staring down into her brimming eyes as he worked the buttons at her waist. He smiled. "How come you're always cryin' when we do this?"

She curled her arms about his neck. "I'm just so happy, Sam."

"Oh, sugar."

Annie pulled Sam's lips down to hers, sank her fingers into his hair, and pushed her tongue inside his mouth, inviting him to take her. Her encouragement was all he needed, and she felt his confident hands pulling down her jeans. A mighty shudder rippling through him, he claimed her in a deep, sure stroke. She moaned in ecstasy, feeling a profound sense of healing at the riveting joining.

"It don't hurt now, does it, sugar?" he whispered raggedly, his hands slipping beneath her to raise her into his devouring thrusts. "It don't hurt now. . . ."

"You're wrong," she sobbed back, kissing his hair, his face. "It's so wonderful, it hurts."

"Oh, Annie."

She clung to him. Never had she felt such sweet, devastating rapture. For an exquisite eternity she rode the crest of a passion so glorious she could not bear it. Sam kissed her breasts, suckling her tight nipple with his hot mouth. She cried out and bucked against him, enhancing her own pleasure as he plunged deeper. At the instant of their shared climax she was left wondering how she had ever resisted him, and through it all she felt certain that if she ever lost him, she would die.

Chapter 27

〜〜⚬GᗅᏚ〜〜

"So where do we go from here, Sam?" Annie asked.

Late that evening after the rest of the band had retired, the two lingered by the central fire, huddling together in the chill night. Annie exulted in being close to Sam, for the balance of the day had been very special for them both. They had made love for most of the afternoon, returning to camp late in the day, still slightly disheveled, with pine needles in their hair. Annie had stopped off to visit with Sits on a Cloud and her baby before the evening meal. After the feast, Annie had again entertained the band with tales of life in the next century.

The hours had been wonderful, but the dilemma facing her and Sam had never been far from her mind. Now she eyed him searchingly as he stared into the flames.

"Do you want to leave?" he asked.

She gazed off at the incredible heavens—black skies and glittering stars framed by snowy Rockies peaks. "I'll admit it's wonderful here. I think I could stay and become an Indian myself."

"You could?" he asked in pleasant surprise.

She nodded. "This simple, natural life appeals to the side of me that misses my youth back on the ranch." Her tone took on an edge of pain. "But then, you don't know much about that side of me, or my life before we met."

He clutched her hand and beseeched her with eyes filled with regret. "Annie, I feel like I know you in the

214

ways that really count. I know you're beautiful, proud, and passionate, good, honest, and kind. I know you give me your soul when we make love. As for your life before we met, you're right, I'm mostly ignorant about that part of you. But we're gonna change that. I was wrong before not to listen. Now I do want to understand everything about you. You just gotta give it some time."

Moved by his heartfelt speech, she reached out, ruffling his hair. "After this afternoon, how can I refuse?"

He wrapped an arm about her shoulders, and they sat in quiet companionship as a wind whipped through the tepees and a coyote began to howl in the distance.

"We still got to decide what we're gonna do, sugar," Sam continued gently. "Whether we're gonna stay here, or—"

"I know," she agreed. "I love this village, but how can I remain, knowing my great-great-grandmother is in such a mess? Besides which, Sits on a Cloud will be leaving the birthing lodge soon. I need to vacate her tepee so she and her family can be back together."

He nodded. "You want to head out in a day or so?"

"Head out and do what?"

"Go to Rowdyville. Try to save your grandma—if we can."

"And how will we do that? Has it occurred to you that my striking resemblance to the real Rosie is not exactly an asset?"

He chuckled, tweaking her chin. "Yeah, I been thinking 'bout that. I'm known in those parts, too, leastwise 'round Central, where I do work for Judge Righteous. Reckon we'll both need a disguise so as not to arouse suspicion."

"What are you suggesting?"

A devilish expression crept over Sam's features. "You know, it's funny, sugar. I keep thinkin' 'bout that preacher's family we run across—and the days when I was still a boy and used to ride along with Grandpa on his circuit."

Annie went wide-eyed. "Are you suggesting what I think you're suggesting?"

He grinned. "Who would suspect a revival preacher and his wife of doin' somethin' underhanded or suspicious? 'Sides which, I heard many a time that Royce Rowdy, bully though he be, has a right pious streak. He wouldn't dare shoot a preacher."

Annie chuckled; she had to admit the prospect was both inspired and intriguing. "Well, I suppose you've got a point. Still, you, a preacher . . ."

"And why can't I be a preacher?" he demanded.

"I suppose you're self-righteous enough," she agreed, her features filled with repressed merriment.

He shook a finger at her. "Woman, you're fixin' to get your butt blistered."

She wrinkled her nose at him. "The day you whip my butt, Sam Noble, is going to be one cold day in hell."

Sam laughed. "That sounds like the day I found you."

Annie had to agree, and rewarded Sam's insight with a kiss. They discussed his brilliant plan long into the night.

Two days later, they parted from the band with great emotion. That chill morning, every member of the small camp arose to bid them farewell at the corral; many brought gifts of food or jewelry.

First Moon Calf stepped forward, solemnly presenting Annie with a charm he had fashioned from sage and multicolored bird feathers. Although he did not speak, Annie could tell from his anguished expression that he was aware she and Sam were leaving. She thanked him, smiled, and touched his hand, and was moved that he didn't recoil. Then she was distracted as Medicine Woman stepped up to give her a beautiful multicolored beaded necklace, and White Owl brought a pouch filled with pemmican.

Next, a smiling Sits on a Cloud came forward with her infant. Annie held the baby for a long moment before returning the child to her mother and giving the squaw a fond hug. She noted that Sits on a Cloud's coloring was excellent, and she showed no signs of having borne a baby only days before.

"Thank you for all your kindnesses toward me," Annie told her friend sincerely.

The other woman squeezed Annie's hand. "May the Wise One Above guide your journeys."

Annie had to smile as she remembered old Windfoot saying the same words to her back in the present. "Thank you. May he protect you and your beautiful family, too."

As the squaw moved away with her baby, Annie glanced over to watch Sam give his grandmother a last hug, then turn and shake hands with Whip. At last his gaze met hers; he nodded, and they went toward their horses.

Annie mounted the magnificent pinto mare Red Shield had given her; Sam had left her other horse in Whip Whistler's care. As the two rode off for the hillside, she glanced back at the many dark eyes watching them; in particular, Moon Calf's emotional stare kindled poignant feelings within her.

"Will the band be all right?" she asked Sam.

"I reckon so. If you like, we can come back and check on them as soon as our business is finished."

"*If* I come back," Annie muttered.

Sam glanced at her sharply. "What do you mean by that?"

"Well, maybe I'm a trifle daunted by the prospect of meeting my own great-great-grandmother. It is quite a paradox, you know."

"What is that?"

"A paradox is a puzzlement, an enigma, something that defies logic."

"Well, you certainly defy logic, sugar," he agreed.

She pulled a face.

He went on more seriously. "What you mean is, it don't make no sense, both you and your great-great-grandma being in the same time and 'bout the same age, when reason argues if you're here, she can't be here. One a'you oughta be dead."

Annie blanched. "Perish the thought. But you're right, our meeting does break all the laws of time and space. What if one of us does disappear?"

Sam shook his head. "Sugar, you say the gall-durnedest things. Ain't you been tellin' me all along that you've got to help her?"

"That's what my instincts keep arguing," Annie admitted with a frown. "I'll just have to pray I'm right."

"Well, if you want to know the truth, this whole business gives me the willies, too," Sam commented with grave concern. "It's dangerous, and seems to me there's plenty of ways I could lose you."

She fell silent a moment. "How long will it take us to get to Rowdyville?"

"I reckon a day or so." He stroked his jaw. "I haven't shaved in a spell—"

"I've noticed."

"So you're bellyaching again?"

She giggled.

"Anyhow, it's for the best that I have a beard—short, but enough to cover my face."

"Ah, yes—our disguises."

"Before we get there, we'll need to stop off at Georgetown, rent a buggy, and buy some respectable clothing." His frowning gaze roved over the shirt and jeans she wore. "You reckon you could make yourself up as a preacher's wife?"

"Oh, I imagine with some black hair dye, a severe hairstyle, and some drugstore glasses, I could give it a good try."

He chuckled. "'Spect you'll need a black silk dress or two."

"Well, I thought that went without saying. That's the standard preacher's wife's uniform, right?"

"And we'll need different names." He scowled a moment. "How 'bout I'll be the Reverend Lemuel Prophet and you'll be my wife, Rebecca?"

"Sounds pretty pious to me."

"I don't suppose you play the piano?" he asked hopefully.

"Nope, I'm tone-deaf. You're out of luck there."

"Well, I reckon we'll make out."

"Now, if you need a world-class barrel racer, I'm your gal," she went on with a grin.

He scowled. "What's barrel racing?"

"Back in the future when I was a teenager, I never missed a major rodeo in Texas. Barrel racing is when you negotiate your horse through an obstacle path of barrels. I won many a blue ribbon in the event."

"Well, that's a talent that might come in handy if we need to leave Rowdyville in a hurry," he commented wryly.

She laughed. "True—I'd likely not mow too many people down."

He fell silent. At last, he spoke with surprising humility. "Annie, tell me more about yourself."

She stared at him, taken aback. "What do you mean?"

"I want to know about your other life, your other world, how you grew up—everything about you."

Annie laughed ruefully. "This has been a long time coming."

His anguished expression beseeched her. "Annie, you know I couldn't afford to ask before—I couldn't become involved. But now I am involved—damn glad to be involved—and you know I believe you, honey."

Annie purred with delight. "Oh, bounty hunter, you're a charmer. When you call me honey it makes my insides melt."

He grinned. "Wanna stop?"

"Do you want a quickie or to hear my story?"

"What's a quickie?"

"We'll do the story," she decided primly.

Annie launched on a long discourse, telling Sam all about her life in the future—growing up on the ranch, gaining her education and beginning her career, losing her parents, her troubles with her brother.

"So you're an orphan except for this Larry?" he asked.

"Yes." She sighed. "In fact, I've been very worried about my brother ever since you brought me here."

He regarded her compassionately. "It musta been real hard on you, losing both your parents."

She nodded. "It's funny, but you kind of remind me of my dad."

He laughed. "Do I?"

Annie's eyes gleamed with pride. "He was a real

rugged individualist, what we called a good old boy back in my time."

"You mean kind of like them legendary ranch hands you told me about?"

She laughed. "Precisely. But I'm afraid my father and men like him have become something of a dying breed. So many of the younger men I met back in the present were—well, urbanized, homogenized."

He frowned. "Don't know what you mean by them words, but I'm right glad that type of man ain't your preference."

Wrinkling her nose at him, Annie continued her discourse, telling him how she'd bought the ghost town. She explained how the venture had become a debacle, with both her contractor and her brother bailing out on her.

When she told him about her legal problems with the Cheyenne and her meeting with old Windfoot, he chuckled. "Hey, that's funny. My middle name is Windfoot."

"You're kidding!"

"Nope. My full name is Samuel Windfoot Noble."

"Do you think you're related to the old codger?"

Sam shrugged. "I kind of doubt it, though Windfoot is a common enough name among my grandma's people."

She regarded him saucily. "Well, Mr. Samuel Windfoot Noble, maybe I need to take you back to the present with me to plead my cause to the Cheyenne." She paused, shaking her head. "Heck, for all I know, my court date may have already passed back in the present, and perhaps my ghost town has already been awarded to the Silver Wind band."

He paled.

"Sam, what's wrong?"

He hesitated before speaking. "Well, it's just odd, I reckon. A few of my grandma's kinsmen are from the Silver Wind band."

"My God!" she exclaimed. "I *do* need to take you back with me to the future!"

He chuckled. "Do you reckon I'd fit in there?"

Annie had to admit the prospect was intriguing. "Oh, I'm sure the citizens of the late twentieth century would find you fascinating. Between your nineteenth-century frontier outlook, your roping and shooting skills, your crusty jargon, and your self-righteous streak—"

"*What* self-righteous streak?" he demanded, glowering.

She rolled her eyes. "Who was it that only two weeks ago was lecturing me on reaping what I sowed and bad girls meeting a bad end? For a big, sexy cowboy, you can be a real prig, Sam."

"A prig? Woman, you're gonna pay for that insult!"

She straightened her cuffs. "I think it's time for me to continue with the story of my life, thank you."

"Please do," he all but growled.

Annie finished with her discourse, telling him everything that had happened to her up until the time he had nabbed her from Deadend.

"That's quite an account," he admitted at last. "And what it means is—"

"Yes?"

He stared at her in awe. "I rode across time to get you, didn't I, Annie?"

"You sure did."

"We were meant to be together."

"Indeed we were."

"Are we meant to stay together?"

"I hope so, Sam."

For a moment they gazed at each other in uncertainty. "You know, it's strange," he muttered. "I don't recall crossing time."

She chortled. "Do you think they put up signposts like they do for the railroads: 'Time Crossing Zone—Proceed with Extreme Caution'?"

He fought a grin.

"It was the wind, silly."

"The wind? You mean that razor-backed blue norther that was a'howlin' the day I come for you?"

She nodded soberly. "I think it's the force that conveyed you across time to me and brought us back here together."

"Then there really is a purpose in our being together."

"Indeed there is."

He scratched his stubbled jaw. "But one thing still troubles me."

"Yes?"

He regarded her with torment and uncertainty. "You're here for a reason, Annie, but you belong to another time. When this is over . . . well, you ain't told me nothing to convince me I ain't gonna lose you."

Chapter 28

~~~~~OO~~~~~

Annie's first impression of Rowdyville hovered somewhere between amusement and horror.

With Sam driving the buggy they'd rented in nearby Georgetown, they plodded down the steep, muddy main street of the small burg, which was nestled high in an Alpine pass between snow-capped mountains. Glancing at Sam, Annie mused that no one would guess from his sober black suit, matching hat, and short, neat beard that he was a bounty hunter, and no one could have known from her severe hairstyle, her large horn-rimmed glasses, her black cloak, bonnet, and gloves, that she had once been his quarry. Annie did feel rather silly in her disguise, as well as uncomfortable in her tight corset, although she had to admit she was proud of the pretend wedding band she wore on her left hand beneath her glove. Sam had bought her the ring during their stopover; they'd also purchased the clothing and Bible needed for their masquerade.

Last night they'd made love out on the trail, lying beneath breathtaking starry skies, holding each other close all night long. Annie shivered with delight at the memories. She and Sam had clung together almost feverishly, neither daring to voice all the doubts in their hearts. But Annie was well aware that both of them were preoccupied with anxieties regarding this expedition to find the real Rosie.

Seeing the community of Rowdyville firsthand gave

her further reason for doubt. On either side of the mud street were strewn several ramshackle saloons, a weathered general store with sagging stoop, a small apothecary, and a modest boardinghouse. Although the town possessed both a telegraph office and a small bank, there was not a church or a jail in sight. The boardwalks were cluttered with the most unsavory-looking characters: scruffy, bowlegged cowboys with Colts ambled along; fallen angels brazenly flaunted their paint, satin, and feathers; flashy men in black sported bullet-studded belts and pearl-handled revolvers that proclaimed them to be either gunfighters or gamblers.

In the street, they passed a grizzled old prospector leading his burro and a peddler in his bright yellow bandwagon. As they approached one of the saloons, Annie was stunned to watch a drover gallop out the doors on horseback! While the confused animal reared and snorted, the drunken rider hollered and waved his gun before riding off.

Eyes enormous, Annie turned to Sam. "My God, this is Sodom!"

He chuckled. "Where's your sense of adventure, sugar?"

"This promises to be a real roller-coaster ride, all right," she replied drolly.

"It's Saturday—I reckon the cowhands are a mite unruly." Sam frowned. "You want to stay somewheres else tonight and come back tomorrow?"

"No, let's bite the bullet now," Annie replied with bravado. "What better time to march into one of those saloons and organize a revival? We need to catch those sinners in the act, don't we?"

He chuckled. "Now you're talkin', though I'll be keeping a watchful eye on you." He gestured toward the saloon from which the rider had emerged. "I reckon we'd best start at the Rowdy Roost. I've heard tell it's Royce Rowdy's main haunt."

"Hmmmm . . . From the looks of the place, Mr. Rowdy and company may not take too kindly to the idea of you organizing a revival."

He regarded her with new concern. "Yeah, sugar, you

got a point. Maybe we should settle you into the board-inghouse first."

She glowered. "Not on your life, Sam Noble! If you can brave the lions, so can I."

His face lit with pride. "That's my girl."

Sam halted the buggy in the street, tucked his Bible under his arm, and came around to Annie's side to offer her a hand. Before they even set foot on the boardwalk, Annie could smell and hear the saloon—her ears were assaulted by bawdy laughter and a tinny version of "Camptown Races," and her nostrils quivered in dis-taste at the odors of flat beer and stale tobacco.

They stepped through the double doors into the kind of scene that had obviously given Rowdyville its name. A haze of smoke cloyed the air, and bullet holes riddled the walls. On a small stage, three hurty gurty gals in skimpy red-and-white striped costumes strutted about in a line, while beneath them two drunkards wrestled on the floor amid an overturned spittoon. Beyond them, three bearded Spaniards in sombreros were playing monte while at the other tables, drovers and prospectors indulged their fancies for everything from poker to blackjack to keno. Practically beneath Annie's nose, a bearded old mountain man was pawing the voluptuous soiled dove he held on his lap; Annie wondered how she could bear his rank odor of sweat, dirt, and soured whiskey, not to mention the chewing tobacco spittle on his beard.

She was soon distracted as Sam hauled out his Colt and fired three shots into the ceiling. Gasps rippled over the room, followed by stunned silence as dozens of belligerent eyes focused in his direction. The piano player scrambled off his stool, and the girls on the stage also beat a hasty retreat.

Annie stared at Sam in horror, wondering if he had lost his mind. Still, she had to admire his daring as he stood there proudly facing down the rabble, his features a picture of righteous indignation.

He held up his Bible and his voice boomed out, filled with fire and brimstone. "Repent, sinners, or God shall smite you as surely as he rained fire on Sodom and

Gomorrah. The Good Book says, 'Seek the Lord, and ye shall live.' "

Sam's words packed so much power, they sent a shiver down Annie's spine. For a moment the crowd did not react, the male customers regarding him with caution or confusion. Then a surly voice called out, "Hey, preacher, why don't you leave us be, and go pound your Bible somewheres else?"

Raucous laughter erupted, and the men quickly ignored Sam's presence and returned to their various amusements. Glancing at Sam, Annie watched him tremble in apparent indignation, and wondered what he would do next.

He targeted the man who had spoken out, a pockfaced miner with mean, bloodshot eyes. Sam charged across to the man's table and kicked it over, sending cards, money, drinks, and liquor bottles crashing in all directions, and forcing the miner and his two companions to scramble to their feet.

Eyeing the furious men, Annie was convinced she and Sam had about ten seconds left to live.

Yet her lover's audacity continued to astound her. " 'The soul that sinneth, it shall die!' " Sam quoted to the men with eyes breathing fire. "I expel you, sinner, just as Jesus banished the money changers from the temple!"

With a grim silence hanging over the assemblage, Annie wondered if the ragtag throng would heed Sam's words or shoot them both. The miner who had challenged Sam appeared primed for murder, his gnarled fingers twitching near his holstered revolver.

All at once the focus shifted to a tall, middle-aged man who walked through the crowd toward Sam. Balding and slightly paunchy, wearing black pants, a white shirt with red bow tie, and a black satin vest accented by a gold watch fob, the man moved with an assured stride that bespoke wealth and authority. His long face was cleanshaven, but sagging jowls and baggy eyes attested to his dissipation; his thin lips were curled in a smile, but something about his dark, nearly black eyes gave Annie pause. It was almost as if she could see through to his soul, but there was no soul there. Watching him approach Sam, she restrained a shudder and protectively approached her "husband."

The man turned to address the crowd. "All right, folks, the excitement's over."

As the men mumbled among themselves and resumed their gambling, the man focused his attention on Sam and Annie. "Howdy, neighbors," he drawled in a mild tone laced with an underlying menace. He nodded toward Sam's holstered gun. "Have we done something to offend you, stranger?"

Sam drew himself up with dignity. "Who am I addressing?"

"I'm Royce Rowdy and this here is my saloon you're bustin' up."

Sam regarded Rowdy sternly. "Well, Mr. Rowdy. Pardon me, but it appears this saloon already has enough holes in it to roost pigeons. I ain't intendin' to damage your property, but I must speak the Word in the presence of evil."

The man chuckled, studying Sam with grudging admiration. "You a Bible-puncher?"

Wrapping an arm about Annie's shoulders, Sam faced Rowdy with dignity. "I'm Reverend Lemuel Prophet, and this here's my bride, Sister Rebecca."

Rowdy glanced at Annie, and she felt a twinge of anxiety as a slow, speculative frown gripped his features. "Have we met, ma'am?"

Despite a suddenly racing heart, Annie maintained a cool facade. "I think not," she answered archly.

Rowdy shrugged, then addressed Sam. "What brings you folks to these parts?"

Sam's features shone with pride. "Why, preachin' the gospel to the prospector on his hillside, the drover out on his range, the farmer at his soddy, even the heathen Indian out on the prairie."

Rowdy appeared intrigued. "You a revivalist, eh?"

"I consider it my mission to save the godless masses."

Rowdy turned to a drover who sat nearby. "Been quite a spell since we've had a preacher hereabouts, eh, Jed?"

"That's shore right, boss," answered Jed, sipping whiskey.

"So, tell me, Mr. Rowdy, do you want to be saved?" Sam asked.

Rowdy's gaze narrowed on Sam, and his voice took on an edge of annoyance. "What makes you think I ain't already been baptized?"

Sam gestured expansively. "Well, this here town has no church, and you're clearly running a den of iniquity."

"Or maybe I'm just givin' the good Lord a helping hand," Rowdy suggested with a sly grin.

"By harboring harlots, drunkards, and gamblers?" Sam inquired in outrage.

Rowdy threw back his head and laughed. "Well, preacher, the heathen can't be saved till they've had their fill of sin. Maybe I'm just easing them along the way."

"Then you won't object if I come back here tomorrow to preach the gospel?" Sam asked, seizing the advantage.

Rowdy hesitated for a long moment.

"You've provided all of Satan's temptations," Sam went on in charged tones. "Surely you won't deny these pitiful transgressors a chance at heaven?"

Glancing about at the sea of "sinners," Rowdy chuckled. "You know, I like you, preacher. You're a right entertaining and enterprising fellow."

"Then let me enlighten all of you at services tomorrow."

His expression sly, Rowdy waved a hand in acquiescence. "Heck, preacher, long as you do your pontificatin' before noon, when the saloon doors open, why should I care? I might even come by to hear you. Should prove amusing."

Though a muscle twitching in his jaw betrayed his annoyance, Sam eagerly shook the other man's hand. "You've got yourself a deal, Mr. Rowdy. May I make an announcement?"

"Be my guest."

Sam strode purposefully through the crowd toward the stage, drawing curious stares in his wake. The hurty gurty gals scampered away long before he hopped onto the platform.

He turned and leveled his grim visage on the crowd. "Brothers and sisters, heed my call!"

Though it took a moment, every voice in the room at last fell silent.

Holding up his Bible, Sam announced, "The Good Book says, 'Ye serpents, ye generation of vipers, how can ye escape the damnation of hell?'"

As he paused for dramatic effect, a voice called out, "Amen, preacher!"

Despite scattered snickers, Sam continued. "Only through salvation can you escape that lake of everlasting fire. Judgment Day is coming, and it'll be here before you know it, brothers and sisters. All those who wish to escape God's wrath, be here tomorrow morning at eleven o'clock to hear the Word."

This time, scattered applause erupted as Sam hopped down from the stage, went to grab Annie's hand, and escorted her out of the saloon.

Chapter 29

"Whew!" Annie whispered to Sam out on the boardwalk. "For a moment I didn't think we'd get out of there with our hides intact."

"Ah, it wasn't so bad," he said, assisting her into the buggy.

Annie rolled her eyes. "What do you mean, it wasn't bad? You walk in there bold as brass, overturning tables and announcing everyone's been damned to hell, then expect that gang of miscreants to accept it all in good grace?"

Hopping in beside her, Sam chuckled and worked the reins.

"On top of that, I was scared to death Royce Rowdy might have noticed my resemblance to Rosie."

Sam considered this with a frown. "Yeah, he seemed taken aback for a moment, but I think you passed muster."

"Well, I can't believe you're being so cavalier about everything."

He spoke sternly. "Annie, I ain't bein' cavalier. Matter of fact, I'm worried about your safety. But if we're gonna pull off this masquerade, it's going be through sheer daring."

"Yes, I suppose you have a point. . . ." She paused, her expression perplexed. "Why do you think Rowdy is letting you preach tomorrow?"

Sam reined in the horses in front of the boarding

house. "I ain't rightly sure, though I've heard he's partial to preachers. My guess is, he wants somethin'."

Annie nodded. "I think he finds you intriguing and diverting, and when he becomes bored, he may just shoot us both."

"Well, he's shootin' you over my dead body."

Quite possibly, Annie mused grimly.

Taking his Bible, Sam climbed out of the buggy and strode around to her side. "Come on, sugar, let's get a room."

She dubiously eyed the small, ramshackle boarding house, with its peeling paint and pots of drooping petunias on the porch windowsills. "What if they don't have one?"

He winked, shoving the Bible under his arm and pulling their two bags out of the boot of the buggy. "We'll try the saloon. Maybe one of them line gals has an extry bunk up in her crib."

"Oh, you're impossible!"

Carrying the bags, Sam followed Annie up the sagging stoop of the plain, Greek Revival–style house. His knock was answered by a plump woman who appeared to be around thirty. Her face was flushed, glossy with sweat. Her brown hair was coiffed in a bun, from which numerous damp tendrils spilled free. She wore a dark blue broadcloth dress and a food-stained apron.

"May I help you, sir?" she asked breathlessly, glancing from the newcomers to their luggage.

"Yes, ma'am." Sam shifted his Bible and gave the woman a moment to notice it. "I'm Reverend Lemuel Prophet and this is my bride, Sister Rebecca. Since we're staying over so's I can lead a revival and preach to the heathens hereabouts, I was hoping you might have a room to let."

The woman let out a gasp of delight and clapped her hands. "Oh, a preacher! My, my, we haven't had your likes around these parts ever since Stinky Hacker up and shot the circuit rider." Watching her guests' faces pale, the woman laughed and waved a hand. "Don't fret, folks. Stinky was a bad-tempered drunkard, but thank God he ate some rancid pork and passed on last spring."

Quashing a smile at her droll humor, Sam replied cordially, "In that case, the wife and I are mighty pleased to be here."

"But it's a flat shame we're full up," the woman continued with an apologetic frown.

"Is there no place for us?" Annie asked.

Their hostess pondered this, then burst into a smile. "Well, I suppose you could have my brother's room in the attic. Dick's off prospecting right now. I'm sure he won't mind, you doin' the good Lord's work and all."

Sam removed his hat. "We'd be mighty obliged, ma'am."

The plump woman stepped back and opened the door wide. "Now, where are my manners? Come on in, you two. I'm Dolly Dumble and I'm right proud to have you here!"

Sam retrieved their luggage, and Annie preceded him inside a barren but cleanly swept central hallway. The comforting aroma of chicken simmering toward the back of the house eased her anxieties about staying here.

"Your room is this way," Dolly called.

With Dolly in the lead, the three proceeded past a parlor filled with rocking chairs and a black horsehair settee, then up two flights of stairs. By the time they wended their way up a third spiral of twisting, narrow steps that obviously led to the attic, Dolly was huffing and puffing.

"Sorry you folks have to be all the way up here, but Dick likes his privacy."

"No problem, ma'am, we do, too," answered Sam dryly.

Annie tossed him a chiding look over her shoulder, but the rogue only grinned.

They followed Dolly inside a drab but spacious attic room, with an iron double bed, a plain dressing table, and a boxy-looking maple bureau. Sunlight spilled in through the front windows, the soft beams illuminating a small eating table with two ladder-back chairs.

Though the accommodations were austere, Annie noted that the bedding and curtains looked fresh, and the bare floor appeared recently swept. In one corner were piled items that obviously belonged to Dolly's prospector brother—a stack of faded shirts and dungarees, a rusted-out wash pan and gritty shovel, a bucket filled with what appeared to be dime novels.

Setting down the bags, Sam glanced about the room with an approving smile. "This'll do right fine, ma'am," he informed Dolly, taking out his wallet. "How much do I owe you?"

She waved him off with a plump hand. "Oh, no sir, I can't take money off'n a preacher. The least I can do is give you and your wife free room and board, you leadin' the revival and all. Why, it's my Christian duty."

"That's right kindly of you, ma'am," Sam replied. "And I'm sure the good Lord will take due note."

Moving over and opening the window, Dolly gazed down at their horses and buggy in the street. "But if you want to give me four bits, I'll have Zach—he's sort of my handyman—take your rig down to the stable and see your horses is tended."

Sam dug in his pocket and handed Dolly two coins. "Much obliged, ma'am."

She accepted the money with a smile. "Heck, we're the ones who are blessed to have you here in Rowdyville, Reverend. I warn you, this is a mighty godless place."

Annie stifled a smile as she watched Sam stick his thumbs inside his vest pockets and fairly preen like a peacock. "Well, ma'am, that's the reason the good wife and me are here, to minister to Rowdyville's sinners."

"Bless you, Reverend. You know, Dick and me used to live in Central and attend Saint James Methodist Church." She sighed heavily. "I sure miss playing the piano for them fine folks."

Sam and Annie exchanged a meaningful glance. Then he asked, "Ma'am, would you be willing to play for us at services tomorrow?"

She clapped her hands. "Why, I'd be right proud! Where will church be held?"

"At the Rowdy Roost," Annie put in.

The woman's hands flew to her face. "The saloon!"

Sam feigned a grim countenance. "We have to minister to the sinner in his den, do we not, Sister Dolly?"

"Well, I suppose." She brightened. "Don't worry, Reverend, I'll be there good and early with my hymnal. Maybe some of them soiled doves Royce Rowdy roosts in his hellhole will repent of their evil doin's and give 'The Old Rugged Cross' a chance. You may be sure there'll be no strutting about to 'Buffalo Gals' while Dolly Dumble is at the piano."

"We're counting on you, ma'am," agreed Sam.

Dolly flashed both her guests a smile. "Oh, I can hardly wait! Now if you folks want supper, it'll be served in the kitchen at five. Or, if you're right tuckered, I could bring you up a tray."

Sam glanced at Annie, and she repressed a smile at the mischief dancing in his eyes. To Dolly, he intoned soberly, "We'd be mighty obliged if you'd fetch up our vittles, ma'am. You see, I do need to work on my sermon."

Dolly made a sound of dismay. "But of course. How thoughtless I am! I'm keeping you from studying your Good Book, ain't I, Reverend? Well, I'll bring up supper for you folks just before five."

"Thank you kindly, ma'am."

Beaming, Dolly swept out in a rustle of voluminous skirts.

Tugging off her gloves and tossing them on the dresser, Annie rolled her eyes at Sam. "Work on your sermon, indeed! Shame on you for taking advantage of that poor woman—conning her out of free room and board, not to mention a supper tray."

Sam laughed, striding to Annie's side and pulling her into his arms. "That 'poor woman' is having the time of her life and you know it."

"Well, she is an effusive sort, I'll admit. But I do feel guilty for imposing. I thought she would pass out after leading us up three flights of stairs."

"What's the alternative, sugar? We need a respectable place to stay. We can't give away our disguises, can we?"

"No, but the supper tray was too much," Annie scolded. "We should go downstairs, mingle with the other boarders, try to find out what we can regarding Rosie—"

He held up a hand. "All in good time, sugar. Reckon breakfast'll be soon enough for us to meet the other boarders."

"But what are we going to do in the meantime?"

An ardent gleam burning in his eyes, Sam ran a hand up and down Annie's spine and inclined his head toward the bed. His voice took on a husky note. "Well, sugar, it occurs to me that's a mighty fine-looking feather tick, and it's been almost eight hours since I've made love to you."

"Sam!" Annie protested, even as her heart hammered with anticipation. "They'll hear us downstairs!"

"Naw," he replied with a chuckle, reaching out to remove her horn-rimmed glasses. "They'll own it up to religious fervor."

"You are incorrigible!"

Yet Annie was laughing as Sam untied the ribbons on her black silk bonnet. He leaned over and nestled his warm lips against her throat. "Besides, you look so damn prim, I'm hankerin' to undo you."

"Well, to tell you the truth, I *am* dying to get out of this corset," she admitted with a groan.

"Ma'am, I'll be happy to oblige." Grinning, Sam pulled her to the bed with him, and they landed side by side on the feather tick. He gazed down into her eyes. "Know what I love about this, Annie?"

"What?" she asked breathlessly.

He raised her left hand to his mouth and solemnly kissed the finger with the wedding band. "Pretending you're mine."

"Oh, Sam." Her heart melting, she curled her arms around his neck.

Sam continued to regard her thoughtfully as he pulled the pins from her hair. "Sometimes, I get so afraid—"

"Of what?" she cut in. "I thought you weren't afraid of anything."

"I'm afraid of losing you," he admitted. "And maybe just a little scared I'll lose myself in you."

She gazed up at him starkly. "Then you still have a choice. I'm already a goner."

A look of fierce tenderness crossed his face. He uttered

her name in a groan as their lips met hungrily. He thrust
his fingers into her hair, holding her mouth to his. A
moment later his impatient fingers began unfastening
the many tiny buttons on her bodice. She sat up, sighing
in relief when he untied her corset, then punching him
playfully when he chuckled and tossed the corset on the
floor. She unbuttoned his vest and shirt and caressed his
muscled chest, leaning over to kiss his smooth flesh and
the tufts of dark, sexy hair. He pushed her camisole aside
and ran his lips over a shapely breast. Annie quivered
with delight as her nipple hardened beneath his skilled
mouth. Currents of desire sizzled down her body to
settle deep inside her, and her back arched in ecstasy.

She smiled as she felt Sam's hand sliding beneath her
skirts, his fingers reaching for the tie on her drawers. She
slipped her hand between their bodies, wantonly caressing him through his trousers, delighting at his tortured
grunt.

"Getting impatient, are you, cowboy?" she teased.

"Impatient to savor every inch of you."

He did, removing all of Annie's clothing, arousing her
entire body with his hands and mouth. He kissed her
ankles, her long legs, her trembling thighs, and slowly
roved his lips over her belly and breasts, exciting her to a
fever pitch until she was famished for him and tearing at
his clothes.

At last he brought her astride him and freed his
burgeoning erection. His features were seized with desire, yet she found his expression every bit as poignant as
it was passionate.

"It would be lovely to have you with me all the time,"
he murmured, his voice tight. "To make love to you in
the sunshine, watch what I'm doing to you, see every
response in your beautiful blue eyes . . ."

"You can see it now . . . can't you?" she replied
breathlessly.

He smiled, then penetrated her in a powerful upward
stroke. She cried out, leaving him surging upright to
claim her quivering lips. She panted, locked in his lap,
transported by the exquisite sensations consuming her,
shattering her with such bliss.

"You all right?" he asked.

She nodded between gasps. "I can take all the love you can dish out, cowboy."

His knowing chuckle hinted she might regret her words. But she didn't as he held her to him tightly, plied her breasts with his mouth and tongue, and rocked her into paradise. Soon her fingernails dug into his spine and her teeth nipped at his shoulder, but her kiss was all surrender as they surged toward their mutual climax. That moment proved so intense that she tossed her head and sobbed once more. Sam quickly recaptured her lips, drowning out the rapturous sounds. Otherwise, Annie mused dazedly, they would have heard her downstairs for sure.

Chapter 30

$\sim$ ∞ $\sim$

Much later, Annie started awake to the sound of a
knock.

"Oh, Reverend Prophet!" came Dolly Dumble's
breathless voice. "I'm here with your supper tray! May I
come in?"

"Sam!" Panicked that she and Sam lay in bed together
naked, Annie yanked the covers up to her neck, prodded
him in the arm, and whispered urgently, "Do something
before she comes in."

Sam shook his head and opened his eyes. Glorious,
naked, and unrepentant, he grinned at her.

"Sam!" she hissed in exasperation.

He cupped a hand around his mouth and called back,
"Sister Dolly, would you kindly leave our tray by the
door? Sister Rebecca and I are immersed in prayer, and
we'll fetch it in just as soon as we finish."

"Oh, yes, Reverend!" called Dolly. "Sorry to have
disturbed your communion with the Almighty."

As soon as she heard the woman lumber away, Annie
punched Sam again. "You scamp! 'Immersed in prayer,'
my foot! You should have said 'immersed in sin.'"

He chuckled and got to his feet. "If you don't quit
your bellyachin', woman, I'm gonna have to teach you a
lesson or two in wifely obedience."

Her eyes sliding over his gorgeous body, she restrained
a wince. "I'm not your wife."

He turned, staring her in the eye. "Want me to fix
that?"

Annie could only stare back, rapt and breathless.

"I could fix it *real* good," he added.

From the look in his eyes, boy, did he mean it! Annie could barely hear him over her roaring heart.

He winked. "Called your bluff, didn't I, woman? Well, at least you've stopped complaining."

"Oh!" Annie threw the pillow at him.

He caught it with a smirk and tossed it back, then went to fetch both carpetbags, setting them on the bed. Opening his bag, he pulled out the dressing gown Annie had insisted he buy in Georgetown. Donning it, he retrieved a nightgown from her bag and tossed it at her. "There, woman. Make yourself presentable so I can bring in our supper."

She pulled the gown over her neck and stared at him dreamily. "You know what, Sam?"

"What?"

She leaned forward and hugged her knees with her forearms. "I don't think I'm really complaining at all."

As confident as a peacock, he strode to the door.

He returned bearing a tray with two filled plates and glasses of tea. The scrumptious chicken fricassee set Annie's mouth to watering. "Oh, that aroma is divine!"

He set the tray on the table near the window. "Then come on, woman. I'm famished."

Annie felt almost shy as she took her place facing Sam at the small table. She realized they'd crossed over some boundary in bed together, that they'd allowed themselves to succumb to fantasies of being a real married couple. It was thrilling and illicit being in the intimate setting with him, with the rest of the world assuming they were husband and wife. And he had excited her when he'd "threatened" to marry her. Oh, yes. Looking at him now, watching the light of the fading day illuminate his handsome visage and shoot golden highlights through his thick dark hair, she wondered how she'd ever be able to let him go. Their future was so uncertain.

Swallowing a knot of painful emotion, she picked up her fork and began sampling the fare. The fricassee was tender and very tasty, the mashed potatoes, green beans, and homemade bread equally delectable. Even the tea was strong and flavorful, spiced with fresh mint sprigs.

Sam took in her solemn mien. "You look mighty serious, sugar. What are you thinking?"

"I'm just enjoying the moment. I'm thinking this is the best meal I've had since you kidnapped me, bounty hunter."

"Wait till I take you to the dining room at the Windsor Hotel," he declared. "The grub there is really fine. You can eat steak and lobster on the finest china, drink champagne in crystal goblets, and sit surrounded by cut-glass chandeliers and diamond-dust mirrors."

"Sounds very elegant," she replied, but with a telltale sadness in her voice. "Will you take me there, Sam?"

Though his features were troubled, his hand tightly clasped hers. "I'd like to, sugar. What do you reckon we'll do, once all of this gets settled?"

She released a heavy breath. "Do you mean what will we do if we are able to find my great-great-grandmother and somehow straighten out her life?"

"Yeah, I reckon."

Annie stared out the window, watching a farm wagon rattle past in the fading light. "Well, I suppose I'd want to at least try to go back to the present—perhaps travel south and see if that same demon wind won't carry me off again. I left behind a host of problems there—plus I'm concerned about my brother."

"You wouldn't want to stay here?" he asked with touching anxiety.

"Are you asking me to?" she replied, her heart in her voice.

He gently stroked her cheek. "You think I don't like having you around, sugar?"

"Oh, I'm sure you do." She released another shuddering sigh. "But you know, Sam, I'll never be the 'little woman' who can stay at home while you go off on your adventures. Now if I could share your life—"

"That would never work out, Annie," he cut in soberly. "I've worried about you enough during this masquerade. But when I'm really hunting down varmints—murderers and rapists, scoundrels who wouldn't think twice about slitting a man's throat—it'd be too dangerous to have you along."

"What if—somehow—I could make it back to the present?" she ventured. "Would you try to come with me?"

He pondered this for a long moment, then slowly shook his head. "My life is here."

She groaned in frustration. "The life you've dictated for yourself. Who says you can't live another way?"

"Who says *you* can't?" he countered.

Annie fell silent, for Sam had raised a valid point. How could she ask him to give up his life when she wasn't certain she could ever abandon her own?

At last, she said, "Sam, there are just so many uncertainties in both our lives. I guess all we can count on is enjoying whatever time we have left."

"Well, if you put it that way, sugar . . ." Sam's bare toes nudged hers beneath the table. "You'd best eat up 'cause I ain't in the mood to wait long."

Laughing in mingled delight and incredulity, Annie tossed her napkin at him. "Sam Noble, you're insatiable! You're going to have to come up with *some* sermon after all this hanky-panky tonight."

His expression turned earnest as he raised and kissed her hand. "Honey, I want you to remember somethin'. What goes on between us ain't no sin. I reckon what we have feels so right, it must have come straight from the angels in heaven."

Annie instantly melted. "Well, if you put it *that* way," she murmured, leaning across the small table to accept his kiss.

Later, while Annie slept, Sam sat at the table with a pencil in hand, his solemn features reflected in a pool of light as he jotted down notes on tomorrow's sermon.

This was gonna be some spectacle, him playing the preacher. He thought back to the days of his youth and remembered his grandfather's sermons, booming orations filled with fire and brimstone, grand discourses on good and evil and choosing the path of righteousness.

Was he a righteous man? He might not darken the

door of a church each Sunday, but those values of his youth were still ingrained in him. He wanted to be a good man.

He wanted Annie, too, wanted to make a home with her, have a baby with her. But did he want her only on his own terms?

Funny how all of his life, he'd never seen himself settling down with such a headstrong female, yet now as time passed, as heavenly Annie lay in his arms each night, he found it increasingly difficult to imagine his future without her. She challenged him, fascinated him, and on some level, completed him. But marrying her would be so unfair to her, considering the vagabond existence he intended to continue living. Plus she hailed from another time and hankered to return there judging from what she'd said. Sadness filled him at the vast chasm between their worlds, a canyon he wasn't sure he could ever bridge. Yet he couldn't deny that it was Annie's very uniqueness, her spirit and outlook, her insistence on sharing his world, that drew him to her so powerfully. Ironically, the very qualities that made him love her would also threaten their future together.

Was there any way they could make it? He knew he was a proud man and pride was a deadly sin. He knew some sort of compromise would be required.

With a sigh, he set down his pencil and turned to gaze at her as she slept. Her gorgeous hair was spread out on the pillow, and her face was as peaceful as an angel's, her long lashes resting against her smooth, pink cheeks. Just looking at her now, remembering her sweet loving, and knowing he might soon lose her, was like a giant weight crushing his heart.

He loved her so! Perhaps he could overcome his own pride, turn his thinking in another direction. Ponder living his life in another way, just as she'd suggested. Perhaps they could find a meeting ground together. Somewhere . . .

Chapter 31

Annie felt as if she were trying to sleep at the OK Corral.

Throughout much of the night, she was jolted awake by sounds of gunfire and men caterwauling in the streets.

The first time, she shook Sam. "Sam, what is that?"

"Just some drovers shooting up the town on their way home," he mumbled sleepily. "Go back to sleep."

"Sleep? How can I sleep through the din?"

Her answer was a soft snore as Sam rolled away from her.

For the next couple of hours, every time Annie drifted back to sleep, the shooting and hollering started up again. At one point she sat bolt upright at the sound of a woman's exuberant yell, followed by more staccato bursts of gunfire.

She shook Sam once more. "Sam! I think I heard a female this time!"

"Sugar, can't we get some sleep?" he mumbled irritably. "You plumb wore me out."

"I wore *you* out?" she demanded, exasperated. "Now wait just a minute, Sam Noble. Whose idea was—"

Annie gave up as another snore curtailed her words. She continued to lie there restively, wondering about the woman's voice she'd heard. She flipped about at each new sound, until finally the clamor abated and she fell into a fitful slumber.

* * *

"Well, good morning folks!" called Dolly Dumble. "Don't you two look handsome in your Sunday black. Come right in and have some coffee, sausage, and grits."

When Annie and Sam stepped into the kitchen, she spotted two grizzled old-timers in overalls and home-spun shirts sipping coffee at the table, and Dolly Dumble standing at the iron stove, an apron protecting her Sunday-best black silk dress. Sam at once strode over to the table and pulled out a chair for Annie.

He flashed a grin at the landlady. "Why, thank you kindly, Sister Dolly. That shore smells good. I reckon my wife could use some of that there strong coffee."

Dolly flashed a compassionate look at Annie. "You ain't ailin', I hope?"

"Oh, no," Annie replied, taking her seat. "It's just that I didn't sleep very well last night."

"Oh, my."

Studying the woman's crestfallen expression, Annie quickly reassured her. "Oh, the room is fine and the bed was very comfortable. It was just all those cowboys raising"—she paused, catching herself as Sam cocked an eyebrow—"er, such an unholy clamor that kept me awake throughout much of the night."

"Oh, I know," commiserated Dolly, heading over to the table with a tin coffeepot. "Saturday nights in Rowdyville are noisier than blasting day at a mine, but we've been putting up with the ruckus so long, I reckon we've gotten used to it by now." She paused. "By the way, folks, these are two of your neighbors, Zach Cramer and Seth Gibbons."

"Pleased to meet you," Sam told the men.

The one named Zach, who possessed a narrow, leathery face and a chest-length beard, inclined his head toward Dolly. "This here the preacher fellar and his wife you been tellin' us about?" he inquired in a nasal twang.

"They are, indeed," Dolly said, returning to the stove.

The old-timer nodded in turn at Sam and Annie. "Welcome to Rowdyville, Reverend, ma'am. We kin use your kind in these parts—ain't that right, Seth?"

"Shore is," agreed Seth, who could have passed for Zach's twin.

"I'm playing the piano for the reverend this morning at church over at the saloon," Dolly called proudly from the stove. "You boys had best put on your go-to-meetin' clothes and come on over."

The codgers glanced at each other, then nodded in unison. "Shore will, Dolly," said Seth.

Dolly ambled back over in a rustle of silk skirts, placing bowls of grits before Annie and Sam. "I reckon I'll say the grace now," he announced.

The small group bowed their heads as Sam briefly intoned the blessing. He looked up and grinned at Dolly. "Looks good, ma'am."

"Thank you."

As Dolly moved away, Annie smiled encouragingly at the two geezers. "You know, this may sound strange, but . . . did either of you hear a woman yelling last night? It sounded like she was galloping through town, hollering and shooting off a gun."

"That woulda been Rotten Rosie," answered Zach.

Annie and Sam caught each other's eye; then he asked, "Who is she?"

"Oh, a little filly that's been givin' Royce Rowdy a rough ride for a couple years now," answered Seth, and both men guffawed.

"Why, she's a murderess and a thief!" declared Dolly, returning to the table with a plate of sausages. "Rustling cattle, robbing the bank, killing Bart Cutter, even if the man was a low-down dog."

"But, Dolly, I hear tell Rosie's helped out that poor starvin' white trash over in Shantytown," put in Zach.

Taking her place, Dolly harrumphed and shook open her napkin. "I hear that, too, but I don't believe it. Why, it's downright sinful, a woman wearing trousers and shootin' off a gun like a man. Rosie should follow the fine example of a good Christian woman like Mrs. Prophet here."

"Oh, yes, you wouldn't catch Mrs. Prophet dead riding a horse or shooting off a gun," commented Sam.

Annie had to give him credit for containing the laughter she could see bubbling up in him.

* * *

Hearing the strains of "The Old Rugged Cross" spilling forth in a saloon that reeked of sour beer and stale tobacco was not an experience Annie would soon forget.

By 11:00 A.M., half of the chairs lined up in rows near the small stage had been filled with an odd assortment of Rowdyville's citizenry. Sitting at the back, holding a brass bowl that Dolly had contributed as a collection plate, Annie had a good view of their ragtag "congregation." In the row directly in front of her sat their fellow boarders, Zach and Seth, both of whom wore respectable brown suits. Nearby several drunkards, who had appeared mainly because they thought the saloon had opened early, sat snoring in their chairs with their hats in their laps. Assorted prospectors, gamblers, and sodbusters had made more of a stab at respectability, showing up clean-shaven, in an assortment of suits, from threadbare to elegant. Even a few prostitutes had trudged downstairs garbed in unusually drab dresses and minus their trademark rouge and feathers, though Annie had to wonder if the soiled doves weren't here mainly out of curiosity rather than out of a true desire for repentance.

She drew little comfort from the motley crew. Indeed, a sense of uneasiness gripped her as she noted the stare of a small, dark Spaniard who sat a few seats beyond her wearing a black jacket, matching trousers, and a large sombrero. The man possessed beady dark eyes and a thin black mustache that he nervously toyed with. Ever since he had arrived ten minutes ago, he had been gazing at Annie in an intent manner that made her uncomfortable, although he was far from the only man in the seamy establishment who had tossed a leer her way!

Clearly, Sam had his work cut out for him.

At least a few well-bred types were present, including a couple of small families and a merchant or two. Glancing behind her, Annie smiled at a young mother in ragged overalls, and the woman acknowledged her overture with a nod. Although the pale, blond creature looked younger than Annie, she had three children with her, a boy and girl who appeared to be around four and five, and a baby girl around eighteen months of age.

Noting that the baby's face was flushed and her nose running, Annie offered the woman her handkerchief. At first the mother hesitated; then she accepted the lace-edged square of linen with a stiff smile.

Turning toward the front, Annie said a silent prayer that she and Sam would be able to pull off this charade. From all appearances, her lover was handling the stress much better than she was. Looking every bit the sober revivalist observing his flock, Sam stood near the stage in his fine black suit, his Bible in hand, his expression proud and pious. If he felt the least bit daunted about perpetrating this fraud, he betrayed no outward sign. Annie had to admire his bravado.

Just as the discordant strains of the hymn ended, the saloon doors swung open and Royce Rowdy strode in, wearing an impeccable brown suit. He was followed by half a dozen drovers in clean white shirts and dark pants, as well as a couple of Mexicans dressed similarly to the Spaniard seated near Annie.

Passing Annie, Rowdy paused, removed his hat, and dipped into a mocking bow. "Mrs. Prophet."

Although her heart hammered with renewed fear that Rowdy might have recognized her, Annie nodded back demurely. "Mr. Rowdy."

Rowdy headed for the front of the saloon and paused before Sam. "Well, Reverend Prophet," he greeted. "Looks like you've got a right fine turnout. You ready to begin?"

"With you here, Mr. Rowdy, I'd be right honored," Sam returned cordially.

While the newcomers seated themselves, Sam hopped up on the stage and raised a hand. His deep voice boomed out. "Brothers and sisters, we have gathered here to hear the Word and to repent of our sins. Praise the Lord, Amen!"

"Amen!" shouted several worshipers.

"Let us all stand and sing praises to the heavens," he continued solemnly.

Sam led the congregation in several rousing hymns— "Bringing in the Sheaves," "Stand Up, Stand Up for Jesus," and "Shall We Gather at the River." Watching

him swing his arms in time, hearing his deep, zealous
baritone voice boom out, Annie actually found herself
caught up in the fervor of the moment. Indeed, even
some of the drunkards around her had stirred and were
joining in the refrain. Sam really was pulling off the
masquerade, she realized with awe. He projected as
convincing an image as any television evangelist she'd
ever seen.

"Be seated, my children," he said when the last hymn
ended. "Hear the Word—and heed it. Let us pray."

Sam launched into a long supplication, beseeching
God to forgive his errant children before the day of
judgment sealed their fates. His sermon followed along
this same theme.

"Brothers and Sisters," he intoned ominously, "hear
the gospel according to Isaiah 13: 'Howl ye; for the day
of the Lord is at hand. . . . And I will punish the world
for their evil, and the wicked for their iniquity; and I will
cause the arrogancy of the proud to cease, and will lay
low the haughtiness of the terrible.'"

Closing the Bible, Sam gazed sternly at the congregation. "I'm here, brothers and sisters, to tell you it's not
too late. You need not perish, like the great city of
Babylon, laid waste by its own corruption. The kingdom
of God is at hand—be saved before His judgment
comes."

"Amen!" shouted several worshipers in unison.

Annie had to admire Sam as he continued to mesmer-
ize the crowd, beseeching all to repent and graphically
outlining the consequences for those who failed to
embrace salvation. Every eye in the congregation was
riveted on him, with many a grimace or gasp following
his bleak oratory on the infernal reaches; even Royce
Rowdy and the mysterious Spaniard seemed suitably
sobered by Sam's ghastly descriptions of hell. One poor
fellow—a perpetual drunkard, judging by his jaundiced
features and bloodshot eyes—sobbed openly, and loudly
blew his nose.

The sermon ended on another long, fervent prayer.
Then Sam smiled at Annie. "Now I'll ask Sister Rebecca
to come forward to take up the collection. And any of

you that's ready to be saved, now's the time to walk up the straight and narrow path that leads to redemption."

Feeling self-conscious, Annie rose with her bowl as Dolly launched into the soft strains of "Whispering Hope." She passed Royce Rowdy, who grinned and loudly tossed in a ten-dollar gold piece, then by his drovers who deposited smaller coins. The Spaniard sneered at her and declined to contribute; Zach, Seth, and the prostitutes gave modest amounts.

Annie hadn't the heart to extend the plate to the young mother, but as she was heading back for the aisle the woman stood and proudly dropped two nickels into the bowl. Annie flashed her another smile and received a second proud nod. Turning toward the front, she watched two drovers shuffle up to kneel before the stage. Sam at once slipped to his knees, laid a hand on each cowboy's shoulder, plaintively prayed over the two, and pronounced them forgiven. After the smiling men returned to their seats, the sobbing drunkard stumbled forth, followed by two whimpering prostitutes.

Observing the vignettes of atonement, Annie was beginning to feel like the worst charlatan. After all of the "saved" resumed their seats, she took Sam the collection plate and slanted him a chiding glance. Appearing unperturbed, he accepted the offering and pronounced the benediction. The worshipers stood; a few shuffled out while others lingered to visit. Annie noted that the young mother and her charges had been among the first to slip away, although the woman had placed Annie's handkerchief on her chair. Picking it up, she felt a twinge of disappointment, since she had hoped to meet the woman.

She returned to Sam's side to see Royce Rowdy shaking his hand. "Splendid sermon, Reverend, if I do say so myself."

"Thank you, Mr. Rowdy."

"You have a talent for describing the bottomless pit," Rowdy continued, his expression sly.

Sam drew himself up with pride. "Are you aiming to avoid the lake of hell, Brother Rowdy?"

Rowdy threw back his head and laughed. "Why, of

course." He winked at Annie. "I ain't hankering to be pit-roasted by Beelzebub. Nossir. Tell me, Reverend, could me and you have us a word later?"

"I'm always available to anyone in my flock."

Rowdy clapped Sam across the shoulder. "I'll count on it, then, preacher."

Watching Rowdy stride away with his entourage, Annie sidled closer to Sam. The man's evil wink had made her skin crawl. "Why do you suppose he wants to meet with you alone?"

Sam's attempted reply was curtailed as Dolly, Zach, and Seth all came forward to gush about his sermon.

Chapter 32

❦

"**A**nnie, honey, reckon it's time for us to leave?"
Annie was seated in one of the chairs, staring at the money-filled bowl that Sam had handed back to her, and feeling miserably guilty. She glanced up at the sound of his voice. "You know, I feel like a criminal."

He sat down beside her and took her hand. "A criminal? But why? Didn't you like my sermon?"

She laughed. "Your sermon was brilliant, Sam. Indeed, you've got to be the best charlatan I've heard since Burt Lancaster played Elmer Gantry."

His features twisted in confusion. "What do you mean by that? I ain't never heard of such a fellow."

"What do I mean?" She gestured her frustration. "Sam, you hornswoggled these people, preaching to them, 'saving' them. Why, you're not even ordained!"

He chuckled. "So that's what's troubling you. Heck, most of what's preachin' in the West these days ain't ordained."

"But at least they're sincere."

He grunted, his expression stunned. "You're saying I ain't earnest?"

"Well, are you?"

He nodded, a formidable scowl settling over his brow. "How do you think I was brung up, sugar? You'd best believe my mama taught me to honor the Good Book and took a switch to me when I strayed. 'Sides, I'll never forget my granddaddy's sermons."

251

"Then you weren't just putting on a show up there?"

He grinned, squeezing her hand in reassurance. "Sugar, the things you fret about. You know, putting on a show is half the fun of being a Bible-puncher. That don't mean I ain't sincere about it. If I can give these people some hope, make them act a mite kinder toward their fellow man, what harm have I done?"

"I supposed you're right," she admitted slowly.

"And don't we have to keep up the pretense if we want to locate your great-great-grandmother?"

She nodded. "That's true. I felt heartened when Zach and Seth mentioned Rosie this morning."

"If we linger around here long enough, we'll find her."

"I hope so." She glanced down at her bowl. "In the meantime, what are we going to do with this money?"

He glanced at the coinage in perplexity. "You mean the offering? Shoot, I don't know."

"We can't keep it, of course."

"No, I reckon that wouldn't be fitting."

Annie released a heavy sigh. "What bothers me most is one of the contributors was a poor young mother with three bedraggled children. I'm sure she tossed in her last two nickels."

Sam snapped his fingers. "Then why don't we give the offering to her and her young 'uns?"

"You mean it?" Annie's face fell. "But we don't know her name or where she lives."

"Someone at the boardinghouse is bound to know. We need to head back there for dinner anyhow."

She regarded him in disbelief. "You mean you can eat after that huge breakfast?"

"Sugar, I been preachin' right hard," he put in solemnly.

Annie had to laugh.

Appearing pleased, he stood and offered his hand. "Come on, let's rattle our hocks before they open up the saloon, and see if we can't do a good deed this afternoon."

* * *

An hour later, Sam and Annie drove out of Rowdy-ville in their buggy. Following Dolly Dumble's instructions, they were heading north, for the area known as Shantytown.

When questioned over dinner at the boardinghouse, Dolly had identified the woman they sought as Sally Mott, a young widow with three children. When Annie informed Dolly that they intended to give Sally that morning's offering, at first the landlady had glanced askance at them both. Then she relented, saying, "Well, I reckon Sally's a decent sort, being a mine widder and all, even if she does live out yonder with the white trash. Still, I reckon her young 'uns could use a handout."

Dolly had even packed up the leftovers of Sunday dinner for them to take to the needy family, and had given Annie an old tea tin to use to carry the collection money. Annie had felt touched when she'd spied Sam adding five dollars of his own to the cache.

Now Sam maneuvered the buggy along a twisting trail carved through a rocky pass. The afternoon air was crisp and clean, spiced with the scent of conifers. On the craggy outcroppings above them, brilliant bluebirds and colorful magpies flitted about from clumps of cedar to stands of Douglas fir.

As they emerged in a gently sloping valley sheltered by ponderosa pines, Annie's eyes widened as she spotted "her" wanted poster nailed to a tree, the paper riddled with bullet holes. She glanced at Sam to see him also staring at the poster.

"Well, would ya look at that!" he exclaimed.

"I know—it's rather sobering seeing 'my' wanted poster publicly displayed," she commented ruefully. "But I suppose it was bound to happen sooner or later."

"Yep. Especially around here." He nodded toward her sedate black outfit and horn-rimmed glasses. "I'm right glad you're wearing that getup, sugar. With your resemblance to Rosie, we need all the help we can get."

Annie forced a wan smile. She knew her disguise was good but still feared being recognized, particularly given the curious stares of both Royce Rowdy and the Span-

iard at church. Still, there was no sense mentioning this
to Sam and causing him to worry even more.

Her thoughts receded as a line of four shacks appeared
ahead of them. She gasped. The pitiful soddies had
sagging roofs, shuttered windows with peeling paint,
weathered doors, and dirt yards strewn with trash.

"Oh, Sam!" she cried. "Dolly says Sally lives in the
first house, and it looks like little more than a tool crib."

"I know, it plum breaks my heart to see folks hafta live
this way," he agreed, reining in the horse. "It's a real
shantytown all right."

He was about to hop down when Annie snapped her
fingers and caught his arm. "Hey, didn't Zach mention
that Rosie helps out the people here?"

"Yep, he did."

"Do you think Sally may know Rosie?"

"Reckon it's possible."

Annie smiled.

Sam alighted and retrieved the food basket from the
buggy's boot. At once a mangy dog from the neighbor's
yard charged forward, barking at him and baring sharp
yellow teeth. Sam stood his ground, casting the skinny
brown-and-white mutt a withering look until it whined
and skulked away.

"Boy, you really are taking your role seriously," Annie
teased as Sam strode around to her side.

"What do you mean?"

"You put the fear of God into that dog."

He chuckled and helped her out of the buggy.

Annie carried the tin with the money as they moved
through the small yard, passing a child's rusty wagon
heaped with scarred building blocks. At the door, Sam
rapped gently; soon Sally Mott opened the panel, a baby
girl in her arms. The young woman glanced from Sam to
Annie in obvious embarrassment.

"Reverend, ma'am, well if this ain't a surprise."

Sam removed his hat. "Mrs. Mott, may we come in for
a moment?"

"I ain't prepared for no company," she replied. "I
ain't got no fancy Sunday dinner to offer you, preacher."

"Oh, we've already been amply fed," Sam reassured

her. He held up the cloth-covered basket. "In fact, there was so much food left at the boardinghouse that Dolly Dumble was wondering if you and the children couldn't take the leftover grub off her hands."

As Sally stared at the proffered bounty, her expression miserably torn, her two older children stepped forward to eye the basket covetously and lick their lips. At last Sally broke the tension, nervously laughing. "Dolly Dumble ain't never wasted a crumb that I know of, but I reckon for my young 'uns' sake I can't refuse. You folks come on in."

Stepping inside with Sam, Annie observed that although the cabin was small, it was clean. The rugged room with its swept dirt floor was furnished with two sagging iron beds and a long table with benches; along a far wall, a fire blazed in an open hearth, with several stools arranged nearby.

Sam set the basket on the table. Nodding toward it, Sally said to her daughter, "Ettie Jean, you feed yourself and your brother while I visit with the preacher."

The little girl's thin, freckled face lit up. "Yes, ma'am!"

Sally gestured toward the stools. "You folks want to sit with me by the fire?"

"We'd be obliged," said Sam.

The adults settled themselves near the hearth, with the baby in her mother's lap sucking her thumb.

"So what brings you folks out here?" Sally asked. "Aside from delivering Dolly's dinner, that is."

Annie smiled at Sally and extended the tin. "Mrs. Mott, we were hoping you and your family would accept today's offering."

The young woman's eyes narrowed on the container, and again Annie watched a pained struggle cross her features. At last, Sally shook her head. "No, ma'am."

Disappointment lanced Annie. "You can't?"

Sally proudly met her eye. "That there box has coins from Royce Rowdy and his riffraff, don't it?"

Annie sucked in her breath, shocked at the venom in Sally's tone. "Yes, Mr. Rowdy and his ranch hands contributed to the collection."

"Then I don't want no part of it," she shot back, lifting her chin. "I wouldn't a'showed my face at his saloon, 'ceptin' one of my neighbors said there was a preacher in town, and I reckoned my young 'uns could use some Bible larnin'."

Annie glanced at the two older children, who were gleefully devouring fried chicken. Sam smiled gently at Sally. "Mrs. Mott, if you don't mind my askin', why do you despise Mr. Rowdy?"

"'Cause he's a big mean bully suckin' the lifeblood out of this here town," Sally retorted. "'Sides, he killed my husband."

Annie and Sam exchanged an alarmed glance. "Would you mind explaining that, ma'am?" he asked.

"Naw, I don't mind. My Jasper was a crew leader at Rowdy's Pine Creek Mine, back before it run dry." She drew a convulsive breath. "Hell, old Royce had that hillside so riddled with tunnels, Jasper flat told me the mine had more holes in it than the Rowdy Roost. He swore to Rowdy that the whole mountain was unstable, but Rowdy made those miners go on drillin' and blastin' anyhow. Kept hoping to find a new mother lode, I 'spect—I never seen no one as sick with the gold colic as Rowdy. Anyhow, that hillside gave way, and Royce Rowdy made widows of me and five other Rowdyville women."

"How terrible!" said Annie, reaching out to clasp Sally's thin hand. "I'm deeply sorry."

"So am I," added Sam.

Although Sally flashed them a look of gratitude, she pulled her fingers from Annie's. "So I 'spect you can see why I ain't wantin' nothin' old Rowdy has touched," she finished tightly. "I ain't acceptin' no handouts offen that slick piece of trash."

Although Annie empathized with Sally's feelings, after glancing at the baby's feet, covered only in ratty socks, she gazed beseechingly at the proud young widow. "Mrs. Mott, does it matter where the money comes from as long as it helps your children?"

Annie watched anger and uncertainty cross Sally's

face. Then, surprisingly, a curious expression settled in. She moved her head about, studying Annie's face from several different angles. "You know what, ma'am? You remind me of someone. Somethin' about you's been nagging at me all day, and I reckon I just figured out what it is."

"Yes?" asked Annie tensely.

"You favor someone—someone else who comes around and brings me food and money."

"You mean Rosie?" Annie asked in a charged whisper. "Can you help us find her?"

At once the woman's mien grew wary. "Why do you want to know 'bout her?"

"Well, I . . ." Annie's voice trailed off as she realized she wasn't sure how to explain her motives.

Sam quickly filled the gap. "Why, we want to bring Rosie our message of salvation. Don't you reckon she's in need of redemption?"

The young woman hooted with laughter. "Mister, you're one fine preacher, but you're tryin' to light a fire in the wrong chimney. You ain't never redeeming Rotten Rosie."

"But she does help you out, doesn't she?" Annie pursued.

"Maybe she do, maybe she don't," Sally replied non-committally. She reached out and snatched up the tea tin. "But I'm thinkin' maybe I'll accept your offering money, after all, ma'am. You're right that I can't let my pride stand in the way of feeding my young 'uns."

"Thank you, Mrs. Mott," said Annie.

Sally laughed. "Why are you thankin' me? You're the ones helping me out."

"Oh, but you've helped *me*," Annie insisted. "More than you can know."

"Rosie helped Sally! I just know she did!"

The ecstatic words left Annie's mouth the instant they pulled away from the cottage.

Working the reins, Sam eyed her in bemusement. "So what if she did?"

"Then she's helping folks—and she can't be all bad!"

"Well, I reckon you've got a point," he conceded with a thoughtful frown.

"If you ask me, it's Royce Rowdy who's corrupt," Annie went on feelingly. "Look how cruelly he treated Sally's husband and the other miners. To think those children are fatherless because of that snake! He's such an oily scumbag. He acts pleasant enough, but there's something insidious about him."

"Insidious?" Sam repeated with a scowl.

"Treacherous."

"Ah, yes. So you noticed that, too?"

She shuddered. "He really gave me the willies when he winked at me this morning."

"He *winked* at you?" Sam demanded, clearly irritated. "The dog."

She grinned. "And it looks like you're starting to come around to my way of thinking, Sam Noble."

"Annie, you know I've never heard good things about Royce Rowdy. But you're right that I'm changing. I ain't condemning Rosie until I investigate things for myself. I ain't makin' the same mistake with her that I did with you."

Studying his earnest, determined expression, Annie felt a welling of admiration and love. "You know what, Sam Noble? You're a good man."

He grinned. "And you're a mighty fine woman, sugar, wanting to help Sally and her kids."

She sighed dreamily. "Who knows? Maybe it's a trait I inherited from my great-great-grandmother."

"Could be," he admitted.

She hooked her arm through his. "And I take back what I said earlier, about your preaching. I think you really do want to help folks. And I'm proud of you for it, Sam."

Sam grinned and wrapped an arm about Annie's shoulders.

Chapter 33

◆◇◆◇◆

When they drove back through town and passed the Rowdy Roost, Sam remarked to Annie, "Reckon I'd best stop in there and speak with Royce Rowdy like he requested."

"You want me to come with you?"

"Nope. You said Rowdy found you familiar-lookin'. No sense havin' you 'round the rascal more than we must."

"I suppose you're right." Spotting the stable just ahead, she ordered, "Hey, pull up."

He tugged on the reins. "What's the matter?"

"You're going to pass the stable."

He pulled the horses to a halt. As the animals snorted and stamped their hooves, Sam protested, "But I'm escortin' you back to the rooming house first."

"Don't be ridiculous," said Annie. "It's only three doors down. I'll walk."

Watching Annie hop out of the buggy, stroll over to the boardwalk, and head off for the boardinghouse, Sam smiled in grudging admiration. How he admired the feisty tilt of her head, the tempting sway of her hips. She was one independent woman. And that was only the beginning of her charms.

"May I help you, sir?"

Sam glanced down to see that the stable boy had stepped outside and was regarding him curiously as he chewed on a piece of straw. He jumped down, handed the lad a coin, and headed off for the saloon.

259

Down the street, Annie was approaching the boarding-house when she was hit by an eerie feeling, as if someone were watching her. She was glancing about in perplexity when abruptly she was seized from behind. Before she could even think, much less scream, a gloved hand was clamped over her mouth and she was hauled over to the side of the house. Deluged with terror, she felt something cold and sharp prick her neck and she froze. She could smell a man's sweat and his stale, tobacco-soured breath.

"Do you know what this is, *señora*?" asked a nasty, Spanish-accented voice.

With the hand over her mouth and the blade at her throat, Annie dared neither move nor speak.

"It's a knife, *señora*," the man continued in a lethally soft tone. "It can slit open your throat faster than you can scream. Now I'm going to remove my hand, and if you make any sound, I'm going to kill you. *¿Comprende?*"

Nauseous with fear, Annie managed the barest nod. As the man lowered his knife but continued to hold her powerless against him, she made no sound at all, save the smallest intake of breath.

"*Muy bien, señora,*" said the man. "Now do not turn around and look at me, or it's the last thing you'll see. *¿Comprende?*"

"Yes," retorted Annie, her voice seething with barely repressed hostility.

"What are you and the gringo doing in Rowdyville?"

"We're leading a revival."

The man's arm tightened about her. "Don't lie to me, *idiota*! You're here about Rosie, no?"

Heart thundering with fear, she confessed, "Maybe."

"Why, *señora*?"

"We just want to help her."

The man's cruel laughter mocked her. "And what makes you think she wants your help?"

Annie had no answer.

"Here's some free advice, *señora*," the man hissed. "Get out of town—or you and the *hombre* will both die."

The man shoved Annie away so violently that she

stumbled and almost fell. By the time she could gather the courage to turn around and look for him, he was gone.

Stepping through the double doors into the Rowdy Roost, Sam spotted Royce Rowdy in a corner playing poker with three cowboys. Raucous laughter erupted from the table, and a haze of smoke curled about the men's heads.

So much for the impact of his preaching this morning, he thought cynically, noting that the entire saloon was again filled with drinkers and gamblers, and the skimpily clad hurty gurty gals were once more strutting about the stage. He gritted his teeth and strode purposefully toward Rowdy's table.

Spotting Sam's approach, Rowdy tossed in his hand. "Afternoon, preacher."

Sam nodded grimly. "Afternoon."

Rowdy spoke to the others. "Boys, reckon we'll give it a rest. Preacher and I need to ruminate."

The other men grumbled but threw in their cards and shuffled off.

"Have a seat, preacher."

Scowling, Sam sat down.

Rowdy picked up a bottle of whiskey. "Care for a drink?"

"Now you know better than to ask that," Sam chided.

Rowdy chuckled and set the bottle aside. "Well, that was some sermon. Folks have been talking about it ever since."

Sam glanced with distaste about the saloon, watching two prospectors at a nearby table scuffle over a bottle of whiskey. "My preachin' don't seem to have changed much hereabouts."

"Give it some time," Rowdy advised. "In fact, that's why I wanted to have our chat."

"So, speak your mind," urged Sam sourly.

A grin split Rowdy's oily face. "How 'bout you and the missus stayin' over a couple of weeks and hostin' a real old-fashioned revival?"

Sam scratched his jaw. "You mean here in the saloon?"

"It's the largest building in town."

Sam laughed derisively. "And the most corrupt. What about the other activities, here—and upstairs in the cribs?"

Rowdy's gaze narrowed. "I ain't shutting the place down, if that's what you're hintin' at. But the Rowdy Roost will be closed during services."

"How generous of you," Sam drawled. "I ain't so sure. I can't preach salvation from the shores of hell."

Rowdy chuckled. "But ain't that where redemption is needed the most? Heck, we can have all the trimmin's if you like, even end off with a mass baptism over at Pine Creek."

Sam regarded Rowdy quizzically for a long moment, taking in his eager though crafty countenance. "What's your stake in this?"

"What do you mean?" Rowdy protested with feigned innocence. "I'm just tryin' to help out the community."

"Pardon my bluntness, but you don't seem the type."

Rowdy laughed, reaching out to punch Sam in the arm. "I like you, preacher. I do."

"Then tell me why you're helping me. There's somethin' in it for you, ain't there?"

Rowdy's dark eyes gleamed. "I'll allow I could profit from some respectability in this town."

"How so?"

"You been over to Central?"

Sam shrugged. "Sure, I've passed through."

Rowdy clenched a fist on top of the table. "Well, there's a judge over there, J. D. Righteous, who would love to see me in the calaboose."

"That so?" inquired Sam casually.

"J.D. and I go back a spell," Rowdy confessed with a frown. "He always claimed I jumped his daddy's claim up around Pine Creek, though he never could prove it, since the codger died somewheres out in the hills. Then two years past, old J.D. was forced to help me out, and it plumb rubbed him the wrong way."

"Mind explaining?" asked Sam.

"Sure, preacher." A malevolent expression gripped Rowdy's face. "You see, a pistol-packing mama named

Rotten Rosie up and shot one of my men for no good reason."

"Rotten Rosie?" Sam repeated, scratching his jaw. "Think I've heard of her."

Rowdy waved a hand in frustration. "Hell, who ain't heard tell of that thievin', murderin' bitch? She's still terrorizing my town to this day. I'd love to shoot the little she-devil, but so far, I ain't been able to catch her. Anyhow, to get back to my story, Rosie shot poor Bart Cutter dead during one of her raids, and Righteous wasn't too happy when he had to hold an inquest in his court. But I had witnesses, and J.D. had no choice but to order a warrant issued for Rosie's arrest. I put up the reward money myself."

"Did you, now?"

Rowdy lowered his voice and confided, "Luckily, the sheriff of Gilpin County, Cal Oates, is a good friend of mine. But I'll allow old Judge Righteous would love to get me on somethin' if he could."

"So you think a preacher might bring this town an air of decency?" Sam posed.

Rowdy grinned. "You got it, Reverend—a preacher, and a church. Figure we could gather enough in offerings to raise the foundation during the revival, don't you?"

"Reckon it's possible."

His expression self-satisfied, Rowdy leaned back in his chair and laced his fingers together behind his head. "You know, I've got ambitions, preacher."

"Do you, now?"

Eyes gleaming, Rowdy confessed, "I ain't spending the rest of my days in this backwater town. Nossir. When I hit my next big strike, I aim to move in to one of them fancy mansions on Millionaire's Row in Denver, rub elbows with the Tabors, the Hills, and the Cheesmans, maybe escort one of them fancy debutantes out to the opera house, even meet the governor. But first I got to become respectable, don't you think?"

"Yes, that would be a good beginning," Sam agreed.

"Then it's a deal." Rowdy filled his glass with whiskey and held it high. "To you, preacher."

Rowdy was about to take a gulp when abruptly the

glass was smashed out of his hand by a whizzing bullet! For a split second both men sat frozen in disbelief as a piercing female whoop rent the air.

Jerking his head toward the sound, Sam was stunned to spot two strangers standing just inside the saloon doors—a small, grinning woman in fringed buckskin jacket, pants, and light-colored Stetson, and a masked Spaniard in a black suit and sombrero.

Each of the intruders held two six-shooters!

"Shit, it's Rotten Rosie!" yelled Royce. "Hit the floor, preacher!"

Sam needed no further prodding. He dived beneath the table just as a deafening barrage of gunfire burst forth. He winced and held his ears as all around them glass shattered, furniture went smashing against the floor and walls, and panicked cries erupted as patrons and hurty gurty gals stumbled about seeking cover. Worst of all was the sound of the female intruder's shouts—her high-pitched cry was bloodcurdling and exuberant, like a Comanche yell.

"I'll get you yet, Royce Rowdy," Sam heard the woman scream over the blast of gunfire. "I'll skin you alive, you low-down viper!"

Then, as quickly as the assault began, it ended, the silence almost deafening. Sam caught a glimpse of the saloon doors flapping after the intruders fled.

Cautiously, he emerged from beneath the table, gazing at Rowdy through a haze of smoke. "That was Rotten Rosie?"

Rowdy was trembling in his rage. "The goddamned she-devil! The nerve of her, bustin' up my saloon on a Sunday afternoon! I'll kill her!"

Yelling orders at his men, Rowdy ran outside. Sam followed, arriving on the boardwalk in time to watch Rosie and her cohort ride off, hell-bent-for-leather, still hollering and shooting into the air. As several of Rowdy's henchmen futilely fired after the riders, Sam shook his head in grudging admiration. He'd only gotten a brief glimpse of the woman—but damn, she looked like Annie!

Annie! Oh, Lord, was she all right? Sam went dashing off for the boardinghouse.

* * *

"Annie, thank God you're safe. Sugar, you ain't gonna believe this, but I just seen your grandma!"

Sam charged into the room at the boardinghouse, only to skid to a halt when he spied Annie's distraught face. She sat on the bed trembling, her features as pale as parchment.

But of course she was upset—she'd likely just heard the gunfire! He rushed over to join her on the bed and gripped her hand, finding her flesh too cool, her fingers trembling.

"Annie . . . sugar, are you all right?"

She glanced up at him in awe. "You actually saw Rosie? Is that why I just heard all that shooting?"

"Yep. Rosie just charged into the saloon, bold as brass, with some Spanish fellar. The two of 'um shot up the place real good—hell, Rosie even blasted a whiskey glass out of Royce Rowdy's fingers."

"Amazing. Are you okay?"

"I'm fine."

"Was anyone else hurt?"

"Nope." Sam smiled at her tenderly. "You know, sugar, I really owe you one big apology for ever thinkin' you was Rosie—though God knows, after seein' her, the two of you could be twins."

"Really?" Annie asked eagerly. "Does she look that much like me?"

"Yep—though she's smaller."

Annie made a sound of frustration. "God, I just wish I could have been there to see her!"

Sam eyed Annie curiously, again noting how white she was. "Did the gunfire scare you bad?"

She laughed. "No more than usual."

"Then why do you look like you seen a ghost?"

She shuddered. "While you were at the saloon, a man accosted me."

"A man? Who?"

Her troubled gaze met his. "I don't know. He came up behind me and I didn't see his face. But he sounded Spanish."

"Damn!" Sam wrapped a protective arm around her. "Did he hurt you?"

"No, but he held a knife to my throat—"

"He *what*?" Sam surged to his feet, eyes wild. "Damn it, I knew I should have escorted you back here! Well, that does it! I'm getting you out of Rowdyville—now!"

Wringing her hands, she popped up as well. "Sam, don't be ridiculous. I told you I'm okay, and obviously we're getting closer to Rosie now—"

"I still won't take chances with your life!"

"Don't you even want to know what the man said?"

Sam scowled at her murderously. "What did he say?"

She groaned. "I think he's onto us."

"Onto us?"

"He knows we're here looking for Rosie, and he warned us to get out of town, or—"

"Or?" he repeated, voice rising.

"Or we'll both be killed," she finished, shuddering.

Sam waved his arms and let out a slew of curses that made Annie's face flame. "That's it. I'm taking you back to my grandma. Then I'll head on back here and shoot these damn sidewinders—"

"Sam, you can't do that," she cut in passionately, fists clenched. "For one thing, you know you're not the kind to take the law into your own hands. Besides which, you'll blow our cover. Can't you see we must be getting close to the truth, or we wouldn't have been threatened? You yourself just saw my ancestor."

Sam began to pace. "Hell, all I know is, Rowdy must already be suspicious, or you wouldn't a'been attacked."

"How do you know it was one of Rowdy's men?" she reasoned. "I really think the attacker was someone who knows Rosie, perhaps the man who was with her at the saloon."

Sam laughed humorlessly. "How could he have been there and here with you, too?"

"He only accosted me for a matter of seconds. I heard the gunfire after I returned to the room."

Sam scowled. "Doesn't Rowdy have some Spanish drovers? I seen 'um at church."

"Yes, that's true. But there was also another Spaniard, a loner, who kept staring at me throughout the services. I think he may have been the one who accosted me—and his message seemed to be that Rosie doesn't want our help."

Sam laughed bitterly. "Yeah, well I got that same message loud and clear down at the saloon."

Annie drew a calming breath. "Did you get a chance to talk to Rowdy at all before the incident? Did he tell you what he wants?"

Sam laughed. "That was real funny. The sanctimonious hypocrite wants us to lead a revival and establish a church here, so's he can turn respectable."

"Then he doesn't know we're searching for Rosie!" she exclaimed, her face lit with new hope.

"Maybe," he said with a frown. "Hell, Rowdy's such a sly weasel, who knows what he's really thinking?"

She moved close to him and clutched his arm. "Sam, we need to play along with Rowdy, host the revival, keep on doing exactly what we're doing—"

"And get you killed?" he half shouted.

"I'm not going to get killed. I really think the man who accosted me today is the one I saw in church, the same man you saw with Rosie. If he's around her all the time, that's why he picked up on my resemblance to her. Besides, I can't believe my great-great-grandmother wishes me any harm."

His gaze implored the heavens. "Well, honey, you ain't seen that pistol-packin' mama in action with pistols in both hands. Your sweet little granny may have cold-bloodedly murdered a man, and 'sides, she don't know you from a bangtailed billy goat!"

Annie grasped his hand. "Please, Sam, don't make me stop now. I promise I'll be careful."

He hauled her close, and his voice came hoarse with emotion. "Careful, hell. I'm not letting you out of my sight again, woman—not even for an instant."

"That's fine with me," Annie replied, stretching upward to kiss him.

Sick with fear, Sam clutched Annie close.

Chapter 34

Over the next days, Sam led the revival in the Rowdy Roost. Royce Rowdy had promised them full use of the saloon on Sunday mornings and each evening from 8:00 till 10:00 P.M. Often at night after the liquor and cards were put away, drunkards and prostitutes remained for the services—some lingering simply to snore in the chairs—the riffraff often joined by a few more righteous souls from the Rowdyville community. Although aware that most of their congregation was there out of curiosity or boredom rather than out of a genuine desire for redemption, the revivalists carried on, with Sam preaching, Dolly Dumble manning the piano, and Annie passing the collection plate.

Each night a few came forward to be saved, weeping loudly on a makeshift mourner's bench, or "anxious seat," as Sam called it, though the depth of the suppli-cants' repentance was questionable. Often the very ones who sobbed the loudest and made the greatest show of atonement were the first ones to grab whiskey and cards once the session ended. Indeed, on the third night, Royce Rowdy himself made a great ceremony of having embraced the Word. His dark eyes breathing fire, he bolted up from his seat and cried, "I have seen the light, Brother Prophet!" As others cheered and stamped their feet, Rowdy strutted forward to the altar and knelt with shoulders heaving as Sam blessed him.

But no sooner had Sam pronounced the benediction than Rowdy popped back up with a mocking grin, and yelled, "It's free drinks on the house, brothers and sisters, in honor of my salvation!"

Sam and Annie repressed their cynical amusement as the worshipers were transformed into sinners once more, storming the bar and even breaking into scuffles in their zeal to guzzle red-eye. They left the saloon that night convinced that Royce Rowdy was a hypocrite of the first water.

Although neither Rosie nor the mysterious Spaniard made an appearance at the saloon during this period, Sam and Annie did learn more about her ancestor's exploits from various citizens of Rowdyville. On the boardwalk, one of Rowdy's drovers described how Rosie repeatedly terrorized the Rowdy ranch, taking potshots at the cowhands, salting wells, and rustling cattle. At the apothecary, the druggist told them how Rosie and her Spanish crony might ride through town at almost any time, shooting off their guns, yelling obscenities, and sparking fear.

Then one afternoon as Sam and Annie strolled the boardwalk, they heard muffled pleas for help coming from the direction of Rowdyville's small bank. They rushed inside to see the safe ajar and three male employees, clad only in long johns, tied to chairs, with gags on their mouths.

As Annie restrained a snicker over the farcical scene, Sam rushed over and ungagged the first man. Clutching Sam's sleeve, he pleaded, "Please, mister, save me!"

"You mean from Rotten Rosie?" Sam asked.

The man gulped. "Nope, from Mr. Rowdy once he finds out Rosie robbed his bank again!"

True to the man's prediction, when Rowdy arrived and surveyed the scene, he flew into such a temper that several of his henchmen had to restrain him to keep him from shooting the three employees. A posse was hastily organized and stormed off, returning later bedraggled and defeated. Afterward, one of Rowdy's hands admitted to Sam and Annie that Royce had repeatedly dispatched vigilante posses to chase or track Rosie, but all of the expeditions had ended in failure, since no one seemed to know the location of her rustler's roost. Even in their own inquiries, Sam and Annie netted no clue as to Rosie's hideout.

Although dismayed by their lack of progress, the couple continued their charade. Rosie's threat to the community was again driven home on Thursday morning when they passed by the Rowdy Roost to see that all the front windows had been shot out. Stepping inside with Sam, Annie grimaced at a foul, charred odor, and saw to her horror that the floor had been singed from just inside the doors all the way to the bar! Toward the center of the saloon, Royce Rowdy stood grimly watching several of his henchmen sweep up broken glass and other debris.

Tugging along Annie, Sam hastened to Rowdy's side. "Brother Rowdy, what has happened here? Was there a fire last night?"

"There was a *spitfire,* that's what there was!" retorted Rowdy in disgust. "That damned Rotten Rosie is at it again! Yesterday the bank, now this. Hell, preacher, you seen her in action. But she's gone too damned far this time! She shot up my town again last night, broke all the windows in this here saloon, then tried to set the place afire by throwing in a lit bottle of kerosene!"

Sam and Annie glanced at each other in dismay. "How terrible," Annie muttered.

Rowdy spoke through clenched teeth. "If me and a few of the boys hadn't been here still playin' poker, you'd be preachin' from a pile of rubble tonight, Brother Prophet. It's a miracle we was able to put out the fire."

"Indeed," murmured Sam.

In his fury, Rowdy kicked over a chair. "That damn hellcat is like a nest of ants in my britches, tormenting me at every turn, robbin' and rustlin' and plunderin'. My men already have orders to shoot the witch on sight. Hell, I'm itchin' to strangle her myself!"

Watching Rowdy turn and storm away, Annie grimly shook her head at Sam.

Later, back at the boardinghouse, Annie expressed her concerns. "You know, I'm worried about my ancestor."

"Worried?" Sam repeated with a disbelieving laugh.

"Yes. I'm afraid Rosie may get herself killed before we can find her. Royce Rowdy seemed very upset."

Sam only shook his head. "Sugar, pardon me for sayin' it, but the man had cause."

"I'm just so frustrated because we can't seem to get close to her," Annie continued. "She's hit the saloon twice now—do you suppose we ought to try staking it out?"

"What do you mean?"

"You know, hide in there and wait for her to appear?"

"Have you gone loco?" Sam waved a hand. "We'd only get ourselves shot or barbecued the next time she stages one of her raids. No, thank you. Hell, I'm gettin' so worried about *your* safety, I'm about ready to cancel the rest of the revival."

"Sam, no!"

He shook a finger at her. "Then I want your promise we ain't takin' no chances, that we're gonna keep on doin' what we're doin' and not lose our heads about this."

"Very well," Annie said heavily.

"Surely if we go on with the revival and winnin' the trust of the people, someone will step forward with some useful information."

Noting that Sam's words seemed to lack conviction, Annie nonetheless flashed him a brave smile. "I hope so, Sam."

Although Annie remained concerned about Rosie's safety, she could understand Sam's reasoning that they must keep up the charade and win the confidence of the people. This was especially true with respect to Sally Mott, whom Annie continued to feel might be their best bet for finding Rosie. The young widow had attended several revival sessions with her children, and she remained passably friendly toward Annie. Each time she saw Sally, Annie sensed the widow had information about Rosie that she wasn't, as yet, willing to divulge.

Thus she felt pleased the next morning when she ran across the woman and her charges at the general store.

With her older girl and boy knelt nearby, gleefully rifling through a box filled with toys, Sally stood at a table of yard goods, trying to hold her squirming baby while perusing fabrics.

"Well, hello," greeted Annie. "Good to see you, Mrs. Mott."

Sally glanced up and smiled, and the baby gurgled at Annie. "Thought I'd make up some new duds for my kids with the offering money."

"That's a good idea. May I hold the baby while you look?"

Sally grinned. "Sure, thanks. This young 'un's a real handful today."

Sally deposited the child into Annie's arms, and she chuckled as the baby cooed while chewing on a cookie. Thank goodness the child appeared much improved today, her nose dry and her coloring normal.

Annie watched Sally carefully examine bolts of wool, broadcloth, and calico. "It's been nice seeing you at the services."

"Brother Sam's a good preacher."

Gathering her fortitude, Annie said, "Mrs. Mott, about what we were discussing on Sunday when we visited your home . . . You know Rosie Dillon, don't you?"

A mask closed over Sally's features. "Maybe I do, maybe I don't."

Biting her lip, Annie decided she may as well take the plunge and try to win the woman's confidence. "Mrs. Mott, can you keep a secret?"

"Sure," Sally replied with a shrug.

Stepping closer, Annie whispered, "I'm a relative of Rosie's, and I'm here to help her. It's critical that I locate her immediately, before she gets herself in even worse trouble."

Sally frowned. "You her kin?"

"Yes. Didn't you yourself notice the resemblance between us?"

"Maybe I did."

"Can you tell me where Rosie is?"

Sally considered this for a moment, then sadly shook

her head. "Look, ma'am, I'm real sorry, but even if I wanted to tell you, I got no idear where she is."

"Could you get her a message?"

Sally hesitated. "Not if I don't see her."

"But what if you do?"

Sally's features grew fraught with turmoil. At last, she confessed, "Ma'am, you been right good to me and my young 'uns, but I reckon I got other loyalties, too."

Annie touched her arm. "I'm not asking you to betray her, only to give her a message."

"Maybe," came the reluctant response.

"Tell her if she wants help, to look up Reverend and Mrs. Prophet at the boardinghouse. Okay?"

"I'll, try ma'am," was all Sally would say.

At the rooming house, Annie told Sam about her meeting with Sally. "I think she knows something, and I'm praying she'll get a message through to Rosie. If only I can meet with her—I know I can make a difference."

Sam gave her a reassuring hug. "I 'spect anything's possible. But I do hope we make some progress soon, since I don't know how much longer we can keep up this masquerade. Sooner or later, one of us is bound to be recognized."

"I know," Annie agreed glumly.

That night when they went to bed, it was quiet at the boardinghouse, almost too quiet, without any of the normal sounds of revelry drifting up from the streets. The very eeriness of the silence put Annie on edge, keeping her wakeful for a long time.

Much later, a low hissing sound made her flinch in her sleep. She jerked awake to face the shimmering light of a lantern. Squinting, she shuddered to find herself looking down the barrel of a gun—a pistol held by a woman who appeared to be her mirror image, a woman whose fierce green eyes were angrily fixed on her! Heart roaring with terror, Annie gasped and sat up, prodding Sam, who at once jerked awake beside her.

As both of them gaped in horror, the intruder perused them and finally spoke, in a frontier twang edged with outrage. "Well, ain't you two a sight for sore eyes. My

twin in bed with a Bible-puncher." She set down the
lantern and leveled the Colt on Annie. "As for you . . . I
oughta shoot you for stealin' my face, sister."

Chapter 35

Annie's first impression as she looked at Rosanna Dillon was overwhelming awe to be in the presence of her own ancestor. Her second thought was, illogically, that the resemblance between them was not as striking as she'd first believed. Rosie's hair, bound in long braids, was strawberry blond, while Annie's was brown. Her eyes were a greenish hazel rather than blue, and were set slightly closer together. Her nose was shorter, the bridge dusted with freckles; her mouth was thinner, and her cheekbones weren't as pronounced.

But the most glaring difference was their size. While Annie was tall even for a twentieth-century woman, Rosie was no more than five foot two in height. Her fringed buckskin jacket and matching trousers and the large, cream-colored Stetson tipped back on her head only accentuated her tininess. Indeed, it seemed ludicrous to Annie that Sam could have mistaken her for this diminutive creature, although she supposed her face would have seemed a close enough match to the black-and-white image on the wanted poster. She also felt amazed that this tiny person had wreaked such havoc and inspired so much fear—although the twin Colts she bore, one in hand and one on her hip, were daunting, especially with herself and Sam the targets, sitting helplessly in bed in their nightclothes!

This last image brought Annie careening back to reality and reminded her that her first priority had to be convincing a very angry woman not to kill them. She looked Rosie straight in the eye and said calmly, "I didn't steal your face, Great-Great-Grandmother. You gave it to me."

The intruder actually appeared taken aback, the huge Colt trembling in her small hand. "What kind of hokum is that? I ain't nobody's granny, and I ain't never handed over my face to no one. It was still attached the last time I peered in the looking glass."

"Then it hasn't been stolen, either, has it?" Annie countered forthrightly.

A charged silence fell in the wake of her question; then she felt heartened when Rosie actually chuckled. But her voice remained filled with menace. "Sister, for a woman staring death in the eye, you shore got one smart mouth on you."

At a loss, Annie turned at Sam. With a long-suffering look, he scolded, "Mrs. Dillon, we're here to help you. If you'll put away that gun, we'll try to explain."

Rosie fell back a step, although the pistol remained firmly in her grip. "I ain't dropping my guard with you two. Nossir. Fact is, if you folks didn't have me so blame curious, I'd shoot first and ask questions later."

"You *are* curious?" Annie asked hopefully.

"Sister, I'm plumb fascinated." Rosie swung her pistol back and forth. "Tain't every day I meet my own reflection, plus learn you two been nosing into my business like we're blood kin or somethin'. All right, spit it out. Who are you folks, why does she favor me, and why have you two been askin' 'round town 'bout me?"

Sam glanced at Annie. "Reckon you should begin?"

Annie sighed. "Okay, I guess I'm going to have to trust you with the whole story."

"You're gonna have to spit it out or I'll shoot you."

Annie hesitated, and Sam squeezed her hand in reassurance. To Rosie, he said sternly, "Can't you please put away that gun? As you can see, we're unarmed."

"Yeah, unarmed, and in your bedclothes," acknowledged Rosie with a cackle. She waved the pistol toward Annie. "After she spills the beans, maybe I'll lower my guard. But not yet."

Sam glanced apologetically at Annie. Giving him a look of gratitude, she turned back to Rosie. "I'll have to begin by asking you something. Do you believe in time travel?"

Rosie's brow wrinkled. "What in tarnation is that?"

"Someone traveling from one age to another—like a person traveling from the future to the past."

Rosie snorted a laugh. "Sounds downright blasphemous to me, not to mention plain crazy."

Annie groaned. "Well, insane though it may sound, I can't tell you my story unless you're willing to believe that traveling through time is possible, that someone—well, like me—could do it."

For a moment, Rosie scowled and muttered under her breath. Then, with a flourish of her pistol, she conceded, "Hell, I 'spect anything is possible. What I know is you gotta be the biggest hornswoggler I ever laid eyes on, sister. But, heck, I can appreciate a good yarn as much as the next fellar. Only when you're through, I reckon I gotta shoot you both for lyin' to me."

Gulping, Annie glanced at Sam, and he said firmly, "Mrs. Dillon, you gotta believe Annie is telling the truth. I didn't believe her at first myself—"

"You mean she traveled through time, but you didn't?" Rosie sneered.

"Yes—well, no, I suppose in a way I did travel through time. But Annie can best explain it." He snapped his fingers. "Hey, sugar, why don't you show her the stuff in your bag?"

"May I get it?" Annie asked Rosie.

Rosie's gaze narrowed. "Where is it?"

"On the table."

Rosie edged toward the table. "Keep palaverin' and I'll have me a gander."

As Rosie sat down at the table and opened the purse, Annie drew a deep, bracing breath. "The truth is, Mrs. Dillon, I'm really your great-great-granddaughter and I'm from a different time, over a hundred years in the future. Sam is a bounty hunter who came across time to nab me, mistaking me for you."

Eyes wild, Rosie dropped the bag and shot to her feet. "Wait just a cotton-pickin' minute, sister! That there's a bounty hunter? I thought he was a Bible-pounder."

"No, he's really a bounty hunter."

With murderous intent gripping her features, Rosie raised her pistol and began to charge. "You mean he's a no-good, low-down . . . Then I gotta kill the varmint!"

"No!" Annie cried, struggling to shield Sam with her own body. "Wait! He's on your side now! He's here to help you! We both are!"

Halfway to the bed, Rosie hesitated for a long moment. At last a sound of raging exasperation escaped her clenched teeth. "Shit and sarsaparilla! If you two hadn't got me so blame confused, I'd shoot you both!"

"It's the truth, Mrs. Dillon," insisted Sam. "We're here to help you. Won't you please at least look inside Annie's bag? Then you'll have proof she's really from the future."

Features set in bristling resentment, Rosie retreated to the table and sat down. Dumping out the contents of Annie's purse, she gasped. "My land, look at all them ditties and doofunnies." Scowling, she examined Annie's container of birth control pills, her sewing kit, hairbrush, and keys, then opened her wallet. She held up Annie's driver's license with a look of mystification. "Well, if skunks don't stink purty. This here says your name is Dillon, like mine, and you're from the year 1996."

"That's what I've been trying to tell you, Great-Great-Grandmother," said Annie with an imploring look.

Rosie tossed down the license. "Now hold your horses! I ain't no one's granny! I'm a widder lady and I ain't never even bore no young 'uns."

"But you will have children someday, or how could I be here?" Annie pursued patiently.

Rosie scowled fearsomely. "You shore do look like me."

"I promise we're related."

"And you got me so buffaloed, I feel like my blame head is fixin' to bust open." With a groan, Rosie pulled off her hat and holstered her pistol. "All right. Let's hear this wild story again. All of it. From the beginning."

Annie patiently spilled out everything to Rosie while her ancestor listened intently, her reactions ranging from frowning skepticism to openmouthed mystification.

"I can't believe we're kin," Rosie acknowledged at last, "though it's plain to see on your face. Still, this traveling through time hogwash—I just ain't sure."

"There's plenty I don't understand, either," Annie said. "Like where I came from, since you're a widow and don't have any children. When I grew up, you were described to me as a great lady who lived in Denver. I even saw a picture of you once—but you were somewhat older, so I'm thinking the picture must have been taken at least ten years from now. No one ever mentioned your having had—er—any troubles with the law."

"Maybe that's 'cause the charges agin' me are false," Rosie suggested.

"Would you tell us about that?" Sam asked.

Rosie got up and began to pace. "It's that bastard, Royce Rowdy! That devil is the root of all evil in my life."

"But you've been accused of killing one of his men," Sam pointed out gently.

She turned to him, her pale eyes seething with outrage. "I killed the slimy sidewinder, but it was self-defense."

"Please tell us," urged Annie. "I promise you can trust us."

"I ain't so sure."

"Please," Annie pleaded. "We really want to help."

Rosie's lower lip began to quiver. "I don't think I can tell you," she confessed with surprising vulnerability. "It plumb breaks my heart to speak of it."

No longer afraid, Annie got out of bed, came to Rosie's side, and touched her arm. "Tell us, Great-Great-Grandmother. I came across time to save you, but we have to know the facts."

Suddenly Rosie was gaping at Annie as if she'd seen a ghost. Drawing her gaze up and down Annie's tall, nightgown-clad figure, the little woman whistled. "Holy hoecakes, sister, what in tarnation did your mama put in your feed bag? You're one huge heifer!"

Annie giggled. "They grow us girls bigger in twentieth-century Texas."

"You mean that's where you're really from?" Rosie asked doubtfully.

"Yes, but more about me later. Sam and I really need to hear your story."

Though she appeared perplexed, Rosie nodded, and the two women sat down together at the table. Rosie tossed Annie a last menacing look. "Well, I reckon I may as well spill the beans. It can't make things no worse. But I swear, if you're lyin' to me, if you two are a couple of no-good fourflushers—"

"We're not," Annie cut in vehemently. "As God is my witness, we're telling you the truth."

"Shit, I don't know why I trust you, but reckon I'll speak my piece." Brushing a strand of hair from her eyes, Rosie haltingly began her tale. "Well, two years ago, I come here to Rowdyville with my bridegroom, Jim, on our wedding night." She sighed. "But 'spect I'd best start back at the beginnin'. You see, Jim and me met over in Denver, where I was beer-jerker at a gambling hall on Market Street." She smiled wistfully. "We plain fell in love at first sight. I knew that man was my salvation from the moment he walked through the door, tipped his hat, and said, 'Ev'nin', ma'am. I'd be mighty obliged if you'd bring me somethin' wet and cold.'"

"He sounds like a real charmer to me," Annie encouraged with a smile.

Rosie's face lit up. "Honey, Jim Dillon was purely a saint. Why he wanted me, the good Lord only knows. Mind you, I weren't no whorin' cyprian, though I'd sashay with the fellars for two bits a dance. Still, I was just a dumb little hillbilly from Tennessee, could barely even read 'ceptin what my grandma lairnt me from her Bible. But Jim—law, that man was fine, a merchant's son from Rolla, Missouri, all polished like and even educated at the School of Mines. He come west to seek

his fortune in gold, and struck his bonanza right before
he met me.''

"Amazing.''

Rosie cackled. "Though the rascal didn't tell me we
was gonna be richer 'n Midas till after we was hitched up
at the Arapahoe County Courthouse. Said he wanted to
be loved for hisself.'' Her expression grew poignant. "If
only he'd a' known I would have loved him if he hadn't
got a boiled shirt to his name. Anyhow, we was drivin'
away from the courthouse when he told me 'bout discov-
erin' his mother lode in the hills north of Rowdyville. He
even showed me a sample. I plumb let out a shout that
nearly toppled the flag poles. Hell, honey, we was happy
as two hogs in a wallow. So we headed out to Central
that very day to file Jim's claim.''

"But you stopped off here?'' Annie asked.

Horror and anguish darkened Rosie's gaze. "Yep, it
got dark, so we let a room at this very boardinghouse,''
she said, sniffing. "Only after we got here, Jim felt kinder
shy, being a bridegroom and all; said he needed a drink
before turnin' in. That was fine by me 'cause I was a
nervous bride. But when three hours passed and my
darlin' didn't come back, I commenced frettin'. So's I
dressed up and went down to the Rowdy Roost, and
that's when . . .'' Rosie's voice trailed off and she shuddered.

"Go on,'' Annie urged, squeezing her hand.

Rosie's tormented gaze met Annie's. "That's when I
found out Royce Rowdy and his thugs had up and kilt
my Jim! Beat my darlin' to a bloody pulp, they did!''

"My God!'' Annie cried, aghast. "But why would they
hurt him?''

Rosie's voice quivered. "Seems my darlin' had one
drink too many and started braggin' 'bout his gold find,
not knowing what a viper Royce Rowdy is. Old Royce
decided to jump Jim's claim, but first he knew he had to
beat the location out of 'im.'' She paused to sniffle, tears
streaming down her face. "Course I lairnt all this later,
'cause my darlin' never told 'um nothin'. But when I first
laid eyes on my Jim all beat to death, I plumb went crazy

and tried to kill old Royce. He grabbed me, laughed, and slapped me silly. Then him and them other bastards started in on me, with my darlin' just a'layin' there all cold. They knocked me 'round but good and tried to make me 'fess up where the gold was. I wouldn't a'told 'um if I knew, and of course I didn't. Jim never told me—said he wanted it to be a surprise."

For a moment no one spoke as Rosie broke down and sobbed, resting her face on her forearms. Annie fetched Rosie a handkerchief, then patted the woman's heaving shoulders and looked on helplessly.

"What happened then?" Sam asked at last.

Rosie looked up and wiped her eyes. "Old Royce didn't get nowheres with me, so he told the meanest one there, Bart Cutter, to take me upstairs, beat and rape the truth out of me." Her eyes gleamed with rabid bitterness. "They never figured a mere female would get her hands on Bart's knife. But I did, and I gutted that piece of low-life trash from end to end."

Annie gasped.

"And that's why you're wanted for murder?" exclaimed Sam.

Rosie nodded.

"How awful!" cried Annie. "Why, your actions were clearly in self-defense. And what about Jim? Why didn't you notify the authorities about his murder?"

"There wasn't no point," replied Rosie with a tortured laugh. "After I kilt Cutter, I peeked downstairs and seen my darlin's body was gone. And I heard one of Rowdy's goons tellin' him the body weren't never gonna be found. So I hightailed it outta there."

"You still could have summoned help," Sam argued.

Rosie waved a hand in deprecation. "Not when I lairnt there was a murder bounty on my head, the reward money paid by Royce Rowdy hisself. After that I didn't care no more. I started terrorizing Rowdy whenever I could—robbing his bank and his stage line, stealing his cattle, shooting at his drovers." She drew herself up with pride. "And I'm still a thorn in his butt. I'm gonna make that miserable bastard suffer a good bit, and then one day I'm gonna cut out his black heart and slaughter his pack of coyotes, too."

Sam whistled. "Two wrongs don't make a right, Rosie."

Eyes gleaming vengefully, she popped up. "But they add up to justice, and so far I ain't got none."

"You can't defeat Rowdy by lowering yourself to his level," Sam maintained.

Standing, Annie turned to Sam. "But Rosie's actions haven't all been self-serving." She smiled at her ancestor. "You've also helped out the needy—like Sally Mott and her children. You've stolen from Rowdy and given to them, haven't you?"

"You think I wanted to keep anything of his'n?" cried Rosie indignantly.

"Let us help you," Annie pleaded.

"How can you help?" she asked with a short, disbelieving laugh.

"Well, if you'd be willing to give up your life of crime," interjected Sam, "maybe we could help clear your name."

"What are you suggestin', bounty hunter?"

"I know Judge Righteous," Sam replied. "J.D.'s a fair man, and he already dislikes and distrusts Rowdy. Plus I know the governor. If you promise me you'll walk the straight and narrow path from here on out, I'll go to Benjamin Eaton and try to get you a pardon. I'm sure Honest Ben will want to see this business remedied."

"He would?" scoffed Rosie. "But how? I ain't given' up so long as Royce Rowdy walks this earth a free man."

"That would be part of the deal," Sam assured her. "Bringing Rowdy to justice."

At this last pronouncement, Annie stared at Sam in awe, but Rosie was shaking her head. "I don't know, bounty hunter," she sneered. "Sounds risky to me. If one of your highfalutin' friends don't agree with ya, I'll be swingin' at the end of a rope by sundown."

Annie touched Rosie's sleeve. "Sam's a good man. If he gives you his word, you can count on it."

Rosie's mouth tightened. "Maybe."

Sam regarded Rosie cynically. "And maybe you're just having too much fun with your life of crime to give it up."

Rosie chortled; Annie was amazed to see the vulnerable woman gone, the ornery outlaw back in her place. "You could be right, bounty hunter," she admitted unabashedly. Grinning, she clapped on her hat. "Well, folks, it's been right interesting, but I'd best scramble before I'm caught—"

"No, please, you can't leave so quickly!" cut in Annie, crestfallen. "We've hardly gotten to talk at all!"

Rosie grinned at Annie. "Don't worry, honey, I'll be in touch."

And as abruptly as she'd appeared, Rotten Rosie turned and dashed out the door.

Chapter 36

❦

"**M**y God—that was amazing," muttered Annie.

"Don't I know it," agreed Sam.

The two sat on the bed together. Annie was sipping a glass of water while Sam sat with his arm around her.

"You're still trembling, sugar," he said anxiously. "You scared?"

She shook her head. "More like stupefied."

"What's it like meetin' your own great-great-grandmother?"

"It's awe-inspiring. I am so glad I finally got to see her face-to-face. She's really something."

"Yep, if I hadn't seen her with my own eyes, I'd never have believed the resemblance between you two." He glanced at her contritely. "Again, sugar, I'm real sorry I ever doubted you."

She kissed his cheek. "Well, looking at things from your perspective, you had cause. Rosie and I do look like we were popped from the same mold."

"Of course, there are differences," he hastily pointed out. "You're much bigger—and prettier."

"You're prejudiced," she accused with a laugh. "But you know, it really did touch me to see how small and fragile my great-great-grandmother is—how vulnerable."

Sam chuckled. "Vulnerable, my foot. Rosie's one tough little spitfire, if you ask me. For a while there

285

tonight, I really did fear she might shoot us both. And her exploits prove she's far from helpless."

"But look what she's been through, Sam," Annie argued passionately. "Watching her husband be killed, having those monsters beat her up and try to rape her! My God, it makes me wild with anger just to think about it!"

"Yep, she's been to hell and back, I'll admit it."

"No wonder she doesn't completely trust or believe us." She sighed. "And she left so abruptly. Do you think she really will get back in touch? Do you think she'll let us help her?"

Sam took her glass and set it on the bedside table. "I don't know, sugar. I ain't exactly convinced Rosie's ready to walk the straight and narrow path. She may have had good cause to stray, but she's been breakin' the law for two years now. A life of crime can be right addictive."

"But she's so worth saving."

"Could be, but a lot of this will be her choice. You know how they say you can lead a horse to water. . . ."

Annie considered this with a frown. "Bless you for saying you'll intervene with Judge Righteous—and even with the governor."

"If Rosie comes around, I'll try my best," he vowed.

"Do you really know Benjamin Eaton?"

"Sure do. You see, the temporary capitol in Denver is right across the street from the Windsor Hotel, where I keep my rooms. I've even taken a swim with Ben Eaton in the Windsor Baths, in the basement of the State House."

"Wow," Annie breathed. "You know, cowboy, you impress me more each day."

"Well, ma'am, I'm willing to try," he replied charmingly. "But if Rosie wants my help, she's gonna have to give up bank robbin' and other mischief."

"She's only trying to retaliate against Royce Rowdy, and who can blame her?" countered Annie. "If only we can bring him to justice, I'm sure Rosie will come around."

"Let's hope so, sugar, though we'll have to have her

cooperation even to get started. Fact is, we're likely to
learn a lot about your ancestor's character in these next
days, beginnin' with whether she keeps her word and
contacts us again. It's gonna take some work to get her
life back on track, and she's gonna have to prove herself
every step of the way."

Annie nodded.

Sam clutched her close. "Come on, honey, it's late.
Let's go to bed."

But even as she lay in bed with Sam tenderly holding
her, Annie's mind still whirled. She relived her astounding moments with her ancestor. Finding Rosie had filled
her with wonder and new purpose. She'd found a great-
great-grandmother who desperately needed her, and she
was not about to shirk her duty to her family history. She
loved Sam with all her heart, yet the two of them had a
mission to accomplish, even though when that purpose
was fulfilled, the future of their own relationship lay in
grave doubt.

In her heart, she supposed she'd known this all along,
had known she'd been thrust back in time for a reason
that went beyond herself, that Sam's love was a miracle
she could count on only for today, that she was involved
in a nobler cause that would require great personal
sacrifice. Still, the prospect of finishing her journey and
possibly ending her adventure with Sam filled her with
great sadness.

Sam, too, felt filled with poignant emotion as he held
Annie close. Resolving Rosie's dilemma would directly
threaten his relationship with Annie. Hadn't she maintained all along that her purpose in being here was to
rescue Rosie? Where would they be left when that goal
was fulfilled? Would the mystical link between Rosie's
world of the present and Annie's life in the future be
shattered? What if the road they followed to Rosie's
salvation ended in a turn that took Annie away from
him?

The questions tortured a heart already heavily laden.
Annie might be here in his arms now—sweet, soft, and
warm—but in a very real sense, she could also be
slipping through his fingers.

Chapter 37

True to Sam's prediction, over the next days, Rosie did not exactly gallop onto the path of righteousness. Annie was dismayed to hear reports that Rotten Rosie had shot out the windows at the apothecary and robbed a supply wagon dispatched from town to the Rowdy ranch.

Even the revival was not immune to the outlaw's antics. On Saturday night as Sam was leading the worshipers in "Onward Christian Soldiers," Annie was startled to hear gunfire coming from the cribs upstairs. Within seconds, hysteria erupted among the crowd. As the worshipers scattered, running for cover, Sam leaped off the stage, grabbing Annie and dragging her beneath a table with him.

"Stay down!" he ordered, as additional shots rang out and screams sounded all around them.

Even with Sam's body covering hers, Annie managed to twist about and catch a glimpse of an amazing parade sprinting down the stairs in the far corner: First came a naked cowboy, vaulting down the steps with his hat shielding his private parts; he was followed by two shrieking line gals in sleazy lingerie; next came Rosie whooping at the top of her lungs and firing off both six-shooters; last advanced her Spanish friend, who was also shooting rapidly.

"Sam, do you see that?" she gasped.

"Keep your head down, damn it!"

Annie's eyes widened as she heard Royce Rowdy yell, "It's Rotten Rosie! Shoot her, boys!"

Annie covered her ears as Rowdy's hands returned fire and the din grew deafening. Sick with fear for Rosie, she watched her ancestor and crony retreat back up the stairs, shooting the entire time.

After what seemed an eternity, the gunfire stopped. Sam rolled off her. "Stay put!"

While several of Rowdy's cronies raced for the stairs, Sam and the others ran outside. At once Annie got up and followed him. On the darkened boardwalk, she hung at the back of the crowd, then heard a man shout, "There they are!"

Squinting, Annie spied two shadowy figures racing across the rooftops several stores down. Her mouth fell open as both leaped off an overhang and landed effortlessly on their horses.

"Kill 'um!" yelled Royce Rowdy.

Annie winced as a new barrage of shots lanced her ears. Given the distance and the darkness, she was pleased to note that the two riders rode off seemingly unscathed.

"After 'um, boys!" ordered Royce.

Royce and his cronies raced for horses and galloped off in a cloud of dust. All at once Annie looked across the boardwalk to see Sam staring at her, his features wan and eyes fierce.

The harsh timbre of his voice made her shiver. "I thought I told you to stay inside. Do you realize you could have been killed?"

"Rosie wouldn't harm me."

Striding closer, he laughed cynically. "Oh, is that so? After she just done such a fine job of showin' her respect for the law."

"She was showing her contempt for Royce Rowdy."

Sam began shaking Annie. "And she could have killed you! Do you hear me, Annie?"

"Shhh!" she scolded, noting a couple of spectators eyeing them curiously. "Someone will hear *you*. It's over now and I'm okay."

"Annie, we ain't gonna be able to help her," he argued heatedly. "She's a lost cause."

"That remains to be seen."

He stared beseechingly at the heavens. "Shit. Reckon we'd best get inside so I can preach . . . if there's anything left to preach to."

After the alarming incident, Sam and Annie argued almost constantly. He insisted they must leave Rowdyville, for the sake of her safety. She begged him to allow them to stay just a few more days, since surely Rosie would relent soon.

Then on Monday night as they entered their room, they spied a familiar figure lounging in a chair near the window, her boots propped on the tabletop. "Well, howdy, folks. Did you like my fireworks on Saturday night?"

"Rosie!" Annie cried in delight.

"You!" Sam exclaimed, charging across the room. "Lady, you have one fine way of demonstrating you want to walk the straight and narrow path!"

"What are you so riled about, bounty hunter?" Rosie demanded.

"Riled? Do you realize you could have killed Annie?"

Rosie chuckled. "Don't get your gizzard in a boil. I seen you folks and I wasn't aimin' at you."

"That was still a damned stupid stunt you pulled!"

Muttering a curse, Rosie shot to her feet. "Well, it wasn't my fault. I never intended to shoot up your revival, preacher."

"Explain that—if you can," Sam ordered.

Rosie hitched up her britches and regarded him impudently. "All right, then, bounty hunter. I'll explain it. You see, my *compadre,* Diego Valencio, decided to visit his ladylove upstairs at the saloon. He figured during your sermon might be the best time to trim the old spurs, if you know what I mean. I was only there to stand guard. But Diego found that trashy little whore of his'n in bed with one of Rowdy's henchmen, and it didn't go down too well, if you get my drift. That's when the fireworks started, and Diego and me chased that coward of a fornicator downstairs. We weren't aimin' at no righteous souls, *Reverend*."

While Annie fought laughter, Sam shook a finger at Rosie. "That was still the most reckless spectacle I ever seen. One day, lady, you're gonna be dangling at the end of a rope, and it's gonna be your own damn fault."

Rosie whistled, glancing askance at Annie. "He sure has got a load of starch in his britches, especially facing a woman with two loaded Colts."

"So you wanted to shoot us all along?" Sam sneered.

"Sam!" Observing the mutinous expression on Rosie's face, Annie clutched his arm. "Come on, you're being too hard on her!"

"She shot up the gall-durned saloon again—with *you* in it."

"Well . . ." Annie flashed Rosie a stiff smile. "Maybe it was just a last hurrah."

"A *what*?" Sam asked.

"You know—a parting shot."

While Sam scowled, Rosie chortled. "Yeah, I like that, sister. A parting shot. That's what it was."

Sam made a growling sound.

Annie glanced at Rosie in admonition. "Actually, what you did was rather foolish. I was very concerned for your safety, and that of others."

"Mighty neighborly of you," concurred Rosie, flashing Sam a fuming look.

"You must also understand that Sam is—well, rather rigid about enforcing the letter of the law," Annie continued.

"Is he, now?" Rosie appeared delighted.

"Oh, yes. You should have heard all the lectures I got when he thought I was *you*."

Rosie cackled.

"That ain't so!" interjected Sam heatedly.

"Oh, yes it is!" she shot back. "All I heard from dawn to dusk was about what a bad girl I was and how I'd have to pay for my crimes." She raised an eyebrow at Rosie. "And don't *ever* go anywhere near his back with a knife. You'll never hear the end of it."

Rosie was covering her mouth to stifle giggles. Sam

leveled a fearsome stare on Annie. "You two through discussin' me like I ain't here?"

"Sorry," she muttered. "You know, we haven't asked Rosie why *she's* here."

Sam turned irritably to Rosie. "So why are you here?"

She eyed him proudly. "Well, I been thinkin' 'bout what you said, bounty hunter—"

"And?" Sam demanded.

With unaccustomed tentativeness, Rosie asked, "Your offer of help still open?"

"Yeah," he all but snarled back. "*I* keep my word."

That comment had Rosie waving a fist. "Shit and sarsaparilla, bounty hunter! When did I promise *you* I'd embrace the law?"

"If you had something besides buffalo chips for brains, you would have done so long before now!"

Annie hastily stepped between them. "Come on, you two, this is totally unproductive. Sam, cool it, will you? Rosie, calm down."

The two backed away, each eyeing the other with resentment.

"So, Rosie," Annie said brightly. "Are you ready to try things our way?"

Rosie set her arms akimbo. "Maybe."

"And what brought about this refreshing change of heart?" mocked Sam.

Rosie gave a shrug. "I reckon there could be more'n one way to skin a sidewinder like Royce. 'Sides, all them gunfights is starting to wear on my nerves. I ain't as young as I used to be."

Annie almost burst out laughing. Rosie couldn't be a day over twenty!

"So, what are you saying?" Sam asked.

"I reckon I'm willing to listen," came the haughty response.

Annie glanced anxiously at Sam. "That okay with you?"

He hesitated, then curtly nodded. "It's an improvement."

All at once, Rosie grinned and tapped Annie's arm.

"He may roar like a big old bear, but he can be tamed, eh?"

Annie sighed dreamily. "He sure can."

"Are we gonna get down to business now or not?" snapped Sam.

Rosie fought laughter. "All right, bounty hunter. If you was *really* gonna help me, tell me the first thing you'd do. . . ."

Chapter 38

"The first thing we need to do," said Sam, "is to find witnesses to corroborate Rosie's story about the night she and her husband stopped here in Rowdyville."

Sam was pacing the room, gathering his thoughts, while Rosie and Annie sat at the table, watching him.

"Witnesses?" Rosie scoffed. "How you reckon we gonna do that? The only bystanders there that night was the bastards that kilt my husband and tried to murder me!"

"Yes, they're all a bunch of animals, Rosie," Sam agreed grimly, "but one thing I've learned chasing down bad men is that one rat will turn on another in an instant."

As Rosie frowned, obviously wavering, Annie said firmly, "Sam's right. He has experience in these matters."

"What we need to do is to target a couple of Rowdy's henchmen who are the most likely to turn on him," Sam continued with a scowl. "Do you remember who all was there that night?"

"How kin I ever forget!" exclaimed Rosie bitterly.

"Do you have any ideas about which ones we might pursue? Perhaps someone who didn't seem real thrilled about what Rowdy was doing to you or your husband?"

Rosie mulled this over for a moment, then snapped her fingers. "Well, there's Willie Wurtz and Charlie Deacon, two of Rowdy's drovers. They didn't appear none too happy when Rowdy and Cutter started in on me." She frowned. "Course Willie's the one that bragged to Rowdy 'bout how my darlin's body weren't never gonna be found. So the two ain't pure as the driven snow, but maybe not quite as low-down as the rest of them vipers."

"We'll target them two, then," Sam decided. "Are they out working Rowdy's ranch each day?"

"Yep."

"Good. Tomorrow I'll see if I can waylay them."

"You can't capture them two by yourself!" Rosie protested.

"That's right," seconded Annie.

"Well, you women sure ain't helping me!" he retorted.

Rosie rolled her eyes. "Ain't that a man for you?" she scoffed to Annie. "They think 'cause they're the ones struttin' 'round with pricks in their britches that they's the cocks of the plains and they kin do anythin' better than a female. Seems to me they're forgitten their mamas used to change their messy diapers and wipe their snotty little noses."

Annie giggled at Rosie's colorful descriptions. Sam glowered.

Rosie waved a hand at him. "Hell, if you're so plumb stubborn, bounty hunter, I'll ask Diego to help you. You can meet up with us tomorry."

"You said Diego's your partner?" asked Annie.

"Yep, he's my *compadre*," Rosie concurred with a grin. "Come across him a year ago when we wuz both trying to rob the same stagecoach. Right comical that was, both of us showin' up at the same time, pistols blazing and kerchiefs over our noses. I couldn't rightly figure out which one of us deserved the pickin's. But Diego was such a gentleman, he let me take the strongbox. '*Señoritas* first,' he says to me."

Sam eyed Rosie reproachfully. "So he's the one you always ride with on your raids?"

"Yep."

Annie snapped her fingers. "Is Diego the one who accosted me the day after we arrived here?"

Rosie nodded. "I told him not to hurt you, jes' scare you a little. You see, I don't cotton to hurtin' folks without no good reason. Now, I got plenty of cause to shoot that miserable coward Rowdy, pit roast him, and throw his meat to the dogs. But with you two just nosing 'round town . . . well, I had my suspicions, mind you, but that didn't give me no call to murder you."

"Well, we're relieved to hear it," Sam put in cynically.

"I'm still curious—was Diego at church two Sundays ago?" Annie pursued.

"Yep—and afterward he come and told me a lady that could have passed for my sister was taking up the offering."

Annie grimaced, rapping her fingertips on the tabletop. "Then he noticed the resemblance between us. Do you think Rowdy has?"

Rosie shrugged. "He only seen me for a short spell that one night. Since that time, I doubt he's glimpsed much more'n the tail of my horse. It's not like with Diego, who sees me ever' day."

"Yes, but your wanted poster is plastered all over these parts, and you and Annie could pass for twins," Sam pointed out. He eyed Annie soberly. "We must still be very careful."

"But we *are* going to help her, Sam," Annie remarked with determination.

"Yeah, we'll help her." Sam crossed the room to Rosie's side. "Do we have a deal, Mrs. Dillon? Will you promise to abandon your life of crime if we'll all work together to clear your name and bring Rowdy to justice?"

Rosie frowned. "Well, I dunno. Not that I ain't grateful, bounty hunter—"

"See—what did I tell you?" Sam interjected to Annie.

"Sam, hear her out!" Annie pleaded.

"Yeah, don't throw a spur," Rosie scolded. "What I'm sayin' is, I'm willin' to give your way a try. If I can make Rowdy pay and still walk away a free woman, hell, there ain't no sweeter revenge. But if it ain't workin' out, I'm hittin' the trail."

"What you mean is, you're not really sure you want to give up your lawbreaking ways," accused Sam.

"That ain't so." Rosie pounded her fist on the table. "I said I'll give it a try, and I meant it. But if things goes sour, I'm sure as hell hightailing it before I attend my own funeral."

"She's got a point, Sam," Annie argued.

He threw up his hands. "Hell, guess we've got a deal . . . of sorts."

"Good," said Rosie, getting to her feet.

Annie also stood and gave Rosie a quick hug. "Thank you for believing us and letting us help you."

Rosie pulled away, regarding Annie skeptically. "Hold it. I ain't at all sure I believe your wild stories." She glanced from Annie to Sam. "Still, my gut says you're good folks, even if the marshal here is purely a pain in the butt."

Sam ground his jaw but refrained from commenting.

"So, I'm willing to give your way a try. But if I ever find out you two have played me false—"

"You won't, Mrs. Dillon," put in Annie adamantly.

"We'll see. And call me Rosie. Well, folks, reckon I'd best mosey along. Bounty hunter, let's get our heads together and figure out where we kin meet tomorry."

"Oh, I'm just so glad Rosie's finally coming around!" Annie declared, clapping her hands.

Seconds after Rosie made her exit, Sam hurled Annie a resentful look. "No thanks to you."

"Sam! What do you mean?"

"You was taking her side instead of mine!"

"But, Sam, you were being so hard on her!"

"Too hard on her after she all but got you killed the other night?" he demanded.

"Well, we explained how that was her last hurrah."

"Yeah, sure."

With a placating smile, Annie stepped close to him and touched his arm. "Now, Sam, please don't be mad at me."

He responded with a forbidding frown. "The two of you was making fun of me."

"Sam! Well, you can be awfully self-righteous."

"So you think I shouldn't enforce the law, huh?" he asked testily.

"You don't have to be so uncompromising about it, especially when we're trying to coax around a hard case like Rosie."

"Yeah, she's a hard case, all right," he muttered. "Well, maybe I don't cotton to coddling criminals."

"But she's coming around."

"Maybe. I ain't at all sure I trust her. But you was treatin' her like Lady Astor, anyhow."

"Good heavens, Sam!" Exasperated, Annie balled her hands on her hips. "We sound like two parents arguing over disciplining the children. That doesn't bode too well for our future together—if we're going to have one."

He scowled, though his eyes held secret amusement.

"Look, I'm sorry for offending your manly pride, all right?"

At last he broke into a grin and hauled her close. "That's better. About time for a little humility from you, woman."

"Oh!"

He ran his hand over her bottom. "So you think I'm pretty well tamed, do you?" He leaned over and nibbled at her throat. "I might still be a lot wilder than you think."

Annie moaned in pleasure. "I'm counting on it, bounty hunter."

Sam ran his tongue over her neck. "Oh, woman, you taste so good. I'm about ready to take you to bed and demand you demonstrate how sorry you *really* are."

Although his nearness was making her wild, Annie managed to push her hands against his shoulders. "Sam, there's one more thing."

He pulled back, regarding her suspiciously. "Yep?"

Taking a bracing breath, Annie blurted, "I want to go with you tomorrow when you meet Rosie and apprehend those men."

"No way in hell!"

"But Rosie's going to be there."

"Only to introduce me to her *compadre*. There's no place for women in this."

With a cry of outrage, Annie shoved him away. "Listen to me, Sam Noble. If you and I are going to make a go of this, you're going to have to quit being such a damn chauvinist. Rosie and I are going along. We'll stay in the background if you like, but we'll be there to back you up if needed. We both know how to shoot a gun. In fact, we might even try some target practice on *your stubborn hide*!"

Sam chuckled. "Sugar, you're some woman. First you apologize, then you try to read *me* the law. Reckon I'm gonna have to wear you out tonight to tame away some of this feistiness. And you'd best be right sweet and agreeable, 'cause I'm about an inch away from givin' you a real good whippin'."

Annie shot him a mutinous look and held him at bay with her hands. "Do Rosie and I get to come along tomorrow?"

"Annie, I'm warning you—"

"Do we?"

"All right!" he retorted in exasperation. "Now kiss me, you willful critter, before I haul you over my knee."

This time Annie did not hesitate.

Chapter 39

Shortly after dawn, Annie and Sam rode out to meet Rosie and Diego at the appointed spot, a small valley two miles north of town. As the two galloped into the grassy dale amid the cooing of mourning doves and the whistle of a cool autumn wind, Annie spotted the pair waiting for them on horseback beneath the shade of a ponderosa pine.

"Morning, folks," called Rosie as the two reined in their mounts. "I'd like you to meet my *compadre,* Diego Valencio."

Diego tipped his sombrero to Annie. *"Señorita."*

Annie recognized the face from church and the voice of the man who had accosted her. "I believe we've already met."

He smiled sheepishly. *"Señorita,* I must beg your pardon. I only sought to protect my dear friend, Rosita."

"Well, see it don't happen again," Sam warned. "I happen to be partial to the lady here."

"Sí, señor, but of course you are," Diego replied diplomatically. He grinned at Annie, displaying even white teeth. "I was unaware that the lady is a distant cousin of Rosita's."

At this pronouncement, Annie slanted Rosie a bemused glance, and the latter shrugged. "Yes, I suppose you could call me that," Annie murmured. Inclining her head toward Sam, she added, "By the way, this is Sam Noble."

"Pleased to make your acquaintance, *señor*," said Diego.

"I reckon I'm obliged to have your help," he replied tightly.

"So what's the plan?" asked Rosie.

Sam replied, "Let's all head out to Rowdy's ranch. Diego, can you show us the way?"

"But of course, *señor*."

"And can you lead us to the two men Rosie told us about?"

"To Wurtz and Deacon? *Por supuesto, señor.* I spied the two just yesterday working the west range."

"It's fall roundup time, you see," explained Rosie. "Them two won't be hard to find. All the hands is busy roundin' up cattle these days for shipment to Denver and on to Kansas City."

"Good," said Sam. "Diego, you ride with me and show us the way." He glanced meaningfully at Annie. "Ladies, hang back at a safe distance, now."

Both women rolled their eyes but didn't protest Sam's order outright.

The men rode off in the lead, the women spurring their mounts and galloping into place behind them. Annie glanced curiously at Rosie. "You told Diego I'm your cousin?"

Rosie cackled. "Should I have told him your cock-and-bull story? Hell, sister, he'd likely shoot us both to put us out of our misery."

"I suppose you have a point," Annie admitted. "Still, you're starting to believe my story, aren't you, Great-Great-Grandmother?"

Rosie's face screwed up in perplexity. "Well, I ain't for sure, though I am thankful to have your help. And would you stop with this 'Great-Great-Grandmother' bunkum? You're making me feel like Methuselah!"

Annie snickered. "What would you like me to call you?"

"How 'bout plain Rosie?"

"All right, plain Rosie," Annie replied, and both women chuckled.

Within an hour, the four had arrived at the western-most boundary of Rowdy's ranch. They clipped the barbed wire and proceeded onto the range, riding over low mountain passes and through wide, grassy meadows. As they approached a high rocky outcropping, Diego signaled for all to halt. From the hilltop, they observed the valley below, where half a dozen drovers were pursuing several dozen head of cattle. With cutting horses prancing and dogs darting about and barking shrilly, the men cut and roped Herefords and longhorns amid vast clouds of dust. Annie smiled at the sight. She hadn't seen cowboys cutting cattle since her days at her parents' ranch, and as always she found there was a certain poetry to the motions of men and beasts.

Rosie pointed at two of the men working on the easternmost fringes of the canyon. "That's Deacon and Wurtz yonder."

Sam frowned. "It's going to be hard to nab them with the others around. Guess we'll have to wait and see if we can catch 'um alone."

The four waited, watching the wranglers and snacking on jerky and crackers. Their vigilance paid off an hour later, when Deacon and Wurtz rode away from the others, pursuing a stray Hereford.

"Aha!" cried Rosie, pointing ahead. "They're gonna chase that heifer up the box canyon yonder. Let's nab 'um when they come back out!"

"Diego and I will apprehend them," stated Sam. Then, noting two sets of rebellious feminine eyes fixed on him, he hastily amended, "You ladies can back us up."

After a bit more grumbling and plotting, the foursome galloped ahead to the entrance to the box canyon. While Rosie and Annie took refuge behind a boulder, Diego and Sam remained on horseback on either side of the narrow pass. Just as the drovers rode back through the opening with the heifer in tow, Diego and Sam converged in front of them with guns drawn.

"All right, stop right there and put your hands up!" Sam ordered.

The startled men reined in their horses and raised trembling hands. "We ain't got no money!" one cried in a shrill voice.

"But we're not *bandidos, señor*—at least not today," Diego answered with a sly grin. Maneuvering his horse closer to the men, he grabbed both their pistols and cut loose the heifer, which ambled off with a loud moo.

As the two men trembled in fear and confusion, Rosie stepped from behind the large rock. "Well, if you two ain't a sight for sore eyes. Remember me, boys?"

"No, ma'am!" exclaimed the second man.

"Don't lie to me, you sidewinders!" She turned to Sam. "Meet Willie Wurtz and Charlie Deacon." She jerked her thumb toward each man in turn. "Well, reckon we'd best get 'um out of here before someone comes along to rescue the snakes. Blindfold 'um, and I'll lead you to my cabin."

"Yes, ma'am," said Sam.

It was easy for Annie to figure out why Rosie hadn't been apprehended in two years. She lived in a deserted miner's shack high in the hills. There was no road to the cabin, only the most circuitous trail, and the hut was surrounded by such a dense thicket of ponderosa pines and Douglas firs that it was impossible to see it until one came upon it.

After Sam removed the captives' blindfolds, the group filed inside. Annie observed that the interior of the log cabin was neat but sparsely furnished, with a single iron bed against one wall, a scarred table and chairs pushed against another, and a makeshift kitchen area crammed into a corner. Without a flower or a curtain in sight, the space seemed utilitarian and impersonal, as if Rosie had no real ties to her life here. And Annie supposed she hadn't any, not after losing her precious Jim.

She watched as Rosie helped Sam tie the ranch hands to two straight chairs while Diego lit a fire in the hearth. For a moment Annie wondered if Rosie and Diego might be more than friends. But another glance around the cabin made her dismiss this possibility, since she spotted nothing that might belong to the Spaniard, only Rosie's lonely narrow bed and her diminutive clothing hanging on pegs around the walls.

Annie studied their two captives more closely. Their faces were pale with terror as they sat with hands tied behind their backs. Willie Wurtz was tall and lanky, with a long, thin face, a scruffy beard, and restive dark brown eyes. His cheeks were heavily pock-marked, his eyes jaundiced. Charlie Deacon was potbellied and balding, with a round face slashed by a huge handlebar mustache. His upper lip continually twitched, revealing tobacco-stained teeth. Both men smelled of sweat, tobacco, and cattle dung.

An appetizing pair, she decided.

While Annie and Rosie sat down together at the table and Diego perched on a stool near the fire, Sam stood before the prisoners. His massive body appeared quite daunting as he loomed with arms akimbo and feet slightly spread.

Nodding toward Rosie, he spoke in charged tones. "All right, boys, we're gonna have us a little chat about the night you murdered this lady's husband."

"Shit, mister, we don't know nothin' about no murders!" exclaimed Charlie in a nasal twang, his upper lip jerking spasmodically. "And the rest of the boys is gonna come lookin' fer us, soon as we don't return."

"They'll never find you," drawled Sam. "And you're not going anywhere until you help this lady."

"But we ain't never even seed this woman before!" put in Willie.

"Hokum and hogwash!" cried Rosie, charging up to confront the pair with a raised fist. "You was both there the night my Jim and I come through Rowdyville, and your boss up and kilt him for no good reason while tryin' to jump his claim."

Willie's guilty gaze darted away from Rosie's. "We got no idear what you're talking about, ma'am."

Rosie pulled out her Colt. "Then you both got sheep dung fer brains and I'm gonna blew your goodfernuthin' heads off!"

"No, ma'am, please don't!" pleaded Willie.

"We ain't no murderers!" wailed Charlie.

Sam grabbed Rosie's wrist and eyed her sternly. "Now let's not take the law into our own hands. How 'bout if I just turn these boys over to Judge Righteous and let old J.D. hang 'um?"

Across the room, Annie turned away to stifle a smirk at Sam's tactics. He and Rosie were really laying it on thick. Forcing a sober expression, she turned back to see the captives cringing in horror. Obviously, *they* took Sam's threats seriously!

Rosie holstered her gun. "Shore. String 'um up. Makes no nevermind to me."

"B-but y-you can't get us for no murder," stammered Charlie.

"We never kilt no one!" insisted Willie. "You got no call to string us up."

"Sure I do," replied Sam with a nasty smile. "You boys is killers, as my witness here will be happy to testify." He wrapped an arm around Rosie's shoulders and all but split his face grinning.

"But she's Rotten Rosie—ain't nobody gonna believe her!" protested Willie.

"Yeah, she's a thievin', cold-blooded killer! Ain't nobody gonna listen to her wabash!" seconded Charlie.

"And I thought you boys claimed you didn't know me!" scoffed Rosie.

Charlie and Willie exchanged a sheepish glance.

"It don't matter," Sam assured Rosie with a wink. "I'm in good with Judge Righteous. If I tell him these boys deserve a fatal bout with hemp fever, he'll be only too happy to oblige."

Both captives gulped in fear.

Sam scratched his jaw and scowled at the prisoners. "Only problem is, boys, they don't got a very good hangman up at Central these days. Last time they had a necktie party in Gilpin County, the executioner didn't hang the fellar quite right and it took the miserable bastard most of an hour to strangle. Poor man turned twenty shades of purple and his eyes all but popped out. I never seen such wild kicking and such." He shook his head and clucked to himself.

Both men were bug-eyed. "Please, you gotta believe us!" cried Willie. "We ain't no murderers!"

"And we ain't aimin' to die!" added Charlie.

Sam ignored the men's pleas and spoke to Rosie. "You know, it's purely a shame, too. If these boys would just help us out, I know I could persuade old J.D. to go easy on 'um, maybe give 'um a year or so at hard labor instead of stringing 'um up."

"We'll help!" cried Willie.

"Yeah, we sure will!" seconded Charlie.

At last Sam turned to the men with an expression of mild curiosity. "Then you boys is willing to admit you seen Royce Rowdy kill this lady's husband?"

"Yeah, we seed it all," blurted Willie, "though we wasn't in on it. Royce and Bart did most of the beatin' and killin'." He paused as Rosie cried out in anguish. "Sorry, ma'am."

She stepped closer, eyeing the men with anger and bitter resolve. "Do you know where my husband is buried?"

"No, 'um," answered Willie. But his guilty gaze shied away from hers.

Rosie pressed the barrel of her pistol to Willie's forehead. As the man cringed, gasped, and even urinated on himself, she yelled, "Spill it out, you no good, flea-brained weasel!"

"All right!" he cried, his yellow, bloodshot eyes beseeching her. "Royce ordered me and Charlie to throw his body down an abandoned mine shaft at Pine Creek."

"Can you take me to his body?"

Willie shook his head and began to sob.

Rosie pointed her pistol at Charlie. "Can you?"

"I'm sorry, ma'am," replied Charlie with a crooked frown. "It was bitter cold that night, and there was too much ice on the road to make it to the mine. So . . . well, ma'am, we reckoned we had no choice but to leave your husband in the woods. We figured the wolves or the coyotes got him."

"Oh, God!" Rosie cried, going pale and almost dropping her Colt.

While Sam grasped Rosie's pistol, Annie rushed forward and grabbed her great-great-grandmother before she collapsed. Holding Rosie's trembling body against her own, she whispered, "I'm sorry. So sorry."

Rosie clung to Annie and shuddered with emotion. After a long moment she pulled away, smiled bravely, and wiped her tears. "'Spect there's nothin' more to be done 'bout my poor darlin', then." Raising her chin with pride, she turned to Sam. "What are you fixin' to do now, bounty hunter? Turn these two in to Judge Righteous?"

"We'll certainly go see J.D. before this is over," Sam replied, "but remember, he's not the one with the power to absolve you, Rosie. So, first I really think I need to take these two to Denver to tell their story to the governor. Then maybe I can arrange your pardon."

"You'd really do that for me?" Rosie asked in quivering tones.

"Didn't I give my word?"

Rosie chuckled and tapped Annie's arm. "Ain't he a piece of work?"

Annie smiled. "He sure is."

"So you're still with us on this, Rosie?" asked Sam gravely.

She shrugged. "Yep—I reckon I'm along for the ride, bounty hunter. Long as I git my revenge, I'm game. Only remember—if you don't git old Royce, I'm gonna."

"We'll get him," Sam vowed, "if you'll just hold your horses while I take these two to Denver. In the meantime, I need to leave you ladies somewhere safe. Perhaps with my grandmother."

"Can't we come with you?" Annie asked.

Sam pinned her with a stern look. "Sugar, are you really thinking of what's best for Rosie? What if we all go to Denver and she is arrested there?"

"Yeah, the bounty hunter's got a point," put in Rosie.

"Besides, there will be nothing for you two to do in Denver except get in trouble," Sam continued. "If you're with my grandmother, that will be the perfect opportunity for you two to become reacquainted."

"I guess Sam is right," Annie conceded.

Rosie nodded. "Yep, it's best we hunker down till the

coast is clear. I ain't aimin' to git hanged for no good reason." She frowned at Sam. "But, friend, you can't haul two wranglers off to Denver single-handed—even if these two is crackbrained idjuts."

While the captives grimaced at being described thus, Sam replied, "Whip Whistler will help me, if necessary."

"Who's he?" asked Rosie.

"A friend."

"You're forgetting Diego," reminded Annie.

All three glanced at the Spaniard, who had sat quietly in a corner throughout the exchange. Now the black-haired man stood and sadly shook his head. "I would love to help you, *señor* Sam, but I, too, am wanted by the law. Rosie and I have created quite a reputation for ourselves in these parts." He bowed to Rosie. "Perhaps, *señora,* now that your family is here to see to your needs, it is best that I return to Mexico." He grinned wryly. "That is, before my luck runs out."

"Whatever you think is best, *compadre,*" said Rosie.

Diego nodded. "*Vayan con Dios,* my friends."

Chapter 40

❦❦**W**e should be arriving at Grandma's camp any time now," Sam called back to the women.

"Good," shouted Rosie. "I'm aimin' to get this mess settled."

"Me, too," agreed Annie.

The five-person caravan wended its way along a rugged trail that snaked through high mountain passes. Above them stretched snow-capped Alpine peaks and vivid blue skies; below them an icy stream rushed over smooth rocks. The weather was brisk and cool, and Annie had noted that the aspens along the trail had turned a deep gold; winter would soon be upon them.

Sam led off the entourage, with a rope hooked around his pommel and tethered to the horses of Willie and Charlie, who rode behind him single file with hands securely bound to their saddle horns. Rosie and Annie, both armed, made up the rear flank.

They had departed Rowdyville with as little fanfare as possible. Before they left, Sam had informed Royce Rowdy that they had to leave town suddenly due to a death in the family. Although Rowdy had been less than pleased to hear of the cancellation of the remaining revival sessions, at least Annie and Sam didn't have to worry about arousing his suspicions. They had returned their buggy to the stable in Georgetown, then met up with Rosie at her cabin, where she and Diego held the captives.

Just as the group was preparing to depart, Annie had started her period, an occurrence that had also reminded her she was almost out of birth control pills. Still, she'd been pleased to have a new woman friend to consult on handling this rather troublesome monthly occurrence here in the past, and Rosie had cheerfully provided supplies for her to use on the trail.

Annie had become much better acquainted with Rosie, and everything she had discovered had only increased her admiration. She had heard of Rosie's humble upbringing in Tennessee, how she had suffered at the hands of a father who had beaten her, and been neglected by a mother who was ill much of the time. She had marveled at Rosie's courage in leaving home, penniless, at the age of fifteen. She had admired her fortitude in working at dozens of saloons and even bordellos, her integrity in never selling her virtue. She had learned how the proud young woman had gradually worked her way west to Denver at the age of eighteen, and more about how she had met and married Jim Dillon—and how her life had been shattered on losing him two years ago. She had learned that, all told, Rosie was a fine human being trapped in a desperate situation, and she needed help to get her life back on the right track.

Annie was determined that she and Sam would provide that help. Smiling at Rosie, she remarked, "Well, Sam should be off to Denver in the morning to see the governor, and I know you'll enjoy being with the Cheyenne band."

"Maybe so," said Rosie, though she frowned skeptically. "I never had no redskin friends before. Where I growed up, all we heard tell was of injuns scalpin' and ridin' the warpath. But I reckon I'm willing to keep an open mind."

Annie stifled a laugh at Rosie's typically outspoken remarks. "Doesn't it feel good to realize you're so much closer to vindication?"

Rosie frowned. "Well, I ain't got no pardon yet."

"Sam will get you one," Annie reassured her.

Rosie sniffed. "I just wish I could bury my poor Jim."

At her last, emotional words, Willie twisted backward

in his saddle and called, "Ma'am, Charlie and me, we're right sorry about that."

"Oh, shet up!" Rosie snapped. "Who's askin' you, anyhow?"

Looking much chastised, Willie turned away.

Rosie pointed ahead toward a large valley. "Hey, is that there the village?"

Annie stretched in her saddle, spotting a circle of tepees in the gentle slope of the distant meadow. "It sure is." She cupped a hand around her mouth. "Sam, do you see it?"

He waved a hand in the affirmative.

As the group filed down into the valley, the Indians ceased their labors and came forward, several waving as they recognized Annie and Sam. Annie smiled as she spotted Sits on a Cloud with her plump infant on a cradle board. She quickly dismounted and rushed over to hug the mother and kiss the baby, thrilled to find both healthy and well fed.

She rejoined the others to find Medicine Woman and Whip at the head of an entourage standing before Rosie and Sam. "Greetings, Grandson," said Medicine Woman, staring from him to Rosie to the two captives still on their horses. "It is an unexpected blessing to have you back with us." She gazed sharply at Rosie. "This is Rotted Rosie?"

While Rosie chortled, Annie said, "Medicine Woman, this is Rosie Dillon, and I assure you she's not rotten at all."

Medicine Woman nodded solemnly. "Welcome to our village."

"Thank you kindly, ma'am," answered Rosie.

Medicine Woman addressed Sam. "Your mission was successful?"

"Yes, ma'am." He jerked a thumb toward Rosie. "We found out Rosie here's been falsely accused of some stuff. And we was hoping her and Annie could stay here with you while I go to Denver to try to clear her name."

"We are happy to have the women among us."

"And what about them two?" asked Whip, jerking a thumb toward the captives.

"They's a couple of bad 'uns," Sam replied. "Reckon they'll be going with me to Denver, as witnesses."

"Need some help with 'um?" Whip asked.

"Likely so," said Sam. "You offering, partner?"

"Sure, friend." Whip stroked his jaw and regarded the prisoners with wry humor. "You know, it's purely a shame. If you didn't need them old boys, we could cut 'um loose and let our braves hunt 'um down and scalp 'um. Our warriors haven't had a scalpin' party in a month of Sundays."

This remark brought grins to the faces of a couple of young bucks standing nearby and prompted the captives to shudder in fear.

Sam chuckled. "Yeah, it sure is a shame, but I did promise the old boys I'd convince the judge to go easy on them for helping us out."

"Too bad," replied Whip while both prisoners breathed a sigh of relief. "I'll get our braves to tie 'um up good in one of the lodges and guard 'um."

"Thanks."

Whip motioned to the two warriors, who strode over and helped him untie the prisoners. Moon Calf edged forward to watch. His bearded features twisted in a combination of caution and confusion, he stared pointedly at each prisoner as he was led away, while Charlie and Willie grimaced at the strange man's scrutiny.

Then Moon Calf turned to Annie, Sam, and finally Rosie. All at once, the sacred idiot appeared as if he'd seen a ghost. He made a wild cry and cringed, flinging his forearms upward to shield his face, as if he'd glimpsed a truth too painful to see. A moment later, he slowly lowered his arms and peered at Rosie in trembling bewilderment.

What on earth was wrong with the man now? Annie wondered. Why had he shown such unusual curiosity about the prisoners, and why was he staring at Rosie in mystification?

Annie was equally astounded by Rosie's demeanor. For she had turned sheet white and was tottering so badly that Annie rushed over and grabbed her arm to steady her. Rosie's skin felt clammy, and never had

Annie viewed such shock and amazement on another person's face.

"Rosie, what is it?" she cried. "What's wrong? Are you ill?"

Impatiently shaking loose Annie's grip, Rosie stepped toward Moon Calf, tears streaming down her cheeks. Moon Calf's eyes were brimming, too, as he stood gazing back at Rosie!

"J-Jim, darlin'!" Rosie cried, her voice raw with emotion. "Is that you?"

"Jim?" Annie repeated in a stunned whisper, her hand flying to her mouth.

Slowly Rosie approached the sacred idiot. For a moment, Moon Calf regarded her in terrible confusion. His gaze darted about like that of a wild, cornered animal, then fixed on Rosie again. At last a hoarse sound escaped him, a primal wail caught somewhere between anguish and rapture.

He reached out and hauled Rosie into his arms. For an endless moment the two stood trembling, tightly embraced, eyes closed in ecstasy while muffled sobs shook them both.

Annie and the others looked on in dazed silence. At last she found her voice. "Rosie, do you mean this man is . . . ?"

Her voice faded away as the couple walked off together and disappeared into a lodge, never once looking back.

"I can't believe it!" Annie cried to the others. "Does this mean Moon Calf is actually Jim Dillon, Rosie's dead husband?"

Bewildered silence greeted her question. Then Sam replied dryly, "Sugar, don't look like he's much dead to me."

"But he's *supposed* to be dead," Annie argued. "My God, the poor man was beaten to a pulp and left for the coyotes. And now . . ." She paused, chest heaving, staring in bafflement at the lodge in which the couple had taken refuge. "I can't stand this! I must go ask them what's going on!"

Even as she started away, Sam caught her arm. "Sugar, this ain't no time to be disturbin' them."

"Oh, you're right, but—" Seething with frustration, she gazed about the small group of Indians still gathered around them. "Can someone explain to me how Moon Calf has been with this band for two years, and no one guessed who he really is?"

Looking much bemused, the Indians consulted among themselves in their native tongue. Then Medicine Woman spoke for the group. "Annie, you are forgetting that when we found Moon Calf, his mind was gone. He was a battered man, both physically and spiritually, and he became reborn, a new man, among the Cheyenne."

"I suppose you're right," admitted Annie, "but this is some shock." Her eyes lighting with a sudden realization, she smiled. "It's wonderful, though. My God, it's a miracle! At last my family history is beginning to make some sense."

"I reckon it is, sugar," agreed Sam. "And no wonder Moon Calf took such a shine to you."

"That's right!" she cried in awe. "He must have wondered if I wasn't Rosie—but in his heart, I'm sure he recognized the differences, too."

Shaking his head, Sam stared off at the lodge. "Boy, I can't wait to hear what them two have to say when they step from that tepee."

This didn't happen for many long hours. Not until the group was gathered for the evening meal did Rosie emerge from the tepee, her face glowing as she tugged Moon Calf toward the others.

Moon Calf, however, appeared almost as helpless and confused as before. He actually recoiled, digging in his heels as the couple neared the circle.

But Rosie merely smiled and gently urged him on with low, clucking sounds. "Come on, darlin'. I reckon you're still flustered, but no one here is fixin' to hurt you. They's your friends, precious, the ones that saved you after you was kilt. 'Member?"

Moon Calf blinked in perplexity, then nodded, carefully taking his place beside Rosie in the circle.

For a moment no one seemed to know what to say.

Indians and whites all wore equally baffled expressions.
At last Annie felt compelled to break the silence.

"Rosie, we're all so thrilled that your husband appears
to be alive after all."

"Thank you kindly," replied Rosie.

"Then he *is* your husband?"

"Shore is. This here is my Jim," she declared proudly,
clutching his arm. She beamed to all in the circle.
"Thanks to these fine folks that took him in."

"Does he remember what happened to him?" Annie
pressed.

"Yeah, I think he do."

"Can you explain it to us?"

"I think Jim should." Rosie eyed him tenderly. "Can
you tell the others, darlin'?"

He shook his head.

"But you trust 'um, don't you?"

He hesitated, glanced furtively about the group, then
nodded.

Rosie raised his hand and kissed it. "Are you still
confused, precious?"

Another nod.

"Can't you say somethin'?"

Jim glanced about the circle again, shuddered, then
finally spoke. "I . . ." His voice trailed off, tears filled his
eyes, and at last a tremulous smile lit his countenance,
shining across his features in a rare moment of lucidity.
"I know this w-woman is my wife," he stammered.

The others cheered, and with a cry of delight, Rosie
tightly hugged Jim. Afterward she beamed at Annie and
Sam. "Bounty hunter, you ain't gotta fret about me no
more," she announced proudly. "I've found my precious
now, it's purely a gift from the Almighty, and I'm a
changed woman. I'm hangin' up my shootin' irons this
very night."

"Good for you, Rosie," replied Sam with a laugh.

"We're so happy for you," added Annie, wiping away
a tear.

Rosie turned to cuddle with her husband again. Jim
said no more that night, as if his one brief speech had

overstrained his returning faculties. Rosie, too, was quiet, her expression radiant as she clung to his side and helped him eat his supper.

After the meal, Annie lingered by the fire with Sam. Watching Rosie and Jim walk off toward their tepee, she sighed dreamily. "I'm stunned, Sam. But, my Lord, I think that's the sweetest sight I've ever seen."

Sam wrapped an arm about Annie's shoulders. "Yep, it shore is a fine sight."

"It seems incredible that Jim could be alive after all he suffered," she continued wonderingly. "But it does reconcile a lot of this mystery in my mind. Who knows? Maybe my great-grandfather will be conceived tonight."

Sam nodded. "Could be, sugar. You know, the Almighty really did smile on them."

"And on us, too, Sam."

"Amen," he murmured, leaning over to kiss her brow. "Darlin', I been thinkin'. . . . Maybe we should all go to Denver."

Taken aback, she asked, "You mean the four of us and the prisoners?"

"Yep. Jim might be the best possible witness to take, and Rosie sure ain't gonna part with him now."

"Can you blame her?"

"Not in the least. Them two have been through enough hell and deserve all the happiness they can find."

"Then you believed Rosie when she announced she's a reformed woman now?"

"Oh, yeah," he replied, staring tenderly into Annie's face. "I seen that light in a woman's eyes before. . . . It's the light of love."

"Oh, Sam." The two kissed blissfully.

Afterward he nestled her close. "You know, I also have a selfish reason for wantin' to take everyone to Denver. I don't want to be away from you, neither, if only for a few days."

She smiled. "I know how you feel. But . . . do you really think Jim can help Rosie's cause? He's still so confused—he could barely get out one lucid sentence tonight."

"Yeah, but he actually made sense for the first time I

can recollect. We'll give it a few days first, till he sorts things out. With Rosie here, I allow it won't take long."

"That's possible."

"I reckon soon he'll be as sane as you and me."

She wrinkled her nose at him. "Are we sane, Sam?"

He chuckled. "We're plumb crazy about each other, sugar, that's for sure." He stroked her mouth with his index finger, his voice lowering a sexy octave. "Reckon we can find a way to be alone tonight?"

Annie cleared her throat. "Sam . . . Well, I'm kind of out of commission right now."

He eyed her askance. "My God—what'd I do to you? Shit, I oughta be horsewhipped."

She laughed. "It wasn't you, silly. There's nothing wrong. I'm just having—well, I think you refer to it as a 'woman's time.'"

"Ah," he murmured, sounding a trifle disappointed. "Then them pills of yours really do prevent you from havin' a young 'un?"

"Yes, but I'm almost out of them."

He grinned.

She eyed him askance. "Were you hoping they wouldn't work?"

He was quiet a moment, looking up at the beautiful, glittering heavens. "I'd be right proud to have you bear my child, Annie, if that's what you're askin'," he admitted in a tight voice. "Hell, what man wouldn't be?"

Annie couldn't contain a joyous smile as she squeezed his hand. "You're a sweetheart, Sam Noble. Still, if I became pregnant—"

"It might make things a mite simpler," he finished for her.

She shook her head. "From my perspective, it would only make things all the more complicated."

"*Only,* Annie?" he asked, an edge of hurt in his voice.

She hugged him close, and hoarse emotion tinged her voice. "Of course I'd be proud to have your baby, Sam. What woman wouldn't be?"

He kissed her cheek. "So you're almost out of them pills, eh? What are we gonna do when you're back *in* commission?"

Annie didn't answer him. What troubled her most was her fear that she and Sam might soon run out of time.

Chapter 41

❦

Over the next couple of days, Rosie worked miracles with Jim. She helped him bathe, and cut his hair and beard. She dressed him in the white man's clothing Sam generously provided. Annie often spotted the couple alone on the hillside, sitting beneath the arms of a spectacular golden aspen, clutching hands and quietly talking as glorious autumn leaves swirled about them. The sight of her great-great-grandparents communicating so tenderly never failed to move Annie. She knew Rosie was gently, patiently nudging Jim back to reality; indeed, with each day that passed, the former sacred idiot appeared more lucid, though he remained almost painfully shy around everyone except Rosie.

Annie felt particularly touched one night when she passed Rosie and Jim's lodge. Hearing the sounds of a woman's soft crooning, she couldn't resist glancing inside through the still open tepee flap. Rosie was kneeling beside Jim, softly singing him the folk song "Black-Eyed Susie" as she tucked him into bed. He was eyeing her with quiet adoration. Annie's heart welled at the poignant scene.

Rosie might call herself "just a dumb little hillbilly from Tennessee," but she was a very wise, incredibly strong woman with a loving heart. She was performing a miracle, healing a man who had been traumatized beyond all known human endurance. Annie could barely absorb the wonder of it all.

The next afternoon, Annie was walking with Sam by

the lake when they were startled to see the other couple
rush up. Annie could scarcely believe the transformation
in both of them. Rosie's face gleamed with happiness,
and for once she looked entirely feminine, wearing a
blue calico dress Annie had lent her, her hair nicely
combed and hanging in loose curls about her shoulders.
Jim appeared handsome, too, his angular face clean-
shaven, his eyes dark and alert; he wore black trousers, a
white shirt, and a leather vest.

Squeezing her husband's hand, Rosie proudly announced, "Jim remembers about his gold bonanza now.
He wants you to take us to Central to file a claim."

"That true, Jim?" Sam asked.

Jim nodded but avoided Sam's eye, and Annie felt a
new welling of sympathy for the miserably reticent man.

"Well, we'll get to your claim in good time, friend,"
Sam reassured him. "First, we all need to go to Denver
to clear Rosie's name. That gold mine ain't gone nowheres in two years, and I reckon it'll be safe for the next
week or so till we get up to Gilpin County." Sam drew a
deep breath. "Jim, I need you to testify to the governor,
tell him what Royce Rowdy and his henchmen done to
you. How 'bout it?"

When Jim hesitated, Rosie flashed him an encourag-
ing smile. "Reckon you can do that, precious?"

Jim seemed to struggle within himself for another
moment; then a tremulous smile lit his handsome countenance. Looking again like a very sane man, he slowly
replied, "Th-This woman is my life. I will do anything
for her."

With a cry of rapture, Rosie fell into Jim's arms. Sam
and Annie looked on through misty eyes.

The journey to Denver took three days. Due to Rosie's
notoriety and the fact that they were transporting two
less-than-willing captives, they avoided towns, traveling
along old mining trails and on abandoned railbeds. They
slept under the stars their first night out. The second,
they were fortunate enough to take refuge in a deserted
logging cabin high in the hills above Denver. While

Annie and Rosie guarded the prisoners, the men went hunting. They returned with a pheasant, which Rosie plucked and cleaned, and Annie helped roast over an open fire in the hearth. While the bird cooked, Sam and Jim fed their prisoners a supper of beans and bacon, then tied them up and bedded them down in the toolshed.

The couples shared their meal on the floor by the fire. Watching Jim offer Rosie a leg of pheasant, Annie reflected on how he was starting to come out of his shell. Today, he had smiled and spoken briefly to them several times, not stammering at all. And he'd even gone hunting with Sam.

Later, as the couples sat quietly sipping coffee, Jim finally told his tale. Staring into the flames and clutching Rosie's hand, he murmured, "You know, it's all becoming clearer now. . . ."

"What's becoming clearer, precious?" Rosie asked.

Distraught, Jim glanced up to regard his wife. "The night I 'died,' and afterward."

Sam and Annie exchanged an amazed glance. "You want to tell us about it?" he asked quietly.

Jim nodded, blinking back a bitter tear. He hesitated as a log settled noisily, sending a spray of sparks shooting up the chimney.

"Yes, I'll tell you," he began at last, raising a trembling hand to his brow. "My Lord, it's hard to believe it happened only two years ago. It seems a lifetime away, an eternity without my darling bride." He smiled tremulously at Rosie.

She squeezed his hands. "It'll be all right, precious."

He swallowed hard. "Christ, I was such a fool that night we stopped in Rowdyville. I was a nervous bridegroom, leaving my wife to go buck up my courage with liquor. If only I'd known . . ."

"How could you have?" asked Rosie.

"The only time I'd ever taken a drink before was at my sister's wedding back in Missouri," Jim confessed. "I made a fool of myself then, and I should have learned my lesson that once. But instead I got liquored up and allowed Royce Rowdy to talk me into a poker game. I started winning, and pretty soon I was spouting off my mouth about my gold find. . . ."

As his voice trailed off in misery, Rosie patted his back. "There, precious, you don't gotta tell us everythin' if you don't want to."

His haunted gaze met hers. "But I must, my love. For two years, I've avoided all recollection of my previous life. I've been like a dead man, buried in my own madness. How can I ever hope to get on with my life, with our lives together, if I can't gather the courage to face those terrible memories?"

"Sure, darlin'," Rosie agreed, sniffling. "Whatever you think is best."

Jim drew a steadying breath, tightly gripping Rosie's hand. "Anyway, like an idiot, I bragged to Rowdy about the fortune in gold I would soon claim, even showed him the sample we were taking to be assayed in Central. All at once, everyone left the saloon except for Rowdy and his bullies, and then they started in on me. . . ." He stared at Rosie through fresh tears. "They beat me savagely and cursed me, kicking me like a dog when I went down on the floor. Still, I wouldn't tell them where my claim was, wouldn't sacrifice our future together."

Rosie reached out to stroke Jim's face, her own features fraught with heartfelt emotion. "Jim, darlin', don't you know you matter to me more'n all the gold in the world?"

"I know that, my love, but my pride and anger got the better of me that night. I felt no man with real courage would give in to those bastards. Besides, if I had told them, I'm sure they would have killed me, anyway."

"You're right," agreed Sam.

"So I endured the beatings and held my tongue. I was mostly dead by the time you came in looking for me." A tormented groan escaped him. "I swear to God I wanted to help you, sweetheart—heavens, I was so scared for you—but I couldn't speak or move, could barely even breathe."

"And I thought you was dead by then!" Rosie exclaimed.

"I hurt enough to be dead," he admitted. "My agony was even greater because I was powerless to go to your aid. After they dragged you away, I heard Rowdy telling Willie and Charlie to take my 'corpse' and dump it down an abandoned mine shaft. I was certain I was done for. But they left me in the woods instead." He shivered. "God, it was so cold. When I woke up, I remembered nothing—not the beating I'd suffered, not the danger to you, not even a single detail of my life up until that moment. Still, when I saw the three Indian braves riding up, I recognized the danger. I started ranting and screaming at them—wild, crazy words. Instead of hurting me, they took me to their band and nursed me back to health. For two years, I lived among the Cheyenne as their sacred idiot. I babbled great ceremonial nonsense and learned to charm animals." He paused, drawing a shuddering breath. "Even when I had my vision that Sam should travel beyond the Numhaisto, I didn't know what it meant. Then Annie came."

He smiled at her shyly, and she smiled back. "You saw something in me, didn't you?"

He nodded. "When Sam first brought you among us, I felt strangely drawn to you, though I didn't know why. Now I know it was because you so resembled Rosie. At the time, you sparked something in my memory, some lost remnant I couldn't seem to find. As with my vision, my spirit seemed to be moving in a direction my mind couldn't fully grasp. I began to feel intensely frustrated, to reach for recollections that weren't even there." He gazed at Rosie through his tears. "After Sam took Annie away, I took refuge in my madness once more. Then when he brought you among us, my love, everything came rushing back."

Rosie and Jim embraced, clinging to each other for a long moment.

Annie wiped away a tear. "What a remarkable story," she said to Sam. "It's a miracle either of them survived."

"Indeed—just wait till the governor hears this," he replied.

"Are you sure he'll see us?" asked Rosie anxiously.

"Damn right he will," said Sam. "Like I told Annie,

Governor Eaton is a friend of mine. We've brushed
shoulders on a number of occasions. And earlier this
year, a gang of bad hombres was robbing banks in
Denver, and you're looking at the man who hauled 'um
in. I know the thieves was an embarrassment to the
governor, with the State House being right there. Anyhow, Eaton called me into his office and gave me a
commendation. He said that any time I needed a favor,
just to call."

Annie gasped in pleasant surprise. "You've received a
commendation from the governor! You never told me!"

He grinned. "There's a heap of stuff you don't know
about me, sugar."

She slanted him a mock-scolding look.

"Then when we get to Denver, we'll all go see the
governor?" asked Rosie.

Sam sighed. "Rosie, you're a fugitive. Why don't you
let me and Jim take the prisoners in for our first
meeting? If all goes well and Eaton is prepared to pardon
you, I'm sure he'll want to do so personally."

Rosie glanced at Jim. "That all right with you,
darlin'?"

He nodded, clutching Rosie's hand. "I almost lost you,
and I'm not taking any chances now." He turned to flash
a look of gratitude at Sam and Annie. "As for you, good
friends, my bride and I will be forever in your debt."

"We're only doin' what's right," answered Sam modestly.

"And we both want to help you," added Annie. "In
fact, that's why I came here."

Jim eyed her curiously. "Can you tell me more about
that, Annie? You know my story now, and obviously our
lives are linked. I'd like to hear more about your life if
you're willing." He glanced lovingly at Rosie. "I mean,
Rosie has tried to explain where you really came from
and how the two of you are connected. Even though my
vision put all these events into motion, it still seems . . .
odd."

"Yep," agreed Sam. "Annie has a stranger tale to tell
than either of you."

"Will you tell us?" Jim asked humbly.

"Of course," she replied.

Annie talked long into the night, telling Jim of the world from which she'd come and how Sam had taken her across time. Both Jim and Rosie asked many questions, and before the night was over, Annie had the feeling that both were now believers.

Chapter 42

Annie had seen Denver before, but never *this* Denver.

This was her thought the next day as the six-person horse caravan proceeded past bustling Union Station, a soaring Victorian marvel with its huge clock tower. Annie's ears were lanced by a cacophony of train whistles blaring, steam engines chugging, and people shouting in a mishmash of different languages. Arriving passengers, many of them immigrants, poured from the terminal, the quaintly clad people towing along everything from children, trunks, and crates to violins, rocking chairs, and even birdcages. The throng stampeded toward the waiting mule trolley cars at the nearby barn of the Denver City Railway Company. Beyond the cars stretched long rows of magnificent three- and four-story Victorian office buildings along Seventeenth Street.

Annie and the others navigated their horses through the crowd, proceeding down Wynkoop to Eighteenth, where they turned south. A jumble of riders on horseback, carriages, trolley cars, even a few brave souls on high-wheeler bicycles, clogged the street. On the sidewalks fronting the brownstone buildings, citizens ranging from scruffy miners and prospectors to gentlemen and ladies in Victorian finery trooped along. On this overcast fall day, Annie was shocked by the brownish gray haze that hung everywhere, a noxious-smelling mix of soot from thousands of chimneys and sulfurous fumes from the smelters north of town. And she had assumed pollution was a twentieth-century phenomenon!

Soon the Victorian splendor of the Windsor Hotel loomed ahead of them. The five-story Gothic marvel, forged of native Colorado stone and crowned by a jaunty tower flying an American flag, proudly occupied the corner of Eighteenth and Larimer.

Amazed, Annie pointed ahead and spoke to Sam. "That's where you live?"

"Yep," he replied proudly, jerking his thumb toward another massive building across the street. "And yonder is the Barclay Building, which houses the temporary State House."

In awed tones, Rosie asked, "Is that where you'll be meetin' with the gov'ner, Sam?"

"Sure is, ma'am."

"How very convenient," murmured Annie. "And I must say I'm impressed by your dapper digs, Mr. Noble."

"Well, I don't get much chance to live in a civilized manner," he admitted with a wry grin.

"So you make up for it when you come here, eh?" As the group reined in their mounts before the hotel, Annie eyed the Windsor doorman in his impeccable red uniform and matching cap, then glanced askance at her own grimy shirt and ratty jeans, and the equally grungy attire of the others. "Are we just going to march in there, all of us looking like the cat dragged us in, and with two prisoners in tow?"

"Sugar, they know I'm a bounty hunter," Sam explained. "Hell, the Windsor's seen the likes of Ulysses S. Grant with his hard-drinkin' ways, and Buffalo Bill Cody. So believe me, they've had more than a few sets of boots spreading manure on their fine imported carpets, and they ain't no snobs about it. It won't be the first time I've arrived here with a desperado in tow. Heck, they sometimes allow me to lock up my prisoners in the tack room of the carriage house till I can fetch 'um over to the county jail."

Willie and Charlie grumbled to each other.

Dismounting, Sam untied the captives but linked the

two men's wrists together with handcuffs. The unkempt group gathered their belongings and marched toward the stately entrance.

Just as Sam had predicted, the doorman smiled and tipped his hat. "Why, good afternoon, Mr. Noble," he greeted Sam in a British-accented voice. "Good to have you back, sir. I trust you and your friends are well today?"

"We're fine, thank you, Mertson," answered Sam.

"Splendid, sir. I'll just summon the stable master to see to your mounts." The doorman glanced dubiously at Charlie and Willie, his gaze pausing on their linked wrists. He coughed. "And I assume you'll want to secure these—er—two gentlemen—in the carriage house for now?"

"You bet." While Charlie and Willie groaned, Sam winked conspiratorially at Annie. "What'd I tell you? Sugar, why don't you, Rosie, and Jim mosey on inside, and I'll join you as soon as I—er—secure my prisoners?"

"Our pleasure," answered Annie, fighting laughter at glimpsing this "refined" side to Sam's nature.

Passing through the ornate door Mertson had opened, Annie, Rosie, and Jim entered the lobby. The scattered gentlemen smoking or reading newspapers in the lavish salon took little note of their arrival. But the newcomers stood transfixed. As if they'd just entered a stately cathedral, none spoke, all overwhelmed by the incredibly opulent setting.

The lobby was gigantic, softly lit, and decorated in muted shades of gold and mauve. Massive crystal chandeliers glittered above tufted velvet settees, brocade-covered walls, and rosebuds floating in sterling silver bowls placed on priceless carved mahogany tables. Beyond the handsome front desk, a massively ornate grandfather clock ticked softly next to a stunning carved staircase that curved toward the upper stories.

Annie and the others tiptoed about, sinking their shoes into plush Wilton carpets and admiring their superbly defined reflections in diamond dust mirrors.

Rosie actually gaped over an ornately carved brass spittoon. "My stars, folks!" she cried. "I ain't never seen a gaboon fancier than a spinster's Sunday punch bowl!"

Jim and Annie were chuckling over her unabashed reaction as Sam reappeared. Gesturing about them, he asked modestly, "Handsome place, eh?"

"Handsome?" scoffed Rosie, turning to him. "Why, Sam Noble, this is the purtiest sight I ever seen in Denver, and I'll have you know I'm countin' Mattie Silks' fancy whorehouse!"

As several gentlemen in the lobby raised eyebrows in disapproval of Rosie's last ribald comment, Annie stifled giggles, and Sam hastily escorted his guests away. They passed the lavish drawing room and stunning ladies' ordinary, then proceeded up the stairs to his suite on the third floor.

Inside the sitting room, Annie, Rosie, and Jim stared in awe at green velvet rococo furniture and a beautifully patterned mauve-and-green carpet. An opened doorway provided a tantalizing glimpse of an elegant bedroom with a satin-festooned brass bed and a white-tiled bathroom with a clawfoot tub.

"My law, ain't this grand!" cried Rosie, plopping down on a velvet settee.

"It is indeed," agreed Annie, joining her.

Glancing at Jim, Sam stroked his stubbled jaw. "I reckon we'd best get cleaned up before we try to meet with the governor. I got a spare suit that should fit you; then afterward we can go downstairs, telephone Ben Eaton, and get us a shave and haircut. How 'bout it, friend?"

"Sounds fine to me," Jim replied. He eyed Annie and Rosie apologetically. "That is, if the ladies don't mind our washing up before they do."

"Mind, my butt!" declared Rosie. "Annie and me can deal with some trail dust for a spell. You boys just go get me my pardon so we can all have us some fun."

"I agree," seconded Annie.

After the men left the suite wearing stylish suits, Rosie and Annie bathed and changed into more respectable attire. Rosie donned the blue calico dress Annie had recently lent her, and Annie put on one of the black silk frocks she'd worn in Rowdyville while pretending to be a preacher's wife.

The two women were visiting in the sitting room when the men returned. Rosie and Annie gasped at the sight of their clean-shaven faces and neat haircuts. "Honey, didn't we choose us a couple of fine-lookin' fellars?" Rosie declared.

"We sure did," Annie answered, admiring Sam in his striped brown suit and gold moiré vest, and eyeing Jim in his equally dapper black frock coat, silver satin vest, and gray trousers.

"While we were downstairs, I registered Jim and Rosie for their own room," Sam announced. "And I called the governor. He said to come right over. He'll fit us in as soon as possible. We'll just fetch Willie and Charlie from the carriage house and be on our way." Sam approached Annie and handed her some cash and the key to the suite. "Why don't you and Rosie go shopping for some pretty new duds? There's plenty of nice department stores over on Sixteenth. With luck we can have us a celebration tonight."

Glancing at Rosie, who appeared delighted at the prospect, Annie nonetheless bit her lip. "If you think it'll be safe for Rosie."

Sam laughed. "Honey, this is a respectable part of town. Ain't nobody lookin' for Rosie here, I'd expect. You two just leave the key under the carpet in front of the door, in case we return before you do—and mind your manners while you're out."

Tossing Sam a chiding glance, Rosie rushed over to hug Jim. "Take care, darlin'. You look so dang handsome I ain't sure I can part with you."

"We'll be back soon, dear," Jim replied solemnly, squeezing his wife's hand. "I promise."

Rosie turned sternly to Sam. "No detours to Market Street, now."

"With you two pretty fillies waiting for us?" Sam asked in outrage. "No way in hell."

* * *

After the men left, the ladies primped a while longer, then departed to go shopping. They strolled over to Sixteenth, where they marveled at all the beautiful buildings—the classically designed post office, the massive county courthouse, the posh new department stores. They lingered for a long moment in front of the Tabor Grand Opera House at the corner of Sixteenth and Curtis. The structure was fashioned on the grandest possible scale, five stories of red brick accented by white limestone. Along the lofty roofline, a stately tower and rows of mock turrets more than satisfied the Victorian fetish for rococo whimsy.

Annie was drawn to the marquee stating that Lillian Russell would perform tonight in Gilbert and Sullivan's *Patience*. "Why don't we surprise the boys and see if we can get tickets?" she asked excitedly.

"Sounds fine to me," agreed Rosie. "I reckon my Jim must miss the finer things. He was brought up right well."

But, to the dismay of both women, the clerk at the box office informed them that the performance had been sold out weeks ago. "Oh, well," Annie said as they walked away. "We can still have a nice dinner tonight, can't we?"

"We'll have us one humdinger of a celebration," agreed Rosie, clutching Annie's arm.

The women stopped at the nearby Fair Department Store to shop for dresses. An hour later, they emerged wearing huge grins and carrying two enormous boxes. They had bought nearly identical gowns, Annie's of blue satin and Rosie's of gold, and had also purchased satin slippers and costume jewelry to complement their frocks.

Spotting a nickel trolley car parked at the corner, Annie exclaimed, "Hey, why don't I treat us to a trolley ride before we return to the hotel?"

"You got yourself a deal!"

The women boarded the car, which luckily was only half occupied. They parked their boxes on one bench and sat together across the aisle, with Rosie by the window. The trolley wound its way past Capitol Hill, the

raised ground Henry C. Brown had donated for a
permanent state capitol, and east through the fashion-
able surrounding area known as Millionaire's Row.
Annie marveled at Rosie's expressions as she gaped at
street after street of mammoth Victorian mansions with
high slate roofs, stained-glass windows, fanciful turrets,
and railed galleries, and at vast manicured lawns sporting elegant sculpture gardens, gleaming fish ponds, and
brilliant strutting peacocks.

"Wait till Jim sees all this!" Rosie gasped. "He'll think
we died and gone to heaven."

Annie squeezed Rosie's hand, feeling a moment of
sublime joy at giving her great-great-grandmother, who
had suffered so much, these moments of innocent pleasure. "I think we're going to have to stop for ice cream
sundaes before we go back," she announced.

They did, stopping in at White and McMahan's Drugstore, joining the Victorian ladies who sat sipping nickel
phosphates in their sedate dresses and feathered hats.

Savoring a bite of ice cream smothered in chocolate
syrup, Rosie glanced at Annie. "How are you doing,
honey?"

Taken aback, Annie replied, "Oh, I'm fine."

Frowning, Rosie set down her spoon. "Well, somethin's been frettin' me."

"What?"

With a sigh, Rosie admitted, "I reckon I've been
downright selfish, lettin' you and Sam solve all me and
Jim's problems and not givin' a thought to yours."

"Rosie, no one expected that, considering all you and
Jim have endured," Annie replied sincerely.

Rosie nodded, but her brow remained furrowed.
"Yeah, I know we been through hell, but things are
looking better thanks to you and Sam. 'Ceptin' I'm
worried about you now."

"Me?" Annie protested, laughing.

Rosie regarded Annie soberly. "Honey, if me and Jim
get our lives all worked out, where does that leave you?"

Annie released a heavy breath. "To tell you the truth,
I'm not sure."

"Reckon you'll marry Sam?"

She smiled, pleasantly surprised by the question. "What makes you ask that?"

Rosie playfully tapped Annie's forearm. "It's plain to see you think that man hung the moon. And Jim says he's sure Sam is plumb sold on you."

Annie nodded. "We'd love to stay together, but it's complicated."

"Figure I'm too ignorant to understand?" asked Rosie with an air of hurt.

"No, not at all," Annie quickly reassured her. "It's just that—well, I'm from a different time—"

"So you say."

"And Sam and I think differently, too. He wants a wife who'll be content to stay home while he goes off on his adventures."

Rosie cackled. "I'll allow that man is prideful and strong-willed, but we both know you're woman enough to tame him."

"I just wish taming him were enough," Annie confessed. "I have no idea what our futures will really hold."

Rosie squeezed her hand. "Honey, you can count on Jim and me. You'll always have a home with us."

Annie smiled with pure gratitude. "Thank you. You're a dear, but . . ."

"It's complicated?"

Annie nodded.

Rosie's expression grew thoughtful. "Honey, have some faith. I know things will turn out all right for you and Sam. If you're doubtful, just take a gander at me. Any fool coulda seen my life was in the slop bucket—but look at the miracle you and Sam brung me, reuniting me with my darlin' Jim."

Annie beamed. "I know. Seeing the two of you back together has been one of the biggest triumphs of my entire life. And it does reaffirm my faith."

Leaning closer, Rosie confided, "Whatever powers brung you here, honey, I don't think the Almighty's ready to drop you in the fat just yet."

Annie smiled. For once Rosie seemed very wise, very much like a grandmother.

When the women arrived back at the suite, Sam and Jim were already there, smoking cheroots in the sitting room. Both hastened to help the women with their boxes, then presented them with bouquets of flowers. Sniffing the festive blooms and spotting the broad grin on Sam's face, Annie knew at once that the visit with the governor had gone well.

"So tell us all about it!" she exclaimed.

Exuberant, Sam turned to Rosie. "Governor Eaton was just wonderful. He wants to see you tomorrow morning. I think he's ready to grant you a pardon."

"Sweet Jesus be praised!" Rosie cried, hugging first Sam, then Jim.

"Oh, this is great!" Annie cried, also embracing Sam. "Now I want you to start at the beginning and tell us all about the meeting."

Sam stuck his thumbs in his vest pockets. "Well, first off, I explained the basic situation."

"You did?" Perturbed, Annie asked, "How did you explain me?"

"Well, I figured it was best to follow Rosie's lead and tell him you and her are distant kin."

"Good thinking," agreed Annie.

"Anyhow, I explained how you and me knew Rosie was in trouble and wanted to help her, how we found her in Rowdyville and learnt her sad tale. Next Jim, Charlie, and Willie all told their stories; then the governor asked a few questions and thought it all over." Sam's face lit with pleasure. "And it appears he's fixin' to see everythin' our way. In fact, Ben said he's been right suspicious of Royce Rowdy for some time, and he'd like to see him face justice."

"Sam, that's fantastic!" exclaimed Annie.

"Kin the governor really do that, make sure Rowdy's arrested?" asked Rosie anxiously.

"He can sure give the authorities a nudge in the right direction," Sam replied.

Rosie hugged Jim again. "Darlin', I'm so happy!"

"And I'm greatly relieved, sweetheart," replied Jim, kissing Rosie's brow. "I just don't know what I would have done if the governor wasn't willing to help us."

"Yeah, but I ain't pardoned yet," Rosie reminded him.

Sam touched her arm. "Don't worry. I think the meeting tomorrow will be mostly a formality. I reckon Ben just wants to be sure you're ready to become an honest citizen."

"We'll hope so," Rosie replied.

Jim squeezed her hand. "Everything will be fine."

"By the way, where are Charlie and Willie?" asked Annie. "Back at the carriage house?"

Sam chuckled. "Nope. I'm friends with the Arapahoe County sheriff, so them two trail rats is languishing at the jail right now. The sheriff promised to have a deputy deliver 'um up to Central in a few days."

"I'm glad we're through baby-sitting those cowpokes," put in Rosie, pulling a face. "They smelt."

As Jim and Annie chuckled, Sam snapped his fingers. "Oh, I almost forgot—Jim and I have another surprise."

"Yes?" Annie asked breathlessly. "I don't see how you can top Rosie being on the verge of getting a pardon."

"Reckon we can come close, don't you, Jim?" Sam slyly asked the other man.

"Reckon we can," Jim agreed.

"What is it, Sam?" Annie demanded.

Mischief danced in his eyes. "Hope you two girls bought some mighty fine duds, 'cause Jim and I have a treat in store for you tonight."

Annie balled her hands on her hips and slanted him a chiding glance. "Will you please end the suspense?"

"Yeah, Noble, spill the beans," teased Rosie.

Grinning, Sam dug in his pockets and pulled out a sheaf of tickets. "How 'bout we all get to watch Lillian Russell perform at the Tabor tonight—from the governor's private box?"

"You're kidding!" cried Annie. "Rosie and I tried to get tickets, but the performance was sold out!"

"Well, the governor and his Rebecca Jane have to miss the opera 'cause they been invited to dinner at the Methodist bishop's house," Sam explained. "So when

Honest Ben offered us the use of his private box, Jim and
me didn't hesitate."

Annie chortled in joy and Rosie clapped her hands.
"So, what are you folks waitin' for?" Rosie cried. "Let's
all get gussied up and step out on the town!"

Chapter 43

Rosie and Jim gathered their belongings and went to their own room to dress for the evening. While Sam bathed, Annie attended to her coiffure and changed into her gown.

Leaving the bathroom in his dressing gown, Sam whistled at the sight of Annie at the dressing table. She was perfection from crown to toe, and his hungry gaze drank her in. Her gorgeous hair was pulled back to one side and spilled in sausage curls onto a creamy shoulder, emphasizing every lovely contour of her face. The soft light shone on the pretty spray of flowers she'd pinned in her hair, illuminating the sculpted perfection of her high cheekbones, her dainty nose and wide mouth, and glittering on her rhinestone ear bobs. Her lovely complexion glowed even without rouge. Her smile highlighted lips as pink as rose petals and danced in eyes that had never appeared a more vivid blue, shaded by exquisitely long, dark lashes.

And her dress! Yards and yards of lustrous, gleaming sapphire blue satin turned the princess sitting before him into an enchantress beyond compare. The low neckline tantalized him with a glimpse of cleavage and a nice sweep of her lovely shoulders. Half sleeves edged with ecru lace trailed over her smooth arms. The folds of satin clung to her full bosom and molded down to her trim waist. From there her skirt spilled free and full, curling into a bustle at the back.

Sam had seen Annie in a dress before, but never had he seen this vision of celestial femininity. He had seen her as a feisty cowgirl and a modest preacher's wife, but now she was a lady beyond compare. Desire lanced him so powerfully, he wondered if they'd even make it out of the room together. They hadn't made love since they'd left Rowdyville, and he was starved for her.

"My God, sugar, I've never seen you look so gorgeous!"

Her demure expression only further stoked his passions. In a rustle of skirts, she stood and came to his side, eyeing him in his gray silk brocade dressing gown. She reached out, her fingertips tormenting the bare flesh beneath his lapel, and he narrowly resisted an urge to pick her up and fling her down on the bed, ruin that hair and shred her lovely gown to pieces. The heavenly scent of her—lavender soap and the unique aroma of a woman's flesh heating silk—rose to further torment him.

Her fingers trailed through his damp, curly hair and teased the cleft in his chin. He drew an agonized breath.

"You look pretty fetching yourself, cowboy," she purred. "I've missed being alone with you."

He hooked an arm about her slim waist, drew her close, and slowly kissed her. Damn, her lips had never tasted so soft and sweet! "At this rate, we'll never make it out the door tonight," he murmured huskily.

She slid away and shook a finger at him. "Oh, no you don't, Sam Noble! There will be plenty of time for mischief later on. We promised Rosie and Jim that we'd meet them in the lobby, and we aren't leaving them stranded."

"We could send down the tickets," he suggested.

"You mean you'd give up hearing Lillian Russell for me?"

He nodded solemnly.

Although her lovely eyes danced with delight, she shot him a saucy look. "Well, forget it. I want to go to the opera and sit in the governor's box."

He shouted with laughter. "Woman, you just broke my heart."

"Yeah, you sound really devastated," she teased. "Get dressed, cowboy."

Despite more grumbling, Sam did her bidding, and Annie admired him in his handsome black suit, red satin vest, and ruffled linen shirt with black string cravat. They grabbed their gloves and his top hat and left the room together. When they walked downstairs into the lobby, Annie knew they made a splendid couple and she felt proud of all the heads they turned.

They found Rosie and Jim sitting on a posh velvet settee; both stood at their approach. Rosie looked beautiful in a gold satin gown fashioned very much like Annie's; she wore pearl jewelry and had styled her red-gold hair in loose curls about her shoulders. Jim still wore the frock coat and trousers Sam had lent him.

"My, don't you two look purty," Rosie crooned.

"You look wonderful yourself," Sam said gallantly.

"You sure do," Annie added, admiring Rosie in her gown.

"Shall we have dinner here before we leave?" Sam suggested. "The Windsor's dining room is world-class."

Rosie reached out to tap Sam's arm. "Heck, we're so hungry, we'd settle for a tough steak. Right, Jim?"

"Right," he answered, and everyone laughed.

Sam led them to the dining room on the second floor. At once a mustachioed maître d' stepped forward to greet them. "Good evening, ladies, gentlemen." His gaze paused on the two women. "Are we honored to have twin sisters among us tonight?"

Both women chortled, leaving the man flustered. "Yeah, we're twins," retorted Rosie. "She's Big Bertha and I'm the runt."

As the poor man's face turned scarlet, Sam said tactfully, "The ladies are sisters in a manner of speaking."

"Now, how 'bout showing us to the grub?" added Rosie.

"Yes, ma'am," answered the chagrinned man.

The maître d' seated them at a table set with the finest Old Paris china, Dorflinger crystal, Tiffany silver, and Belfast linen. A handsome, two-tiered brass-and-frosted-glass chandelier glittered above them, illuminating the lovely table. Annie mused that the magnificent room appeared more like a lavish Paris salon with its twenty-foot ceiling accented by a stunning gold frieze, its soaring windows with silk pouf shades, its diamond-dust mirrors and handsome Wilton carpet.

While Annie discreetly eyed other elegantly dressed diners at nearby tables, Rosie struggled over the menu. At last she tossed it down in disgust and turned to Jim. "Honey, I'm plumb lost as a hog in a blizzard with all this highfalutin' French. You order for us, will you?"

"I'd be happy to," Jim replied.

Rosie glanced askance at the array of silverware surrounding her plate. "And you'll have to lairn me which fork to use and when. Hell, all I know is eatin' beans and bacon on a knife." As the others chuckled, Rosie grinned at Annie and Sam. "Jim was brought up decent. By the time we build us a grand mansion on Capitol Hill, he's gonna see I'm schooled in all the social graces. Ain't you, darlin'?"

"I like you just the way you are," he answered, "but if there's anything you'd like to learn, I'm here to teach you."

"You bet I'm just bustin' to lairn. And honey, I seed just where I want to build us our house today. Annie treated me to a trolley ride through the neighborhood. Precious, they got struttin' peacocks and fountains shootin' six-foot geysers."

Laughing with the others, Annie mused that these two intrepid souls might well be accepted into Denver's society. If Rosie gained a bit of refinement, she could avoid the trap of Molly Brown, who would be snubbed by Denver's uppercrust only ten years from now.

When the waiter appeared, Sam suggested Jim order for everyone. He proudly selected oyster soup, lobster thermidor, rice pilaf, green peas à la français, and champagne.

Over soup, Annie remarked to Jim, "I'm surprised that everything is coming back to you so well. To look at you, to hear you rattle off that order to the waiter, you'd never know you'd been through such an ordeal."

"I have the Cheyenne to thank for that," Jim said solemnly. "Although I was confused while among them, I realize now that my mind desperately needed that quiet, pastoral time to heal. I will never forget all your grandmother's people did for me, Sam. They are my friends, and I'll be indebted to them for the rest of my life. I will find a way to repay them, you may be sure."

"It's good of you to offer," replied Sam, "but I'm sure they don't expect nothin' from you."

"They are giving to us all," declared Jim, "by preserving a way of life the white man is trying to destroy, a way of life I want my children to appreciate."

"I'm with you there, precious," agreed Rosie.

"And we are greatly indebted to you and Annie, as well," Jim continued to Sam. "After I file my claim, we'll see you're suitably rewarded for helping us."

"We don't expect nothin'," protested Sam.

"Indeed not," seconded Annie. "We just want to see you and Rosie happy."

"Well, you already done that," piped in Rosie. "The gold is just icing on the cake, and we'd like to share it with you."

Annie glanced quizzically at Jim. "Are you certain you still remember where your claim is?"

"Oh, yes," he replied with a laugh. "The location is emblazoned on my brain. All I need to do is have a sample assayed in Central to prove I've discovered precious metal; then I can file a claim with the county recorder."

"We'll get you there," promised Sam. "It'll be the first thing we do when we get up to Central, even before we see Judge Righteous."

"Thanks, Sam." Jim lifted his champagne glass. "To Sam and Annie, for all your help and your faith in us."

Annie raised her glass. "And to Rosie and Jim—to your future happiness."

"To yours, honey," said Rosie feelingly. "Yours and Sam's."

The couples toasted each other and ate their succulent dinner. All were feeling slightly giddy by the time they emerged onto the front portico, where the doorman hailed them a hackney cab that bore them the several blocks to the Tabor Grand Opera House. They arrived mere minutes before the curtain was raised, and hastily took their places in the governor's box.

Annie was stunned by the opulence of the opera house. Their private stage box was on the grand tier, at the center of a whimsical, three-story arrangement of loges that culminated in a high, pointed roof and gave the apparatus the look of a trilevel gazebo. They sat on red velvet chairs overlooking the magnificent stage with its lavish oil-painting mural over the proscenium. Many stories above them stretched an awe-inspiring ceiling with square after square of gilded plaster fretwork swirling about a huge circular mural of painted clouds.

Glancing down at the auditorium, Annie was enthralled by the lavish costumes of the gentlemen and ladies in the audience. She glimpsed more than a few sets of opera glasses focused on them. Of course they would seem a curiosity, she mused, since they occupied the governor's box.

She glanced at Rosie and Jim to gauge their reactions. Jim was calmly perusing the program and taking it all in stride; Rosie sat gaping at their surroundings with an open mouth. Annie restrained a chuckle.

"Enjoying this, sugar?" Sam asked.

Annie nodded happily. She glanced down at her program, headlined with the name of Lillian Russell. "I feel as if I'm living a moment of history."

Indeed, at the back of the program, Annie was delighted to read a short history of the opera house, built by Horace Tabor in 1881, and Denver itself, which had last year celebrated its first quarter century of existence. She read how Eugene Field had been present at the opening night of the opera house, how Denver had been visited by such notables as Walt Whitman, Oscar Wilde, Carry Nation, and Grand Duke Alexis of the famous Russian Romanov dynasty. She learned how the city had been built on the railroads, how scions like Horace Tabor, Henry Brown, Nathaniel Hill, and Walter Cheesman had brought commerce and respectability to the bustling community.

Annie enjoyed the sprightly music and melodramatic performances. Lillian Russell stole the show. The buxom blond beauty was perfect as the milkmaid Patience and delighted the audience with her brilliant soprano voice, her campy exploits lampooning the lovesick maidens, and her shameless flirtation with the two male leads.

Sam, Rosie, and Jim appeared to be every bit as captivated by the performance as she was. Rosie got so caught up in the melodramatics that by the second act, she was whistling and shouting encouragements to the people on the stage, prompting many a raised eyebrow from the other patrons. Several times, Annie had to cover her face with her program to hide her giggles. Later, everyone stood and cheered when Russell and the others made six curtain calls.

As the couples left the theater, Rosie remained agog. "I never heard such purty caterwaulin' in all my life," she declared to Annie. "I thought that woman was fixin' to bust her bodice."

"She definitely rattled the chandeliers," agreed Annie.

The foursome emerged into a cool, starry night to the soft gleam of the gaslights along Sixteenth Street. Rosie let out an exuberant whoop and tossed her program into the air. Wearing a grin, Jim went tearing off after it.

"Well, folks, I can't remember when I've shared a finer occasion," Rosie declared. Watching Jim approach with the retrieved program, she took it and purred, "Thanks, precious."

"You're welcome, ma'am," he replied, wrapping an arm around her shoulders. "You folks ready to return to the hotel?"

"Heck, the evenin's still young," protested Sam. "What's say we go dancing on Larimer Street?"

Rosie pulled a face. "I told you fellars no detouring to the red-light district."

"But there should still be a respectable dance hall or two over on Larimer," argued Jim.

Rosie appeared skeptical. "I don't know—there's too many temptations in that part of town. The last time I was there, I think I spied the devil hisself."

While the men chuckled, Annie said wistfully, "I

really would like to see what a nineteenth-century dance hall looks like."

Rosie waved a hand in acquiescence. "All right, then, if you folks is so set on it. But I'm warning you to be on your best behavior. I ain't aimin' to end up in jail for the night. I reckon that won't go down so good with the governor."

"Yes, ma'am," agreed Sam.

They stopped off at Gold Dust Sal's, a lavish dancing parlor where couples sashayed about to piano music on the ground floor and cardsharps fleeced wealthy miners and businessmen on the mezzanine above. Even as the foursome took a corner table, Rosie stared about suspiciously.

"I don't like the look of this place," she grumbled.

Annie glanced at the well-dressed dancers, the crystal chandeliers, the flocked red wallpaper, and the ornate mirrors over the bar. "Why not? It think it's perfectly charming."

Rosie harrumphed. "This ain't no place for decent folk to be seen."

A blond, buxom waitress in a sleazy gown strolled up to their table, sidling close to Jim and batting her eyelashes at him. Leaning toward him in a generous flash of cleavage, she purred, "Well, good evening, sir. What can I get you folks?"

Jim was about to open his mouth when abruptly, Rosie popped up. Features livid, she grabbed a handful of the woman's hair. As the waitress shrieked and cowered, she yelled, "Just what do you think you're doin', you cheap cyprian, ogling my man!"

"Ma'am, I didn't do nothin'!" the woman wailed.

While Sam and Annie looked on in disbelief, Jim pleaded with his wife. "Sweetheart, please, I don't think the—er—lady meant any harm."

But Rosie didn't seem to hear him as she continued to lambast the waitress and yank on her hair. "Don't you lie to me, you two-bit line gal! You was making a play for my Jim!"

As scandalous murmurs sounded all around them, a

tall, thin man with a mustache rushed up. "Ma'am, is there a problem?" he asked Rosie.

"Yeah, you bet your buttons." Rosie thrust the waitress away. Hurling Rosie a blistering look, the woman scrambled off. "That piece-of-trash hussy was making eyes at my husband."

The man appeared chagrined. "Well, ma'am, I'm sorry. I'll see that the bartender serves you."

"Yeah, see that he does." With a curt nod, Rosie sat down.

There was a moment of charged silence at the table. Struggling to keep a straight face, Annie cleared her throat and regarded Rosie's seething countenance. "Er—Rosie, don't you think you overreacted a bit?"

"What's that?" she demanded.

Sam laughed. "What Annie means is, you popped your cork when you shouldn't have."

Rosie's fist slammed down on the table. "You got no cause to say that, bounty hunter! I told you we never should have come here. Now look what you folks made me do!"

"What *we* made you do?" exclaimed Annie.

"Yeah, you brung us to this Satan's lair," Rosie bristled.

By now, even Jim was fighting laughter. "Dear, I really don't think the waitress was trying to steal me away from you."

Rosie patted his hand. "There, there, precious. You only say that 'cause you're innocent as a lamb and you got only pure thoughts in that purty head of yours." She sneered at Sam. "Shame on you for exposin' my darlin' to such a bad girl."

Sam was shaking with mirth. "Yeah, and you've never been bad a day in your life, have you, Rosie?"

"You take that back!"

"Why should I?" Sam asked.

"'Cause there's a big damn difference between robbing banks and stages, shootin' at folks, and being a *whore*!"

Annie groaned and covered her face with her hands. She knew by all the gasps that Rosie had mortified *everyone* by now.

At last she dared a glance at Sam and was amazed to find him sporting a quizzical frown as he faced down Rosie.

"You're right," he said at last. "I apologize, ma'am."

"Well, it's about time." Setting her jaw, Rosie sat back in her chair.

Another tense moment ticked by; then Jim cleared his throat and braved a smile at his wife. "Dear, would you care to dance?"

As if she hadn't just flown into a jealous snit, Rosie all but purred as she took her husband's arm. "Why, sure, precious. I thought you'd never ask."

She sashayed off with him looking pleased as punch!

As soon as the two were out of earshot, Sam and Annie burst out laughing. "My God, Rosie was right!" Annie declared. "We never should have brought her here."

"I know—for a moment there I thought that bouncer was going to summon the sheriff," Sam put in.

"And she would have blamed *us*, too!"

Sam shook his head. "Jim is going to be in for one helluva adventure with that woman. Boy, does Rosie have a short fuse. No wonder you're so feisty, with *her* as an ancestor."

Annie's mouth fell open. "Now wait just a minute, Sam Noble. You can't make me responsible for this."

The two continued to banter playfully as Sam ordered champagne from the bartender. After they shared a glass, he asked Annie to dance. Hand in hand, they strolled to the dance floor. Annie gloried in her moments waltzing with him to the lovely, sentimental strains of "Sweet Genevieve." His arms felt so strong and warm about her, and he smelled so wonderful. As he glided her into a turn, she caught a glimpse of his face—his dark eyes gleaming, his lips lit in a tender smile, and she thought of how incredibly handsome he was, how lucky she was to have him . . . at least for now.

"I think this is the first time we've waltzed, cowboy."

"I've long anticipated the pleasure, ma'am."

"And you didn't even want to go out tonight."

"I couldn't wait to have you in my arms," he said, drawing her closer. "And now I've gotten my wish."

She sighed. Over his shoulder, she glimpsed Rosie and Jim kissing back at their table. "Thank God! Looks like Rosie is finally settling down."

"She has made the evening pretty lively."

"True, though she's taking her redemption *very* seriously. I do feel so good about all we've been able to accomplish for her and Jim." Annie felt her throat tightening. "Thank you for that, Sam," she said with heartfelt sincerity. "Thank you for believing in me, and for helping me help them."

"They're lucky to have you, Annie."

She pulled back slightly, staring up at him with love. "I'm lucky to have *you,* Sam. You've been a prince, and I'm really in your debt."

"A debt I'll be delighted to collect on, ma'am."

Annie stretched upward to kiss him. "When you do, cowboy, I'll be the one who's blessed."

Chapter 44

❧ ⌘ ❧

Back at the hotel, Sam and Annie bid good night to Rosie and Jim in the lobby, and Sam stopped to ask the desk clerk to send champagne up to their suite. Minus their shoes but still in their evening clothes, he and Annie sat on the sitting room settee sipping the bubbly brew.

"You really are aiming to get me looped tonight, aren't you, cowboy?" Annie teased.

Sam had removed his jacket. Looking dapper in his red satin vest and white ruffled shirt, he sat with one arm draped over her shoulders. "What do you mean by 'looped'?"

"Tipsy."

He chuckled. "Well, we haven't had much chance to enjoy ourselves these past weeks."

"I don't know about you, but I've enjoyed myself a lot."

"I won't argue with a lady there," he replied, kissing her jaw. "But I really was bustin' my buttons tonight, I was so proud to take you out for an elegant evening and show you off."

"You really enjoyed that, didn't you?"

"I knew I was the envy of every man tonight—with the exception of Jim, of course."

She thought over his words. "In a way it surprises me that you would feel at home during this type of evening—and in these posh surroundings. Have you ever thought of settling down here in Denver, perhaps

348

becoming an entrepreneur like Horace Tabor or Walter Cheesman?"

He considered this. "Annie, I enjoy my time in Denver, but after a while I get to feelin' like a caged animal. I have to get out on the trail again, smell them pines, look up at the stars, feel the wind on my face."

"Wrestle desperadoes?" she suggested.

"Yeah, somethin' like that."

"I suspected as much," she said with a sad smile. "You look troubled, sugar. Why?"

She sighed. "I just have the feeling my adventure here is almost over. Rosie's and Jim's lives are becoming resolved . . . and I find myself thinking more about the mess I left behind me in the present. I don't know whether I can make it back there or not, but I need to settle matters regarding my ghost town—*if* it's still my ghost town. And I'm still worried about my older brother, Larry. I don't even know where he is."

"He's a grown man, ain't he? He don't need you changin' his diapers. Why can't you stay here?"

"I just can't, Sam! I can't live in the same time with my great-great-grandmother. It's too much of a paradox. Besides, I just don't *feel* I belong here permanently."

He lifted her hand and kissed it, his troubled gaze holding hers. "I feel you belong with me."

"That's different," she agreed, regarding him tenderly. "I feel I belong with you, too. But we're star-crossed, Sam, not to mention the fact that our lives are focused in different directions. You're always going to be the adventurer, and I'm never going to be your little homebody wife. And knowing our worlds could never truly mesh— well, I think it would be just too painful for me."

"But you said you're not even sure you can make it back to your own time."

She drew a heavy breath. "I know I have to try. Perhaps the Hevovitastamiutsts will take me back again."

He whistled. "Where did you learn the Cheyenne word for 'whirlwind'?"

She smiled. "Your kinsman, old Windfoot, taught me

that word before I left the present. Maybe the same forces that brought you across time to me, and brought me here to resolve Rosie's life, will carry me back once my mission is completed."

He took her glass and set it with his on the tea table. "Sugar, let's not try to settle everything tonight. We still have a long way to go, you and me. . . . Don't we?"

"I hope so, Sam."

Sam leaned over, trailing his lips over her bare shoulder, raising gooseflesh. "Maybe we won't have to face those choices at all. Maybe we'll just make this night last forever."

"Oh, Sam, I wish that were possible," she breathed raptly.

"You traveled across time, didn't you? Perhaps if you want something enough, anything is possible."

"Is it, Sam?"

His gaze burned into hers, bright and filled with turbulent emotion. He rose, took her hand, and pulled her into the bedroom with him. Just beyond the door, they embraced and kissed ardently. Annie eagerly undid the buttons on Sam's vest and shirt, loving the image of him in partial dishabille, with coarse dark hair peeking out from the V of his neck. She ran her fingertips over his muscled flesh and listened to his ragged moan. She pressed her lips to the coarse expanse, kissing his chest, then running her tongue over a nipple, which hardened beneath her wet caress.

He caught her to him. "Sugar, I want you so bad."

His mouth caught hers in a drowning kiss. His tongue plunged deep, claiming her utterly. She ran her fingertips up his corded neck, caressing the cherished lines of his smooth, handsome face. She sank her fingers into his thick, soft hair and melted her mouth into his.

He pulled back, breathing hard, eyes nearly black with passion. As he reached for her hand, she knew a moment's hesitation.

"Er—Sam?" she questioned.

"Yes, sugar?"

"Aren't you forgetting something?"

"What?"

"I'm out of pills."

He only grinned.

She laughed. "Now wait a minute, you rascal! What if I do end up back in the present . . . and pregnant?"

His response shocked her as he swept her up into his arms and looked down at her with fierce determination. "What if I don't let you go?"

Before Annie could reply, Sam's demanding mouth slashed down across hers again. He stood there for an endless moment, holding her, kissing her until all doubts and resistance melted in the pit of aching desire deep in her belly.

"Sam, Sam . . ." His name left her lips in a plea.

"Any more doubts?"

"No."

He carried her to the bed. The satin of her dress rustled against the smooth fabric of the counterpane as he laid her down. Staring at her, he gently pulled the flowers from her hair, sniffing the fragrant blooms. She sat up to aid his efforts and was rewarded with another searing kiss. His hand cupped her breast, kneading gently. Her fingers reached out to stroke his hardness through his trousers. His breathing roughened and his kiss grew ravenous.

He pushed her down beside him. Tracing his lips over her cheek, her mouth, her neck, he raised her skirts, sliding his hand up a white silk stocking, toying with the lacy garter. "So sexy," he murmured, then reached upward for the tie on her silk drawers.

Annie sucked in a breath of pure delight. "Impatient, aren't we, cowboy?"

His fingers were already undoing the bow. "I want to make love to you with all your laces and petticoats intact," he said huskily. "I been thinkin' 'bout nothin' else ever since I laid eyes on you tonight. You won't need these, though." He drew the undergarment off her.

"Oh, Sam." His boldness was very sexy, and Annie could feel her womanhood throbbing in painful hunger. As his fingers slid between her thighs, she cried out,

moving wantonly against his touch. Her lips roved his
face, his neck, his chest. His free hand tugged down her
bodice, and he caught a tautened nipple between his
teeth.

Annie reeled, arching her back, rapture radiating from
her tender breast to the hot core of her where his fingers
probed. Sam reached down between their bodies to
unbutton his trousers. His eyes devoured her and his
voice was rough. "So pretty with all them ribbons and
laces. So open to me. Damned if I can't resist you."

She was sure he was going to take her then, but instead
he teased her with his manhood, rubbing his hot hardness against her intimate folds until she was left half
sobbing with frustration. Then abruptly his body slid
down hers, and his mouth claimed her throbbing
mound.

Annie cried out and bucked at the unexpected, brazen
pleasure. Sam's lips were already probing deep, crumbling her resistance, his tongue finding the tiny, sensitive
peak of her desire, gently stroking as his mouth drew and
devoured. Annie was left gasping, clenching her fists,
and finally succumbing to a pleasure so devastating it
brought her to tears. Then Sam's mouth was covering
hers again, comforting, his rigid manhood poised to
enter her.

Annie shuddered at the sudden, pleasurable pressure
of him. His penetration was so tantalizing and deliberate
that at last she surged forward to take all of him with a
greedy wiggle. He slid a hand beneath her and rocked his
loins against her, shutting his eyes, his features fierce, as
if savoring the feel of her warm tissues throbbing and
squeezing about him. With the two of them locked as
tightly as two people could be, she looked up to see a
smile on his face, but his eyes were bright with tears.

"I love you, Annie," he said hoarsely.

"I love you, Sam," she whispered back achingly. "So
much."

His mouth seized hers, and over the next moments,
both of them more than demonstrated the depths of
their feelings.

                         *   *   *

Later, lying naked in bed with Annie cuddled against him, Sam relived their rapturous moments making love. He kissed Annie's hair and breathed in her lovely scent. His hand cupped the shapely breast he had devoured with his mouth. He did love her so—with all his heart and soul. She was a jewel beyond price, proud and passionate, brave and loving and strong.

Yet, remembering their previous conversation, he felt sad. How could he give Annie the life she deserved? More important, could he share his future with a woman on equal terms? And what if she did leave him and go back to the present? What if she carried his child with her?

Aching sorrow and fierce possessiveness warred within him. Holding her incredible sweetness against him, he soon found a single thought dominating his mind, his emotions, the very words he'd said to her before making love: He couldn't let her go now. He just couldn't. He wasn't sure how or where they would make it, but he knew this woman was his life now, and his heart was totally committed to her.

Somehow, they had to find their way together, whatever sacrifices that meant. But surely they could prevail. Heck, he had tracked down the fiercest desperadoes on this planet, had looked death in the eye more than once and survived it. Surely he could find a way to build a bridge between their worlds, to secure a future for himself and the woman he loved.

Even as the heartfelt realization filled his chest with aching emotion, Annie stirred and began trailing her lips slowly down his body, tantalizing him. Her mouth settled on his manhood, drawing him in as she sucked gently. Sam clenched his teeth in tortured arousal. Oh, she had a wicked mouth, wet and hot. He'd already given her his life and his heart—in the next moments, he poured out his soul to her, as well.

Chapter 45

⟨∽⟩‿⟨⟩⟩

The following morning, the two couples sat awaiting the governor's arrival, their chairs arranged before Benjamin Eaton's massive mahogany desk in his office at the Barclay Building. The spacious room exuded an air of officialdom with its U.S. and Colorado flags, as well as the state seal and a portrait of President Grover Cleveland hanging on the wall above the governor's desk.

Sam and Jim sat on either side of Eaton's desk, the women wedged between them. Sam and Jim wore suits, while Annie and Rosie were frocked in dark, understated dresses. Although all four appeared serious, Rosie in particular was fretful, twisting her gloves in her hands and worrying her lower lip with her teeth. Annie mused that if someone even breathed on her, poor Rosie would likely jump out of her skin.

"Are you sure the governor is fixin' to pardon me?" she asked Sam for the third time.

"Rosie, just be yourself and I'm sure everything will be fine," he replied. "Like I told you yesterday, Ben wants to meet you to ensure you're ready to become a respectable citizen."

While Rosie nodded, Jim smiled reassuringly at his bride and Annie patted her hand. "It'll be all right, Rosie. I'm certain of it. We haven't come this far to fail."

Even as she finished the words, a door to their left swung open. All four stood as a handsome man in a black suit entered the room. Sizing up Benjamin Harrison Eaton, Annie felt pleased by the sympathetic air he exuded. His longish face was dominated by a well-defined brow and blunt nose; alert, intelligent, and friendly eyes peered out at them from beneath bushy brows. His graying brown hair and long silvery beard proclaimed him to be a man in his early fifties. His stride was purposeful, his manner assured.

He greeted them in a booming, confident voice. "Well, Mr. Sam Noble," he began, "are these the folks you told me about?"

"Yes, sir," replied Sam. "Governor Benjamin Eaton, I'd like to introduce Annie Dillon, and her—er—cousin, Rosie Dillon. You've met Mr. Dillon."

The governor shook hands with each of the three. "Welcome to Denver, ladies. I can certainly see the familial resemblance in you two."

All three murmured thank-yous.

To Rosie, Eaton added, "You're fortunate, Mrs. Dillon, that your fine cousin has come to your aid."

"Yes sir, I agree," said Rosie, her chin bobbing in emphasis.

Eaton grinned. "Do sit down, all of you, and we'll have a chat." After everyone complied, he asked, "Are all of you enjoying your stay in Denver?"

"Governor, we can't begin to tell you how much we loved the opera last night," Annie answered. "Lillian Russell was wonderful. Thank you so much for giving us tickets for your private box."

"My pleasure," Eaton replied. "Actually, I was delighted that the tickets would be put to good use. You see, my Rebecca Jane is best friends with Mrs. Henry Warren, the bishop's wife. An invitation to dinner at the Warrens' was not an event we could decline."

"Yessir," agreed Sam dryly. "You shore don't want to get them Methodists on your bad side."

Eyes twinkling, Eaton replied, "Last night, we were all discussing the possibility that the Supreme Court may soon settle Henry C. Brown's lawsuit contesting the title of the new capitol grounds. Seems Henry can't decide whether he wants to give us that land or not. But who knows? Maybe I'll be privileged to move into a fine new office while I'm still governor."

"This is a mighty fine office, too," piped in Rosie.

Eaton turned his shrewd gaze on her. "Thank you, Mrs. Dillon. You know, I'm pleased that we're having this opportunity to speak frankly."

"Yes, sir," replied Rosie, twisting her gloves. "I'm right beholden to you for hearing my case."

"You should thank Mr. Noble, as well as your cousin, for acting as your advocates. Since Sam Noble is a man I much admire and respect, when he and your husband brought me your sad tale, I was compelled to listen."

"Yes, sir," replied Rosie, giving Sam a look of gratitude.

"And what a shocking story it is," Eaton went on, shaking his head. "Greed, torture, betrayal." He glanced at Jim. "You know, Mr. Dillon, as a young man, I, too, tried my luck as a miner, and came away from two years' hard labor without a nickel in my pockets. My hat's off to you on your find—although God knows you've suffered enough for it and deserve all the success you can earn."

"Thank you, sir," murmured Jim.

Seeming to relax a bit, Rosie hooked her arm through Jim's and grinned at the governor. "My darlin' was right well educated at the School of Mines in Rolla, Missouri. He knows all about finding gold and such."

"I'm happy for you both, Mrs. Dillon," said Eaton. "And I must also tell you that I'm deeply sorry that you and your husband have suffered so grievously. I'm eager to do anything in my power to see that the man who wronged you both, Royce Rowdy, is brought to justice."

"Yes, sir."

Eaton stroked his bearded jaw. "But the fact of the matter is, ma'am, you've broken the law. Your actions went well beyond self-defense."

"Yes, sir," Rosie humbly admitted, "and I'm right sorry for all that."

The governor nodded. "That's all well and good, but I must have your promise that you'll never again break the law."

"Yes, sir, you have it," said Rosie. "Cross my heart and hope to die."

"And I must also order you to make financial reparation to anyone who may have suffered due to your thievery—excepting Royce Rowdy, of course."

"Yes, sir, I give my word. We'll do whatever you say." Rosie inclined her head toward Jim. "Heck, governor, once my Jim files his claim, we're going to go right respectable. We're gonna move us right over to Capitol Hill, within spittin' distance of your purty new capitol, and build one of them fine mansions complete with struttin' peacocks and statues of nekkid men."

Everyone laughed. "We could use your kind of spunk in our community," commented Eaton with a chuckle.

"If you'll just help us set things right, me and Jim'll be grateful to you for the rest of our lives," Rosie replied sincerely.

"That's what I want—grateful constituents," concurred the governor.

"Then you're prepared to pardon Rosie fully?" asked Annie.

Eaton nodded. "You've convinced me, folks. I'll sign the papers this afternoon. And I'll write a letter for you to take to Judge Righteous, urging J.D. to issue an arrest warrant for Royce Rowdy."

"Thank you, sir," said Sam. "You've been of tremendous help."

"No more than you've been to me in the past," replied Eaton. "Besides, it's always a great satisfaction to see justice done."

Rosie and Jim stared at each other with stark joy. "Hot damn, sugar!" she cried. "We made it."

The two embraced while the others laughed. "Sam, I'd be pleased to have you and Mr. Dillon join me for a swim at the Windsor Baths before you leave town," added Eaton.

"Yes, sir, we'd be right honored," replied Sam. "Then after tomorrow, it's gonna be Mr. Royce Rowdy who's in right deep water."

Chapter 46

~~~ ∽◯◯◯ ~~~

Two days later, the couples were seated in yet another office, that of Judge J. D. Righteous, in Washington Hall, the courthouse of Gilpin County. Holding hands with Sam, Annie thought over the exciting events of the last twenty-four hours.

They had arrived in Central City yesterday, taking rooms in the elegant Teller House hotel just across the street from the courthouse. At once Sam had telephoned Washington Hall, speaking to Judge Righteous's clerk and making an appointment for the four of them to meet with the magistrate this morning. Afterward Sam and Jim had prepared to leave to go mark the boundaries of Jim's claim, post a notice, and bring back a sample of ore for the assay office.

Rosie and Annie had begged to accompany the men, but both had adamantly refused. Sam had argued the safety issues, pointing out that until they actually met with Judge Righteous and fully cleared Rosie's name, she might still be subject to arrest in Gilpin County. Jim had cited additional concerns, reminding the ladies that until his claim was actually filed, the danger wasn't over, and the less they knew about its location, the better.

Although disappointed that they would have to wait before seeing Jim's fabulous treasure, the ladies had kept each other company at the hotel until the jubilant men had returned with a chunk of gold the size of an apricot.

Sam in particular had appeared awed by his first glimpse of the mine. "Ladies, just wait till you see it," he'd declared with eyes aglow. "You'll think you died and gone to heaven—a paradise paved in gold." After the four had shared a victory glass of wine, the men had left again, taking the ore to the nearby assay office for grading and afterward carrying the assayer's certificate and the plat Jim had drawn of his claim to the courthouse for filing.

By supper time, Jim's claim had been secured, and the foursome again celebrated with a discreet dinner at the hotel. Over champagne, Jim had related to the women how delighted he'd been to learn from the county clerk that his claim was free and clear, the mine site having been abandoned over two decades ago.

Rosie and Jim's lives were almost completely resolved, Annie mused. Now they were all waiting impatiently for Judge Righteous to conclude his morning court docket, so they could fully clear Rosie's name and address the issue of bringing Royce Rowdy to justice.

All breathed a sigh when the door creaked open and J.D. Righteous appeared. Annie stood with the others. Yet her relief proved short-lived in the face of the judge's formidable presence. Striding into the room in his black robe, a law book in hand, the tall elderly man cut an imposing figure. His hair was snow white, his face craggy and intelligent, his brows bushy, his eyes ice blue and penetrating. He exuded uncompromising authority and rigid discipline, a far cry from Ben Eaton's laid-back friendliness. Yet there was also a benevolence in Righteous's smile as he spotted Sam, and Annie sensed that while this judge could be stern and principled, he did possess a fair heart.

"Sam Noble, how good to see you again," Righteous greeted, his gaze quickly flicking to Rosie and Annie. "And heavens, this must be Rotten—My God, where are my glasses? I'm seeing double!"

Sam rushed forward and shook the judge's hand. "Don't fret over your specs, J.D. You're seein' just fine. I'd like you to meet Rosie and Jim Dillon, and Annie Dillon, a—er—relation of Rosie's."

Righteous leveled a stern stare on Rosie, then Annie.

"My word, the resemblance between these two is . . .
Then you've nabbed Rotten Rosie, have you, Sam?
Shouldn't you have taken her straight to the calaboose?"

While Rosie gasped and went pale, Sam extended
some papers toward Righteous. "J.D., I reckon there's
been a change of plans. We've a long story to tell you.
And as you'll see when you read these here documents,
Rosie has been pardoned by the governor."

Righteous regarded Sam in amazement. "You can't
mean Honest Ben Eaton pardoned Rotten Rosie?"

"He had good reason, as I'm sure you'll agree, if you'll
read the papers," urged Sam.

"Well, I'll be deuced," muttered Judge Righteous. He
waved a hand at the others. "Very well, I'll listen. Have a
seat, folks."

Over the next tense moments, Righteous sat scowling
fearsomely as Sam and the others explained what had
really happened to Rosie and Jim. Donning his steel-
rimmed spectacles, Righteous then carefully examined
Rosie's pardon and read the letter Ben Eaton had
written, urging him to arrest Royce Rowdy.

Removing his glasses, Righteous frowned thoughtfully
for a long moment, then nodded to Sam. "If this isn't a
story to beat all. But you've got me convinced, Sam."

As all four visitors broke into smiles, Sam exclaimed,
"Thank God."

"Yes, it appears that Mr. and Mrs. Dillon have the
Almighty to thank for their very lives." He flashed a
compassionate look at Rosie and Jim. "Folks, I can't
begin to tell you how sorry I am regarding all you were
forced to endure. Truth to tell, I've never liked Royce
Rowdy. He's a mean, oily money-grubber, and that town
of his is a hellhole. Always figured that slick sidewinder
jumped my daddy's claim and hastened his death,
though I never had any proof." Righteous sighed heavily. "But my suspicions alone weren't enough to bring
down Rowdy. I also swore to uphold the law, and in your
case, Mrs. Dillon, my hands were tied. Rowdy had half a
dozen witnesses swearing you were a murderess, plus
you had taken flight and were continuing to break the

law. I had no choice but to issue the warrant for your arrest."

"Yessir, Your Honor, I understand," Rosie put in humbly. "And I admit I ain't been innocent as a baby's smile. But now that I have my Jim back, I'm a changed woman. And I'm tellin' you what I told Honest Ben Eaton: You have my word I ain't never breakin' the law again. I'm gonna be Colorado's most upright citizen from now on." She paused, shooting a haughty glance at Sam. "I ain't even darkening the door of no dancing parlors. Nossir. I got my standards, unlike *some* I know."

While Sam and Annie chuckled, Righteous grinned. "Good for you, Mrs. Dillon. Considering that the governor of Colorado has pardoned you, and taking all the other facts into account, I'm more than happy to vacate the order for your arrest and issue a new one for the apprehension of Royce Rowdy."

All four visitors cheered, and Rosie and Jim happily embraced. "Your Honor, can we be there to see old Rowdy get his comeuppance?" Rosie asked hopefully.

Righteous drummed his fingertips on his desk. "Well, ma'am, that is an unusual request."

"Oh, purty please!" she pleaded.

The judge fought a smile. "I suppose the sheriff might agree to deputize Sam, as we've done on a few occasions before. If so, I don't see why the rest of you can't accompany him to Rowdyville—if I have your word that you'll let Sam do the apprehending and not take the law into your own hands."

"Yes, sir, we promise," vowed Rosie.

"Just let me give Cal Oates a call at the jail and ask him to come over," said Righteous, reaching for the telephone on his desk.

The group visited for the ten minutes it took for Sheriff Oates to appear. Annie stifled a chuckle when he stepped in, for the middle-aged, blond lawman exuded an almost comical air with his ambling, bowlegged gait, his thumbs shoved into his pockets, and his huge potbelly pushing against his food-stained white shirt. The man's dour expression was underscored by an exaggerated handlebar mustache streaked with tobacco juice. His oversize Stetson hat practically swallowed up his forehead.

The sheriff stopped in his tracks and gaped at Rosie and Annie. "Leapin' lizards, judge, I'm seein' twins. Is one of them females Rotten Rosie?"

"She's not rotten anymore," replied Righteous. "As these folks have just explained to me, she's been pardoned by the governor of Colorado." He gestured toward his guests. "Cal, meet Mr. and Mrs. Jim Dillon and Miss Annie Dillon. You already know Sam."

Though he scowled suspiciously at Rosie, Oates dutifully removed his hat and nodded to the newcomers. He turned back to Righteous and spoke in a hoarse undertone. "I don't understand, J.D. Who are these strangers with Sam, and how come Rosie's been pardoned?"

Righteous briefly explained the situation to Oates. "And now I'm ordering you to arrest Royce Rowdy for assault and attempted murder," he finished.

Oates shifted from boot to boot. "Judge, I ain't so sure 'bout that. I count Rowdy a friend. I don't cotton to arresting no *compadres.*"

Righteous lifted a bushy brow. "Are you saying you'll not enforce my order, Cal?"

The sheriff avoided Righteous's harsh stare. "Your Honor, I don't mean no disrespect. I'm just saying it don't sit well, puttin' a friend in the hoosegow."

Righteous grinned cagily. "Then why don't you deputize Sam here, round up a few boys to help him, and let them do the dirty work while you mind the jail?"

The sheriff hesitated a moment, then glanced at Sam. "That all right by you, Noble?"

"It'd be my pleasure."

Oates nodded. "Reckon that's how it should be, then, Judge."

Chapter 47

Early the following morning, eight people on horse-back left Central City. Amid the brisk coldness of the fall morning, the riders wended their way along misty mountain passes where a few brave arctic gentians and harebells still bloomed, and across grassy valleys where male bull elk and bighorn sheep rutted, locking horns in an annual autumn mating ritual.

Sam had informed Annie that they should reach Rowdyville by afternoon. Wearing a deputy sheriff's badge, her lover now led the caravan, followed by Jim, Annie, and Rosie, and four other hastily sworn deputies who comprised the rear guard. Sam had recruited the taciturn group at the Teller House bar, mostly through a generous display of gold coins. The four, Joe, Red, Ted, and Earl, shared in common the lanky, bowlegged frames of seasoned cowboys, as well as an aversion for bathing and shaving and a fondness for chewing to-bacco.

Annie worried that the hastily gathered posse might be insufficient for nabbing a scoundrel like Royce Rowdy. But Sam felt their numbers were adequate; he had argued that a smaller group was less likely to be detected and could maintain an element of surprise. Sam felt it should be a relatively simple matter to apprehend Row-dy, most likely by just striding inside the Rowdy Roost, nabbing him, and riding out of town before anyone much knew the difference.

Annie sorely wished she could share Sam's confidence, yet she feared he was maintaining a positive facade mostly for her and Rosie's sakes. After listening to tales of the horrors Rowdy had inflicted on Rosie and Jim, Annie was fully aware of what a dangerous brute their quarry was.

The riders were navigating down a gorge lined with rocks, yucca, and cedar when suddenly a bullet whizzed past, tearing off Jim's hat! As the women gasped and Jim instinctively pressed a hand to his head, Sam yelled, "Take cover! Everyone! Now!"

No additional prompting was needed as a new barrage of gunfire erupted. Even as Annie was struggling to dismount, Sam was at her side hauling her off her horse. "Shake your hocks, sugar, before them bastards blow several holes in you."

Amid the whiz and sputter of more bullets, the two ran for a stand of pine and fir, pulling along their horses. Tethering her mount to a tree, Annie craned her neck and spotted the men of the posse seeking cover in a large clump of cedar while Rosie and Jim took refuge behind a pink granite boulder about ten feet away. Cupping a hand around her mouth, she called in a tense whisper, "Is Jim okay?"

Rosie popped up. "Yep, it was only his hat that got blowed off!"

Rosie had no sooner uttered the words than she screamed as a bullet bit into the rock mere inches from her nose. Jim yanked his wife back down behind the boulder. "I'm fine, folks!" he yelled. "For heaven's sake, stay low!"

Meanwhile, Sam had cocked his revolver and was peering down the ravine. "I think the ambushers are holed up in that brake of aspen near the bottom of the gulch," he told Annie, and began returning fire.

Squinting at the distant trees, Annie spotted telltale wisps of smoke but no signs of movement. "Who are they?"

"I reckon they're Rowdy's henchmen tryin' to slow us down a bit," Sam replied, then fired off several more rounds.

She grimaced at the roar of Sam's pistol. "But how can they even know we're coming?"

"I'll bet good money that weasel Cal Oates warned 'um," muttered Sam grimly. "Most likely by telegraph. If it turns out I'm right, his days of law enforcement will be over once J. D. Righteous gets wind of it."

Annie recoiled as a bullet sailed past within inches of her nose. "That's not exactly helping us now."

Sam placed his Colt in her hand. "Honey, for chrissakes stay behind that there tree. I'm grabbing my rifle and a couple of the boys. We'll sneak around them lowdown bushwackers and see if we can't get the drop on 'um."

"No!" Annie cried. "You could be killed."

"I'll take care, honey," he promised, leaning over and kissing her cheek. "You just lay low and return fire if you need to."

Annie watched with her heart in her eyes as Sam hunkered down and worked his way into the clump of cedar where the posse had taken refuge. For several agonizing minutes, she didn't see or hear him. She clutched Sam's Colt tightly but was afraid to return fire, fearing she might accidentally hit him or another deputy.

At last she heard a new battery of gunfire and a yelp. Peeking out from behind the trees, she watched as half a dozen strange men galloped off, while Sam, Red, and Ted raced into view on the trail, firing after the fleeing men.

Annie heaved a huge sigh of relief.

By the time Sam, Red, and Ted strode back up the trail, the rest of the party was there to greet them. Sam grinned at Annie. "We killed one of 'um and spooked the rest. We'll bury the unlucky bastard and get back on the trail."

Jim stood with his arm protectively about Rosie's shoulders. "But the others will still be able to go back and warn Rowdy, won't they?" he asked Sam.

"Unfortunately, yes," Sam acknowledged.

"Maybe we should ride back to Central City and get more help," Annie suggested.

Sam shook his head. "Nope, we've come this far, and the longer we wait, the more likely Rowdy will take off for the badlands or somethin'. Reckon we'd best keep on going."

"What if we're ambushed again?" she demanded.

"We'll take care," he replied. "After all, *we've* been warned now, too."

Hours later, Sam's expression was grim as the armed posse charged into the saloon with guns drawn, cursing, kicking over chairs and tables, and causing drunkards, gamblers, and prospectors to flee in panic while painted prostitutes shrieked and ran for the stairs. At the door, Annie and Rosie stood watching and holding rifles; Sam and Jim had ordered the women to remain outside, but they had followed the men anyway.

Sam approached a man he recognized as one of Rowdy's cohorts. Leveling his Colt on the cowering, grizzled ranch hand, he demanded, "Where's Rowdy?"

The man raised trembling hands. "Er—well, hello, preacher, what'er you doing back in town?"

Sam cocked his revolver with a deadly click. "I ain't no preacher, and if you don't tell me where your boss is—now—you're gonna be dispatched to the hereafter a mite sooner than you expected."

The man gulped. "I reckon the boss is holed up out at the ranch house."

"And where is the ranch house?"

The man hastily supplied directions.

"Holed up is right," muttered Sam.

The group was crouched behind a string of boulders on a mesa overlooking the big house at Royce Rowdy's ranch. In the gentle valley beneath them, the one-and-a-half story native stone house appeared much like a fortress; two guards with shotguns were positioned on the porch, and several other armed men marched about the yard, barn, and outbuildings.

"We can't charge the ranch house now," said Jim. "They'll pick us off like ducks in a pond."

"We'll have to wait for darkness," said Sam.

Rosie laughed. "What makes you fellars think they'll drop their guard then?"

"Damn that traitor, Cal Oates," Sam muttered.

Jim snapped his fingers. "I think I have an idea. Sam, may I have a word with you?"

Rosie and Annie watched, perturbed, as Sam and Jim moved away from the others and spoke intently. After a moment, Sam laughed and slapped his sides; then the two continued their animated discussion.

Rosie and Annie glanced at each other in perplexity. "What in tarnation do you reckon them two is plotting?" Rosie asked.

"Beats me."

Finally the two returned, both appearing proud as strutting cocks. Sam addressed the posse. "Boys, can you watch the ladies for a spell? Jim and me need to make a run back to town for supplies."

"Supplies?" Annie protested. "What supplies?"

Sam winked at her. "We just want all of you to sit tight till we return. No jumping the gun now. Understood?"

"Sam, what on earth are you two up to?" Annie demanded.

"Yeah!" seconded Rosie with a glower. "Spill the beans, fellars!"

Jim grinned at his wife. "All in good time, dear."

"Let's just say there's more than one way to catch a skunk," Sam added.

Chapter 48

❦

Annie and Rosie endured a long, boring wait as night spread its chilly tentacles over the landscape. The four deputies took turns watching the ranch house and playing poker by a small fire they'd built in the shelter of a boulder. Sam and Jim didn't reappear until the moon had risen well into the night sky. When at last they rode up, Jim had in tow a large burlap bag, which he handled most gingerly as he dismounted.

Watching the two men stride up to join them, Annie glanced askance at the bulging bag. "Where in blazes have you two been? Rosie and I were getting worried."

"Yeah, and what's in the bag?" added Rosie.

Jim lifted a hand in warning. "You don't want to look inside, honey."

"Why not?" she demanded.

"Because there's a skunk in the bag."

Rosie and Annie sucked in horrified breaths while three deputies playing poker nearby kicked over the coffeepot as they scrambled away with their cards and money.

"A skunk?" Rosie repeated in a charged whisper. "Have you two gone plumb loco?"

"For heaven's sake, you could end up with rabies or something" Annie scolded archly, "though it sounds like you're already stark raving mad!"

Sam chuckled. "We didn't even touch the skunk, sugar."

"Then how did you bag it?" Rosie demanded. She

jerked a thumb toward the sack. "And why is the critter being so docile?"

Sam grinned at Jim. "You wanna tell 'um?"

"Sure," he replied. "You see, dear, I had this idea. I thought the best way to smoke out Royce Rowdy would be to put a skunk down his chimney."

Stunned silence fell. Then, pulling a face, Annie asked, "Won't the skunk burn?"

As Jim hesitated over her question, Sam strode toward the edge of the mesa, glanced down at the darkened house, and returned to join the others. "Nope, there ain't no smoke comin' from the big-house chimney tonight," he announced.

"Well, thank heaven for that," Annie muttered.

"Anyway, I knew I could charm a skunk into coming close," Jim continued, "because I used to do so when I lived among the Cheyenne. But I wasn't sure how to get the creature to cooperate after that." He grinned at Sam. "That's where Sam came in."

"We sneaked back into Rowdyville and begged some ground-up steak off Dolly Dumble," Sam explained. "Then we bought us some sleeping powders at the apothecary. You should have seen the druggist's face when we asked him how much of the stuff to give a skunk."

Annie giggled. "And what did the man say?"

Sam replied, "He said, 'I reckon that depends on whether you're hankering for the critter to wake back up.'"

Everyone laughed as Jim once again took up the story. "So we came out here, set out our bait laced with sleeping powder, and I charmed in a skunk. After the animal ate the meat and fell asleep, Sam and I carefully drew the burlap bag over it."

"And how do you reckon getting it down Rowdy's chimney?" asked Rosie.

"We'll fix up a sling to lower it," Sam explained. "The bag ain't cinched up tight, and when that essence peddler awakens . . ." He whistled.

"You're forgetting something," said Annie. "Are

Rowdy's guards just gonna let you march right up and climb onto the roof?"

Sam laughed. "Sugar, Jim and I didn't spend our time with the Cheyenne without learning how to move about as quietly as ghost dancers. Rowdy's guards ain't never gonna hear or see us."

"That's right," seconded Jim.

"Well, if this don't beat all," muttered Rosie.

"Amen," added Annie.

The women watched with grudging admiration as Sam tore a large square strip from a blanket, then tied each corner with a long rope. He and Jim positioned the sling beneath the sack holding the skunk. Afterward, with each man gripping two pieces of rope, they practiced lifting and lowering the animal.

"There—just like falling off a log," Sam drawled to Annie. "That's how she goes down the chimney."

"How do you know it's a she?" she simpered back.

He grinned so wickedly that, had he not been holding a skunk, she would have kicked him.

Sam glanced at the four deputies, who were gathered a safe distance away. "You fellars cover us now."

"Shore, boss," replied Earl with a nervous nod.

"Long as we don't got to go with you," added Joe, and all four men guffawed.

Annie rolled her eyes. "Good luck, boys."

She and Rosie watched the men slip away into the night shadows.

"So what do ya think?" Rosie asked Annie.

She shook her head. "If that skunk ever wakes up, he's gonna be one unhappy camper."

In less than an hour, the men returned. "Success!" Sam exclaimed. "Now we just have to watch and wait."

Sam assigned guards for the night, taking the first shift himself while the others slept. Shortly before dawn, he awakened everyone. The eight huddled together in a circle to hear him.

"You men will all need to come with me," he began. "We'll take out the guards and tie them up, then hide in the stand of pine not far from the porch. Hopefully by sunup, Rowdy will make a run for it." He nodded toward Annie and Rosie. "You ladies stay put. If the rest of us get in trouble, get the hell out of here and go straight back to Central. Understood?"

"Sure, Sam," said Annie.

The women hugged their men good-bye and wished them luck. After the posse crept away, Annie spoke up to Rosie. "If they get in trouble, we'll back 'um up, right?"

"Right," replied Rosie.

Sunrise brought with it a scene Annie would never forget. Indeed, Rosie and Annie could *smell* victory before they ever saw it.

Annie was perched on a rocky ledge beside Rosie. "Yuck! Is that what I think it is?"

Rosie waved a hand in front of her face. "Honey, that's a wood pussy if I ever smelt one."

The two intently watched the big house. Seconds later, they heard the muffled sounds of men hollering inside. A ranch hand came hurtling through the front window, groaning as he rolled off the porch. Next the front door flew open and six men, including Royce Rowdy, bolted outside yelling as if their britches were on fire. Instantly all were surrounded by men with guns—Sam, Jim, and the rest of the posse.

Annie and Rosie nearly split their sides laughing at the spectacle.

"Well, I'll be hanged!" cried Rosie, clapping her hands in glee.

"They went out with a whimper, all right," said Annie.

Holding their noses, the women hastened down to join the others. Annie chuckled at the sight of the skunk emerging through the open front door, making a beeline off the porch, and tearing off for the hills, its striped tail waving high. By the time she and Rosie reached Sam and the others, the stench was unbearable.

"Phew!" Rosie declared, gazing in disgust at Royce Rowdy. "Do you boys stink. I reckon we'll have to dunk

you in tomater juice before old Judge Righteous'll even
have you. Or maybe we oughta just shoot you and put
you out of your misery."

Although his hands were held high, Royce Rowdy
trembled in fury. "You'll pay for this!" he declared in a
shrill voice. "Especially you, *Reverend*. You traitor!"

Sam only laughed. "Well, Mr. Rowdy, I did promise
all you sinners that you'd get your comeuppance. This
here is Judgment Day."

As Rowdy stared at Sam in seething hatred, Rosie
took Jim's arm. "Yeah, you big bully, it's your turn to
pay! Do you recognize this fine man standing here beside
me?"

"Why should I?" Rowdy sneered.

"'Cause you thought you kilt him two years ago, you
miserable bastard!" Rosie retorted. "Now he's risen
from the dead to see you rot in hell."

Rowdy gazed at Jim and gulped. For once, he appeared visibly shaken. Still, he retorted with bravado, "I
ain't got no idea what you're ranting about, woman."

"That's okay, 'cause the judge is gonna understand
ever' word," Rosie replied. "You're gonna pay for all the
harm you done me and my husband. I'll see your no-
good butt planted in a hole deeper than Hades, with the
devil's pitchfork just a'itchin' to tear the flesh from your
bones. Hell, you'll be wishing you had a skunk for
company."

"Yes, you're going to regret the day you ever met Rosie
and Jim Dillon," Jim added.

"Believe me, I already do," muttered Rowdy.

Chapter 49

Two days later, the couples stood on a narrow ledge perched on a craggy hillside in the isolated mountains north of Rowdyville. Annie sadly noted that the countryside surrounding them showed the ravages of placer mining decades before: Mine heads crumbled along the canyon beyond, massive piles of tailings spoiled the beauty of the landscape, and the pollution of heavy metals had turned the Alpine stream below them an ugly yellow brown.

Before them yawned the dark opening to a deserted mine, a mine that now belonged to Rosie and Jim. To the left of the aperture stood the small wooden sign Sam and Jim had posted several days before; the placard was carved with Jim's name and the notice of his claim. The men had also marked and pegged the boundaries of the mine.

Excitement had gripped Annie when Jim and Sam had finally agreed to show her and Rosie the mine, yet in another sense she felt apprehensive and sad, fearing her journey here was truly about to end. Royce Rowdy and several of his cronies—including former sheriff Cal Oates—were safely locked away in jail now, awaiting Judge Righteous's justice. Rosie's and Jim's lives had become successfully resolved. Annie sensed her purpose in the past had been fulfilled, and her gut kept arguing that it was time to try to return to the present and the problems she'd left behind there.

If she could return!

Assuming she could, where did that leave her and Sam? She glanced at him now, and though he smiled back, the same anguish and uncertainty darkened his eyes.

Jim held up his lit kerosene lantern. "You folks ready? Ladies, be careful, now," he warned. "The timbers in this mine are over twenty years old."

"Yeah, we don't want one of you gettin' hurt," added Sam. "Lead away."

Single file, they entered the dank, dark tunnel, the lantern flashing eerie shadows on the brown walls, the men stooping to avoid hitting their heads on the low roof.

"Hey, Jim, tell Annie how you found this place," Sam suggested.

Over his shoulder, Jim called, "Sure, Sam. Well, Annie, when I first came out here from Missouri, I started scouring some of the abandoned mines in the area. You see, as a geologist, I'm aware that, in their reckless haste to become rich, miners often miss valuable deposits of ore. For instance, it was only due to Will Stevens's persistence in poking around the deserted gold mines in Leadville that the huge lode of silver was discovered there."

"It certainly helps if you know what to look for," agreed Annie. "And with your background, you'd have an edge."

"The day I came upon this mine, I saw a burro outside and came in to investigate. I heard a man calling out for help. Deep in the shaft, I found an old prospector lying beneath a pile of debris. The unfortunate codger could barely speak, but his story was pretty straightforward. He had just discovered a vast geode of gold when the cave-in got him. I tried my darnedest to help him, removing the rocks and boards and feeding him a few sips of water, but he was very badly hurt, both legs broken, and coughing up blood. I suppose I only made his final moments a little easier. Anyway, he told me he'd spent his whole life searching before he'd finally found his bonanza in this mine. Now it was too late for him to file a claim."

"What a sad story," said Annie.

"I'll never forget his last words. 'Sonny, all my life I've grubstaked myself and I don't owe nothing to no man. It's too late for me now, but you been mighty kind. All I ask is you bury me proper and take good care of my jenny. I want you to file a claim on this place, for there are riches here beyond King Solomon's mines. Jes' look behind the cave-in.'"

Annie whistled. "How fascinating. What did the prospector mean by his 'jenny'?"

"His burro," explained Jim. "Anyway, I did what the man asked, burying him in a pretty valley with a nice view of the mountains. I gave his burro to a farmer who promised to treat her right. Afterward, I went back to Denver, met Rosie, and she and I arranged to wed. As you know, we were on our way to Central to file the claim when we made our fateful stop in Rowdyville."

"And Royce Rowdy interfered before you got to enjoy your fabulous treasure," muttered Annie.

"But it's ours now," finished Rosie proudly.

At the end of the narrow corridor, the four proceeded single file down a rickety ladder into a cool lower tunnel. At last they reached a dead end where a pile of rocks and timbers barred the way.

Jim handed the lantern to Rosie and gestured toward the pile of debris. "After I discovered the geode, I reinforced the timbers, then blocked the entrance to discourage the curious. After Sam and I obtained the sample the other day, we again camouflaged the opening." He hunkered down by the heap. "Sam, if you'll just help me move this rubble aside . . ."

"My pleasure," said Sam.

Over the next moments, Rosie and Annie stood tensely waiting as the men painstakingly freed the entrance. Both women became compelled to place bandannas over their noses due to the cloud of dust rising from the men's labors.

"At last," muttered Jim, wiping his sweaty brow.

He took the lantern from Rosie and illuminated a narrow, irregular-shaped opening. "It'll be a squeeze, folks, but I think we can all make it."

"Sure we can," concurred Sam. "I'm the biggest, and I made it in fine the other day. Still, it might be best for me to go first. . . ."

Annie watched anxiously as Sam got down on his hands and knees and clawed through the tight opening. She heaved a breath of relief when she heard him call, "I'm in. Pass me the lantern."

Grinning, Jim knelt and handed the lantern through to Sam. He stood and brushed off his pants. "Ladies, you're next."

"I'm game," said Annie with a grin, dropping to her knees.

Although their side of the opening was shrouded by darkness, Annie guided her movements by the wan pool of light flickering at the edges of the opening. She pushed her body into the aperture with little effort and soon felt Sam's hands gripping hers, pulling her into the next room.

"You all right, sugar?" he asked.

"Sure."

He pressed the lantern into her hands. "You hold this while I help the others."

Sam assisted first Rosie then Jim into the chamber. Jim took the lantern from Annie. "All right, everyone, you can stand up now. There's plenty of headroom here."

He stood and held the lantern high as Sam helped the women to their feet.

"My God!" gasped Annie, staring in awe.

They stood inside an enormous vault of gold. At least thirty feet high, ten feet wide, and twenty feet deep, the cavern was strewn with vast, sparkling rocks and gleaming spears of the precious metal, and sported walls teeming with gold flakes and crystals. Never in her life had Annie seen such fabulous riches. The old prospector had been right when he'd said this treasure was more fabulous than King Solomon's mines. The expanse was so dazzling, she felt as if she'd arrived in a glittering utopia.

Rosie had picked up a large crystal of gold and was staring at it agog. "Holy hog bellies, precious, what is this place? I knew you struck gold, but I ain't never dreamt of nothin' like this! If the devil didn't go and shit gold bricks!"

Both men chuckled. "Miners call this a 'vug,'" Jim explained. "In geological terms, it's like a vast geode, with crystals forming inside the cavity of a huge rock, somewhat similar to a lava tube. A rare occurrence, and a true marvel of nature."

"And now it's all ours and worth millions!" cried Rosie, dropping the crystal and hugging Jim. She winked at him. "You wanna tell 'um, honey?"

"Tell us what?" asked Annie.

Wrapping an arm around Rosie's shoulders, Jim announced, "Rosie and I have decided to deed you half ownership in our mine."

"But that's not necessary," insisted Sam.

"No way!" protested Annie.

"It *is* fittin'," Rosie argued. "You saved our lives and got the two of us back together. If not for you, there would be no mine—and no future for my darlin' Jim and me."

Her expression bittersweet, Annie stepped forward and touched Rosie's hand. "Thank you so much, but I must decline. Maybe you can talk Sam into accepting half ownership, but I have a journey to make and I think I'm going to have to travel light."

"What journey?" Sam's voice was hard.

Sadly she turned to him. "Sam, I'm sorry, but you know how I feel. I wish I could stay with you, but I just don't see how Rosie and I can continue to share the same time."

He regarded her in turmoil.

"My purpose here is fulfilled, and I must at least try to go back to my own century and to the responsibilities I left behind there. It's time for me to leave."

Even as he tried to protest, Rosie cried, "No! You belong here with us! Why, we'll build us twin mansions in Denver!"

Annie regretfully shook her head. "I'm sorry, Rosie, but you're wrong. This is *your* time, not mine. Although you don't like to hear it, I *am* your great-great-granddaughter, and it's too much of a paradox for both of us to remain. I'm worried about what might happen to our family history."

Rosie didn't reply, though her lower lip trembled and she wiped away a tear.

"But how would you return to your time?" asked Jim.

Annie shrugged. "I don't know. All I can do is ride south and hope I'll meet up with that same blue norther again."

"If you're riding south, woman, I'm coming with you," put in Sam obdurately.

Annie regarded him in pleasant surprise. "But what if we both end up back in the present?"

His intent gaze did not waver from hers. "Then so be it, woman. I'll stay with you there."

"Sam, I can't ask you to make that sacrifice!"

He gripped her shoulders. "Listen to me, Annie. I'm going with you. We've come this far, and we'll finish this journey together. My mind's made up, and I ain't lettin' you go. You got that?"

Annie grinned at Rosie. "I guess the gentleman has spoken."

"Isn't there anything we can do for you?" asked Jim.

"As a matter of fact, there is," Sam replied. "You can look after my grandmother and her people."

"Rosie and I were already planning to do that," he protested with a laugh.

"Yeah, after the way your granny took care of my honey," added Rosie, "we'll buy them folks their own ranch if they cotton to it."

"If you'll just keep an eye out, make sure they have provisions and a place to roam, I'd be much obliged," said Sam.

Jim nodded. "Consider it done, my friend." He extended his hand toward Sam. "Well, guess this is good-bye, then."

As the men shook hands, Annie turned to a teary-eyed Rosie and felt a keen twinge of guilt and disappointment at having to leave her. "I'm sorry we can't stay, but I know this is for the best."

"*You're* the best, honey," replied Rosie in quivering

tones, squeezing Annie's hand. "And I wish you and Sam all the happiness you deserve. Though I've been right ornery about admittin' we're kin, I want you to know I'm right proud to be your great-great-granny."

"Thank you," said Annie hoarsely. "I'm proud to have you."

"Still, it do give a body pause," Rosie continued in awe. "When you think about it, honey, you ain't even been born yet."

Annie laughed. "I will be. I have faith in you and Jim."

Rosie nodded. "I reckon you're right that you belong back in your own time—though it plumb breaks my heart." She sniffed. "I'm sure gonna miss you."

"Oh, Rosie." With arms that trembled, Annie fiercely hugged her. "I'll miss you, too. So much. My life has been so enriched through knowing you and Jim. Seeing all you've overcome has renewed my faith in life, and in love. I'm sure we'll all meet up again someday—if not here, then in heaven."

Rosie clutched Annie close. "Thanks for everythin' you done for us, honey," she whispered. "And Godspeed."

"May God protect you and Jim, too." Bravely wiping away a tear, Annie turned to Rosie's husband. "Don't charm too many skunks now," she teased, giving him a fond hug.

"You two come back and visit us if you can," he replied.

Eyes bright with love, Annie glanced at Sam. "Who knows. . . . Maybe we will." She laughed. "In fact, if we can't find a certain demon wind, you may see us again a lot sooner than you think."

Chapter 50

By the time Sam and Annie rode off on their long and uncertain journey, the day was beginning to wane. Only an hour later, they stopped in a sheltered canyon to make camp.

Dismounting, Annie hugged herself as a cold wind whistled through the gulch. She gazed up at ominous gray clouds framing the canyon. "Think it will snow tonight?"

Scowling, Sam glanced overhead. "Could be." He pulled Annie into his arms. "Don't worry, sugar, I'll keep you warm."

She snuggled closer to him. "You know, I miss Rosie and Jim already."

"They're fine folks and I'm happy we was able to help them," he agreed. "But I think you're right that you don't belong here."

"Really, Sam?"

His arms tightened about her. "I didn't want to accept it, but now I've been forced to see the truth or lose you."

She reached up to caress his cheek. "And what about you, Sam? Where do you belong?"

"With you."

She sighed. "Are you really committed to riding south with me?"

"I'm committed to *you*, woman. With all my heart."

"Oh, Sam." Feeling a welling of love for him, she nestled her head beneath his chin and breathed in his comforting scent. "I'm committed to you, too. But I feel like you're giving up your life for me."

He rubbed her back with his hand. "Annie, I understand your feelings about going back. All I know is, I don't have a life if I lose you."

"Do you really mean that?" she asked in a small voice.

"I realized how much *you* mean to me that night in Denver. I love you, sugar. Heck, I don't even know if I can make it in your time, but I'm gonna give it a try. Who knows? This might be the greatest adventure of our lives."

"Could be," she agreed.

"No matter what happens, we belong together."

She hugged him close. "Oh, Sam. I love you, too. So much. And I pray you're right."

Luckily, the snowfall that night was moderate. The next day, Sam and Annie continued south, stopping briefly to say good-bye to Sam's grandmother and the Cheyenne band. Sam explained the situation to Medicine Woman and advised her that Jim and Rosie would see to the needs of the band from now on; Medicine Woman agreed that Sam should leave with Annie to find his place with the woman he loved. In an emotional moment, she blessed the two travelers and bid them farewell.

The journey back to the Texas Panhandle took an exhausting seven days. Once they were delayed by rain, another time by a heavy snowfall.

On a blustery, cold morning, they had just entered the vast red mesas of Indian Country, when Annie heard the harsh keening of the wind and stared ahead to spot dust devils dancing and tumbleweeds swirling.

"My God, I think that's the whirlwind," she muttered to Sam. Anxiously she caught his eye. "This could be your last chance to turn around."

Sam's reply was vehement. "Sugar, you've seen my world and lived in it. Now I'm gonna take yours by storm. Come on, woman, let's ride!"

Annie's laughter echoed over the plains as the two

galloped off into the powerful, wailing wind, and into their destiny together.

"We're back! I think we're back!"

Several hours later, Sam and Annie galloped into Deadend. The wind was still howling ferociously, stirring up torrents of red dust, rattling shutters and windowpanes along the old storefronts.

Holding on to his hat, Sam glanced at the deserted main street. "Yep, this looks like the ghost town, all right. But what century are we in?"

"Follow me, and we'll soon find out," she called.

She led him back behind the saloon. Her blue sports car, still intact but covered with red dust, was parked where she'd left it. Oh, she couldn't believe it! They'd traveled back across time.

"We made it!" she declared. "We're back in the twentieth century!"

"Well, I'll be hanged," said Sam, staring mystified at the strange vehicle. "If that ain't the queerest lookin' buggy I ever seen."

"Cowboy, you ain't seen nothin' yet!"

He grinned. "Let's get these horses stabled."

Both dismounted and led their horses next door, where Annie was surprised to see a familiar, battered old pickup truck, which Sam also gaped at.

"Well, look at this—Mr. Windfoot's pickup," she remarked. "I wonder if he has returned to the saloon. Heck, as far as I know, he and his people may own the place by now."

"And this is his trusty mount?" Sam asked dryly.

Annie winked at him. "Something like that. She's old and temperamental."

Sam looked at Annie as if she'd lost her mind.

They unsaddled the horses and rubbed them down, then navigated through the violent wind to the saloon. Sure enough, as they stepped through the double doors, they spotted old Windfoot. Looking almost precisely as he had the day Annie had first met him, the old Indian sat at one of the tables whittling a bird.

Sam managed to shut the doors against the force of the wind.

"Mr. Windfoot?" Annie called.

The old man glanced up at her, perturbed; then his gaze fixed on Sam. A raw cry escaped him. Appearing as if he'd just seen a ghost, he dropped his work and staggered to his feet, knocking over his chair in the process.

"Thomas!" he cried, holding on to the table to keep his balance. "Praise Maiyun, is that you?"

Sam glanced askance at Annie; she rolled her eyes heavenward and tapped her temple as if to say, "He's touched."

Sam regarded the old man in alarm and uncertainty. "You think you know me, mister?"

Even as the old man struggled to reply, a spasm of pain crossed his features and he clutched his chest. "Thomas!" he repeated in a hoarse whisper.

Sam rushed forward and gripped Windfoot's arm. "Sir, you're lookin' right peaked there. Reckon we'd best set you in a chair."

Sam retrieved Windfoot's chair and helped the old man sit down. Pale and breathless, Windfoot blinked back tears and stared intently at Sam. "It *is* really you, isn't it, Thomas?"

"Well, I ain't rightly sure," muttered Sam.

Annie frowned at the old man. "Mr. Windfoot, are you okay? And what on earth are you talking about? This man is Sam Noble."

"No, no, it's Thomas!" insisted the old man, surging back to his feet.

"Mr. Windfoot, are you sure you should be standing right now?" asked Annie, grasping his arm.

But the old man impatiently threw off her touch. "I'm fine, young lady. And I tell you, this is my beloved grandson, Thomas, who disappeared into the wilderness at the age of fifteen. Yes, he has grown, and his manner of speech is somewhat different now, but I'd know his face, and the timbre of his voice, anywhere."

Annie pulled a face at Sam. "Do you have any idea what he's ranting about?"

Sam shrugged.

Pulling out his wallet, the old Indian moved closer to Sam. "Grandson, much time has passed, and I'm sure you must have become confused by your ordeal." He drew out a snapshot and held it up with trembling fingers. "But pictures don't lie. I tell you, you are Thomas Noble Windfoot."

Sam and Annie gaped at a faded photo of a teenage boy with longish hair and brown eyes, a boy who could have been Sam fifteen years ago.

"Well, I'll be damned," muttered Sam.

"The resemblance is uncanny," agreed Annie.

"Then you remember now?" asked Windfoot, eyes gleaming with wild joy. "My dear grandson, welcome home!"

The old man threw his arms about Sam. Sam slanted Annie a perplexed glance but didn't resist the embrace, while she stood on the sidelines shaking her head.

At last Windfoot released Sam. "You must tell me all about your journey, grandson."

"Yeah, that'll be some tale," Sam agreed dryly.

"I'm so glad I never gave up on you," continued Windfoot. He gestured expansively at the saloon. "So grateful I never abandoned my cause in trying to reclaim this property for you."

"Oh, my God, the property," cried Annie. "Did the case go to trial while I was away?"

Windfoot shook his head. "No, miss, your attorney secured a continuance after you disappeared." Wry humor shone in his eyes. "I told the judge you likely were off on your quest for spiritual enlightenment."

"And how," agreed Annie drolly.

"But I remain determined to win back this land for my grandson."

"Wait a minute, mister! Are you the one that's been trying to take the town away from this here lady?"

"That is correct," affirmed Windfoot.

"You're trying to steal it from her to give it to me?" Sam cried in disbelief.

"It is your Cheyenne birthright, Grandson," Windfoot protested.

Sam fell silent for a long moment, scowling and stroking his jaw, while Windfoot waited anxiously. All at once Sam snapped his fingers and wrapped an arm about Annie's shoulders. She threw him a confused glance, but he only grinned.

"And what if I marry this here lady?" Sam asked Windfoot. "Will you quit pestering her?"

Windfoot considered this with a frown. "You wish to marry her?"

"Damn tootin'."

The old man hesitated a moment, then sighed. "In such an event, your woman will become a part of our people, too. The Silver Wind band will drop their lawsuits."

Sam grinned and shook the old man's hand. "In that case, just call me Thomas."

"You're not really old Windfoot's grandson, are you, Sam?" Annie asked.

They sat alone at a table discussing their remarkable meeting with Windfoot and trying to decide what they would do with the rest of their lives. "Nope, sugar, I'm not his grandson," Sam replied with a dry chuckle, "but there's no doubt we're distant kin. I'm looking at this as a sign—a sign that you and me are meant to make a go of it here, a way to make an old man happy—"

"And to establish a new identity for yourself," she finished with awe.

"I reckon you're right," he murmured with wonder. "You know, sugar, you spoke to Rosie about how you felt you belonged in the present, how her and Jim's time was in the past. Perhaps old Windfoot was tryin' to tell us that *our* time is now."

"Perhaps he was." She leaned toward him intently. "Sam, do you really think the two of us can make it here? Will you be happy to give up your other life— bounty hunting, being wild and free—forever?"

He clutched her hand and stared into her eyes. "Sugar, let me tell you something. I think I must have loved you almost from the first moment I laid eyes on you. But you were so feisty and headstrong, a real handful, and you're right that it took me a spell to accept the notion of having a really strong female for a wife, a woman who would demand more from her man than I was ready to give. All my life, I've yearned for adventure, but now I know you're my adventure, a woman challenging and spirited enough to keep life interesting till death us do part. Hell, I've had more fun these past weeks with you than during the rest of my life thrown together. By the time we reached Denver, I knew I could never give you up. Old Windfoot only confirmed what I already knew in my heart." He squeezed her hand and gazed at her with utter love. "Somehow, you and me are gonna make it. This world is gonna be our new frontier, and I can't wait to explore it with you."

"Oh, Sam." Laughing in delight, Annie flew across into his lap, almost knocking over his chair as she blissfully kissed him.

Epilogue

A year later . . .

"**G**ather round, folks, and I'll tell you about the fiercest desperado I ever nabbed."

Annie stood at the back of the refurbished saloon, watching Sam on stage giving a one-man show for a group of enthralled tourists. Her husband wore a white Stetson hat, a blue-and-white-checked western shirt, jeans, and a bullet-studded gun belt. Strapped to his thigh was the Colt revolver he used in shooting demonstrations for visitors to their ghost town. Her cowboy looked handsome and fierce, good enough to devour—which she must be sure to do tonight, she decided wryly.

Annie smiled as she thought over the amazing events of the past twelve months. It seemed so ironic to her now that she and Sam had returned to Deadend with few prospects and little more than the shirts on their backs—or so they had thought. Yet since that time, fortune had smiled on them in every way.

First, just as old Windfoot had promised, the Silver Wind band of the Cheyenne had dropped their lawsuits claiming Deadend as part of their tribal lands, and the new state highway had pushed through as planned. On contacting her office in Dallas, Annie had learned from her partner that while she was away, the huge ranch she'd been trying to market for so long had finally sold for a fat price, netting her a hefty commission that had not only gotten her and Sam on their feet financially but had also helped them finish the renovation of Deadend. Many of the Cheyenne had also chipped in to help with the project; indeed, a number of the Indians were now employed here, giving demonstrations of Native American ways.

Sam had established a new identity for himself as Thomas Noble Windfoot, although he would always be Sam to Annie. Only weeks after their return, the two had married right here in town, with many of their new Indian friends surrounding them. After the ceremony, they had renamed their town Windfall, in honor of their changing fortunes and their ties with the Cheyenne.

They'd been blissfully happy since then, and Annie was so proud of her man. From the moment he had arrived here in the 1990s, Sam had been amazed by the twentieth century, and he had become a voracious learner and reader of history books. He had been the one who had come up with the idea of giving one-man shows, in the tradition of Will Rogers, once their ghost town opened for tourist trade.

Annie supposed what astounded her most was the success of their town, and especially Sam's show. How she had fretted close to their opening date, wondering who would want to come see an attraction in the middle of nowhere. "We've made a terrible mistake," she would rant to Sam. "No one's going to want to come out to this godforsaken place."

Her husband had only laughed, and she chuckled at the memory. All along, she should have counted on the charisma and magnetism of the man she had married. For they had rebuilt their town, and the people had simply come—come to see Thomas Noble Windfoot, as Sam was now publicly known. The guests beheld a true gem of the Old West, as well as a living history Indian exhibit organized by the Silver Wind Cheyenne.

Since Windfall had opened four months ago, all of the attractions had been smashing successes. In particular, Sam's reputation for riding, shooting, roping, and telling tall tales had become legendary. Rave reviews of his astounding one-man show had appeared in newspapers all over Texas and beyond. Annie remembered one quote in particular: "Mr. Windfoot's act has a real ring of verisimilitude, all the gore and grit of a forgotten era. If this reporter didn't know better, he would swear Mr.

Windfoot had been magically transported here from the *real* Wild West."

Annie knew better: Her cowboy was the genuine article! Even now she chuckled as she listened with the others, hearing him speak of his exploits tracking down murderers and claim jumpers, and even of the time he had rescued a bobcat cub from a tree for a group of frantic children. Of course, most of the audience thought Sam's stories were pure invention, but Annie knew the truth.

Given the popularity of their attraction, bus tours had been organized out of Amarillo, bringing people to Windfall to experience a day in the Old West. Already, Sam had offers to appear on television, and he was warming to the idea of taking their show on the road— with Annie by his side, of course.

Their lives had been blessed in so many ways. Even Annie's family problems had been resolved. For, at this very moment, her brother Larry sat with old Windfoot at a table only a few feet away. The two men were whittling wooden animals as several captivated children watched.

Soon after Annie and Sam had returned to their town, Larry had simply appeared one day, apologizing for leaving Annie in the lurch, for going off honky-tonking when the renovation project became too stressful. He'd also offered to help her finish restoring the town. Annie had introduced Larry to old Windfoot, and since that time, her brother had spent countless hours talking to the Indian or whittling with him. Larry had given up drinking and had found his niche making wooden sculptures for the gift shop here at the ghost town.

Annie was truly amazed by the transformation in her brother. She felt such a sense of closure to be staring at this man with her hair, her father's face, and her mother's eyes. Their lives had come full circle now, and she felt her parents would have been pleased to see both their children settled and content.

Annie also thought frequently of her other family— Rosie and Jim. She and Sam often spoke of them and missed them dearly. She remembered once when Sam had asked, "If we're here now, and alive, does that mean Rosie and Jim are dead?" Annie would never forget her joyous, tearful response: "No, darling, Rosie and Jim are alive, alive in our hearts, our spirits, and imaginations, forever." Clutching her close, Sam had tenderly agreed.

Sam didn't know the half of it, Annie mused with wonder. For she had two glorious secrets to share with her husband tonight. In a very miraculous way, their lives were *still* linked with those of Rosie and Jim.

This morning, she'd received an astounding letter at their mailbox here in Windfall. She pulled the envelope out of her pocket and caught a tremulous breath. The parchment was aged, with a faded two-cent stamp in the upper right-hand corner—and a postmark from Denver dating to 1900! Amazingly, there'd been no explanation from the post office as to why the letter had been delayed almost a century, and no return address was listed.

The contents were even more mind-boggling. There was no note or letter included, only a brief newspaper article. But what an article! Annie removed the yellowed clipping, which had been cut from the July 5, 1900, edition of the *Denver Post,* and reread the piece in awe.

TURN-OF-THE-CENTURY CELEBRATION

Popular scions of the Denver community James and Rosanna Dillon hosted a turn-of-the-century picnic and reunion on the grounds of their magnificent mansion in Capitol Hill. In attendance were many of the city's elite families, including the Hills, the Cheesmans, the Tabors, and the Moffats. Mr. and Mrs. Dillon's three rambunctious children enlivened the day.

Also in attendance were Mrs. Dillon's distant cousin, Annie, who came from Texas with her husband. The couple brought along their two small children, one but a babe in arms. . . .

The most singular guest of the day was a very old Cheyenne medicine woman, accompanied by her equally ancient white escort. . . .

Replacing the clipping in the envelope, Annie could only shake her head. Just wait until she showed this to Sam! So they *would* get to see Rosie, Jim, their children, and Medicine Woman at least one more time—and they would take along their own two children!

What amazed and moved Annie most of all was that right before she'd received the letter this morning, her home pregnancy test had confirmed that she carried Sam's child. Come summer, their first baby would be born. The very thought brought blissful tears to her eyes, especially as she imagined Sam's face when she told him. Oh, she loved him more than life itself. How blessed she was to have both her wonderful cowboy and his baby growing inside her, plus such marvelous future bounties for them all to look forward to.

Her husband's voice again broke into her thoughts. "Like I said, folks, I've tracked down bad ones, all right. Will Rogers once said he never met a man he didn't like. Well, I never met an outlaw I couldn't catch. But to tell you about the fiercest desperado I ever nabbed . . ."

Rope in hand, Sam hopped off the stage. While the crowd issued a collective gasp of breathless expectation, Sam threw his lasso high over their heads. Seconds later, the loop landed square around Annie's hips to the applause and cheers of the spectators.

Annie grinned as Sam gently reeled her in. With his arm about her waist, he announced to the audience, "Here she is folks, the wildest, orneriest outlaw I ever tamed. My beautiful bride, Annie. The love of my life and the keeper of my heart. And I ain't *never* lettin' her loose."

Avon Romantic Treasures

*Unforgettable, enthralling love stories,
sparkling with passion and adventure
from Romance's bestselling authors*

SUNDANCER'S WOMAN by *Judith E. French*
77706-1/$5.99 US/$7.99 Can

JUST ONE KISS by *Samantha James*
77549-2/$5.99 US/$7.99 Can

HEARTS RUN WILD by *Shelly Thacker*
78119-0/$5.99 US/$7.99 Can

DREAM CATCHER by *Kathleen Harrington*
77835-1/$5.99 US/$7.99 Can

THE MACKINNON'S BRIDE by *Tanya Anne Crosby*
77682-0/$5.99 US/$7.99 Can

PHANTOM IN TIME by *Eugenia Riley*
77158-6/$5.99 US/$7.99 Can

RUNAWAY MAGIC by *Deborah Gordon*
78452-1/$5.99 US/$7.99 Can

YOU AND NO OTHER by *Cathy Maxwell*
78716-4/$5.99 US/$7.99 Can